THREAD AND BURIED

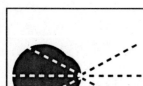

THREAD AND BURIED

JANET BOLIN

WHEELER PUBLISHING
A part of Gale, Cengage Learning

GALE
CENGAGE Learning·

Detroit • New York • San Francisco • New Haven, Conn • Waterville, Maine • London

GALE
CENGAGE Learning

Wheeler Publishing Large Print Cozy Mystery.
The text of this Large Print edition is unabridged.
Other aspects of the book may vary from the original edition.
Set in 16 pt. Plantin.

LIBRARY OF CONGRESS CATALOGING-IN-PUBLICATION DATA

Bolin, Janet.
 Thread and Buried / By Janet Bolin. — Large Print edition.
  pages cm. — (A Threadville Mystery) (Wheeler Publishing Large Print Cozy Mystery)
  ISBN 978-1-4104-6255-8 (softcover) — ISBN 1-4104-6255-2 (softcover) 1. Large type books. I. Title.
PS3602.O6534T45 2014
813'.6—dc23   2013035537

Published in 2014 by arrangement with The Berkley Publishing Group, a member of Penguin Group (USA) LLC, a Penguin Random House Company

Printed in the United State
   1 2 3 4 5   18 17

*To the librarians and booksellers
who know which books we love
and help us find more . . .*

ACKNOWLEDGMENTS

Welcome back to Threadville!

As always, I thank my friends and mentors, Krista Davis and Daryl Wood Gerber, who also writes as Avery Aames. They always have time for my questions, plot problems, and silly remarks. And Daryl was the first to suggest the title *Thread and Buried.*

Many thanks to my friend, Sgt. Michael Boothby, Toronto Police (Retired) for his comments and suggestions. Any errors are mine — and maybe my characters'.

Thanks also to Sisters in Crime, especially the Guppies Chapter and the Toronto Chapter, and to Crime Writers of Canada.

And then there are the conferences where I meet so many supportive and (yes) very funny fans and mystery writers — Malice Domestic, Bloody Words, and Scene of the Crime. I wonder if the volunteers who put these conferences together understand how much we appreciate all the hard work they do.

I couldn't have written this without the capable aid of my editor, Faith Black, and my thanks go to her as well as to the talented Berkley team, including Annette Fiore Defex, who is responsible for the cover design of the original publisher's edition, and Tiffany Estreicher, who designed the interior text for the same edition.

I'm lucky that Robin Moline does the paintings that become my cover art. Many readers have told me the paintings alone make them want to read the books. Thank you, Robin!

I'm still pinching myself about landing the always-helpful Jessica Faust of BookEnds, LLC, as my agent.

Joyce of Joyce's Sewing Shop in Wortley Village, Ontario, again provided the first tip at the end of the book. Thank you, Joyce, both for the tip and the laugh.

I thank my family and friends. They're beginning to understand why I do sinister things like plot, predict doom, and envision worst-case scenarios.

And I thank you for returning to Threadville. Welcome back!

1

Clay pointed at a squarish, rusty thing sticking out of the sand near the bottom of the excavation. "Do you know what that is, Willow?"

"A box?" At noon on the first day of summer, the sun was hot and directly overhead, but I shivered. How long had this mysterious box been hiding underneath my backyard?

Clay grinned down at me. I loved having to look up into a man's face. I was nearly six feet tall, and Clay was taller. He asked, "Shall we find out?"

"Sure." Another of the many things I liked about Clay was the way he was willing to include me in his schemes. And to play along with mine.

He threw a shovel into the hole and offered me a hand. "Will you be okay in those sandals? There could be nails and glass down there."

His grip was firm, his hand warm and callused. Fortunately, I'd worn jeans, not a skirt, to work at my machine embroidery boutique, In Stitches, that morning. We skied, scooted, and leaped down the slope into the excavation where Blueberry Cottage used to be.

The cottage was now on a sturdy new foundation higher in my backyard, finally safe from floods. Clay had been burying the old foundation stones when his front-end loader had scraped against metal, and he'd fetched me from my apartment underneath In Stitches. I'd been about to fix lunch.

He picked up the shovel and eased it into the earth. The muscles in his bare arms bulged. Could he have found the long-lost Elderberry Bay Lodge treasure?

Yesterday, one of his employees had unearthed skeletal remains on the grounds of the newly renovated lodge. This morning, the women in my machine embroidery workshop had discussed almost nothing besides that skeleton. They said it had been found with a silver belt buckle engraved with *Z*s. Everyone guessed that the remains were Snoozy Gallagher's.

Snoozy had owned the Elderberry Bay Lodge. About thirty years ago, when he'd been in his sixties, Snoozy had disappeared along with the contents of the lodge's safe — a substantial amount of cash along with several hundred thousand dollars' worth of jewelry belonging to the lodge's patrons.

The heist had occurred during the afternoon *before* the final banquet at a jewelers' convention, and each of those jewelers' wives had arrived at the lodge prepared to outshine all the others.

It must have been an interesting evening.

For years afterward, everyone assumed that Snoozy had fled the area, but yesterday's dreary discovery showed that he'd been buried on his own property, instead. Could his treasure have remained in Elderberry Bay, also, underneath the cottage that I'd bought, along with my shop and apartment, only a couple of miles from Snoozy's lodge and final resting place?

Clay gently brushed sand off the box. It was almost big enough to hold one of the sewing and embroidery machines I sold in my shop.

He stood back and leaned on the shovel. "I found the chest on your property," he said. "It's yours. You open it."

The sun beat into the sandy pit. I knelt beside the box. Above us, Clay's front-end loader stood silent, its bucket high and filled with soil. Without the gallant hero by my side, I might not have tried to budge the warped lid off the chest — I was afraid of finding someone's bones.

I was even more afraid when I saw the wadded-up black plastic garbage bag inside the box. Swallowing hard as if gulping could give me courage, I touched the twist tie. It broke and fell away.

Barely breathing, I eased the top edges of the bag apart.

I smelled the mildew before my eyes adjusted to the gloom inside the bag, and then I couldn't believe what I saw.

The bag seemed to be full of small leather and velvet pouches, discolored and thinned by damp.

Carefully, I lifted out a black velvet bag. It was heavy considering its size. I unlooped a fraying silken cord and peeked inside.

One thing about platinum and diamonds — they don't tarnish or disintegrate, even after thirty years of being tied in a plastic bag and buried in a steel box in the sand.

2

I couldn't manage even one tiny word. Overwhelmed by amazement and a shocked thrill that sent tremors through my arms and legs, I pulled out a diamond necklace and arranged it on top of the pouches.

Clay dropped his shovel and squatted beside me. "I wonder what happened."

Sun hammered down on the back of my neck. "Snoozy buried the treasure, and then died?"

Clay brushed a forefinger across the necklace's pear-shaped central diamond. "I was only about seven when he disappeared, but everyone said a detective followed his trail as far as Cleveland, where he supposedly bought a bus ticket to Mexico. Rumor had it that he didn't take much luggage with him, and everyone watched for him to come back and lead them to his stash, but no one ever saw him around here again."

Until yesterday . . .

"Maybe he did go to Mexico," Clay continued, "and then he came back and couldn't find his treasure. You know how ice knocked Blueberry Cottage around during winter floods?" He stood and pointed at the pit's walls. "Snoozy could have dug under the northeast corner when the treasure was really under the southwest corner. The moral of the story? Don't abandon your treasure on a flood plain."

I stood, too. "I'll try to remember that. And Snoozy might not have been able to do a thorough search. He might have worried that someone would hear him." The Arts and Crafts–style building that housed my shop and apartment could have been a private home when Snoozy came sneaking back for his treasure, but the buildings on either side of In Stitches would have housed stores with apartments above them, even then. Besides, people could have been living in Blueberry Cottage. "Or he might have been afraid that someone might come along the trail." The Elderberry River hiking trail ran behind my property. Beyond the trail, the river separated the village from the state forest. The thick hedges between my yard and my neighbors' could have been here thirty years ago, though perhaps not as tall. The jewels had been buried in a secluded, but not completely isolated, spot.

Sparkling and glinting beneath the sun's fierce rays, the diamonds at our feet almost seemed to dance. I itched to peek into all the other pouches.

Clay and I both removed phones from our pockets.

"Great minds," Clay said. "Do you know Chief Smallwood's number?"

"I've programmed it into my phone." A little drastic, perhaps, but I'd been known to need Elderberry Bay's only police officer at times when the situation didn't warrant dialing emergency.

She answered on the first ring. "Willow Vanderling. What's wrong?"

What made her ask that? Did warning lights flash whenever my name showed up on her call display? "Clay and I found something in my backyard. We think it could be Snoozy Gallagher's treasure."

"That's better than some of the things you've found, Willow." The tiniest of smiles eased into her voice. "I'll be right there."

I thanked her and disconnected the call. "Right there" could mean a few minutes or a half hour. She had jurisdiction over the village of Elderberry Bay plus the rural area surrounding it. When she wasn't on duty, troopers from the Pennsylvania State Police

15

kept an eye on things.

In that hole in the ground, sounds from outside were muffled. My blood rushed past my ears, and although I wasn't touching Clay, the warmth of his bare arm near mine needled my skin like sparks. He'd spent all of last fall, winter, and spring restoring the Elderberry Bay Lodge, and I'd hardly seen him. I hadn't been inside the lodge yet, but he'd done a fabulous job of bringing the majestic inn's exterior back to its reputed glory.

As if he might be reading my thoughts — about the lodge, anyway — he said, "I really like Ben Rondelson, the new owner of the Elderberry Bay Lodge. He's holding an opening celebration at the lodge next Friday night, dinner and everything. I think he and Haylee should meet each other. How about if you and Haylee go to the party with me? But let's not tell Haylee or Ben about our matchmaking."

"That sounds great." With any luck, Ben Rondelson wouldn't be married or a criminal — one of the guys Haylee had dated had been both.

Besides, having her along would take some of the pressure off me. I liked Clay, but we were only friends and had never gone out together. If I thought of the evening as a

16

real date with just the two of us, something horrid could happen, like I wouldn't be able to think of a thing to say. Haylee would keep us chatting.

I inched away from him and pointed at the diamond necklace. "Too bad I can't wear that." Even though I knew the necklace would probably go from the hole in my yard to a police vault to its real owner, I was already designing the perfect black dress to wear with it, perhaps based on the pattern of the bright coral scoop-necked blouse I was wearing. I'd used one of my machines to embroider a simple flame stitch around the neckline of the blouse, but the black dress would be unadorned, to show off the necklace.

Clay looked down at my throat. "Mmm. You look fine the way you are."

Men! There was no way I was going to a gala banquet in jeans. But I wouldn't care if *he* wore jeans. He always looked great. I'd seen women do double takes when they caught a glimpse of his square-jawed face, chocolate brown eyes, and easy smile. He never seemed to notice the effect he had on them, which, as far as I was concerned, made him even more attractive. I inched farther from him.

He asked, "Will your assistant mind that

you're away from In Stitches so long?"

"I've still got three quarters of my lunch hour left."

Up the hill on Lake Street, a car door slammed. The gate leading into one of my two side yards clanged.

Naturally, even though I expected Chief Smallwood, I pictured Snoozy Gallagher, stooped, wrinkled, freshly returned from Mexico, and dangerously determined.

Demanding his treasure. Perhaps at gunpoint . . .

3

Chief Smallwood appeared on the lip of the excavation. "Whoa!" she exclaimed. "That is some necklace. If no one claims it, you'll get to keep it, Willow."

"Clay found it." I blushed at visions of Clay and me dining out every night for weeks. Each time, I would wear a different set of jewels and a gorgeous new outfit that I would make and embellish with tiny touches of tasteful machine embroidery. To attend that many elegant dinners, we might have to go on a long (and romantic — my imagination was spinning out of control) cruise.

Smallwood dampened my optimism. "On the other hand, if it turns out to be part of Snoozy Gallagher's trove, you two could be charged for possessing stolen goods."

I finally knew her well enough to realize she was kidding.

Clay only encouraged her. "It's on *Willow's*

property," he deadpanned.

Smallwood slid down into the hole with us. I envied her those heavy black police officer boots. Protected only by sandals, my toes were gritty. As usual, Chief Smallwood managed not to mess up her neatly pressed navy blue uniform or her pert blond ponytail. She was shorter than I was, about average height. Her faultless peaches-and-cream complexion always made her appear barely out of her teens, though she had to be in her late twenties or early thirties. She wasn't trying to look super-tough at the moment, and was very pretty.

She put on plastic gloves, nudged the diamond necklace aside, and peeked into another pouch.

Blurting something improper and improbable about the nocturnal behavior of catfish, she jumped to her feet as if she'd been burned. "Emeralds, too. They look real to me, but we'd better call in experts. Meanwhile, we'll have to treat this as a crime scene." She pointed toward the grassy part of my yard. "Up you go."

With her right behind us, we clambered out of the excavation. She radioed the state police and said that a pair of civilians had found evidence that could be related to the case of the skeletal remains from the day before.

She ended the call and told us, "They'll send Detective Gartener. He's the lead detective investigating the old skeleton that Fred Zongassi dug up."

The satisfaction in her voice made me hide a smile. In addition to being handsome, Gartener was kind, fair, and capable. Smallwood and Gartener had been partners as state troopers, but when Gartener had been promoted to detective, Smallwood had left the state police and become Elderberry Bay's police chief. She was supposed to call the state police whenever she needed backup of any sort, and it seemed to me that she often asked for a detective.

Gartener was frequently the detective on duty for our part of the county . . .

I glanced at her ring finger. No engagement ring — yet.

She turned to Clay. "You'll have to stop excavating." She included me in her glance. "And stay away from that hole and the treasure in it while I go get some tape. Don't let anyone else in, either." She ran up to the street and came back with yellow police tape.

Before Clay and his employees had started moving Blueberry Cottage, they had rolled back the chain link fence on the river side of my property so they could drive their heavy earth- and cottage-moving equipment from the wide, flat trail into my yard. Because of my dogs, they'd temporarily bridged the gap in the fence with orange plastic snow fencing.

The yellow tape that Chief Smallwood draped across the orange mesh gave it a strangely festive look. She pointed at the gate leading from my yard to the trail. "You can still come and go through your gate, Willow, and use that side of your yard." She ran the tape up to Blueberry Cottage, across its riverside porch, and back down to the orange snow fencing.

Clay asked her, "Do you know yet if the bones Fred discovered yesterday were Snoozy Gallagher's?"

Smallwood bit the tape off the roll and tied the end to the fence. "Not yet."

Clay had another question for her. "Did you find any hint of how he died?"

"They're not sure what bashed in his skull. Maybe it was Fred with your bulldozer." Smallwood often found ways of sounding ever so slightly accusing.

Her tone didn't seem to bother Clay. He gave her a lazy grin. "It would have been an unusual accident. Fred sifts through the earth with that bucket as gently as if he were using a spoon."

I suggested, "Wouldn't a new fracture in a skull look different from an old one?"

Smallwood agreed that it would, and that this break had looked old to her. "But the lab will tell us, and will also give us an idea about how long ago the deceased was buried. You have to admit that ending up six feet under about the time he was supposedly hightailing it to Mexico could make his death look suspicious." She pierced Clay with one of her famous glares. "How long has Fred Zongassi worked for you?"

4

Clay became serious. "Fred's worked for me for a couple of months."

Smallwood took a notebook from her pocket. "What made you hire him?"

"He had the experience I needed, and he's really good with earthmoving equipment. He lived in Elderberry Bay as a kid, and after years out west, he wanted to come back."

Smallwood flipped back toward the beginning of her notebook. "Here's the thing. Thirty years ago, when Fred was in his early twenties, he was head gardener at the Elderberry Bay Lodge. A day or two before Snoozy disappeared, Fred had a noisy argument with Snoozy, quit his job, and wasn't seen around here again until recently." She looked up at Clay. "It gets worse. Yesterday, Fred didn't call me, or any law enforcement, as soon as he discovered those bones. He went off somewhere, first. We know that because other people heard his bulldozer shut off and saw him drive away about an hour before he called us, and he didn't return to the site until after that. Could he have found the treasure near the skeleton, and come over here during that hour, and buried the box?"

I shook my head. "The dogs and I were in the yard most of the time from twelve to one. Clay was the only one here from Fraser Construction."

Smallwood waved my comment aside. "Zongassi drove away from his bulldozer at one, and he called me shortly after two."

"Clay was here all afternoon," I protested.

He contradicted me. "Sorry, I wasn't. I took off from one to two. I borrowed Willow's new kayak, paddled up the river, and ate my lunch."

I'd told him to use that kayak anytime. I was hoping he'd like it so much that he would buy himself one, and we could go kayaking together. However, if I was going to daydream about boating with him, maybe I should aim for the cruise ship I'd been imagining earlier.

Smallwood asked Clay, "Did anyone see you?"

He shrugged. "Some ducks."

She gazed toward the river as if expecting

those ducks to waddle up the bank and corroborate what Clay had said. "Zongassi didn't need to come during his lunch hour, I suppose. He could have hidden the chest in his truck when it was parked at the Elderberry Bay Lodge, and then driven over here at night. How well do you know him, Clay?"

"Not well, but he's been an excellent employee."

Chief Smallwood's eyes became a steelier shade of blue. "Don't you find it strange that one of your employees dug up bones at the lodge yesterday, and you found a possibly related treasure here today?"

Clay waved toward his bright yellow front-end loader. "Digging up related things in different places could be strange, but it's not odd that Fraser Construction was involved in both, since we are the only people around here with this kind of equipment."

Smallwood only grunted.

Clay's jaw tightened. "I'll talk to Fred."

"No need." Smallwood flicked her ponytail over her shoulder. "We already have questioned him, and will again if we need to."

"I guess we shouldn't have touched that chest," I admitted. "But before Clay dug it out, the ground around it didn't *look* like it had been disturbed."

"I didn't think so, either." Clay propped his shovel against the front-end loader. "It was straight down from where that grass is over there. Besides, the box is rusty, and the sand around it was discolored, with rust, I thought."

Smallwood grunted again. "It's going to be hard to pile up grains of sand the way they were."

I had to admire her skill with sarcasm.

Squinting against the sun, she looked up at our faces. "Can one of you stick around until Gartener and his team get here? I don't want anyone accusing me of helping myself to any of those gems."

"You wouldn't do that," I said. My relationship with her had been rocky, but I was as certain of her honesty as I was of my own and Clay's. Wealth — and that included diamonds and emeralds — didn't matter to any of us as much as living with our own consciences. I added, "I'll stick around, but first, I'd better go tell my assistant what's keeping me."

Leaving the other two to keep an eye on the unburied treasure, I ran up the hill past Blueberry Cottage, which was now firmly bolted to its new foundation and ready for the renovations Clay and I had been planning. I slid open the glass door leading from my patio to my apartment. My dogs, Sally-Forth and Tally-Ho, greeted me with wagging tails and pointedly hopeful glances at the backyard. They loved Clay. They also loved to investigate recent excavations, but this would not be a great time for one of their mining projects.

I told them to stay, and as always, they obeyed. Keeping them inside, I slid the patio door closed and gave each of them a home-baked dog biscuit.

My open-concept great room with its compact but convenient kitchen was aboveground, with floor-to-ceiling windows overlooking Blueberry Cottage, my treed yard, the hiking trail, the Elderberry River, and the state forest beyond it all. I loved the view but would probably want to make drapes, especially if I succeeded in renting Blueberry Cottage to tourists.

The fun thing about drapes would be the amount of embroidery I'd be able to add to them. I'd keep it simple like the rest of the embroidery in the apartment. My basic color scheme was white, but I had embroidered soft furnishings for punches of color. For June, my accent colors were yellow and navy. I planned to replace the yellow with red during July — I was a sucker for red and white stripes, and I'd been embroidering white stars on navy fabric. For August, I would switch to cooling greens and blues, maybe with wavy designs embroidered on them.

I trotted up the stairs, opened the door at the top, and almost ran into Haylee. She and I were the same age and size, and although she was blond and her face wasn't as long as mine and her eyes were a more vivid shade of blue, many folks thought we were sisters. An expert tailor, she sewed all of her clothes, and today's printed jean jacket and matching skirt were gorgeous. She demanded, "What's Chief Smallwood's cruiser doing in front of your place, Willow?"

Looking concerned, Ashley, my sixteen-year-old summer assistant, hovered nearby.

No customers were in the shop at the moment, but I lowered my voice, anyway. "Clay found something in my backyard —"

Haylee clapped her hand to her mouth. "Not —"

"Nothing *bad*," I explained. "But it *could* be the Elderberry Bay Lodge treasure, so we reported it to Chief Smallwood."

Ashley gasped. "The Elderberry Bay Lodge treasure? *Really?*"

Haylee insisted on a full description.

I gabbled about gems and precious metals and lovingly crafted pouches.

Ashley breathed. "I can't *wait* to tell people that my boss found the treasure the whole world has been looking for, like, forever!"

Haylee agreed. "Ever since yesterday when they heard that Snoozy's remains had probably been found, everyone's been making conjectures about where that treasure could have ended up." She gave me a stern look. "They're saying Snoozy may have been murdered. You be careful. Don't get yourself into danger."

"Snoozy disappeared thirty years ago," I pointed out. "He may have come back later, but even if he did, his killer would be long gone by now." I would tell her Smallwood's comments about one of Clay's employees later, when Ashley wasn't around to hear and spread the news.

Haylee relaxed her shoulders. "If you aren't going to be careful, like late at night walking your dogs, bring me along for the fun."

"Okay." The dogs always needed exercise, and so did we, and if our walks late at night just happened to coincide with a necessary bit of snooping, could we help it?

"Maybe you should change the name of

your shop," she teased. "Yours merits the name of The Stash more than mine does, now."

Ashley giggled.

Haylee added, "I wish I could stay to see *your* stash, Willow, but customers may need me in mine."

I watched her trot across Lake Street to her fabric store at one end of a row of textile arts shops on the ground floor of a perfectly maintained redbrick Victorian building. The other shops sold yarn, notions, and quilting supplies. Even before I'd first opened In Stitches, those four shops had given Elderberry Bay a nickname that was now familiar for miles around — Threadville.

I asked Ashley if she could hold out and take her lunch hour a little later if mine lasted longer than usual. She said she'd be fine. "And if I run into problems, I'll just holler out the back window for the police."

I laughed. I was lucky to have her working for me full time during the summer. In addition to her sense of humor, she had enormous talent with thread art. Stitching freehand with her mother's old zigzag sewing machine, she'd been the only contestant in Pennsylvania to place higher than honorable mention in a major international machine embroidery competition.

I thanked her, ran downstairs, whipped up a lunch for three, and carried a tray outside. Fortunately, the table and chairs I'd set up near Blueberry Cottage's original location were beyond the taped crime scene. I plunked the tray down on the table and called Chief Smallwood and Clay.

We finished our sandwiches and were about to dig into a tin of my secret recipe chocolate chip cookies when Detective Gartener, wearing jeans, T-shirt, and a blazer, arrived with two uniformed state troopers. Gartener nodded at Smallwood, and then shook Clay's and my hands. "Good to see you both again." A smile lurked behind his dark brown eyes, quite a change from the first time I'd met him, when he'd been stern, inscrutable, and just plain scary.

All six of us munched cookies while Smallwood briefed Detective Gartener and the two younger troopers. Commenting on the marks that Clay had drawn in the sand with his front-end loader and his shovel, the troopers helped Gartener carry the box out of the pit. They set it on the grass. Detective Gartener opened the top few pouches.

It didn't take him long to decide that the jewelry probably was real and must have come from the Elderberry Bay Lodge robbery. "Before we take this away," he said, "I want you all, including Clay and Willow, to help me inventory what's in this treasure chest. I don't want any questions later about what was or wasn't there." He had the deepest, most resonant voice of any human outside a film studio.

After a look at my eyes, which had to be wide with anticipation, Smallwood laughed. "This will be fun," she said.

5

With Clay, Detective Gartener, and the two troopers watching us, Chief Smallwood and I took turns emptying the pouches, one at a time, into each other's hands, which we held over my outdoor table. We didn't want to drop stray gems onto the grass.

Well, maybe I'd have *liked* that, but I wasn't about to do it.

None of the pouches held stray gems, though. All of the stones were set in bracelets, rings, necklaces, earrings, brooches, and tiaras. With knowledge and enthusiasm, Smallwood described each piece of jewelry and made certain that one of the uniformed troopers transcribed her words perfectly into his notebook while the other trooper took photos. Gartener labeled the pouches.

After we'd itemized everything, Clay pointed out that according to local legend, a large amount of cash had also been stolen from the safe at the Elderberry Bay Lodge.

"But we got to the bottom of the box. There's no money."

One of the young troopers glowered at Clay and me as if he believed we'd taken the cash before we'd called the police.

Gartener pointed out, "Whoever emptied that safe may have spent the cash but hidden the jewels until the hue and cry died down." He gave Clay and me a friendly look. "Thanks for your help. You two can go."

I picked up the tray of plates and glasses and left the remaining cookies behind. Walking up the hill with Clay, I studied my lawn with new interest. "Did you notice anything resembling buried treasure when you excavated the new foundation for Blueberry Cottage?" I asked.

He glanced down at me with a glint of teasing appreciation in his eyes. "Want to dig up the rest of your yard after the police are done with it?"

"Sure!" I was only partly joking.

"Let me know when we're allowed in your yard again. And next Friday night, how about if I pick you up at six thirty for the gala?"

"That would be great." I had seven days to figure out what to wear.

"I'll go ask Haylee to come with us." Clay

waved and strode uphill toward the gate leading to the front yard.

Humming, I jockeyed my tray of dishes and glasses through the door to my great room and past two snoopy dog noses. I dashed upstairs and thanked Ashley for looking after the shop for so long. She lived only a few blocks away with her parents and younger sisters and brothers, and usually went home for lunch. I told her to take until half past two if she wanted.

She was back long before that. When our afternoon workshop ended, we stitched new designs with our embroidery machines. Our fervor nearly always intrigued browsers. Ashley had a flair for describing the features of all of our fun machines, so I let her do that while I measured, cut, and sold natural fabrics, gave advice about embroidery-gone-wrong, and helped match thread colors to designs.

Usually, the Threadville tour buses left shortly after our shops closed, but it was the summer solstice, and Threadville was staging its first Midsummer Madness Sidewalk Sale. Both busloads of Threadville tourists, one from Erie, and one from eastern Ohio, were staying for the evening.

After our customers took off for supper, Ashley and I gathered and priced items for the sale, then set up long, folding tables in the opening between the pillars near the top of the porch steps. Ashley left for supper, and I went downstairs to eat with Sally-Forth and Tally-Ho.

Haylee phoned. "I got the strangest invitation today."

"Going to the lodge's opening gala with Clay and me? I hope you can make it."

"Don't you want to be alone with him?"

She knew me pretty well.

"I might run out of things to say! Come on, it will be three friends going out together."

"Okay." She quickly got to the important stuff. "What are you going to wear?"

"I'll think of something." I told her that Clay and I had been allowed to help make an inventory of the jewels.

"Wow," she said. "I'd loved to have seen them. And touched them."

"You had customers."

She heaved a sigh. "You're right. See you at tomorrow's picnic, if not before."

I finished my supper, then leashed the dogs and took them out through the patio door. Smallwood waved at us from the other side of the police tape. Sally-Forth and Tally-Ho whimpered, but Smallwood didn't come closer. From the sounds, I guessed the chief was watching people dig with shovels. Clay's front-end loader, with Clay's shovel still leaning against it, sat alone and unneeded.

I urged the dogs up to the gate. From the front yard, we could see the shops across the street. Tables were set up in front of The Stash, Tell a Yarn, Buttons and Bows, and Batty About Quilts. On our side of Lake Street, tables waited for merchandise on the sidewalk in front of the old-timey hardware store and the home décor boutique.

We headed down the hill. Threadville tourists thronged Pier 42's outdoor patio, and several of them were having picnics in the park that connected the sandy beaches along the river with the more extensive Lake Erie beach. A few hardy people braved the cool June waters.

I took the dogs home and then carried sale items to the tables on my front porch. Ashley returned and helped me arrange them.

At eight, the Midsummer Madness Sidewalk Sale began.

At five after eight, the sale lived up to the madness part of its name.

6

Across Lake Street, shrill voices rose in anger. I grabbed a porch pillar and stood on tiptoe to see over the crowd.

At Haylee's table in front of The Stash, two women tugged at opposite corners of a remnant. The stouter one with the maroon curly hair wore a red polo shirt. The taller woman's long blond hair straggled down the back of a teal tank top, but that was all I could see of the women. I didn't recognize them.

Opal, Haylee's mother, left her sale tables at Tell a Yarn, eased into the melee next door, and must have said something calming. The shouting stopped.

Haylee went into The Stash and came out with a bolt of fabric in each arm, obviously a peace offering.

Opal returned to her tables, and I went back to selling embroidery hoops, precut stabilizer, adorable little scissors shaped like birds, and embroidery thread in luscious colors. Making room for new merchandise was always a bonus.

Several of the regular Threadville tourists oohed and aahed over embroidery thread I was offering at half price. "It's old stock," I warned them. "Thread can dry and become brittle. I've kept it out of sunlight and dust, but it may be more likely than new thread to fray and break."

They were happy, anyway. One of the problems with machine embroidery, if we could call it a problem, was that each design seemed to require colors we didn't have, and we had to buy more.

"Fishing line?" a man asked in a deep voice. Tom Umshaw showed me the spool of gray monofilament nylon thread in his hand. He was one of the fishermen who sold their catches down at the wharf. I'd bought a batch of Lake Erie yellow perch fillets from him recently.

"Maybe if you're angling for minnows," I joked.

"Hardly." Tall and broad-shouldered, he had a deep tan and creases beside his eyes from time spent in the sun and on the water. His hair was prematurely salt-and-pepper, and so thick it probably wouldn't lie down even if he wore a fisherman's cap over it all day. His gray eyes seemed bleached by the sun, yet accustomed to searching the horizon for signs of storms. "What's this stuff for? Do you sew with it?"

"Sometimes," I answered. "If we want our stitches to be almost invisible on dark fabrics."

He bought the thread. This past winter, when ice prevented him from going out in his commercial fishing boat, he had enrolled in Haylee's sewing classes. She'd told me that he had started calling himself a "seamster" and was very good at the actual sewing, but ignored the instruction sheets that came with patterns. He claimed he liked the challenge of figuring out how the pieces should go together. Maybe I could interest him in machine embroidery next time he had to tie up his boat for the winter. Machine embroidery had more to do with manipulating pictures on a computer screen than reading fine print.

"How was that perch?" he asked me. "Did you cook it the way I told you?"

"It was fine." The fish had been great, but even though I'd followed his (verbal, not written) instructions, it had curled and the batter had fallen off and made odd little dumplings in the hot oil. Both men and women could become seamsters, but I suspected that men were, somehow, better at frying fish.

"Cookies, anyone?" Smiling, Neil Ondover, the owner of La Bakery, held out a platter of yummy-looking treats. I loved peanut butter cookies, and although I baked them nearly every week, I couldn't resist one of Neil's. Ashley turned him down, but everyone else helped themselves.

Tom took a handful. "Thanks, bud," he said. "When are you coming out in the boat with me?"

Neil looked a little green around the gills. "Never."

"What's wrong?" Tom laughed. "The waves go up, the waves go down. You get used to it."

Neil, who was short and wiry, grinned up at his friend. Neil appeared to be in his mid forties, while Tom looked a little more weathered. It was easy to see that they'd been teasing each other for years. Neil challenged, "You come to La Bakery and bake and decorate a wedding cake, and I'll go out in your boat."

Palms up as if to ward off evil, Tom backed away. "Huh-uh, no. Don't give me anything to do with weddings."

Neil laughed. "One of these days, one of your babes will net you."

Tom shook his head. "Nope." He joined the crowds milling in the street.

Carrying his tray of cookies, Neil ambled off toward the hardware store. Most evenings, local men gathered inside The Ironmonger, but tonight they hung around outside. Like the beaches, restaurants, snack bars, and souvenir shops, the hardware store was a refuge for those who, for some incomprehensible reason, weren't interested in sewing, knitting, crocheting, quilting, embroidering, home décor, or the latest Threadville offering, costumes.

Georgina, one of my regular customers, approached our table. She lived in Elderberry Bay, and always seemed to dress in only one color at a time. Tonight's elegant outfit was a silvery tunic and matching slacks that she had embroidered all over with a machine she'd bought from me. She reached for a spool of magenta silk embroidery thread.

A skinny blonde in a teal tank top jostled her and grabbed the spool.

Goose bumps spiked up the back of my neck. I was almost certain the blonde had been one of the two women involved in the ruckus in front of The Stash.

Georgina usually said what she thought, but this time the thin line of her mouth and the flush on her cheeks made her self-control obvious. Without saying a word, she stepped back, away from the thread and the straggly-haired blonde.

I told Georgina, "I'll get you another spool of thread like that from inside."

The blonde flung the spool down and drifted away without buying anything. I *gave* Georgina the thread.

In the crowd, I caught a glimpse of the blonde talking to a maroon-haired woman in a red polo shirt. Were the two women friends now, or about to start another fight? A shorter woman joined them, but I could see only part of her back. She had short, light brown curly hair and wore a pink plaid shirt. Together, all three of them drifted down the hill toward the beach.

Across the street, Haylee and Opal and the two women who had helped Opal raise Haylee were still selling everything from fine crochet cotton to cozy, high-loft quilt batting.

Fairy lights in trees added a celebratory touch, while Threadville's streetlights, with their gas lamp styling, were charming. However, by ten o'clock, when we'd scheduled the Midsummer Madness Sidewalk Sale to end, none of the outdoor lights were bright enough for making change or checking signatures against charge cards, and the Threadville tour buses chugged away. Women waved and called through open bus windows.

Haylee and her mothers tidied the sidewalks in front of their stores. People meandered down Lake Street toward the beach, where the almost full moon and puffy clouds could be putting on quite a show. Ashley and I had sold most of what we'd offered, so we had little to do besides fold the tables and lug them back into the storeroom.

Before long, I would need to start opening In Stitches for a full day of Saturday browsing and sales. I loved my store and my life in Threadville, but not for such long stretches. This June's midsummer madness was over. What a relief.

And Sally-Forth and Tally-Ho wanted relief, too. I leashed them and we walked Ashley home.

I watched until she let herself into her house and turned to wave good-bye, and then the dogs and I started back.

On Lake Street, Haylee and all three of her mothers had put everything away, and their flower gardens again dominated the fronts of their stores. Spirea and roses glowed under streetlamps. Although Haylee's mother and her friends had lived together from the time Haylee was born, looking after Opal's fatherless child together, taking turns going to school and work, they now each had their own apartments above their stores, and Haylee's store and apartment were the largest. All four apartments were lit with a homey glow.

Opal and her two best friends had met in kindergarten. When they read *Macbeth* in junior high, they began calling themselves the Three Weird Sisters. Haylee naturally referred to them as The Three Weird Mothers, which didn't bother them at all. They thought Haylee was just about perfect. They were very perceptive women.

As always when I thought about Haylee and her three mothers, I smiled. I wasn't sure that Haylee's mothers always remembered that I wasn't also their daughter. Having these four good friends living across the street was wonderful — and often comforting, especially when things went wrong in my yard or my shop.

I took the dogs through the gate and down the slope to the patio outside my great room. In the warm night air, the heady sweetness of linden blossoms was almost overwhelming. Blueberry Cottage waited quietly for renovations that Clay and I would have to delay until the investigators were done with my yard.

None of the investigators were around at the moment, but beyond the tape-festooned snow fencing, a man and woman sauntered along the riverside path. The moon glinted in patches on the river. The couple turned toward the water, and she rested her head on his shoulder.

Only seven more days, I thought. *An evening with Clay.*

7

I'd fallen asleep thinking about Clay and my date with him. I woke up counting the days. This was Saturday. Our date was next Friday. Six and a half more days. But I would also see him and his band at the community picnic, only hours away. Fraser Construction had grown since I'd first met Clay. Discovering that nearly every one of his employees played an instrument, he'd started a band. Clay played the trumpet.

All morning and afternoon, everyone in my shop was in a holiday mood, looking forward to the picnic and crowing about the bargains they'd bought at the sidewalk sale.

After my last customer left for the evening, I closed In Stitches, leashed the dogs, and took them out to my backyard. We were able to stay on the correct side of the police tape and go through the back gate for a quick stroll along the riverside trail.

When we returned, I eyed Clay's front-end loader. Digging holes in my yard with that thing could be fun.

The dogs probably had similar ideas, though they might prefer slightly more primitive tools. I took them inside.

I put on jeans, sneakers, and a navy blue T-shirt with the Elderberry Bay Volunteer Fire Department logo on the front and *FIRE* screen-printed in huge white letters across the back. Leaving my dogs behind, I took off for the picnic.

The temperature was perfect. I wouldn't swelter in the firefighter's outfit I'd promised to wear for the first part of the evening. From the hill above the beach, the aromas of vanilla, cinnamon, and boiling oil — the good kind — whetted my appetite for funnel cakes and French fries.

The picnic appeared to be a hit with children. They shouted inside a bouncy castle, petted baby farm animals in a pen surrounded by hay bales, and ran around with their faces painted to resemble cats, flowers, and superheroes. Emergency medical technicians gave tours of the ambulance. Chief Smallwood sat in the driver's seat of her cruiser, showing excited kids the gadgets built into the car. She must have found time to buy supper. Plates of deep-fried Lake Erie yellow perch fillets, asparagus salad, and strawberry shortcake balanced on her dashboard.

Wearing her firefighter's jacket unbuttoned over her official department T-shirt, Haylee helped a squirming toddler up into the fire truck's passenger seat.

I opened one of the truck's storage lockers, grabbed a pair of firefighter's pants, stepped into them, and snapped my suspenders. Kids laughed. I toed my sneakers off and slid my feet into the clumsy boots. Like Haylee, I didn't bother fastening my jacket. Finally, I plopped a helmet on my head without bothering to tuck my hair underneath it. The kids found that funny, too.

Our new fire chief blasted the siren for a second. Haylee and I jumped. Our pint-sized audience laughed harder. "It startles me every time," one mother said.

We lifted children into and out of the fire truck until every kid at the picnic who wanted to sit in a fire truck had done it, some of them several times, and the fire chief announced that it was the truck's bedtime. Haylee and I stowed our gear. Everyone under four feet tall rowed up along the curb and gazed wistfully as the bright red fire truck, siren blaring and lights strobing, roared up the hill toward the fire station, a little more than a block away. The ambulance left, too, at a speed that caused the children to lose their bereft expressions and jump around in impromptu dances.

Eating strawberry shortcake, Chief Smallwood leaned against her cruiser. She waved a fork. We waggled our fingers at her and took off toward a tent labeled *Tom's Fish Fry*.

Tom piled fillets of fried perch on my plate.

"That looks lots better than when I cooked it," I admitted.

He pointed his slotted spoon at his deep fryer. "Nothing beats deep frying. You have to cook these suckers really fast. A little light breading, then into the pot, and right back out."

I ordered onion rings to go with mine, and Haylee chose sweet potato fries. We bought drinks and wended our way between families to Opal, Naomi, and Edna, who were beckoning to us from a table close to the beach.

Opal had given birth to Haylee when Opal and her two best friends were only seventeen. Haylee's three mothers had celebrated their fiftieth birthdays recently, but they were fit and always teasing each other, and appeared much younger than they actually were.

Opal was almost as tall as Haylee and looked a lot like her, complete with the long blond hair, but while Haylee tailored her own clothes from fabrics she sold at The Stash, Opal knit or crocheted every garment she owned. Tonight, she wore a pale aqua T-shirt and matching slacks that I'd seen her crocheting with cotton yarn during her Friday night storytelling evenings at Tell a Yarn. She stared at our firefighter T-shirts in pretend shock. "Willow and Haylee, those are *lovely* T-shirts! So creative and original."

Edna, the shortest of the three women, almost never ventured out without some of the embellishments she sold at Buttons and Bows. With red and blue tapestry trim running down the outside seams of her red capris and tank top, she resembled a toreador. A headband she'd made from the tapestry trim corralled her hair, sort of. Crimson and navy points of hair stuck up all over the top of her head. She pointed her fork at me. "Printed, Willow, not machine embroidered?"

I had to grin. Although I tried to restrain myself, I used my machines to embroider almost every garment I owned. I thought of it as marketing. Neither Haylee nor I were advertising our shops at the moment, but the white *FIRE* across my back made me feel important. If anyone needed help at the picnic, they could easily find Haylee or me.

Naomi, who always stood up for everyone, complimented us. "No one else looks as good as you two do in jeans."

I could think of someone who looked much better in jeans. I would soon see him in his shiny band uniform . . .

I thanked Naomi. She owned Batty About Quilts, and nearly everything she wore had been pieced together from several colors and patterns of fabric. For winter, she added batting and backing, and quilted all the layers together. For summer, she simply sewed the cottons together in interesting ways. She wore a long skirt, all pastel batiks, with a pale yellow cotton T-shirt she had crocheted during storytelling evenings. Despite Edna's frequent hints and suggestions about hair colors, Naomi was letting natural gray highlight her brown hair. She had, however, obtained big sequins from Edna and had stitched them to both her top and her skirt, so she wasn't completely immune to Edna's brand of flamboyance.

Edna examined the food on Haylee's and my plates. "You two didn't get any asparagus and bocconcini salad. You should before it's all gone. It's delicious. I poured some of their hot pepper vinaigrette on mine."

Naomi shuddered. "Opal and I can't understand how Edna and Haylee can stomach asparagus."

I confessed that I loved it. "But let me see if I can eat all these fried goodies, first. And someone around here is making funnel cakes."

Haylee said, "La Bakery is serving strawberry shortcake. With fresh strawberries."

I muttered, "Life is just full of tough decisions."

The perch and onion rings were delicious, and Haylee shared her sweet potato fries.

Opal, Naomi, and Edna left, probably to gather in one of their apartments to gossip, play with needlework, and drink beverages that weren't available at the family-oriented picnic.

Greeting old friends and making new ones, Haylee and I headed to the salad tent. A placard advertised asparagus salad, coleslaw, potato salad, and macaroni salad. Unfortunately, though, the last serving bowl was being carted away.

By a woman with maroon curls. She hopped up into the back of a large white van with no windows except for its windshield.

I elbowed Haylee and whispered, "Is that one of the women who fought over the remnant?"

"I think so."

Tripping over heavy-duty electrical cords strung across the lawn, we hurried to the rear of the van, but all we saw of the woman was a flash of her navy blue long-sleeved shirt and her hand as she pulled the back door shut. Seconds later, the van rumbled away.

The sun was still high above the horizon. The time for salads might be over, but there was plenty to do. Funnel cake or strawberry shortcake?

Fresh strawberries. And Neil's shortcake would be the real thing. Besides, I'd had enough fried food to last me awhile. Decisions weren't that tough, after all.

A tiny, energetic woman I'd never seen at La Bakery worked the cash register. "Hi," she said. "Are you two from around here?" She looked maybe all of twenty-one. Some of her light brown curls had popped out of the holes in her hairnet, giving her a whimsical look, like she'd decorated her head with randomly placed springs.

We explained that we owned some of the shops in town.

She snapped her fingers. "You serve cookies in your shops, right? You must spend a lot of your free time baking." Her gray eyes were guileless, her skin freckled and young. "I'm Cassie, La Bakery's new manager, and I have an idea for you. Can I come by your shops tonight after the picnic?"

"Sure," I said. "How about if all three of us meet at In Stitches around ten?"

Haylee and Cassie agreed.

Neil heaped strawberries and whipped cream on round, flaky shortcake, then handed us our mountainous desserts. Despite creating all sorts of wonderful baked goods day after day, he somehow managed to stay thin. He beamed at Cassie, but she was looking at us, not at him. Was he thinking of her as a potential girlfriend? He must be more than twice her age, but he probably seldom met women who didn't tower over him, and she was short. Was she avoiding his gaze in hopes of fending off his advances?

I felt suddenly protective of the girl. I'd obviously spent too much time around Haylee's mothers with their penchant for looking after everybody and everything. I handed Cassie the correct change. "These smell wonderful," I said.

Spooning whipped cream and strawberries into our mouths, Haylee and I sauntered toward the bandstand. The Fraser Construction Marching Band weren't marching, but they were warming up.

Clay looked yummy in that red and white uniform with gold braid crisscrossing his chest. He marked time with his trumpet, and then the band launched into a Sousa march.

We finished our shortcake. I was going to stay and listen for the rest of the evening.

Someone behind me touched my elbow. I turned around.

Chief Smallwood stared at the band. "See the gray-haired clarinet player in the high-top sneakers?" she asked.

He was hard to miss. One of his white satin pant legs was caught in the top of one of those black sneakers, and he was gazing at Chief Smallwood as he played. I couldn't be certain, but if I was hearing his clarinet, he was really good.

"That's Fred Zon . . . Fred Zhong . . ." Chief Smallwood's face was pale, tinged with green. Perspiration stood out in droplets all over her forehead.

"What's wrong?" I whispered to her.

"Shh. Don't make a fuss, but come with me."

8

"Come with me quietly." Chief Smallwood turned toward Lake Street. "Please." It came out, "pleesh." She stumbled. "Help me to my cruisher."

Haylee and I reached for her arms, but she shook us off. "Just walk beside me. Don't call attention to me."

Did she think that a washed-out, staggering policewoman in her uniform, complete with bulletproof vest, wouldn't be noticed?

Frantically, I looked around for help, but the fire and ambulance personnel had left. Haylee's mothers must be in one of their apartments sharing a bottle of wine. Like Haylee and me, Clay was a volunteer firefighter. He seemed capable of everything, including resuscitating the near-dead, but he was playing his trumpet and leading his band in another rousing march. Chief Smallwood probably wouldn't appreciate my interrupting the concert and making it clear to all of Elderberry Bay that she was under the weather.

"What's wrong?" I asked her again.

"Shick." Yes, it was obvious that she was sick.

"You can't drive," Haylee informed her.

"Have to." She ran the words together.

"My apartment's up the street," I reminded her. "Lie down until you feel better."

"Call 911," Haylee said to me. "She's sweating and shivering."

"No!" Smallwood protested. "I don't want *anyone* seeing me like this. I'll be fine." She took a wobbly step, sighed, and halted. "Okay, Willow. I'll go to your place, but let's take the trail. Maybe no one will see us."

One thing about Chief Smallwood — she was determined. Chin up, eyes focusing straight ahead, breaths shallow, she walked between us, and probably managed, except for her greenish face, to look almost normal.

I asked her, "Why did you point out that clarinet player? Is that Fred Zongassi? Clay's employee?"

"Yes."

"Did Fred make you sick?"

"No. I don't know. Do not trust him."

Promising her that I wouldn't, I opened the gate. We crept up the hill. "Why did the

investigators stop working?" I asked Smallwood.

"Almost done. Comparing our inventory
to list of stolen jewelry. They should release
the scene soon." She slurred the ss. By the
time we'd climbed the hill to my back patio,
Haylee was holding her up. I dashed inside
and shut the dogs into my bedroom. Haylee
led Smallwood, now greener than ever and
trembling, over the threshold.

We helped Smallwood into my guest
room. "You'll be my first guest," I told her.

"I can't lie on that beautiful bed in my
uniform!" Smallwood could look fierce even
when she was about to faint.

I turned down the white embroidered duvet and plumped the pillows. "Don't worry
about it." I'd had my parents in mind when
I'd decorated the room and its en suite
bathroom in embroidered whites, but my
mother was always too busy in the South
Carolina House of Representatives to stray
into the northern reaches of Pennsylvania,
and my father always stayed home, putter-
ing with his inventions and occasionally
emerging from his workshop to barbecue a
steak. Fortunately, they had a housekeeper
who shopped and cooked for them, or
they'd have gone hungry.

Smallwood dashed to the guest room's en

suite bathroom. Eventually, she crawled out on her hands and knees. We helped her sit on the edge of the bed. With great concentration, she unloaded her gun, then carefully tucked the cartridges into a pocket and stashed the weapon underneath a pillow. Finally, apologizing for creating problems, she flopped down with her head on the pillow, one hand covering her eyes, and her booted feet hanging over the side of the bed. She didn't object when Haylee and I each tackled a boot and untied it.

A siren sounded in the distance. All three of us tensed. "Can't be a fire truck," Haylee said. "The whistle on the station didn't go off." She pulled off one of Smallwood's boots.

I tossed the other one to the floor. "And it's not Chief Smallwood's cruiser. She's here."

Smallwood muttered, "Would you stop calling me that? My name's Vicki-with-an-i-no-e. And anyway, that's an ambulance."

How could she tell? I hoped she'd radioed for one for herself, but the siren dwindled off into the distance.

I asked Vicki if she had any family in the area.

"No."

I straightened her boots near the foot of

the bed. "Friends?"

She opened her mouth and closed it again.

I pulled the duvet over her. "What about Detective Gartener?"

She gasped. "No! Don't you dare call Toby. I'll . . . I'll . . . well, you'll wish you hadn't."

"But he has always been helpful," I said. It was true, except for the first time I'd met him, when he'd frightened me half to death with his penetrating, accusing silences.

"I don't want him seeing me like this."

I hadn't guessed that our police chief would have this vain streak.

Vicki managed to be assertive even when whispering. "And don't tell your boyfriend, either."

I denied, "I don't have —"

She waved my words aside. "Clay Fraser. He might tell Toby. I have my radio, so if there's an emergency, I'll either respond to the call or ask for help from the state police. Meanwhile, don't tell *anyone* until I'm back on my feet. Just knowing that I'm temporarily incapacitated could cause folks to drive around like maniacs and *cause* police emergencies."

She looked so pathetic that I agreed I wouldn't tell anyone she was in my apartment. *Unless you get worse, Vicki.* I put my fingers on her wrist. Her pulse felt strong.

Her complexion gained the tiniest tinge of pink, and her ragged breathing became more rhythmical. Softly, I told her that if she wanted to change out of her uniform, she should look in the closet for the waffle weave summer bathrobes — embroidered, of course — that I'd hung there for guests. She didn't respond. Maybe she'd wake up totally recovered in an hour or two and would be able to drive her cruiser home. She wasn't going to like leaving it on Lake Street.

Haylee and I tiptoed out of my guest room. I closed the door and let Sally and Tally out of my bedroom.

Sally went straight to the guest room door, wagged her tail, and whimpered.

"You can't go in there, Sally," I told her. "Chief Smallwood needs to rest."

Sally curled up next to the door. Haylee and I sat on my comfy couch and shared a pot of tea. Shortly before ten, we went upstairs to my shop for our appointment with Neil's assistant. Tally came with us, but Sally, who seldom departed from Tally's side, stayed beside Vicki's room. I left the stairway door open so I would hear Vicki if she called, then unlocked the front door.

"I hope we don't all come down with the

flu," Haylee said.

My sea glass chimes jangled and Cassie trudged in. She looked exhausted. She'd taken off her hairnet, but many of her curls were still flat while others sprouted like wild cartoon hair.

I said to Haylee, "Maybe it's food poisoning." Although I had spent very little time around my mother recently, I'd listened to her carefully years ago when she'd still been a family physician. Like other doctors' children, I probably thought I knew all about medicine and health.

Cassie slapped a brand-new red notebook onto my cutting table. "Please don't call it food poisoning," she said. "Several people got sick at the picnic, including Neil. He helped me put everything away, but all of a sudden, he could barely stand. It *wasn't* food poisoning, but even if it was, it did not come from La Bakery." Despite her rather wonky logic, challenge sparked from her eyes. Tally had been standing in front of her, his tail held low but waving gently back and forth. He backed into his pen and stomped a nest, around and around, in his bed.

I understood why Cassie might be upset. This sudden epidemic had occurred right after she'd become La Bakery's manager, and she was probably afraid that people suspected her of causing the problem. "Tell Neil to get better quickly," I said. "And don't worry about food poisoning coming from La Bakery. Haylee and I gobbled every bit of your strawberry shortcake. We're fine."

"Then, can I bring you each a couple dozen cookies, free, first thing Tuesday morning? If your customers like them, I can deliver them to your shops as often as you like until you tell me to stop."

Haylee and I both accepted the offer, but after Cassie dashed out, running her hand through her curls and probably making them more unruly, Haylee and I agreed that if Neil was sick, maybe we didn't want his cookies until after he had completely recovered.

"What did Vicki Smallwood and Neil eat that we didn't?" Haylee asked.

I straightened a bolt of lightweight mint green linen that my students and I liked to hem and embroider for tea towels. "Vicki had perch, asparagus salad, and strawberry shortcake on her dashboard. And she had an insulated cup of something as well. Coffee?"

Haylee held up fingers, one for each food item. "You and I had perch and strawberry shortcake. We had canned drinks. And we didn't have any of that asparagus salad."

I gnawed at my thumb. "Edna did."

Haylee hauled out her phone and punched in numbers. "Hi, Opal." She called all of her mothers by their first names.

Opal's response came clearly, even to me, and I wasn't right beside Haylee. "Edna's sick!"

Haylee asked questions and ended the call. "Edna has the same symptoms that Vicki has, and she refuses to allow Gord near her."

The village's popular older doctor was dating Edna. He insisted that Haylee and I call him by his first name. Like everyone else, we thought he was fabulous, so we'd learned to stop calling him Dr. Wrinklesides and to treat him as another member of our extended family.

"Opal and Naomi are fine," Haylee went on. "They're with Edna. They suspect the asparagus salad, too." She glared in the direction of the beach. "That salad lady was furtive, climbing into her van and then shutting the back doors. Because we were coming?"

"Maybe, but she drove off, so she could have simply been using that door to get into the truck, not to escape us. She must have gotten to the driver's seat from the back."

Haylee squinched up her mouth in annoyance. "She was up to something, joining that blonde in a seemingly unnecessary fight."

I clapped a hand over my mouth.

"What?" Haylee asked.

"I saw the salad lady and the woman she fought with later last night, talking together as if they were friends, with a third woman. I'm sure the third woman was wearing the same pink plaid as that shirt Cassie had on under her jacket just now. And the third woman was about the same size as Cassie, and her curly hair was the same shade of light brown."

"Maybe it was only a similar shirt worn by a different petite woman with brown curls."

I agreed that was possible. I couldn't imagine why a sweet girl like Cassie would hang around with those two women.

Suddenly, Detective Gartener burst into my shop. Handsome as ever, he scowled in a particularly ferocious way. "Willow, I need to talk to you."

Haylee eased toward the front door.

"You, too, Haylee," he barked.

She paled and stopped. Tally had tiptoed out of his bed and now leaned against me, warming my legs through my jeans.

Gartener asked in a voice as sharp as the

blades of my best embroidery snips, "When did you two last see Chief Smallwood?"

Haylee turned toward me and lifted an eyebrow. Vicki had specifically told us not to let him know she was in my guest room. I stammered, "She was at the picnic this evening, showing her cruiser to kids."

"After that." He held his arms loose, elbows out, obviously ready for anything. "Don't lie to me, Willow."

I opened my mouth to protest that I would never do such a thing, but was silenced by his unyielding, dark eyes. Another time, I thought I had successfully lied to him, and had discovered later that he'd seen right through me. Everything had worked out that time, but . . .

"She was observed with you two," Gartener accused. "Holding on to her, and heading toward the trail that runs along the river, and that also conveniently leads to your property, Willow. Chief Smallwood's cruiser has her leftover dinner in it. That's not like her."

I stalled. "Don't throw that food away. It should be tested for food poisoning."

Gartener grated out, "I don't care about spoiled food. I need to find Chief Smallwood. Do I have to haul you two in for

questioning about the mysterious disappearance of a police officer?"

9

Gazing into Detective Gartener's angry eyes, I imagined and discarded about a thousand ways to evade telling him the truth about Chief Vicki Smallwood. I came up with a lame, "You don't have to *haul* us anywhere for questioning."

"I could arrest you both!" Judging by those piercing eyes, he wasn't bluffing.

Downstairs, Sally barked, two sharp yelps. Tally spun away from me and raced toward her.

I balled my hands into fists and hid them behind my back. "I do know where Chief Smallwood is," I conceded, "but she asked me not to tell anyone." *Especially Detective Gartener.*

He probably thought I was crossing my fingers. He stepped closer. "I've reported her to the state police as possibly missing, Willow. You could be in a lot of trouble."

"She's sick," Haylee said.

Gartener moved a smidge away from me.

"Chief Smallwood, I mean," Haylee corrected herself.

"She doesn't want anyone to see her," I added desperately, still trying not to break my promise.

Gartener stood straighter than ever and folded his arms across his chest. "I'm afraid I'm going to *have* to see her. Or arrest you."

Finally, when I was considering going to jail to prevent myself from betraying Vicki Smallwood's secret, she hollered from downstairs, "I'm fine, Toby. Leave them alone."

Gartener rushed toward the doorway to my apartment. I didn't try to stop him. Not that I could have.

Vicki yelled, "Don't come down here, Toby!" A door slammed.

Gartener thumped down the stairs. Jumping over every other one? Was I going to end up looking after a sick police chief *and* a detective with broken arms and legs?

Haylee and I pounded down after him.

At the bottom, Gartener stood with his face mere inches from my closed guest room door. His feet had to be a dog's width away from the door, however. Sally had positioned herself where she would enter the guest room before he could. "Vicki, let

71

me in." Gartener's order had a hard edge that would be hard to ignore. He rattled the doorknob.

Vicki had locked the door.

Sally whimpered and sniffed the crack between the door and the jamb. Tally stood nearby, his tail down and his toffee brown eyes worried.

Vicki shouted, "No! Stay out. I'm fine. I mean I'm *not* fine, I'm sick, but Haylee and Willow didn't kidnap me. They've been keeping me alive."

It was an overstatement, but at least it took the fight out of Gartener's posture. "Your cruiser's parked out on the street where anyone can get to it."

"Move it for me?" she asked him. "Put it in my garage?"

"And it's got rotting food in it," he added in genial tones. "Crawling with maggots."

Sally wagged her tail. She probably liked the satisfied sound of his voice. And maybe what he was saying, too. I wasn't sure that I did.

Vicki retorted, "It's too soon for maggots." Apparently, she was feeling better. "Get every last bit of that food tested. Something made me sick. And bring me a clean uniform. They're hanging in the closet in my bedroom."

"Give me your keys."

Her answer was far from gracious. "Go away! Willow can bring them to you."

I nodded my agreement at Gartener and, to make everything perfectly clear, pointed at the stairs.

He marched up toward my shop. His radio crackled. He said very distinctly, "Call off that SWAT team."

Haylee and I traded horrified glances. Had he really believed we would have kidnapped our police chief, or anyone else?

The guest room door opened a crack. Vicki whispered, "Is he gone?"

"Yes," I said.

Tail wagging madly, Sally wedged her snout between the door and the frame.

Vicki thrust a jangling set of keys at me. "Can you please give these to him, Willow?"

"Okay, but are you sure you don't want to talk to him yourself?"

"Positive. I look horrible!" Gently, she pushed Sally aside and closed the door.

With Haylee right behind me, I trotted upstairs and handed the keys to Gartener.

"Thanks, Willow. The next time you kidnap a police officer —"

"I did no such thing!"

He raised an eyebrow, but I finally recognized a spark of humor in the depths of

73

those dark eyes. "Try not to *appear* to do it ever again. But I'm sure that Chief Smallwood appreciates your loyalty."

"Maggots," I scolded. "How could you say such a thing to someone whose stomach is upset?"

He tossed Vicki's keys in the air and caught them. "How was I supposed to know what's wrong with her? She deserves it, don't you think, for involving you in a crackpot scheme that could have landed you in jail?"

"No, I don't agree that she deserves it. If you'd seen how sick she's been, you'd have been more considerate."

He looked serious then. "I was very worried about her." He gave us a slightly apologetic smile. "Sorry for mentioning maggots — call it cop humor. I'm sure the chief understood. And will find a way to get me back. Driving her cruiser after she left fried fish in it for a few hours on a warm evening won't be pleasant. She'll get her revenge."

Haylee asked, "Do you need someone to follow you to her place and bring you back to your own car? My truck's across the street."

He actually gave her a nice grin. "Thanks, but I called for backup when I was trying to find the chief. State Trooper Jeffers is already in the area. She can give me a lift. She often takes over on Chief Smallwood's days off."

I folded my arms. "And that was your SWAT team? One trooper?"

"Two, counting me." His nice grin turned wicked. "Gotcha!"

"I knew he was joking," Haylee murmured, but Gartener couldn't have heard. With a wave over one shoulder, he was out the front door and running down my porch steps.

I tapped my toe on my beautiful walnut floor. "I hope he has to personally clean the leftover fish out of her cruiser."

"And that there *are* maggots," Haylee added.

We high-fived each other.

Our celebration was short. Gartener raced back into my shop.

"Hey, you two!" He looked from me to Haylee. "Come with me."

10

Why was Gartener ordering us to go somewhere with him? Wrinkles creased his forehead and his lips were thin with something
like stern disapproval, but I could have
sworn he was trying not to smile.

"I can't go anywhere," I apologized.
"Chief Smallwood may need me."

"Your dog is doing an excellent job of
making certain that no one goes near her,"
Gartener said drily. "Okay, then, Haylee,
you come with me."

He opened the front door for her and they
went outside and turned toward the beach.

A few minutes later, Haylee breezed in by
herself. She was laughing. "Go down to the
chief's cruiser, Willow. You've got to see this.
I'll stay here and listen for her. I'll tell Opal
to meet you there." She pulled out her cell
phone and punched buttons.

"Opal?" I asked.

She waved me toward the door. "Go on."

I hesitated. "Maggots?"

"There are no maggots. Go!"

I ran outside, jumped over my porch steps, and dashed down Lake Street. All vestiges of the picnic had been cleared away.

However, between the almost full moon and the streetlights, it was easy to see what was going on. Mona, the curvaceous and flirtatious forty-something divorcée who owned the home décor shop, Country Chic, was laughing with Ralph from Disguise Guys. Ralph's son Duncan was there, too, beside Gartener and a tall, redheaded female state trooper. I'd seen her patrolling Elderberry Bay on Vicki's days off. She had to be Trooper Jeffers.

Both Ralph and Duncan made costumes. Ralph, who was about ten years older than Mona, was short, round, and garrulous. Duncan was about my age, which made him about ten years younger than Mona. Tall and all angles, he barely resembled his father, and seemed too shy to say more than a few words. While Mona and Ralph laughed, Duncan stood back, staring at Vicki's cruiser as if bewildered.

And no wonder. The cruiser was completely engulfed in a car-sized sweater.

I'd heard of yarnbombs, but this was the first one I'd seen. Yarnbombs were art installations, often crafted offsite so they could be thrown over something public, like a statue, in only moments, and then the yarnbombers could flee the scene without being caught.

The people who had decorated Vicki's cruiser must have been watching for an unattended car, and they had lucked out and found an actual police cruiser.

The sweater resembled, sort of, a police car. Although it was knit of haphazard diagonal stripes of red, taupe, turquoise, black, purple, and pink, the passenger door was white, with *PEACE* embroidered in black yarn on it. The roof was white except for a scarlet section covering the light bar.

The trooper snapped photos of the car.

Opal ran down the hill. I asked her, "How's Edna?"

"Trying to keep water down. Naomi's with her." She peered beyond me. "Yarnbombing! I never expected this in sleepy little Elderberry Bay."

Gartener walked closer to her. "Also known as *Thread*ville. Do you recognize any of this yarn, Opal?"

Opal shook her head with certainty. "Those are cheap craft yarns. I sell quality yarns, much too expensive for yarnbombing."

"Can you ladies help me remove it?" Gartener asked. "Can we pull a thread and unravel it?"

Between guffaws, Ralph gasped. "Don't do that! Give it to Duncan and me. We can turn it into a costume that four people can wear together."

Now *that* would be something.

Gartener apologized to Ralph and Duncan. "Sorry I can't give it to you. We may have to file charges."

Duncan folded his arms and stared mutely at the car.

I told Gartener, "These things are designed to be thrown on quickly, so we can probably just lift it off." I couldn't help admiring the yarnbombers' crafty work. "But you don't have to take the yarnbomb off the car to drive it. The yarnbombers thoughtfully left openings for the windshield and windows." I walked around to the driver's side. "Check this out —" I fingered the "button," about the size of a doorknob, but covered in crocheting, just below the driver's window. "They fixed it so you could open the door, get in, then reach out the window, button the sweater again, and drive off." Someone had crocheted a nice big yarn loop to go over the enormous button.

Without taking his eyes off me, Gartener

shook his head. His mouth twitched.

I added sweetly, "Wouldn't it be nice to leave Chief Smallwood's car decorated like this in her garage? As a welcome-home surprise when she gets back?"

That got him. He laughed. "Sorry, I can't. She might need to respond to an emergency." A glimmer of mischief crept into his eyes. "But don't tell her about this, okay? I may be able to arrange something that won't slow her down."

"You'll be there when she finds it, right?" I suggested. "So you could drive her anywhere she might need to go?"

He grinned. "You'll have to help make sure that *I'm* the one who takes her home."

I agreed. I was certain that Vicki wouldn't mind having him as her chauffeur when she was well enough to leave my apartment.

I had been right — removing the yarnbomb was easy. Careful not to dislodge the side mirrors, Opal and I, plus Ralph, Duncan, and Gartener, lifted the gaudy creation off Vicki Smallwood's shiny black and white cruiser.

Gartener turned to the trooper. "Let's put it in your car, Jeffers. We wouldn't want all this yarn to absorb the odors of spoiled fish that might be in hers."

We all helped shove the recalcitrant car

sweater into Jeffers's backseat. I asked Gartener, "Was that thing on the car earlier, like immediately before you came to my shop looking for Chief Smallwood?" Surely, he would have mentioned it.

"It appeared during the ten minutes or so while I was talking to you."

I persisted. "Did anyone see the yarn-bomber? Maybe he or she arrived in a truck that blended in with other trucks that came to collect tents and things after the picnic."

"I didn't see anyone," Mona said quickly, managing to ogle Ralph, Duncan, and Detective Gartener all at once. "I was in my shop."

Jeffers closed the back door of her squad car. "As far as I know, all of the trucks had left by the time I arrived, but I did see someone in a floor-length cape run to a motorboat down by the river and zoom away. The cape had a hood, pulled up. I didn't see the person's face. He ran like a man."

"What kind of motorboat?" Gartener asked.

"Small," she answered. "A rowboat equipped with an outboard motor. No windshield or anything like that. Just basic aluminum. And I don't think it had running lights."

"What color was the cape?" I asked Jeffers.

"It was too dark to be sure. Some light color. Maybe gray. Kind of splotchy."

Detective Gartener watched me as if guessing what my next question would be.

"What kind of fabric?" I asked.

Detective Gartener hid a laugh with a cough. I shot him a quelling look.

Jeffers bit her lip. "It was too far away, and, as I said, it's dark out here."

"Did it shine like plastic or float like cloth?" I probed. "Or could it have been stiff, like paper?"

"Cloth," she answered.

"Which way did the motorboat go?" Detective Gartener asked.

She pointed north. "Toward the mouth of the river."

"And then?" he prompted.

Jeffers's blush showed up under the streetlights. "I'm sorry, I should have taken the guy's picture, but all I could think of was capturing the squad car on film. I mean pixels. Thinking back on the sounds I heard, though, I think the boat turned west after it got to the lake, and then accelerated, you know, that sound of the hull crashing between waves."

Detective Gartener focused on me again. "What's west of here?"

"A long sandy beach lined with cottages, then the main harbor, the fishing wharf, and the marina. Beyond the harbor, the Elderberry Bay Lodge has its own beach and, I've heard, a new, long dock. West of that are sandy bluffs, no beaches, and nowhere to moor a boat or pull it up onto the sand." Opal nodded as I mentioned each feature.

Gartener turned to Jeffers. "Let's go have a look." In an overly theatrical gesture, he pinched his nose between his thumb and forefinger before opening Vicki's car door. He shut himself in, turned on the ignition, opened the windows, and sped off, with Trooper Jeffers in her state police cruiser right behind him.

Opal and I walked up Lake Street together. "That yarnbombing can't have been done by my regulars," she said. "They're much too practical and well-behaved."

She looked tired. I asked how she felt.

"Fine. But in case this thing is the flu, not food poisoning, you and Haylee need to be careful. Naomi and I will take turns keeping Edna hydrated, starting with little sips of water. Tell Haylee not to join us."

I asked, "What if *you* get sick?"

"Edna will be well by then, I hope. Right now, all she wants to do is lie there and moan."

That did *not* sound like Edna. Ordinarily, she complained only if she ran out of rhinestones or beads to trim garments she was making for herself.

Opal rushed off to force a quarter teaspoon of water on her.

At In Stitches, Tally-Ho greeted me like I'd been gone for weeks. Haylee told me she hadn't heard a peep from Vicki or seen a hair of Sally-Forth. I relayed Opal's message about staying away, but Haylee ignored it and headed toward Edna's.

I peeked downstairs. Sally gazed up at me and wagged her tail, but she didn't budge from her post.

Finally, I could play with my embroidery software. I kept my own, private computer in the part of the shop that had been penned off for the dogs, where no one could accidentally tamper with my embroidery designs. Tally settled near my feet. I checked my e-mail first. Two new commissions for embroidered wall hangings had arrived. One customer had e-mailed me a formal photo of her multi-turreted home, and the other had sent a snapshot of an adorable golden retriever puppy with a ball of yarn. I'd begun my machine embroidery business by selling my own original designs online, and those designs still provided a substantial percentage of my income. I opened my embroidery software and began transforming the photos into embroidery designs.

Someone knocked on the glass of my front door. Sally barked but didn't come upstairs. Tally galloped to the door and whimpered. On the front porch, Trooper Jeffers held Vicki's uniform on a hanger in one hand and a cosmetic bag in the other.

I opened the door and accepted Vicki's things. "How long will you be taking over for Chief Smallwood?" I asked.

She leaned forward to pet my exceedingly friendly Tally-Ho. "Until she's well enough to come back to work. I have the first shift, and other troopers will take over until she's better. Don't worry, we've always got you covered."

I saw her out, locked the door, turned off the shop lights and went downstairs. Beside the guest room door, Sally thumped her tail on the floor.

I tapped gently. No answer. Giving the dogs a hand signal to stay, I opened the door. The dogs sat. Tally wagged his tail, but Sally looked up at me pleadingly, as if asking to be let in to wash the chief's face.

"Willow?"

I hoped Vicki was stronger than her voice. "Yes. May I come in?"

"Just you?"

"Yes."

"Okay," she said.

Sally gave me very reproachful looks as I shut her out of my guest suite.

Vicki had left her uniform on the floor, replaced it with a bathrobe, gotten back into bed, and pulled the duvet up almost to her shoulders.

I set her bag near the bed and hung her clean uniform in the closet. "How are you?" Silly question. Of course she was not all right.

Perspiration gave her greenish face an unhealthy sheen. She struggled up onto her elbows. Her eyes were bloodshot. Wayward tendrils of her usually neat hair sprouted from her ponytail. "I heard your voice. Were you talking to Toby Gartener again?"

"No."

"Don't let him come in. I look terrible."

"I'm sure he's seen worse."

She fell back on the pillows. "Yes, but they were *already* dead."

Illness hadn't taken much of a toll on her sense of humor. "Can I get you anything? A tiny sip of water?"

She wrinkled her nose in disgust, but agreed to try it.

I dumped an entire half teaspoon of water

into a pretty liqueur glass and took it to Vicki. I didn't realize that Sally had followed me into the sickroom until I heard her tongue washing Vicki's hand. "Sorry, Vicki," I said. "I didn't mean to let the dog in."

"That's okay. Your dogs are sweet." She sipped a little water, then let her head loll back. "I'd like more, but let's just see . . ."

"Do you mind if I leave your door ajar so I can hear if you call? The dogs may come in."

She rubbed Sally's ears. "That's fine."

I went to bed and set my phone to wake me up in half an hour. Before its alarm went off, however, Sally came whimpering to me. She and I gave Vicki another sip of water.

In the kitchen, I poured ginger ale into a glass, then I went back to bed. I forgot to reset the alarm, but I didn't need it. Sally got me up and led me to our patient. I started Vicki on flat ginger ale.

The next time Sally woke me up, she went and looked out the patio door. The poor doggie had been inside with her patient for so long that she probably needed exercise. Without turning on lights, I let her out and crossed my fingers that she wouldn't en-counter a skunk.

In his machine-embroidered doggie bed, Tally muttered in his sleep.

A few minutes later, Sally-Forth pawed to be let in. Everything, both inside and out, was dark and silent. I stumbled to the door and slid it open. Sally trotted into Vicki's room. I snuggled underneath my duvet.

With more whimpering, Sally came out of Vicki's room and batted the patio door with a front paw. She had to be suffering. Usually, she didn't need to go out at night even once. Yawning and blinking in the darkness, I let her out, and then back in a few minutes later. Once again, she headed straight for the guest room. At least Vicki was sleeping. Tally-Ho, too. This time, he didn't stir.

But it turned out that Vicki wasn't sleeping, after all. She was . . . sobbing?

11

Was Vicki sicker? What was making her cry?
I leaped out of bed and skidded into furniture in the darkness. In addition to the gasping noises, I heard strange squeaks and a raspy sort of rumbling. What could possibly have gone wrong? I'd thought that Vicki was improving, yet she sounded like she'd gone downhill. Bumping into corners, I dashed into her room.

"W-W-Willow," she managed. She wasn't crying. She was laughing. "Turn on a light and see what your dog brought me."

I switched on the nightstand lamp.

Vicki lay on her back, under the duvet except for her arms, which were wrapped around two kittens. The kittens were black and white, and marked a lot like Sally, except that Sally didn't have a black mustache like one or a black bow tie like the other.

I checked again. Yes, they were kittens,

not baby skunks.

The kittens purred madly, Vicki had a giggling fit, and Sally-Forth stood proudly beside the bed, wagging her tail and gazing up at me for the praise she expected.

"Good doggie," I said. "Where did you get these little darlings?"

Sally wagged her tail harder and stared toward the patio door, which she couldn't see from the guest room.

"You asked me to let you outside so you could bring home kittens?" I asked her.

The tail flew faster.

"Outside?" Vicki asked. "Did you let your dogs out into your backyard?"

I clapped my hand over my mouth. "I'm sorry. I was half asleep and forgot about the crime scene. The crime was thirty years ago. And it was only Sally. And she came right back in."

I asked my attentive dog, "Were there any more kittens out there?"

Sally was very good at looking sad. Silly me. Of course there weren't more, or she would have insisted on bringing every one of them home.

"Did you take them from their mother?" I asked.

Sally gave the closest kitten a kiss with her tongue. I had a better look at the kittens.

They seemed old enough to be away from their mother, but Sally apparently didn't think so, and had appointed herself — and, apparently, Vicki Smallwood — the job of looking after them. They were still damp from being carried in Sally's gentle mouth.

I put my hands on my hips and asked the kittens, "What are we going to do with you two?"

They closed their eyes and purred more loudly.

"They can stay where they are," Vicki said. "They won't keep me awake."

"They might be hungry. They need a litter box. They might have fleas." Oops, I was nearly as bad as Gartener with his threats of maggots.

Vicki closed her eyes. "I believe your dog will look after them."

That wasn't exactly true. Sally wouldn't bring them food. At least, I hoped she wouldn't.

However, the kittens seemed perfectly content, and I was tired. I went back to bed.

When I got up in the morning, Sally-Forth was cuddling the kittens in her embroidered doggie bed. I heard the shower running in the guest bathroom. If I had designed my apartment myself, I might have made do with only one bathroom, but Haylee and

Clay had planned the building's renovations while I still lived and worked in New York City, and had given both bedrooms their own bathrooms. That morning, with two of us needing to get ready for work at the same time, I appreciated Haylee and Clay's foresight.

Clay. A little shiver rippled through me. Thanks to a lucky set of circumstances, and Haylee's maneuvering, I'd met him.

The first I'd ever heard of the building that was eventually to become my shop and home was when Haylee called me in New York and told me to come see this property that had just "happened" to come on the market. I'd fallen in love with the shop, the apartment underneath it, Blueberry Cottage, and the long, sloping yard leading to the trail and the river. I'd also fallen in love with the idea of opening the embroidery boutique I'd been dreaming of owning. I had never regretted the decision I'd made that day to move to Threadville.

Now I also had two dogs and, until I found their rightful owner, two kittens. I opened a can of tuna, plopped a spoonful of it onto each of two bread plates, and set the plates on the floor. Sally-Forth stood back and watched her small charges eat. Tally seemed interested in both the kittens and their food, but with a little growl, Sally warned him away. Looking perplexed, Tally sat down and watched.

The kittens gobbled the tuna, and then used their paws to wash their whiskers. Unsatisfied with their hygiene, Sally gave both little faces thorough baths.

I showered and put on a khaki skirt and top I'd made and decorated with embroidery around the hems. I slipped my feet into sandals, and then padded out to the great room with its wall of windows overlooking the backyard.

Vicki was outside in her fresh uniform. A kitten in each arm, her ponytail wet and flying behind her, and her face still so pale she looked panicky, she charged up the hill, away from the yellow police tape, and past Blueberry Cottage. The dogs galumphed toward my apartment, too.

I went outside and called to Vicki, "Sorry the animals got out."

"My fault," Vicki yelled back. "I didn't realize I had to slide the door all the way closed." She was probably usually in good shape, but this morning she seemed to be panting from the exertion of running uphill.

She'd probably also been chasing the animals. I should have warned her about that door. If I ever left the tiniest gap, my naughty dogs slid it open and sauntered off. This time, they'd apparently encouraged the kittens to help them invade a crime scene.

And that wasn't all they'd done. Sally-Forth had a stick in her mouth. Tally-Ho ran toward her, but she spun away from him and collided with Vicki, who, still clutching those kittens, tried to grab her. Sally-Forth dashed out of reach. Wagging her tail, she turned to face Vicki. Was she trying to teach the kittens a new game? Or, now that Vicki had recovered, had Sally merely reverted to being her usual self, a young dog with plenty of energy and enthusiasm?

Vicki ran toward Sally-Forth, which was exactly the wrong thing to do if she wanted Sally to halt or come to her.

Turning her head and watching Vicki out of the sides of her eyes, Sally dodged. The stick glinted in sunlight. It was very straight and smooth, and strangely shiny. Purple, too.

I hollered, "My dogs are not really good at fetching."

Vicki shouted back. "Oh, yes, they are. Look at what they fetched."

I beckoned to Sally-Forth. Tail wagging, she came.

"Don't touch it!" Vicki's command had an odd quaver.

I gaped at her.

She thinned her lips. "It will have to be fingerprinted."

12

"Drop it," I told Sally.

My clever dog placed the "stick" neatly at my feet.

It was a purple aluminum knitting needle, a much finer gauge than had been used to make the yarnbomb that had been on Vicki's cruiser.

"Your other dog has one, too." Vicki had regained some of her usual, crisp speaking manner, but she was out of breath and looking everywhere at once, as if she expected an entire posse of crafty pets to leap out of the shrubbery.

Nose high, tail wagging, a purple knitting needle in his mouth, Tally-Ho pranced to me. He obeyed me and let it go. I praised the dogs and then shut them and the kittens into the apartment. Although afraid to find out why Vicki wanted to fingerprint knitting needles, I slipped outside and joined her.

Standing with her back to my patio door, she spoke into her radio. "Tell Toby Gartener I need to talk to him."

So he could drive her home, I hoped, but unease crowded into my stomach.

"I *know* he's a detective," Vicki said crossly into the radio. "I've got something here that I want him to see. ASAP."

The unease grew. I wanted to sit down, inside. Maybe go to bed and pull the covers over my head.

Vicki gave my address and added, "Trooper Jeffers should be nearby. Tell her I need her here right now, also." Head turning right and left like she was scanning my hedges for more rogue craft supplies, Vicki walked away from me, down the hill.

Curiosity conquered the queasies. I followed her as far as the yellow police tape surrounding the excavations in my yard.

Last night around eight thirty when Haylee and I had walked Vicki to my apartment, the orange plastic mesh fencing beside the riverside trail had been upright.

Since then, something had flattened it.

In the pit that used to be underneath Blueberry Cottage, there was a . . . a *what?*

A huge white cocoon, like a monster grub that had just emerged from the depths of the earth?

I gasped.

Vicki turned around. "Sorry, Willow." And she actually did look sorry. "It looks like we've found a body in your yard."

A body? Against my will, I looked at the "cocoon" again. Someone had wrapped a humanlike shape in quilt batting, pinned the batting shut with knitting needles like oversized purple straight pins, dumped the thing into the pit, and then had tossed a few shovelfuls of dirt over it.

"How do you know there's a body in all that?" I asked.

"I ducked under the tape and went down into that hole to find out what your dogs were finding so interesting."

"Are you sure the person is dead?" It was a dumb question, but someone could have been playing a prank, sort of like yarnbombing, but gruesome.

"Are you kidding? That was the first thing I checked. It's a corpse, all right, and it's been dead awhile. It's cold. Did you see or hear anything unusual out here in the night? Or more recently?" Again she eyed my hedges.

No one committed suicide and then wrapped himself or herself in quilt batting. This person must have been murdered, and the killer might be hiding in those thick hedges. My heart outdid itself with scared, nervous beating. "Only Sally," I managed. "Wanting to bring in those kittens. One at a time." Had the kittens and the dog startled the killer? Was that why he hadn't finished burying the victim? He must have hoped to cover the wrapped-up body completely, and also planned that no one would notice that the pit had become slightly shallower during the night. And maybe no one would have.

My hand shook as I pointed at dirt heaped up around the excavation. The victim's feet must have dragged, plowing a pair of wavering furrows in the sand. Doggie footprints were all over the place, but I thought I could see partial prints from shoes — sneakers, maybe — and boots, too. Police had swarmed this area yesterday, and some of the prints must have been Vicki's from a few minutes ago.

I asked her, "Do you know who the victim is?"

She stared off toward the river. "We'll have to get a positive ID and notify next of kin before we go blabbing names around." She looked at me. My anxiety must have shown on my face. "Don't worry. It's not one of your close friends. It's a male."

The gate leading to Lake Street from my

side yard clanged. I jumped about a mile, and Vicki whirled to face uphill. She placed her right hand on her holster.

Whistling, Clay strode down the hill toward us. I was so glad to see him alive and healthy that I had an urge to run to him and hug him, but my leg muscles felt like they'd been knit from cotton thread.

Vicki challenged him, "What do you think you're doing here?"

Clay stopped and raised one eyebrow. "Checking to see if I can work here today, but I see you still have the yellow tape up." He must have noticed the expression on my face. "Is something wrong?"

"Don't go near your excavation," Vicki told him. "This is a crime scene again. I mean still. I mean an even *worse* crime scene than before." She didn't usually get this flustered.

"What is it?" he asked.

"It's not a what, it's a who," Vicki said. "Except now, it's become sort of a what."

"She's been sick," I explained.

Vicki brushed that aside. "I'm not sure how the who and the what got here, but it looks like they came from the trail. Did you see or hear anything unusual around here last night or this morning, Clay?"

He shook his head. "Until now, the closest I've been since Friday afternoon when we inventoried the jewelry was the bandstand, last night." He glanced toward me as if about to ask a question.

I mumbled, "Sorry I didn't stay."

Vicki asked him, "Do you have any idea what that employee of yours, Fred Zongassi, is doing today?"

I gave her a sharp look. Last night, when she'd been about to collapse, she had pointed out Fred and his high-top sneakers. Did she suspect that Fred had something to do with the corpse in the odd shroud? I controlled an involuntary shudder. Perhaps she knew that Fred *was* the corpse in the shroud.

"We're digging the foundations for some new cottages beyond the state forest," Clay told her. "Fred should be out there. I'll go check." He patted his shirt pocket. "Or I could try his cell."

"Don't. Detective Gartener will likely send someone from the state police to talk to him."

So the corpse wasn't Fred. Who was it, anyone I knew?

She again assessed the lower part of my yard as if expecting someone to jump out at us. "You two can go. Keep the kittens and dogs out of the yard, Willow, and open your shop. Business as usual."

I glanced toward the hazy blue sky, but all I could think of was the batting and what it concealed. "Usual. Right."

Clay walked up the hill with me. "Kittens?" he asked.

I kept my answer short since we both had things we needed to do. "Strays. Sally-Forth rescued them during the night."

"Your dogs are really something. Let me know when we can work in your yard again, okay?"

"If *ever.*"

He squeezed my shoulder. "Don't worry. See you Friday, if not before." He loped toward my gate.

Glad that Clay wasn't annoyed at me for leaving while his band played, I opened the patio door only enough to sidle through and greet my excited dogs. They were undoubtedly proud of themselves for discovering a body and helping unpin its weird wrapping. Sally's little charges, however, had gone to sleep in her bed. They yawned, opened their eyes, and blinked at me, but they must have been too drowsy to get up. I locked the patio door to prevent any of the pets from squeezing out again.

I felt sad about the person who must have met an untimely end and would surely be missed. Again, I thought back over the night. I hadn't heard anything unusual besides Sally's insistence on being let out and in twice, Vicki's giggling fit, and the kittens' mewing and purring.

Who was rolled up in that quilt batting?

And where had the batting — and the knitting needles — come from? Vicki was probably asking herself the same questions, but Vicki was guarding the crime scene. She wouldn't want me endangering myself or giving the murderer any hint that we, I meant *she,* was on their trail, but she should allow me to ask trusted friends a few questions.

I didn't need to open In Stitches for at least a half hour. I sprinted across the street.

Edna was already switching her sequined sign from *Come Back Later* to *Welcome.* She opened the door and poked her head out. She'd washed most of the red and blue from her hair, leaving only a few purplish streaks running through the blond.

I ran to her. "How are you feeling?"

"A million times better. I couldn't stand the thought of hiding upstairs and missing the fun of selling all these great notions."

She'd feel worse if I told her what Vicki had found in my backyard. I trotted to Batty About Quilts.

The small front room of Naomi's shop was a gallery of finished quilts and everything one could possibly quilt, including multi-pocketed tote bags and adorable little dresses. Wearing another of her summery pieced dresses, Naomi was in the sales area immediately behind her art gallery. She hummed as she slotted a new bolt of batik between others already on her shelves, and smiled at me like I was a long-lost daughter. "Willow, I'm glad you didn't catch the flu that's been going around."

"Not yet. Have you recently sold quilt batting to anyone?"

She was too polite to comment on my abrupt change of subject. "Lots of people, but Duncan was probably the most recent. He said his dad wanted it to pad a dinosaur costume. That boy's so shy he could barely whisper his request. Why do you ask?"

"I think Chief Smallwood is going to want their names."

"Why?"

"She found a body wrapped in quilt batting in the excavation in my backyard this morning." Did I have to be so blunt? Naomi would have found a tactful way of saying it.

"Oh, Willow, no! Not on *your* property again. You poor thing!"

She was, as always, very sweet, but I

wasn't the one who needed sympathy. "I'm much better off than the guy in the batting. I don't know who he is, or was, but Chief Smallwood said he was male, and not one of my close friends." I quickly added, "And I just saw Clay. He's fine."

"What about —" She bit her lip. Tears glistened in her eyes.

"Gord Wrinklesides," I finished for her. If anything had happened to Gord, Edna would be devastated.

Naomi picked up her phone, dialed, and asked the person who answered if she'd seen Dr. Wrinklesides during the past few minutes. Naomi nodded, thanked the person, disconnected the call, and smiled at me. "His receptionist must have thought I was peculiar, but she said she was looking right at him. So that's okay." Her eyes even shinier, she shook her head. "Wrapped in quilt batting . . . That means . . ." She hugged herself. "Did someone do him in?"

"Chief Smallwood's treating it as suspicious."

She perked up. "Maybe the quilt batting didn't come from my store! I don't keep track of names unless they charge their purchases. Come into the back room with me. Maybe if I'm surrounded by my rolls of different types of batting, I'll remember who all besides Duncan bought some recently."

Walking between bolts of colorful fabrics toward her back room was a bit like touring the inside of a rainbow. The quilt fabric that Naomi sold was cotton, lightweight, and dyed in luscious colors with prints that could be put together to make striking quilts.

Monster rounds of batting hung on industrial-strength rods fastened to shelves in Naomi's back room. She touched each roll as she passed. Near the steel-clad door leading to the parking lot, she stopped, put her hand on a bare metal shelf, looked up at the empty cardboard tube on the rod above her, and let out a little gasp.

"Someone took all the batting off that tube," she said. "I didn't."

13

Of course Naomi would know if a roll of quilt batting wasn't there. No one could misplace something that large. Ever the great interrogator, I asked her, "When did you last see it?"

She squinted toward the window overlooking the parking lot. "Friday afternoon, shortly before our Midsummer Madness Sidewalk Sale. I was cutting smaller pieces off that roll for table runner kits when I heard a customer come in, so I left the end of the batting just hanging here, and ran to the front of the store. After the sale that night, I noticed that I'd neglected to lock my back door." She tested it. "It's been locked ever since."

"Was the batting there then?"

Lowering her chin, she pursed her mouth. She was obviously giving herself a silent scolding. "I didn't notice. You'd think I would have. But that must have been when they took it. No one could have carried it out through the front of the store without my noticing them."

True. But why would anyone steal quilt batting? Because they needed it for a quilt?

Or because they had a more devious plan for it?

I told Naomi, "The batting around the body was pinned together with knitting needles."

We traded glances and ran from that room, past long-armed quilting machines and the rainbow of fabrics in the next room, through the gallery where Naomi showed off her students' work, and out through her front door.

We jogged past Edna's shop and burst into Opal's. Usually, the first thing Opal's cat did was purr around my ankles and beg for a cuddle. This time, Lucy opened her mouth and stuck her face against my shin, her method of sniffing where the kittens had been. I picked her up. She purred.

Since it was June, most of the yarns Opal had on display were cottons, linens, and silks in whites and pastels. Pretty and very tempting, but I was still working on a scarf I'd started months before, and I was determined to finish it before I bought more yarn. I did my knitting on Friday evenings at Opal's storytelling events, and the scarf was taking a while.

Smiling, Opal came out of the back room she used as her dining room and also as a cozy meeting place for classes and storytelling night. She was wearing a skirt and top she'd pieced together from flowerlike granny squares crocheted from pink, lavender, and white cotton.

Naomi surprised me with her directness. "Are you missing any knitting needles?"

Opal cocked her head. "It's the strangest thing. I put out a bunch of needles at the sidewalk sale, and seven pairs disappeared. All of my size three aluminum needles. No other size. Not the bamboo size threes or the double-pointed or circular needles. Only the size three aluminum needles. I must have put them somewhere, but I can't figure out where. How could I lose seven pairs?"

My shoulders tensed. Lucy squirmed. I offered her to Opal. "What colors were the seven pairs of needles?"

"Purple." Opal snuggled the cat against her shoulder. "All of them. All seven pairs."

Naomi looked at me and lifted an eyebrow.

"I know where they are." My voice came out dead flat. I explained it all to Opal.

Opal stroked her wriggling cat. "So someone shoplifted those needles during the sidewalk sale. I wondered but didn't want to believe it." Lucy butted her head against Opal's jaw and increased the volume of her purring.

Naomi asked in her usual gentle way, "How would someone hide knitting needles?"

"Seven *pairs*," Opal repeated. "Fourteen needles. And they were in packages."

"Maybe they put them in a violin or gun case," Naomi suggested.

I asked, "Did either of you see anyone carrying either of those?"

They hadn't, and neither had I.

"Maybe they stuck them up a sleeve?" I guessed.

Naomi raised a foot and pointed at her ankle. "Or into a sock."

Opal's trill of laughter was always contagious. "I hope whoever did it got *poked*. I hate to think of anyone shoplifting in Threadville. It can't be our usual customers. They never do anything like that."

There could always be a first time . . . "Remember those women fighting over remnants at Haylee's table?" I asked.

"I didn't see them," Naomi answered, "but I heard them."

"Harpies." Opal seldom sounded that disgusted.

I reached out and chucked Lucy under the chin. "Do you know who either of them was?"

"No," Opal said. "And after Haylee offered them similar fabrics, they both left without buying anything."

I told Opal and Naomi that one of those women had seized a spool of thread before Georgina could close her hand around it. "But when I said I'd get Georgina an identical spool, the woman suddenly didn't want thread or anything else. She went off — and I think she joined the woman she'd been fighting with earlier. It was like they were going around causing disturbances just for fun."

Opal stroked Lucy. "Maybe they had a reason, like, I don't know. This sounds silly, but what if they caused the disturbance at Haylee's sale so that another accomplice could grab knitting needles from my table?"

"That doesn't sound silly, Opal," Naomi reassured her. "That's as good a theory as any."

I agreed. "They left the sale with a smaller woman in a pink plaid shirt. Cassie, Neil's new assistant at the bakery, was wearing a shirt like that on Saturday."

Opal stuck a forefinger up into the air. "Aha! Could Cassie be their accomplice and our shoplifter?" Lucy stretched out her neck and rubbed her gums on Opal's finger.

Naomi looked pained. "I've only been in the bakery a few times since Cassie started working there, but she seems like a sweet girl. I can't picture her shoplifting."

"Or carrying a whole roll of batting," I pointed out.

Naomi turned a shade of pink that matched some of the triangles on her pieced dress. "It wasn't a whole roll."

"Was there enough left to wrap up a . . . you know, a *person*?" I hated to use upsetting words like "corpse" when talking to Naomi. She was too likely to take on other people's worries and cares.

"There would have been enough for *that*." She clapped her hand across her mouth and said between her fingers, "I hope Chief Smallwood doesn't think that Opal or I had anything to do with killing anyone!"

"She couldn't possibly," I said.

Opal nodded and kissed the dark gray M on Lucy's forehead.

But as I crossed the street toward In Stitches, I looked down the hill at the spot where Vicki's yarnbombed cruiser had been parked. Detective Gartener hadn't seemed positive that Opal was innocent of that yarnbombing.

Even worse, someone had fled that scene wearing a blotchy, whitish cape that floated like fabric.

Quilt batting?

I knew for certain that Opal and Naomi weren't murderers, but would the police believe they weren't involved?

Was someone trying to frame my friends for murder?

14

I dashed the rest of the way across the street, opened the gate, and started down into my side yard. Perched on the front edge of one of my Adirondack chairs near the foot of the hill, Vicki looked tiny and alone. I called to her and she ran up to me.

Knowing I needed to open In Stitches soon, I babbled about Naomi's stolen quilt batting and Opal's missing purple knitting needles.

Predictably, Vicki reminded me that I wasn't supposed to be sticking my nose into a homicide investigation. Then she took out her notebook and had me go through it all again, slowly, while she wrote it down. "Can you describe the two women who caused the disturbances during the sidewalk sale?" she asked.

"The street was crowded, so I only caught glimpses. One of the fighting women was sort of scrawny, but a ropy sort of muscled kind of scrawny, and very tan. She wore a teal tank top and had straggly long blond hair. I got a look at her when she fussed about some thread I was selling. Her face was drawn, and her eyes were calculating and mean-looking."

"What color?"

"I didn't notice. The other woman's hair was curly, an odd shade of maroon that clashed with her bright red polo shirt."

"And you think these two women, the one with the maroon hair and the blonde, may have staged a fight to create a diversion so that a friend could steal quilt batting and knitting needles?"

I nodded. "And I think the friend may have been wearing a pink plaid shirt like the one Cassie, Neil's new assistant at La Bakery, was wearing last night when she came to offer a free trial of cookies to Haylee and me. She was wearing a jacket over it, but —"

Vicki's face went still, and she blanched. Maybe I shouldn't have mentioned food to her quite yet. She again stared at my tall and bushy cedar hedge. "You know your fabrics — I suppose you'll be telling me the fiber content of Cassie's shirt next."

I grinned. "When you were a little girl playing with toy guns and police cars, I was making doll clothes. The pink plaid shirt or shirts were mostly cotton, I'd guess, from the way the fabric draped."

She rolled her eyes up to the sky before aiming that cool, direct gaze at me again. "Okay, but are you *sure* that the plaid you only glimpsed in a crowd on Friday night could be the same plaid you saw worn under a jacket last night?"

"I'm not sure," I admitted. "And from the little I've seen of Cassie, she doesn't seem like a shoplifter."

"Trust me, lots of people don't *seem* like shoplifters. Or other criminals. We solve cases using facts and evidence, not appearance and hunches."

I had to agree that her method was better. "But what woman wears the same shirt two days in a row? It can't be Cassie."

"You spout the oddest theories, Willow. Maybe it *was* Cassie, and she's like me and wears identical shirts every day." She paged through her notebook. "Okay. The batting and knitting needles apparently went missing Friday evening." She pointed her pen down the hill toward the excavation. "But the body didn't appear for at least twenty-four hours. I was sick when you and Haylee brought me through your backyard after the picnic last night, but I would have noticed a corpse."

"I would have, too. And because of the dogs, I would have also noticed if the snow fencing had been knocked down."

"It wasn't," she agreed. "And I saw the victim alive and well at the picnic. But that was a couple of hours before you brought me here."

I held my breath, hoping she'd tell me who the victim was, but she didn't. "The method of disposing of the body sounds premeditated," I suggested.

"It sounds positively *weird.*"

I wanted to tell her that the yarnbomber might have worn a cloak made of quilt batting when he fled, but Gartener had asked me not to tell Vicki about the yarnbombing. She hadn't been home yet, so she wouldn't have seen whatever surprise he might have arranged for her. I clamped my lips shut.

The gate near the street clanged. Half expecting a murderer disguised in a quilt batting cloak, I whirled, but Detective Gartener strode down the hill toward us. "Need a ride home yet, Chief?" he asked Vicki. He turned his head so she couldn't see his face but I could. He winked.

I managed not to laugh, but my smile might have been a little big. If he had put that car sweater on her cruiser in her garage, or maybe on her couch in her living room, his mind was on that yarnbomber, and he would likely connect the quilt batting with the yarnbomber's escape getup. If not, I'd make sure he did, later. Or that Vicki did, after she saw the hand-knit creation, which, judging by the mischief I'd detected in Gartener's wink, would be as soon as he could possibly engineer it.

She gave him a bleak smile. "I wish. Come down to the foot of Willow's yard and see what I found."

Dismissed, I charged up the hill, through my apartment, and to the shop's front door in time to let Ashley in.

A venturesome kitten, the one with the bow tie, peered around the corner from the stairs leading to my apartment. Ashley swooped down, picked it up, and crooned to it. "Where did he come from?" she asked me.

The one with the mustache dashed to Ashley and began climbing her jeans. She picked that one up, too. Sally-Forth sat at Ashley's feet and gazed up into her face.

I explained that Sally had found the two strays and brought them inside during the night.

Ashley's eyes widened, maybe because Bow-Tie was clinging by his little claws to the top of her head and gnawing on her ponytail. "I thought your yard was a crime scene. Did Sally go out there?"

"I forgot and let her out. But I won't forget again. Now it's a worse crime scene than yesterday."

"Huh?"

"You don't want to know." But I relented and told her.

Naturally, she was frightened and wanted to know who the victim was. She'd lived all of her sixteen years in Elderberry Bay, so if the victim was from the area, she probably knew him. We all probably did.

To distract her, I suggested, "Let's make posters about the kittens." We worked together until we got an adorable snapshot of them, then Ashley sat down at my computer and whipped up a poster. That girl had oodles of design talent.

Assuming that someone would be frantic about losing the kittens, I sent Ashley out to visit other stores and put up posters while I took over teaching the morning class. I loaded the kittens' pictures into my embroidery software, then my students and I used the photos to create embroidery designs. We had great fun trying different fill stitches to make our embroidery resemble fur.

During our break, my students helped

themselves to lemonade and cookies and greeted Sally and Tally, who had learned not to beg for cookies but had *not* learned to turn off their particularly cute and hopeful expressions.

The dogs' pen kept them corralled. The kittens could easily slip out between the upright spindles supporting the railing. Whenever they did, though, Sally whimpered, and they returned to her. Soon, looking extremely pleased with herself, my motherly dog had the kittens snuggled next to her on her doggie bed, which was now a doggie and kitty bed. I didn't dare think about what would happen if the kittens' owner claimed them. Sally might bring home baby skunks or porcupines to fill the void.

Ashley returned and phoned animal rescue organizations and local newspapers. I loved having a full-time assistant, especially one as capable as Ashley. I would miss her in September when she started eleventh grade and would be available to work only after school and on weekends.

Concentrating on my students' many creative ways of making lifelike stitched designs of kittens, I almost forgot about the batting-wrapped body, but when I glanced out the back window, the morning's horror came back in a startling rush. Strange-looking aliens covered from head to toe in baggy white outfits were wandering around my yard.

Of course my students noticed my pained grimace, and once again, I had to admit that a crime had been discovered on my property.

Rosemary, the driver of the Threadville tour bus that came from Erie, asked, "Crime? A death?"

I managed a curt nod.

Rosemary suggested that death didn't necessarily mean murder. "Maybe someone collapsed from this flu that's been going around."

I asked her, "Has the flu been going around Erie, too?"

She gestured at the group surrounding us. "Not as far as I know, but I heard on the radio that lots of people in this corner of the county came down with stomach flu."

"You're all very brave," I told Rosemary, "coming here when something may be infectious."

"Ha! Nothing short of the plague could keep us away from Threadville."

I grinned. Rosemary had a way of making me feel better. And of encouraging everyone to return to their embroidery machines.

During my lunch hour, I took all four animals out to the upper section of my yard, the only part that wasn't off limits. I kept Tally-Ho and his energetic exploring habits on a leash, but Sally-Forth spent the whole time keeping the kittens from straying and didn't need a leash.

Shortly after our customers left for the day and we closed In Stitches, Ashley kissed all four animals and went home. We were both disappointed that no one had called about the kittens and they couldn't yet be reunited with their owner.

Opal charged into the shop. "Where are the kittens from the poster that Ashley brought me?" She hardly needed to ask, since both of the tiny charmers were attacking her sandals and toes. She picked them up. "Aren't you two naughty little ones?" She said it lovingly, and they responded by purring. "When you get a spare moment, come over, Willow. I've got things they can use." She handed them back to me.

Inside their warm fur, their bones felt hardly more substantial than needles, which strengthened my desire to protect the kittens. "Maybe their owner will claim them —"

"Sure, sure." With a wave, she was out the door.

After Sally and Tally helped me give the kittens another outing, I left them all in the apartment and ran across the street.

As usual, Lucy was Tell a Yarn's official, and very vocal, greeter. Opal gave me a small bag of kitty litter, six cans of cat food, a package of cat kibble, and four toy mice that she had knit and filled with catnip from her garden. Lucy's comments became louder.

Opal cooed, "Now Lucy, you have a dozen catnip mice scattered around the shop. Why don't you see if you can find them? You might have to actually look *underneath* things." She bundled everything into a grocery sack. "Do you have a disposable baking tray you can use for a litter box until you get a real one, Willow?"

"I do. Good idea. It won't be for long. Someone is sure to claim the kittens."

"Don't count on it."

"How old do you suppose they are?" I asked her.

"About two months. They're just babies. Shame on people for dumping them." She turned away, and the emotional pain of her situation hit me like a blow to the lungs. When she was sixteen and became pregnant with Haylee, Opal's parents had kicked her out.

I thanked her for the kitty supplies and ran back to In Stitches, which still needed its evening tidying. I let my entire menagerie into the shop and began dusting sewing machines.

My front door chimes jingled. Long before I'd met him, Clay had made the chimes from driftwood and sand-roughened glass that he'd found on the beach, and I pictured him nearly every time I heard them.

But he wasn't my visitor. Vicki was. Both kittens galloped to her and began ascending her pant legs. Sally nudged the kittens as if warning them against hurting the police chief.

Vicki whisked a bouquet of small red roses from behind her back. The roses contrasted nicely with her navy uniform and made her look younger than ever. "Listen, Willow, I can never pay you back for all you did for me. If you do catch the flu, let me know and I'll look after you."

"Flu?" I asked. "Wasn't it food poisoning, from something you folks ate at the picnic?"

"It would be easy to jump to that conclusion, but people who didn't attend the picnic were rushed to the hospital with similar symptoms, but worse than mine. Ambulances were busy all night." The kittens batted at the roses. Vicki handed them to me. "My cottage has climbing roses blooming everywhere, so I cut some for you."

Thanking her, I rubbed Sally-Forth's ears. "Even if I do get sick, I've got my little nursemaid dog."

Vicki smiled. "She is really something. Both of your dogs are great."

I agreed.

"But these little guys . . ." She captured the kittens on her bulletproof vest before they could vault onto her shoulders and into her hair. Holding them against her cheeks, she demanded, "What do you know about yarnbombing?"

I realized with a start that she was talking to me, not the kittens. "Not much. Have you —" I had to figure out how to word it without spoiling any of the surprises Gartener could have left for her. "Ever *seen* any yarnbombing?"

"Ha! As if you didn't know! My car was bundled in a hideous yarn *thing* when I got home."

"How would that have happened?" I asked, all innocence. "Who could have gotten into your garage?"

She narrowed her eyes at me. "So you *do* know."

"I know you asked Detective Gartener to

park your car in your garage."

"He did. And then he yarnbombed it."

"Oh, but he wouldn't," I said. "He knew you could be called to an emergency."

"He made certain he was with me when I saw the car. He helped me take the thing off it. *After* he took a picture of me gaping at it."

I burst out laughing. "I'd like to see that picture."

She glared.

I could tell she was faking her outrage, but I changed the subject anyway. I pointed toward my rear windows. "What's going on with the crime scene?"

"They're sifting through it for clues. They've taken the body away."

"Do you know who he was?"

"Yep, and I might as well tell you, now that we've contacted his family. All he has . . . all he *had* was his mother, in Florida. It's Neil Ondover. The baker from La Bakery."

15

I nearly fell onto an expensive sewing and embroidery machine. Neil the baker was dead? Neil, who'd been nearly as sweet as the treats he'd baked? "Neil was sick, too," I managed. "Cassie said he was one of several people who got sick at the picnic. Did the illness you had actually *kill* people?" The idea was frightening. Edna and Vicki had survived the disease, but the rest of us could come down with it. "Do you know yet what caused your illness?"

Wrestling with two kittens who seemed determined to search for prey underneath her hat, she told me that testing hadn't been completed. "As I said before, people who didn't attend the picnic are reporting similar symptoms, so we can't be sure it was food poisoning, and we don't know what virus it could have been."

"It was so contagious that a whole bunch of you got it, while the rest of us didn't."

She glanced at me under half-closed eyelids and twisted her mouth to one side. "Not yet."

I waved my hand in dismissal. "I feel fine."

"I did, too. It came on suddenly. Don't let yourself get too far from home."

A home that, thanks to someone leaving a corpse in the backyard, was not as comfortable as it should be. I glanced toward the back windows.

Neil. Who could have wanted to hurt sweet, gentle Neil?

"Maybe someone found Neil after he succumbed," I guessed. "And then panicked and disposed of the body in a really strange way."

Vicki maneuvered little kitty claws out of the heavy nylon covering her bulletproof vest. "You said that batting was stolen Friday night, right?"

I nodded.

"And you said Cassie told you that Neil became ill after the picnic, last night, which was Saturday. And he certainly seemed fine when I bought my strawberry shortcake from him."

"He was fine when we bought ours, too. Maybe someone wanted to make a quilt, but then found a different use for the batting." Even as I said it, I knew it wasn't a plausible explanation. But nothing was.

Neil. I let out a sigh.

"People are strange." She glanced at me sideways as if checking my mood, then added lightly, "And to think I wanted to be a cop so I could drive fast cars."

I knew that joking could be one way of coping with the darker seams of life, so I teased her. "But hand-knit sweaters could slow your cruiser down with all that wind resistance."

"Maybe I'll let it wear its sweater in parades." She faked a shudder. "And community picnics. I'm not sure I want to project a warm and fuzzy image, though."

Sometimes she couldn't avoid it, especially when cuddling a couple of black and white kittens.

She handed me the kittens and took out her notebook. "Do you know Cassie's last name or where she lives?"

"No. I got the impression that she moved to Elderberry Bay recently, but I don't know where. I met her for the first time Saturday night. She was serving strawberry shortcake —"

Vicki made another exaggerated shudder. "Don't keep talking about strawberry shortcake! Tell me again about the two women you thought you saw her with — the ones who were going around starting commotions."

I described the two women again. "I think the one with maroon curly hair was the same woman who was carrying empty bowls away from the salad tent at the picnic, but I didn't get a good look at her. She hopped into the back of a white van and closed the doors."

"I know who you mean. I bought asparagus salad from her. Did you notice what she was wearing that time?"

"A navy blue long-sleeved shirt, and, I think, jeans. Who is she?"

"I don't know her." Vicki gave me a stern look. "But I'll do the investigating. You keep out of it."

"Don't worry." I had no intention of snooping into Neil's death and the subsequent peculiar disposal of his body. However, if I *happened* upon more evidence, it would be helpful if I learned as much as possible so I could pass it on to Vicki accurately, wouldn't it? I had liked Neil. The entire community would mourn him.

Vicki gently lifted Bow-Tie away from my ponytail, confined him against her bulletproof vest, tickled him under the chin, and commented in tones that were painfully too casual, "I saw your posters. Has anyone phoned about losing the kitties?"

"No. If no one claims them, would you like them?"

She pocketed her notebook and rescued me from Mustache, who had apparently decided that one of my dangly earrings was a toy. "They're tempting, but I'd hate to take them away from Sally-Forth. If anyone does claim them, though, let me attend the reunion. I'd like to see who managed to misplace kittens in your yard around the time someone dropped off a body."

Speaking of dropping, I nearly had to pick my chin up off my knees. Surely, whoever dragged Neil into my backyard had not brought kittens along.

Vicki straightened her own ponytail and resettled her hat on her head. "First yarn-bombing," she murmured to the kittens. "Then quiltbatbombing."

I covered my mouth. Despite the horror of Neil's sudden death, I was finding cop humor funny. Maybe I was coming down with something. I spoke between my fingers. "I wonder if the supposed yarnbomber was wearing that quilt batting when he ran off and hopped into a motorboat." If only I'd seen that cape on a running person, I might know if it had flapped like quilt batting or like an old sheet or blanket.

"Neil?" she asked. "And he wasn't sick after all?"

"Probably not Neil. On Friday night, he turned green when Tom Umshaw teased him about going out in boats."

"Tom Umshaw?"

"He sells fish down at the wharf. He had the fish fry tent at the picnic."

"*Must* you keep reminding me of the things I ate last night? Including the perch I didn't manage to finish so I'd have room for strawberry shortcake?" She groaned.

I grinned.

"Okay," she said. "I'll tell Gartener. He'll probably go find Cassie, the two fighting women, and this Tom Umshaw, and have a word with them all." She pointed her pen at me. "And remember, Willow. Police investigate crimes. Civilians don't." She quickly amended that to, "At least they *shouldn't.*"

"Sorry for reporting the treasure trove of jewelry," I teased. "What's happening with that?"

"Every item matches something in the insurers' lists, so all of it will eventually be turned over to the insurance companies. At the moment, the jewelry and the box it was buried in are being kept as evidence during the investigation into Snoozy's death. Sorting everything out could take a long time."

She cocked her head and gave me one of her police officer assessing looks. "Thirty years ago, rewards were posted for the return of the jewelry, so it's possible that you and Clay may get a windfall."

"I won't hold my breath." But I couldn't help wondering if my dream of a cruise might come true, or if I would be practical, instead, and make early mortgage payments.

After Vicki left, I phoned Haylee. She was as shocked and sickened about Neil's death and the disposal of his body as I was. "What killed him?" she asked.

"If Vicki knows, she's not telling me. Maybe it was the gastrointestinal whatever that Vicki and Edna had. He must have had it, too. Vicki thinks it was the flu, not food poisoning, since people who didn't attend the picnic also got sick."

"So Vicki won't be upset if you and I sort of *accidentally* look into the possibility of food poisoning?"

I played along. "How would we do that?"

"Visit local asparagus farms, for a start?" I heard the grin in her voice.

"I'm running low on fresh produce," I said. "And I'm totally out of those cinnamon rolls from that one farm stand."

"My nice red truck or your boring car?" Haylee teased.

"My car doesn't call attention to us like your red truck does — your truck with its sissy automatic transmission."

"You could teach me to drive a stick shift, but then you'd have nothing to act superior about."

"Ha. We need to save my *boring* five-speed for times when we don't want people recognizing us, like when we have to snoop around after dark."

"We'd never do that," she said.

I laughed. "I'll walk the dogs and then meet you at your truck in a half hour."

What was the point of fencing in my backyard if the poor dogs couldn't run around freely in it? After a short outing with all four animals in the part of my yard we were allowed to use, I let Sally help me round up the kittens, then took the dogs for a brisk jaunt to the beach and back.

Hoping I wouldn't return to shredded furniture, I shut the animals into my great room, and then Haylee and I set off in her cherry red pickup truck. She turned to me. "Have you talked to Tom Umshaw since Neil's death?"

"No. I should offer my condolences."

"I need to do that also, and I could use some fresh fish for supper. Mind if we head for the wharf, first?"

"We should," I agreed.

She drove out of Threadville and west on Shore Road. "Do you know anything about Neil's family and his other friends besides Tom?"

"Vicki said that his only family was his mother, in Florida. And he must have other friends besides Tom. But I think he usually started his working day around two in the morning, which would have kept him from many evening activities, like hanging around with the regulars at The Ironmonger."

Haylee turned her pickup right on a road leading down a hill to the Elderberry Bay Lodge, the marina, and the wharf. "During sewing classes," she told me, "Tom said that he heads out very early some mornings to get to the really good fishing spots. He was glad that our courses were held in the daytime. He said that even during the winter, he started yawning by seven. So he wouldn't hang out with the Ironmonger crowd, either. No wonder he and Neil were friends. Our lunchtime would just about be . . . have been . . . their suppertime."

Neil had seemed like an outgoing, contented, and generous man, but I hadn't known him well. He'd lived in the apartment above La Bakery, and I'd never seen anyone else around who might have shared that apartment with him. I felt sorry for his mother. And for Tom and for Neil's other friends, too, who would be grieving over his loss. Life was too short, especially for Neil.

To our left, the Elderberry Bay Lodge, resplendent in fresh white paint, nestled among trees above lawns sloping down to the beach. The bright blue sky reflected on water lapping at the sand. A couple of motorboats were tied up at a spanking new dock, while canoes, kayaks, and paddle boats were on the sand above the waterline.

Haylee turned right again, onto Beach Row. We passed a marina that was colorful with flags flying from yachts.

Beyond the marina, Haylee could have continued along Beach Row, which would have taken us back home. Instead, she parked in the lot that served the marina, the public boat launch, and the wharf.

Tom's shop was the largest on the wharf, and the closest to Beach Row. It was built of weathered wood with a rustic sign over the door, *Tom's Fish Shack,* and a hole or two gnawed through the wood near the pavement.

Head down, Tom came out of his shop and headed for a pickup truck with a windowed cap over the bed.

Jumping out of Haylee's truck, I called to him.

His eyes were red-rimmed, his face puffy. With obvious effort, he turned the corners of his mouth up in a smile that didn't match his sad eyes.

Haylee clambered out of her truck, too.

Awkwardly, we asked if we were too late to buy fish.

"Of course not. Come on in." He turned around, led us to the building, and rammed the wooden door with his shoulder. "It sticks," he apologized. "I was going to fix it, but . . ." His voice trailed off as if Neil's death had robbed him of his energy.

"We're sorry about Neil," I managed.

Tom nodded, accepting the sympathy if not the reality. "We were friends since grade school. I can't believe he's gone."

It occurred to me that Haylee and I should offer Cassie our condolences, also. I blurted, "Do you know what's become of Neil's assistant?"

Tom looked blank.

"Cassie?" I prompted.

"What's become of her?" he asked. "Nothing, I hope." He shook his head as if to clear cobwebs. "Sorry I'm so slow. I was laid up with the stomach flu ever since Saturday night, and then I heard about Neil, and I'm still not really on my feet. Maybe Cassie's sick, too. Or maybe she went back home. Cleveland, I think Neil said." He went around to the other side of his sales counter. "Poor kid. She seemed so eager to run that bakery better." He opened the glass door at the back of the refrigerated display unit. "What kind of fish do you want and how much?"

It was a relief to discuss fish and not murder. He sprinkled ice chips over our fish to keep it fresh, wrapped it, and saw us out.

Sobered, we climbed into Haylee's truck. She drove back past the marina and lodge and up the hill to Shore Road.

Years before, my Brownie leader took our troop on what she called "penny hikes." The plan was that whenever we came to a crossroad, we flipped a coin and scampered down that street until the next crossroad, where we flipped a coin again. Sometimes, we ended up at my leader's house in only a few rather disappointing minutes. Once in a while, though, the leader had to pocket the penny and direct us to the quickest route home to prevent concerned parents from laying siege to her house. After one memorably long hike, the leader began carrying a compass.

That was sort of how Haylee and I did

our shopping at farm stands. We seldom flipped a coin, though. We tended to take routes we hadn't traveled before, and if we found something particularly good, like those cinnamon and pecan breakfast rolls, we returned to that stand on our way to the grocery store for whatever was still on our shopping lists. So far, we hadn't needed a compass.

Haylee drove south, away from the lake. Stands that had been selling only asparagus were closed for the season. We bought lettuce, spinach, strawberries, new potatoes, goat's milk cheese, free-range eggs, and, of course, the cinnamon rolls we'd come for. We also bought muffins and artisanal bread at that woman's stand, too, and cookies to supplement the baking that we would have to continue doing on Mondays.

Haylee had driven only about a mile toward home when a certain farmland aroma made us close the pickup's windows. She pointed. "There've been times in my life when owning a manure spreader might have come in handy or been a lot of fun." The manure spreader twirled like a small but jolly merry-go-round. All it needed was the music to go with it.

Asparagus grew in the field. The stalks were longer than the ones we commonly saw in stores or bought directly from farm-ers, but they hadn't yet branched out into their ferny greenery. I asked, "Do you sup-pose someone sold asparagus after spread-ing manure on their fields, and the salad lady bought some? She served it raw. What if she didn't bother washing it?"

Haylee nodded. "Food poisoning, maybe? How about if we do the rest of our shop-ping at the supermarket, go home, put away our groceries, eat supper, and later, when it's dark —"

I finished the suggestion for her. "We'll use my nicely nondescript five-speed car and bring the dogs out for a ride and their late-night walk."

16

Haylee and I had our after-dark snooping down to a science. If we had questions, we took the dogs for a ride wherever we thought we might end up with answers. Usually, the dogs scored a walk. Sometimes, we found evidence. Occasionally, we landed ourselves in trouble.

We had learned to be careful.

I put away the groceries, ate supper, and played with embroidery until dark, which, only two days after the summer solstice, was late. I left the kittens to sleep or vandalize my apartment, then walked my dogs down Lake Street to my car. They hopped into the backseat.

Haylee strolled uphill from the vicinity of the bandstand. Like me, she was dressed in black from head to toe. We got in, and I started the car and eased out of Threadville.

Haylee asked me, "Did anything go missing from your table at the sidewalk sale

Friday night?"

"No. I had Ashley with me, and that girl sees everything. And no fights broke out over my merchandise. I don't know why," I teased, "since it's every bit as nice as yours."

Haylee grunted. "The shoplifter or shoplifters may have hit me as well as Opal and Naomi. I remember putting out a small box of water-soluble thread. It had nine or ten spools in it, last I knew. Today, Ralph came over from Disguise Guys. He was in a panic because he'd run out of the stuff, and I couldn't find it. That poor guy! He loves creating costumes, the more original the better, but he hates ripping out basting stitches. He was miffed, too, because Duncan had apparently refused to shop in my store."

"Duncan's shy."

"I don't know how Ralph, who is so outgoing, managed to raise a son who, although he must be over thirty, can barely string two words together."

I suggested, "Maybe Duncan likes you."

"That's what his father implied, but I think it was wishful thinking. He muttered something about Duncan never working up the courage to ask anyone out, so how was he, Ralph that is, ever going to have grandchildren to make costumes for?"

I laughed. "Has Ralph been spending time with your mothers?"

She turned toward me. I took my eyes off the road for a second. She was grinning. "Makes you wonder if they could be conspiring to matchmake, doesn't it? It's not going to work, though. Duncan's handsome in a sort of nerdy way, and probably very nice, but how would anyone get to know him?"

"What do you think happened to the missing thread?"

"Either I put the box away in a very strange place, or someone stole it. Poor Ralph will have to rip out basting stitches until I get more water-soluble thread for him."

"A lot of those costumes he makes look like they shouldn't be dunked in water. The fur might mat."

"He claims he has tricks up his furry sleeves."

I slowed for a corner. "Maybe the blonde stole it. She was the one who tried to pick a quarrel about thread — embroidery thread — at my sale table. What a *strange* coincidence." Sarcasm twisted my tone. "Opal's knitting needles, Naomi's quilt batting, and your box of thread all went missing around the time the blonde and the salad lady attracted our attention."

"And then the salad lady went and poisoned half the village? If that woman knowingly harmed Edna, I'll —"

I interrupted her. "And I'll help you. Ugh. I wonder if your thread was used with the batting and knitting needles to wrap up Neil's body."

Haylee sighed. "I hope not. But I'd better be prepared for weird accusations from Chief Vicki Smallwood and the state police."

Asparagus could tolerate dry, sandy soil, and most of the asparagus farms we'd patronized during our penny-hike shopping expeditions were close to the lake.

First, I drove to the farm where we'd seen the manure spreader at work earlier in the evening. All was quiet in the moonlight, but the smell had not diminished. The dogs raised their noses and sniffed. We closed the windows. I kept driving.

Not much farther down the road, we spotted a dark, banged-up minivan teetering on a slope beyond the shoulder. Concerned that the van might be in danger of rolling into a ditch, I slowed the car.

We couldn't see anyone in the van, but Haylee pointed toward the field. A hefty man was quickly gathering asparagus stalks and stuffing them into a white plastic bag.

"It's a funny time to harvest," she commented.

"Both the time of year, when the asparagus is past its prime, and the time of day," I agreed. "I mean night." I nodded at a piece of farm machinery parked at the back of the field. "And most asparagus pickers use those things."

We'd seen the homemade harvesting contraptions often during the asparagus season, and I'd asked one farmer what they were called. He'd thought awhile, and said he called his an Easy Ride, but he wasn't sure what others might call theirs. Their construction varied, and most appeared to have been homemade, welded together at the farm where they were used. Most were centered on lawn tractors with winglike extensions on their sides. Seats and footrests dangled from the wings. As the Easy Ride trundled down a field's rows, people sitting on the low seats reached between their raised feet for the spears. Canopies protected the harvesters from the worst of the sun and rain. Although picking the spears all day would still be hard work, doing it from an Easy Ride had to be more comfortable than walking and stooping like the figure in the moonlight was doing.

We'd spent so much time using each

other's vehicles as our snooping headquarters that we both knew where to find the important tools. Haylee opened my glove compartment and took out my flashlight.

It was small but powerful. Haylee opened her window and aimed it at the figure in the field. He turned away, even though his hood shielded most of his face from view. Like us, he was dressed in black.

I drove until we would be out of his sight, then turned around and flicked off my headlights, which I didn't really need the night after the full moon, anyway. I urged the car forward at a crawl.

The man had returned to the van. He opened the driver's door, threw his bulging plastic bag inside, hopped in after it, and roared off. He'd kept his hood up, and neither of us had recognized him.

The night air was redolent of recently spread manure. I muttered, "Don't tell me someone's going to poison *more* people with unwashed asparagus." I was tempted to gun the motor, but I held back in the hope that my lack of headlights would prevent the thief from noticing we were following him.

Apparently having satisfied themselves that whatever had created the prodigious amount of manure was nowhere near us,

Sally and Tally flopped down on their seat.

Ahead of us, the road ran flat and straight, a ribbon of gray in the moonlight. The van's taillights diminished, but I kept them in my sight and dropped back. We left the smelly field behind and opened our windows.

The van turned off the main road onto one that would lead him straight to Elderberry Bay.

I glanced in triumph at Haylee. "We'll find him." I pressed harder on the gas.

17

We were almost at the intersection where the van had turned. Wind whipped into the windows, blowing our hair into our faces, but we only laughed.

A dark monstrosity lumbered out of a field and onto the road in front of us.

An Easy Ride.

"Farmers work long hours," Haylee commented.

Yells came from the machine. "Farmers' sons *play* even longer hours," I said.

As far as I could tell, five teenage boys were riding on the thing, each of them brandishing a bottle of beer. Instead of boxes for vegetables between the seats, the Easy Ride carried cases of beer. The entire monstrosity, welded superstructure and all, took up both lanes of the country road.

Surely, the kids would pull into a field any moment.

They didn't. They kept their Easy Ride

chugging along, filling my car with exhaust fumes. We closed the windows.

Unless I could pass the Easy Ride, I had no hope of catching up with the asparagus thief and his load of probably tainted asparagus, no hope of finding out where he lived, who he was, or warning him to wash that asparagus thoroughly.

No. I wouldn't talk to him or let him see us. Whoever had poisoned the community could have killed Neil, directly or indirectly. I would tell Vicki about the asparagus thief and let her do the interrogating.

But first, I had to find that van, which meant I had to pass the Easy Ride. The shoulders weren't wide enough to drive on them safely, but the Easy Ride could have made an abrupt right turn onto the shoulder. The thing's wings would then be parallel to the road and I would be able to pass it. Although I was certain they knew we were behind them, I honked and turned on my headlights.

The boys knew we were there, all right. They turned around, waved their bottles at us, shouted something I couldn't make out, which was probably just as well, and kept going, continuing to block both sides of the road.

If the tractor propelling the Easy Ride had

a headlight, it didn't cast any light that I could see. What if an oncoming vehicle didn't see the Easy Ride, and plowed into it?

I dropped back.

I was glad I had when bottles flew from the Easy Ride and smashed on the pavement in front of us.

Broken glass, just what I needed to drive through. I still had a snow shovel in the trunk. And I always carried plastic garbage bags.

I pulled off the road and we all tumbled out. Haylee walked the leashed dogs up and down the shoulder and snickered as I shoveled up bits of glass from the asphalt and dumped them into a garbage bag.

A car barreled up from behind us and stopped beside me.

Vicki Smallwood, in her cruiser without its gaudy sweater, opened her passenger window, and leaned down so she could see us. Sally-Forth and Tally-Ho wagged their tails.

Vicki looked pointedly at the snow shovel in my hand and raised a delicate eyebrow. She hollered over the sound of her engine, "Snow too deep for you?"

Silently, I held up the garbage bag.

Vicki covered her mouth, but her eyes

gleamed with mischief. "Stoop and scoop? I hope that shovel's overkill."

I shook the bag. It rattled, but she probably didn't hear that. I walked to her car and bent to speak through the open passenger window. "Glass. The kids in front of us were throwing bottles."

Wrist draped over her steering wheel, Vicki peered out her windshield. "I don't see anyone."

Sure enough, the road was empty.

I explained, "They were riding on one of those asparagus-picking contraptions, drinking beer, and tossing the empties. That contraption takes up both sides of the road. I couldn't pass. They must have pulled off. You'll find them in a field or barnyard." If she hurried.

She didn't. Abandoning her casual pose, she gripped her steering wheel and gave me one of her stern police officer glares. "Were you driving without lights for a while back there, Willow?"

I shuffled my feet, which of course she couldn't see from inside her cruiser. "I forgot them at first. The moon is bright." Not a great excuse for "forgetting" the headlights, I knew.

"Taillights can keep you from being rear-ended." She scrutinized my face.

I tried to maintain a neutral expression, for all the good that did. I managed not to say anything.

She looked past me to Haylee and called, "How did you get here so fast, Haylee?"

The dogs had given up on any sort of outing and were lying at Haylee's feet. Hanging on to leashes with one hand, she raised the other one, palm up, to show she didn't know the answer to Vicki's question.

"She didn't get here fast," I answered for her. "We were creeping along behind the harvesting thing. I probably reached speeds exceeding six whole miles an hour."

Vicki tilted her head in question. "But I saw Haylee in Elderberry Bay only ten minutes ago. She was in a silver BMW with a Norse god."

"Impossible," I said. "She's been with me for almost an hour."

"An *hour*?" Vicki scowled. "You two aren't playing detective again, are you?"

"Of course not. We drive around most nights and walk the dogs."

"On the shoulders of roads. And maybe in ditches. Lucky dogs." She had definitely recovered from her illness.

"Most of my yard is still out of bounds," I reminded her. Telling her about the man picking possibly contaminated asparagus in the moonlight would be too much like a confession of snooping, so I didn't. If Haylee and I managed to collect real facts, we could give them to our police chief. For the moment, I was happy enough to discuss something else. "Are you sure it wasn't Opal you saw?" I asked Vicki. "She and Haylee resemble each other."

"So do you and Haylee, but I can tell you apart. This woman was not Opal's age and looked almost exactly like Haylee. I wondered who the hunk was and how long Haylee had been hiding him from the rest of us."

"I wish," Haylee joked.

Just wait until Friday night, I thought. *Clay has a plan . . .*

Vicki promised, "I'll go look for those kids and their undoubtedly unlicensed contraption and beer bottles. Don't forget your headlights on your way *home.*" Her emphasis on the word "home" was far from subtle. "You might accidentally puncture your tires on broken glass." She peeled away into the night. I hoped *she* would watch for fragments of glass.

Haylee, the dogs, and I piled into my car. I turned on the headlights and drove at a sedate speed, though by then we would have been no more than two pinpricks of light in

Vicki's rearview mirror.

"Vicki hinted rather broadly that we should head home," I said.

"Let's." Haylee could be very agreeable. "The asparagus thief turned toward Elderberry Bay."

Grinning, I followed the road the van had taken. I drove slowly so we could check driveways, but neither of us saw the old van.

How were we going to prevent people from eating unwashed and recently fertilized asparagus if we didn't know who had picked it and where he lived?

"Could the asparagus thief have been the salad lady?" Haylee asked.

"Maybe, if she'd strapped on stilts and shoulder pads."

"Perfect for harvesting asparagus!"

I had to laugh. "Did the salad lady's truck or tent have a company name on it?"

"A sign at the tent said 'salad.' I think the truck was unmarked."

"Who helped Mona organize the picnic?" Mona was very good at delegating, which was why Haylee, her three mothers, and I had not accepted her invitation to join the organizing committee.

Haylee laughed. "Don't you mean, 'Who *actually* organized it?' "

"Yes. Someone on her committee must

know who brought the salads."

Haylee suggested, "It's kind of late now, but shall we talk to Mona tomorrow?"

"Sure." Vicki wouldn't be able to complain, at least not much, about our interfering with an investigation if all we did was ask Mona for a name.

"How about tomorrow? I have appointments with fabric representatives most of the day — planning what to stock next winter. But I left a couple hours free at lunchtime. Can you bring the dogs to the park for a picnic, and then we'll tackle Mona?"

"It's a deal." I drove down Lake Street, parked the car, and took the dogs home to a pair of kittens who were more than ready to get up and play. They were still tackling my toes when I drifted off to sleep.

18

Even though it was my day off, sleeping late wasn't an option. My four young pets were raring to start their morning fracases. I'd set up a litter tray inside, so I took only the dogs for a leashed run on the beach. When we arrived back in the apartment, the kittens barely stirred from Sally's bed. Their nighttime activities must have tuckered them out. I carried my breakfast upstairs to my front porch and latched the gate in the picket fence surrounding my front yard. Tally was happy to come out onto the porch with me, but Sally needed a little convincing to leave her sleeping charges and join me and Tally.

Birds sang in trees under a sky soft with haze. I loved In Stitches and barely thought of it as work, but it was nice to have time to relax with my morning coffee and the latest machine embroidery magazines while the dogs snoozed beside my comfy chair.

After breakfast, I swept the porch and washed the shop windows and the glass in the front door. Awake again and energized for new games, the kittens batted at me from the other side. I had to clean their paw prints off, too, but they were so cute and funny they could get away with nearly anything.

Needing to water the begonias in the urns on my porch, I went inside and filled the watering can. The dogs curled up on their beds in their pen, but Mustache and Bow-Tie were not ready for naps. With both kittens skirmishing around my feet, I carried the sloshing watering can toward the front door.

I was used to having strangers appear in my store. I shouldn't have been shocked when a man appeared on my porch and just kept coming until he was inside.

But it was Monday, the embroidered sign on my door said *Closed,* and Vicki had discovered Neil's body in my backyard only a day before.

I stopped dead, weighing that watering can and its contents as possible defenses. Squealing, the kittens skittered away, heading, from the sounds of things, to Sally-Forth's comforting presence.

The man removed his aviator sunglasses.

He had to be Vicki's Norse god. Tall and rangy, he was blue-eyed and firm-jawed. A horned helmet would not have looked out of place on his thick blond hair.

Instead of a shield and a spear, he carried a camera, an expensive one. A reporter coming to question me about Neil's death? Just what I did not need.

I saw a question in his eyes, the look of someone trying to figure out whether or not I recognized him.

I didn't, but he looked familiar, maybe because of Vicki's nickname for him.

"I'm Max," he said, holding out a hand.

Okay, so I would switch the watering can to my left hand and shake the god's hand with my right, but I wouldn't be interviewed about a suspicious death in my backyard.

Tally and Sally got up, stretched, stared intently at the man calling himself Max, and wagged their tails. My guard dogs.

Of course, I did have attack cats, and they had overcome their bashful moment and were climbing Max's jeans.

"Max *Brubaugh*," he said, as if I should know the name.

It didn't ring a bell.

I guessed I was supposed to say something. I managed, "I'm Willow," and pulled my hand from his clasp.

"What can you tell me about Threadville? That's what this village is called, right? Unofficially?"

"Yes, because of the needlecraft shops here."

"I hear there was a yarnbombing incident here Saturday evening."

He was here to learn about yarnbombing, not mysterious deaths or food poisoning? "Yes, a police cruiser was covered in knitting."

He touched his camera. "Could you direct me to it so I can get a picture?"

I shook my head. "The chief needed her cruiser."

"Any idea who did the yarnbombing?"

I might have shrugged if I hadn't been burdened by a watering can. "I'm afraid not."

He turned and looked out my front window. "Is Tell a Yarn a yarn store?"

"Yes."

"I thought maybe it was a bookstore." *So why did he ask if it was a yarn store?* He had a really nice smile, but I wasn't about to be swayed by his many charms, even if he did pluck those kittens gently off his jeans and cradle them in his hands on either side of his camera.

"The proprietor has storytelling evenings

there some Friday nights."

"Sounds like fun. Does she knit or crochet?"

I wasn't about to let that winning smile trick me into saying too much about my friends. "Yes."

"So she could have done the yarnbombing?" Maybe he was a plainclothes detective, and the state police were looking into the possibility that the yarnbomber and the quiltbatbomber were the same person. Maybe the camera was only a prop, and that was why he didn't seem to notice that the kittens were swatting at each other around the long lens.

"She *could* have, but I'm sure she didn't."

He tilted his head and raised one eyebrow in a way that could be endearing, almost doglike, if I trusted him. "Sure?"

"Positive." I was not being the most entertaining conversationalist in the world, but I didn't want to be. I had no idea what information this man was actually after, and I wasn't about to divulge anything I'd regret later. Besides, it was my day off.

"Why?"

I mentally gritted my teeth while giving him my best friendly-but-not-too-friendly look. "She was taking care of a sick friend when it happened."

"I was just wondering because we've had a spate of yarnbombings in the Pittsburgh area, and some in Slippery Rock and Meadville, and now this. I thought the yarnbomber might have moved here."

The only new Threadville shop was Disguise Guys, but Ralph and Duncan had wanted that hand-knit cruiser so they could make it into a costume for four people. If they'd taken time to knit the thing, wouldn't it have been simpler to keep it in the first place, and not risk having it confiscated by the police? But I merely said, "Opal's been here a few years. I can't imagine her playing pranks like that." Opal would prefer crafting creative outfits for herself. "But you could go ask her."

Without moving a muscle, Max had become tense and watchful. "Opal, you say?"

Oh, no, what had I done? But it would have been easy enough for him to discover her name on his own. He'd only need to look up Tell a Yarn's website. I nodded.

That only encouraged him. "Does she have children?"

What a strange question. My suspicion of the man's motives must have shown on my face.

He actually blushed. "Like little ones who might be eating breakfast at the moment so

I shouldn't bother her right now?"

"Only if you count Lucy," I said.

His face softened. Had he met the personable and talkative cat? "Lucy?"

I'd told him enough. "Here, I'll take my pests." Mustache and Bow-Tie were nestled in Max's arms and purring very loudly. In case he hadn't understood my hints, I added, "So you can go talk to Opal and meet Lucy."

"Okay, thanks. I'll talk to her." He handed me the kittens, who had gone all boneless, warm, and sleepy. Sally-Forth sat up straighter, ready to cuddle them into naptime, no doubt.

Max left. I carried the kittens into the dogs' pen. Sally-Forth trotted to her bed and lay down. I placed the kittens next to her, and she gave them a vigorous washing.

Outside, a silver BMW, with Max at the wheel, eased away from the curb. Why had Max said he was going to talk to Opal, and then driven away?

He did not, I noticed, have a passenger. He must have left the girlfriend at home.

I ran across to Tell a Yarn, opened the unlocked door, went in, and called out a greeting. Meowing, Lucy dropped a bedraggled hand-knit catnip mouse at my feet. Eyes going all blissful, she fell shoulder-first onto the mouse, and in a very deliberate and intricate choreography, proceeded to roll around on it.

Wearing a yellow crocheted dress, Opal came out of her back room. "Willow, good morning! Nice to see you so early."

"A man was just in my shop implying that you could have been behind the yarnbombing."

"Well, I wasn't. I have better things to do with my time. And better yarns, too. Who would want to touch that plasticky stuff? Yuck." She folded her arms.

"That's what I told him, though not quite in those words. But the strange thing was that I told him to bring his questions to you, and he said he would, but he drove off without coming over here. I think he may have been a detective or a reporter."

Opal became very still in a way that reminded me of Max's sudden silent watchfulness.

I added, "He said he wouldn't bother you if you were feeding your children breakfast. The name Lucy seemed to ring a bell with him."

"What was his name?" She almost flung the words at me.

"Max, he said. Max Brubaugh. Chief Smallwood must have seen him driving around the village last night. She called him a Norse god and she was ri—"

I was talking to thin air and to a cat who was only slightly stupefied from the effects of her catnip mouse.

19

Opal had flung the back of her hand across her mouth and dashed away, into her dining room, and from there, it appeared, into her kitchen. A door slammed.

Stunned, I stared at the doorway into Opal's dining room. I had never before seen Opal run away in the middle of a conversation.

Haylee's mothers always treated me kindly, as if I were a member of their family, and I would never upset one of them if I could help it. But now I had, and I wasn't sure how I'd done it, and wished, too late, that I hadn't. I took a step toward Opal's inviting dining room, and then halted. I didn't want to make things worse.

I turned toward the front door and stopped again. In Opal's lovely shop, with morning sun flowing into her front windows and her cat murmuring in catnip-inspired ecstasy at my feet, I began to understand.

First, Vicki had reported seeing a Haylee lookalike. Then, when I'd met Max, I'd sensed that I might have already encountered him, but I hadn't been able to figure out where.

Max resembled Haylee, and Opal, too. A relation?

Opal never mentioned her family, and Haylee had never met them and didn't talk about them.

If I stayed where I was in Tell a Yarn, I could keep one eye on Opal's shop and the other on In Stitches, which was also unlocked. I pictured my little embroidery boutique being invaded by about a thousand more mysterious strangers, some handsome, some dangerous, and some both.

As I watched my front porch for these imagined intruders, a door behind me unlatched. I whirled around.

Head down, Opal stumbled toward me. "Sorry, Willow," she muttered. "I was a little surprised by what you said."

I intended to be gentle. Instead, I blurted, "Do you *know* Max Brubaugh?" After the words were out, I couldn't retract them. Miserably, I held my breath. I'd probably made a bad situation worse. Would she dash away again?

She raised her chin and patted her eyes

with a tissue. "Could he be the same Max Brubaugh we sometimes see on the Erie news? On a program originating from their Pittsburgh parent station?"

That's why he'd looked familiar, besides resembling Haylee and Opal. "Aha, yes. Is he a relative of yours? He has that Norse god look."

"Well *I* don't." She blew her nose.

"Goddess," I corrected myself. "Haylee has it, too."

"I had a nephew named Max Brubaugh." Her lips quirked in a tenuous attempt at a smile. "I probably still have one. He was about three the last time I —" She broke off and grabbed another tissue from a box behind her sales counter. "My big sister's kid. Of all the people in my family, I was most surprised that my sister cut me off. The others, well . . ." She shrugged. "That's what they were like. If it hadn't been for Naomi and Edna, I don't know what I'd have done. They gave me back my confidence and self-esteem, and they have always done everything they could for me. And for Haylee, too, of course. Sisters couldn't be closer. My real sister wasn't close, as it turned out."

She stood tall and looked out at the street, but I suspected she was seeing into a different world and a different time. "Little Max was adorable. I babysat him often. He didn't pronounce Opal well and called me 'Auntie Elbow.' Not seeing him ever again, not being able to watch him grow up, tore my insides apart." She half turned from me and dabbed at her eyes.

I asked, "Did he have a sister?"

She faced me. Behind her glistening eyes, I saw both fear and hope. "Why do you ask?"

"Last night when Haylee and I were out with the dogs, Chief Smallwood said she'd seen Haylee with him. Since Haylee had been with me, I guessed that the woman Chief Smallwood saw was Max's girlfriend, but now, because of the family resemblance, I suspect the other woman could be related to him, like maybe a sister."

"I wondered if Pearl might have been pregnant last time I saw her, but I wasn't sure." Opal tossed her tissues away. "I'd better go talk to Haylee, Edna, and Naomi, so none of them will be as shocked as I was if he shows up again."

Would he? Or had he gathered the information he wanted and driven off with it?

As we left Opal's store, I turned around. On the other side of the glass door, Lucy pawed at the catnip mouse until it flew up into the air. Rump high, the gray tabby scooted after it, and probably batted it underneath the counter.

I jogged across the street to In Stitches, went inside, and looked out my front window at the shops across the street.

Opal stood stiffly with Haylee at the door of The Stash. Naomi marched toward them. Beside her, Edna took little hops between steps to keep up. They all went into The Stash.

Would Haylee eat lunch with me at the park, and talk to Mona afterward? Or would her plans change?

I spent the rest of the morning baking cookies, with disruptions involving two unruly kittens and two importunate dogs. Investigators milled between the crime scene in my backyard and vehicles parked on the hiking trail.

Shortly before noon, I took all four animals out to the patio and the flower gardens surrounding it, where Sally-Forth supervised the kitties and Tally-Ho pulled at his leash, undoubtedly planning to trot down the hill to meet the investigators.

Inside again, I put a sandwich, some carrot sticks, and a box of juice into a lunch bag that I'd made and embroidered for myself, then leashed the dogs and walked them to the park.

Haylee was already sitting on one of the benches lining the knee-high walls of the bandstand. She'd brought a bowl of salad.

I fastened the dogs' leashes to the leg of a bench and gave Haylee's salad a suspicious glance. "No asparagus?"

"None. And I washed everything thoroughly under briskly running water. *That* should scare all the germs away." Although she was joking, strain wrinkled the skin between her eyebrows.

"Did Opal tell you about the man who came to my shop?" I asked.

Haylee stabbed at a piece of cucumber. "What nerve. How *dare* they?"

Her vehemence startled me. Maybe my report of Max's visit had disturbed Opal more than I'd realized.

Haylee pointed the speared cucumber at me. "They kicked Opal out when she needed them, and then when she's made a nice life for herself, they come waltzing back. What are they going to do, try once more to destroy her?"

"Max was three years old when it happened," I reminded her. "And there's no way they can ruin her life. She's strong, and she loves what she's doing. Don't we all?"

"Someone put him up to it." Haylee

hunched over her salad. "I refuse to even think of them as my grandparents. Disowning can work both ways."

Sally-Forth sat up, rested her chin on Haylee's knee, and stared with a worried expression up into Haylee's face.

I didn't know what to say. My parents were distant, emotionally as well as geographically, but they loved me in their way and had raised me with care. Besides, I'd spent my summers with doting grandparents, and they'd always made me feel secure.

Haylee's father didn't know she existed, and she didn't know her grandparents, but the three women who had raised her adored her. Everybody probably had dark little holes in their existence that could have been filled with more love, but neither Haylee nor I had cause for complaint.

We ate in silence except for the panting of Sally and Tally at our feet. I finished my lunch, then said fiercely, "Opal has us — you, me, Naomi, and Edna. None of us will let anyone hurt her."

Haylee stuffed her empty salad bowl into her lunch bag. "Opal has two weird sisters, two weird daughters, and one weird doctor who is almost a brother. Gord will rally around any cause of Edna's. And Opal has got to be one of Edna's causes."

I smiled. "Unless Edna continues to hide from Gord."

"Edna says she's almost ready to let Gord see her again." Haylee's love for her three mothers seemed to have fueled her anger at Max Brubaugh and his family. Maybe she was also jealous because Opal had probably never stopped loving Max, or at least her memories of the boy. I was sure that Opal didn't blame the long-festering pain of rejection on a three-year-old.

If Haylee had any other inner demons to wrestle, she apparently wasn't about to tell me about them. She stood up. "Let's go talk to Mona," she said.

20

Certain that Mona wouldn't want dogs in her shop even on Threadville's day off, I asked Haylee to help take them to my apartment. We had to greet the kittens properly before Sally-Forth herded them away from the door and toward her inviting embroidered doggie bed.

Haylee and I went down the street to Country Chic. Mona was alone, and thrilled to show off her latest merchandise. I'd already bought lawn furniture from her and didn't need more, especially if huge sections of my yard were always going to be barricaded behind police tape. Mona had stocked some very pretty things, including a whole new line of bird-houses, pastel garden urns, and Adirondack chairs painted in floral designs with matching tables and umbrellas.

She had a way of shaking her head at the end of every phrase, as if everything she said distressed her, even though she was busily praising her merchandise. When she stopped for a breath, I asked her who had provided the salads for the community picnic.

She stared off into the distance. "Some woman. That little girl from the bakery found her. Such a pity about Neil."

Haylee and I agreed.

Mona murmured, "Don't let them accuse that little girl from the bakery of murdering Neil. Cassie, that's her name. She's much too tiny."

I backed away from Mona. "I'm leaving the investigating to the police." Maybe saying it aloud would make me actually do it.

"Even if that hunk of yours is involved?"

I guessed Mona meant Clay. "How could Clay be involved in Neil's death? And anyway, Clay's not *mine.*"

Mona took a deep breath. "He's not? Whenever you want to push him *my* way . . ."

Haylee quickly objected. "She's not going to. But why would anyone say that Clay had something to do with Neil's death?"

"Murder." Mona rolled the *r*s dramatically. "You might as well call it by its proper name. That new guy in town, Fred Zongassi, found Snoozy Gallagher's skeleton, right?"

I wasn't about to tell Mona about Vicki's interest in Fred. "Yes. Though last I knew, they're still not certain it was Snoozy."

Mona shook her head vigorously. "Who else could it be?" She pointed her hand like a gun at my face. "Fred works for Clay. Fred used to live in Elderberry Bay. Check into it. People are saying that Fred had a knock-down, drag-out brawl with Snoozy, and then fled just about the time Snoozy was murdered."

I resisted pointing a finger back at her. "And you're saying that Fred murdered Snoozy, buried him, and then came back thirty years later and unburied him? Why would anyone do that?"

Mona tugged at her tight dress. "I'm not saying that's what happened, but then, the very next day, didn't Clay dig up the treasure that Snoozy owned?"

Naturally, I had to defend Clay. "It's not surprising that Fred and Clay both made finds while digging. Clay's company is the only one around with earth-moving equipment."

Mona blew at the tip of her finger. "See? That's exactly what I'm saying. Someone tried to bury Neil in the excavation in your yard. And who can drive those earth movers?" She gave me a triumphant smile. "Clay and his employees. Like Fred."

It wasn't nice, but I enjoyed puncturing her theory. "No one used an earth mover to bury Neil. They threw a few shovelfuls of earth over him, that's all. The murderer could have been anyone who found a convenient hole in the ground."

Mona ran a hand over a cast-iron garden bench. Every curlicue had been painted a different jewel tone. "Well, maybe Clay somehow knew about the skeleton and the treasure. He's Fred's boss, so maybe Clay told Fred where to dig."

I deflated her theory even more. "The new lodge owner and I were responsible for where Fred and Clay dug on our properties."

That distracted her. She asked breathlessly, "Have you met the new lodge owner?"

"No," I answered. "Have you?"

She pouted. "Not yet. But he's going to need decorating help, and I'm going to make certain that he uses my talents." She gestured at the merchandise in her crowded shop. "There's lots more where this came from, and I know just where to find it. At prices that will allow me a decent markup as the designer."

Clay had told me that he and Ben had restored the lodge, inside and out, to reflect its Victorian origin. The name of Mona's shop, Country Chic, described her style perfectly, a style that didn't seem Victorian to me. I asked, "Don't you think the new owner will have completed the lodge's interior design by now?"

Mona dismissed that with a wave of her hand. "People can never have enough artwork, and I can teach him how to change it with every season." Arching her neck, she looked about to burst with a secret she was dying to tell. "He probably needs help with taste. I hear he's single." She peered around as if to check for eavesdroppers in the corners of her shop, then shielded one side of her mouth with a hand and whispered, "Widowed."

I spluttered, "Lots of men have good taste."

Mona only placed one forefinger against her lips.

Haylee tried, unsuccessfully, to hide a grin. "I wonder if he was around when Snoozy Gallagher died. Maybe he, and not Fred or Clay, had something to do with Snoozy's death and burial."

Mona stomped a foot. "Impossible. Whoever killed Snoozy Gallagher must be long dead. If he was alive, would he have left the treasure there all these years? No way."

I didn't tell her Clay's and my theory about ice or floods having shifted the treasure during the years since it was first dumped underneath Blueberry Cottage. I merely answered, "So according to that logic, Fred Zongassi didn't murder Snoozy." And Clay had nothing to do with it, either, but I didn't bother telling her that.

Mona tightened her mouth in a peeved expression.

Haylee came up with another conjecture. "Maybe *Snoozy* buried the treasure, and someone else found out and demanded to know where it was. Maybe they fought, and Snoozy died."

Mona flattened that idea with a downward sweep of her hands that threatened a garish purple and orange porcelain Shih Tzu. "That would be stupid, like killing the goose that laid the golden egg."

I steadied the Shih Tzu. "Stupid happens, especially among thieves and murderers."

Mona crossed her arms and glared at me. "*Stupid* is you and Clay digging up that treasure and then giving it away to the cops."

And finding the treasure, not reporting it, and then being arrested for possessing stolen goods would be . . . what?

"Finders keepers, losers weepers," Mona

parroted in a girlishly high voice.

Haylee glanced at the flower-bedecked clock on Mona's wall and brought the conversation back to our original question. "So, will Cassie know who made the salads for the picnic?"

"Cassie wrote down the woman's phone number for me. It should be on my desk." She glanced toward her office. Her desk had to be underneath those piles of paper.

I asked her, "Do you have any idea how we can reach Cassie now that the bakery is closed?" Tom had pointed out that Cassie could have caught the flu or gone back to Cleveland.

If we managed to get in touch with Cassie and she didn't know anything about the salads at the picnic, we could at least give her some sympathy about her boss's death.

"I should have her cell number on my desk, too." Easing around chairs, tables, trellises, and garden gnomes toward her office, Mona raised her voice so we could hear her. "She said she was staying at Lazy Daze, the campground west of here, a few blocks from the beach, you know, just up the hill from the ice cream stand and on the way to the Elderberry Bay Lodge." She scrabbled around in her office. Finally, she emerged and made her way back through aisles crowded with merchandise. Head shaking, she handed me two slips of paper that appeared to have been torn from the same notepad. "Here you go. The numbers Cassie wrote down for the salad caterer and for herself. No way Cassie's a murderer."

One slip of paper said, *Yolanda can make the salads,* and gave a phone number. The other said, in the same printing, *Cassie,* with a different phone number.

We had to admire about ninety more of Mona's treasures before we left.

We sauntered up the hill toward In Stitches. Haylee said, "I've got another fabric saleswoman coming this afternoon, and then I need to bake several dozen cookies. But shall we take a walk on the beach tonight?"

"Great idea. We'll probably need some ice cream." The ice cream stand Mona had mentioned sold delicious homemade ice cream. The proprietors had purchased equipment and recipes from the 1940s, and when they said "cream," they meant it. Ever since Memorial Day weekend, when the stand had opened for the summer, Haylee and I had discovered many reasons to walk the dogs to it.

Haylee grinned. "Yum, yes."

■ ■ ■ ■

After supper, I leashed my dogs and took them to the parking lot behind Haylee's apartment. She made fusses over the wriggling dogs and took Sally's leash from me.

We could have used roads and sidewalks to get to the ice cream stand, but all four of us preferred exploring the beach. We could always return by way of Beach Row and the Lazy Daze campground. The dogs plowed through the soft sand more easily than we did. Finally, we removed our flip-flops and padded along hard, damp sand near the water's edge.

Sally and Tally seemed to think it was their job to drink all of Lake Erie, and when they weren't attempting that, they wanted to chase the haughty seagulls stalking along just beyond reach.

The evening sun was warm and relatively high. Although it was Monday, many cottages were obviously in use. Strolling past their backyards made us feel part of the cottage community, which was always fun. A few cottagers waded and played in the shallows. Others tended barbecues on sandy lakeside decks, roasted marshmallows over campfires, or lounged, drinks in hand, in lawn chairs. They called to each other and greeted us. The fronts of those cottages would face Beach Row, which we explored only when blowing sand and spray kept us off the beach.

Sally and Tally watched a border collie stare at a Frisbee its owner held up in one hand. Obviously, Sally and Tally wanted to play with that dog. The border collie, however, saw only the Frisbee and the man about to throw it.

On the way to buy ice cream, I always carried on a debate with myself about flavors. Mint chocolate chip often won, but last time, the ice cream stand's owners had made sweet woodruff ice cream, flavored by one of their garden herbs. It had been delicious.

I found a flat stone and skipped it. *Plop.* Well, I *tried* to skip it. "Maybe they'll have double dark orange chocolate fudge tonight," I said.

The ice cream stand was on Beach Row. We turned up a public walkway between two cottages. My bare feet sank into luxuriantly warm sand.

I was thinking, *On the other hand, you can't lose with vanilla . . .*

Haylee stopped and grabbed my arm. "Is that them?"

21

"Is that Vicki's so-called Norse god?" Haylee asked in a sarcastic whisper. "Max? And the woman she saw with him who supposedly looks like me?"

Without thinking, I said, "She does look like you."

Haylee made a growling sound deep in her throat. Tally couldn't have sounded more forbidding. "Let's go. We'll come back another night."

"But —" No vanilla or double dark orange chocolate fudge? No mint chip or ginger or pineapple?

Apparently not. Haylee led Sally toward the beach, and Sally was all too willing to take a closer look at seagulls riding the waves. And Tally insisted on keeping up with his sister. I had no choice. Still carrying my flip-flops, I had to go with Tally.

We caught up.

Haylee wasted no time putting distance

between us and the people who might be her cousin or cousins, and Sally was probably eager to get home to the kittens she had adopted. We kicked up sand and water.

I puffed, "We're burning enough calories for double scoops next time."

Behind me, a man yelled, "Willow!"

I couldn't help turning around. Max loped toward us. The blond woman jogged easily behind him.

Haylee stood like a statue beside me. The dogs sat at our feet.

Max took off his sunglasses. His wide smile almost outshined the golden sun behind his left shoulder.

He ran closer and stretched his arms out like he was about to hug Haylee. "Auntie Elbow," he said. "I've missed you."

Auntie *Elbow.* He had to be Opal's long-lost nephew. Who else would have known that nickname for Opal? Always liking happy endings, I was excited about the prospect of a reunion between Opal and the nephew she'd loved.

The dogs stood up and wagged their tails.

Haylee spluttered, *"Aunt?"* Head up, she turned and marched away, taking Sally with her, east down the beach toward home. Sally looked back at Tally and me and whimpered.

Behind me, the woman giggled. I turned around. It was no wonder that Vicki had mistaken her for Haylee. She was a tiny bit shorter than Haylee, and her eyes were brown, not blue, and while Haylee was a natural blonde, this woman's highlights were too evenly spaced to have grown that way. She was close to our age, and slender like we were.

Max stared dumbstruck at the rapidly retreating Haylee. He dropped his arms.

The woman punched him in the bicep. "Max, you doofus! That woman's too *young* to be our aunt. You insulted her."

"But she looks like I remember Auntie Elbow, I mean Aunt Opal. Aunt Opal was sixteen, and that woman's definitely older than Aunt Opal was the last time I saw her."

"And so are you, doofus! Aunt Opal would be about fifty now. There's no way that woman you insulted is fifty. Run after her and apologize."

I put my hand out to stop him, which was difficult with Tally-Ho tugging at his leash and eager to follow Haylee and Sally-Forth. "No, don't. Who are you and what do you want and why didn't you go talk to Opal after you talked to me? You drove away." I hadn't meant to sound accusing, but maybe it was just as well. Haylee could be right

185

that this pair were only trying to hurt Opal.

Max managed to look apologetic. "I'm sorry. I went back to fetch — oh, sorry, I should introduce my sister. Willow, this is Zara Brubaugh. After I picked up Zara, we drove back to Tell a Yarn. The door was locked. No one answered."

I remained stiff and, I hoped, unyielding. "Our shops are actually closed on Mondays. Did you say you're looking for an aunt?"

"Our mother's little sister. Her name is Opal Scott. She ran away from home when I was three, shortly before Zara was born."

Opal Scott didn't run away. She was banished. I wasn't about to correct him, though. If he and his sister were fakes, the inaccuracies in their story would alert Opal not to trust them. Like Haylee, I wasn't about to let anyone hurt Opal.

Max continued, "For the past few years, I've tried to find her. Do you know how many Scotts there are and how many *Opal* Scotts? I saw the name on Tell a Yarn's website, so we drove up here to see if it could be her." Tightening his lips, he gazed at Haylee, who was behind me, probably very far behind me. He focused on me again, and I read a plea in his eyes. "Please tell me, is that woman we just met, I mean *almost* just met, a relation of Opal Scott's?

She looks so much like I remember my aunt, and like the rest of our family."

I was torn between wanting to give him good news and letting Opal tell him. And letting her decide *what* to tell him.

Loyalty won. I was fairly certain there couldn't be two Max Brubaughs who called their Aunt Opals "Auntie Elbow," but the story wasn't mine to tell. I clamped my lips shut.

"You know them both, right?" he coaxed. "That woman running away down the beach, and the Opal Scott who owns Tell a Yarn?"

I relented, if only slightly. "How about if I get Opal to phone you?"

"Okay." He pulled a card from his wallet. "Here's my home address and cell phone number. We're staying at the Elderberry Bay Lodge, so she can try my room or Zara's there. We were heading off for ice cream when we saw you. Can I buy you a cone?"

"Thanks, no, I'd better let this fellow catch up with his sister." Whining, Tally-Ho was adamant about possibly dragging me home along the beach. "But I recommend the ice cream."

"We heard that," Zara said, "from people at the lodge."

"How is the lodge?" I asked. "Do you like

it there?"

"I'd give it four stars," Max said.

Zara wrinkled her pretty nose. "Our first night there, they found a body."

"A skeleton," Max corrected her.

"That's no better," she told him.

Promising to ask Opal to call Max, I left them to their arguing. They strode away, discussing why chocolate ice cream was better than strawberry, and vice versa.

I jogged down the beach. Tail up and waving madly, Tally wanted to run much faster than I could. How did dogs, with their shorter legs, manage to scoot along at such lightning speeds?

Haylee and Sally were almost out of sight when I glimpsed movement in a cottage window. Maybe my imagination was working too hard, but I thought I saw Cassie appear at a window, then quickly back away until all I could make out was a pleasant sunroom set up as a dining room. If the cottage had an address, the number would be on the front, facing Beach Row. It was a cute little cottage, sided in gray, between a small pale yellow cottage and a two-story robin's-egg blue cottage. It should be easy to find the gray cottage from Beach Row. Tally and I kept running.

The border collie was still flying after the

Frisbee. The dog's exhausted-looking owner tossed the Frisbee back the way I'd come. The dog charged after it, caught it, and trotted back.

Beyond the determined border collie, a tall blond man strolled toward me. Had Max changed his mind about ice cream? He stopped near the cottage where I thought I'd seen Cassie, then turned and looked out over the water. Pretending he hadn't been following me?

Feeling persecuted and almost as annoyed as Haylee had been, I let Tally pull me toward where he'd last seen Sally and Haylee.

We caught up with them on Lake Street, heading up the hill from the beach. "Aunt!" Haylee complained. "He's older than I am."

"And you're older than Opal was the last time he saw her. Opal was sixteen, then." I handed her the card Max had given me. "Maybe Opal should be given the chance to communicate with him."

"I don't like him. Or his sister." She shook her hair out of her face. "I guess I'm being childish and selfish."

"Want me to come along when you give Opal that card?"

"Would you? They're at Naomi's."

She whipped out her phone and asked

Naomi if we could visit. Of course Naomi said yes, and to bring the dogs. We walked around the post office to the parking lot behind the Victorian row of shops. Smiling and murmuring about how pleased she was to see us, Naomi let us in through a door next to the steel-clad one that, when it was unlocked, would open into the back room where she stored her rolls of quilt batting. We climbed the stairs to Naomi's apartment.

Everything in her apartment that could possibly be quilted was, including window blinds and upholstery. A glass of wine in one hand, Opal nestled in a wing chair. Edna snuggled with Gord on one of Naomi's two love seats.

Gord rose to his feet and sang, quietly for him, in French. His song sounded very welcoming. He loved opera and had an amazing voice, even when he tamped it down by barely opening his mouth.

When he finished, we applauded. He bowed, sat down beside Edna, and tucked her against him.

"How are you feeling, Edna?" I asked.

"All better!" she chirped.

She certainly looked fine, though the glitter-coated silver spikes in her hair did make her appear wired for sound, and not exactly as cuddly as Gord seemed to think she was.

I asked him, "Any idea what caused the outbreak?"

"Maybe a virus," he said. "Could have been food poisoning."

That led to my next question. "If asparagus had been fertilized with fresh manure shortly before it was harvested, and then not thoroughly washed and served raw, could that have caused symptoms like the people around here had?"

"Sure it could." He frowned, obviously perplexed. "That's why they fertilize asparagus plants *after* the harvest each year, and also why they compost the manure before they spread it."

"But," I persisted, "what if they used fresh, uncomposted manure, and someone didn't notice that the asparagus they picked had been too recently fertilized with un-composted manure, and then they served it unwashed and raw?"

"Yuck, please!" Edna frowned in an exaggerated way that showed the discussion wasn't bothering her as much as it might have the day before.

Naomi asked, "Uncomposted manure? Who could fail to notice that?"

"You're right," Haylee confirmed. "It's

impossible to miss. But we saw — and smelled — someone picking asparagus in a field that reeked of manure. Maybe if we want to know who gave half the community food poisoning, we should search for someone with no sense of smell."

Opal shook a finger at us. "You two shouldn't search for anyone."

Haylee corrected herself. "I meant we should tell the *police* to look for someone with no sense of smell." She walked toward Opal. "Speaking of things that don't smell quite right, we met this guy on the beach. He thought I was his aunt. Auntie Elbow, he called me." Watching Opal's face, Haylee thrust Max Brubaugh's card at her.

The red drained from Opal's cheeks. "Elbow?" she faltered. She took the card but didn't look at it, just ran her fingers across it as if feeling the expensive card's raised ink. She glanced from Haylee to me.

I tried to calm the apprehension I saw in her expression without raising false hopes. "He's the man I told you about earlier. He seems nice," I said. What an inane comment. "He has a sister with him. Zara. They're staying at the newly restored lodge."

Opal swallowed. "For how long?"

"Probably until they get whatever they

came for." Haylee's voice was filled with scorn.

"Haylee," Naomi cautioned.

Edna's laugh broke the tension. "He thought you were our age, Haylee? No wonder you're miffed."

Slowly, Haylee began to smile. "It is sort of funny, isn't it?"

Gord shook his head. "Men. No sensitivity at all."

Edna sat up straight and looked him in the eye. "Gord! That's not true. You're very sensitive."

He only gave her a smile and toasted her with his glass of wine. And with his eyes.

Running a thumb around the edges of Max's business card, Opal stared at me as if I could make everything come out all right for her.

But how could I? I needed to ease away from the unwanted burden that I probably only imagined she was putting on my shoulders. "I'd better go," I managed in a small voice. "I've left those two kittens alone far too long. No telling what they may have done."

"I'll come, too," Haylee said.

Naomi offered to see us out, but we told her to stay with her guests. Not that any of the three of them appeared to be paying

Naomi much attention at the moment.

We clattered down the back steps and out the door into the parking lot. I muttered to Haylee, "I hope I haven't caused Opal trouble."

She took Sally's leash from me. "*You* haven't. If anyone has, it's those people."

I let Tally pull me down the alley behind the post office. "You don't mind about Gord?" I asked Haylee.

"Mind what?"

"That he's always with Edna and often with your other mothers."

"Of course I don't mind. He's a good person. Edna deserves someone like him."

We passed the front of the post office and started up Lake Street. I thought aloud. "I wonder if we could find men for the other two."

"Ha. Believe it or not, my father was the love of Opal's life. Can you imagine? A summer love. He was eighteen. He went off to college and after a few letters, she never heard from him again. Then her parents disowned her, and Naomi and Edna joined her to help raise me. When I was about eight, Naomi got engaged. I liked the guy. He was going to be my brand-new father. Then some drunk driver put an end to Naomi's and my dreams, and Naomi hasn't been interested in anyone since. Someone asked her out recently, but she turned him down."

"Who?"

"She wouldn't say. But you know her. She felt guilty for possibly hurting his feelings."

I laughed. "Poor Naomi. She's too sweet for her own good. Why did Edna wait so long? She seems to love having a man in her life."

"Edna was dedicated to her work in chemical research and to helping with me. She never took time just for herself. She deserves some fun now. And maybe she was waiting for the right guy. Gord is good for her."

"And she for him."

We angled across the street toward In Stitches. There was more I wanted to know about Haylee's three mothers, but I caught a glimpse of someone on my front porch. I nudged Haylee and stopped talking.

22

The sun hadn't quite set. The porch roof cast shadows, and the person I'd seen was mostly eclipsed by fat pillars. Sniffing the air, tails high, Sally-Forth and Tally-Ho pulled Haylee and me up the stairs and onto the porch.

Cassie was hunkered down in one of my rocking chairs. She sat on her feet and had her arms wrapped around her chest as if she were cold. The now-familiar pink plaid shirt wasn't covered by a jacket, and was short-sleeved. But the evening was still warm.

Although on leashes, Sally and Tally ran to Cassie. She uncoiled her legs, plunked her feet on the floor, and bent forward to pet the dogs. "I saw you on the beach heading this way. So I followed." She glanced toward us, then away. "I thought maybe we could hang out . . ." Her voice, hoarse and slightly muffled, dwindled to a sigh.

The poor thing must be lonely and nearly friendless in our small village. Her boss was dead, and maybe she didn't even know those two women I may have seen her with, the ones who had fought over Haylee's fabrics at the Midsummer Madness Sidewalk Sale. Haylee and I could be the closest thing to friends that Cassie had here. With a pang of sympathy, I unlocked the front door. "Come in. Haylee and I were about to have tea and cookies."

Haylee didn't refute my sudden plan. I closed the door, unsnapped the dogs' leashes, and urged everyone downstairs to my great room.

Busying myself with mugs, plates, cookies, setting water to boil, and greeting the kittens, I sneaked glimpses at Cassie, perched on the front edge of my couch. Her mouth was thin, her shoulders were tense, and she held her arms close to her body as if trying to keep her feelings inside a fortress. I wanted to say something comforting, but I was afraid she'd crumble if anyone mentioned Neil. If she'd come to talk about his death, she would. I didn't need to prod.

Haylee relaxed in one of my cushy chairs across from the couch. Rubbing Tally's ears, she was obviously as aware of Cassie's distress as I was.

I knew Cassie wouldn't want me talking about food poisoning, so I asked her if she'd caught the stomach flu that was going around.

"Maybe a bit of it, not a bad case like Neil had."

We both told her we were sorry about Neil.

She acknowledged our condolences with a watery smile, then leaped from the couch and paced, commenting on my handmade and machine-embroidered decorating touches. "Someday —" Her voice caught. "I'd like a place like this. Of my own." She plunked down on my couch again and slumped forward, her head lowered and her white-knuckled hands clasped between her knees.

Mustache and Bow-Tie climbed into her lap. Nudging the kittens with her nose, Sally leaned against Cassie. If those animals couldn't cheer the girl up, nothing could. She unclenched her hands and stroked the kittens. Sally wormed her snout underneath Cassie's hands so that Cassie couldn't help petting her, too.

I swished boiling water around inside the teapot to warm it up. "I didn't get this place until I was thirty-three," I told her. And I'd worked extremely long hours on Wall Street while running an embroidery business on the side for ten years to make it all happen. I dumped the hot water out, then added tea bags and filled the pot with more boiling water. "You have a few years yet."

"Managing La Bakery was my dream job." She lifted her head. "Why did Neil have to go and die on me?"

Her wording was strange enough, but the simmering rage underneath her tone put me on high alert. Haylee darted a look at me.

"I don't know what I'm going to do," Cassie wailed. "With no job, I won't even be able to stay where I'm living." She peeked at me between her lashes as if checking whether I believed her, then added, "Lazy Daze Campground."

I asked, "Didn't I see you inside a cottage at the beach this evening?"

She looked down at the kittens. Her answer took a millisecond too long. "It wouldn't have been me."

She seemed scared. Of being caught in a lie? Maybe she was afraid that Neil's murderer would come after her. Meanwhile, what about Neil? Didn't Cassie have sympathy for him? Restraining myself from pointing out that all of his dreams had ended permanently, I imitated Naomi, and tried to encourage Cassie. "You got that job. You'll land another one."

"It took me a whole year to find that one. I graduated from college last June."

Haylee must have been channeling her mothers, too. "The Elderberry Bay Lodge has just opened. Even if they've hired their permanent staff, they could probably use help at the gala this Friday. You should apply."

"I suppose," Cassie mumbled.

"And you helped Mona organize the community picnic, right?" I asked her. "That will look good on your resume."

"Knowing Mona, you did most of the work," Haylee added.

That got a weak grin from Cassie. "I didn't care."

I put a plate of cookies on the coffee table. Sally and Tally knew they weren't allowed to help themselves to anything from the low table and didn't try. I hoped that the kittens, who were nodding off in Cassie's lap, wouldn't wake up and discover that cookies worked as pucks in a rousing game of floor hockey.

Haylee leaned forward and counted on her fingers. "You rented the bouncy castle, found people to paint faces, got that adorable petting zoo to bring their animals, and enlisted caterers."

I had to admire Haylee's interrogation methods. "That's a lot," I said.

Cassie waved the notion aside. "It was fun. And the caterers were easy — Neil was glad to provide the desserts, and everyone said that Tom did the best fish fry around." She shrugged with one painfully thin shoulder.

She'd left at least one caterer out. On purpose? "Who provided the soft drinks?" I asked.

"Mona arranged that."

"And there were funnel cakes. And corn dogs," I prompted.

Cassie shrugged again. "I found them on the Net."

"And salads," Haylee said. "From a white van."

"Mona got her . . . I mean *them,* to supply salads."

I held my breath, and Haylee probably held hers, too.

Cassie looked down at the sleeping kittens. "I gave Mona a brochure from someone I met on the beach. Maybe that's who she called. I don't know."

Brochure? Mona had handed us slips of paper with Cassie's number and a number for someone named Yolanda who could make salads, and I was pretty sure that the same person had printed both numbers. Who besides Cassie would have done that? Mona hadn't mentioned a brochure.

To hide my skepticism, I turned around and poured tea into our mugs. The kittens slumbered on. I handed Cassie her mug. "The kittens seem to like you, Cassie." Again, I sounded like Naomi.

Cassie sniffled. "Cats always head for the most allergic person in the room."

I immediately apologized. "We can take our tea and snacks outside."

But Cassie said it was fine, she wasn't that allergic, and she would hate to wake them up. "I saw your posters. How did you get the kittens?"

"I think someone dumped them." I couldn't hide my scorn for whoever might do that.

While we ate cookies and sipped tea, we discussed suitable punishments for people who left pets to fend for themselves.

Cassie stood up and handed me the warm, dozy kittens. "I guess I'll go back to the campground now." She gazed around as if memorizing every corner and every bit of machine embroidery in my great room. "This is a fab apartment. I'm jealous. You wouldn't consider renting a room, would you?"

Behind Cassie, Haylee glared at me, but I didn't need the warning. I didn't know Cassie. She was not remotely like the honest and upright Chief Vicki Smallwood, and there was no way I would offer to let her stay with me.

I shook my head. "Wouldn't work. You're allergic to cats."

"Oh, I thought you were trying to get rid of them." She let the last word hang in the air like a question.

I hugged the fragile, purring little bodies closer. "If they were dumped, they're staying with me. Want us to walk you back to Lazy Daze?"

She paused as if weighing the offer. "No, thanks, I've got my car."

It was still dusk at this time of night in mid-June. I set the kittens on the couch, took Cassie upstairs, turned on lights in the shop, and let her out the front door. The streetlights had already come on, and the air had the softness of warm spring evenings at the exact moment when night-blooming flowers release their scents. Cassie should be able to find her way to her car, wherever she'd left it.

I turned around in the doorway and nearly bumped into Haylee and my complete four-animal zoo.

"Make sure you lock that door tonight," Haylee muttered.

At the sidewalk, Cassie waved and turned north toward the beach. I counted to three, then tiptoed out onto the porch. After convincing all of the animals to stay inside, Haylee joined me.

Cassie disappeared down the hill. We didn't hear a car door slam or an engine start. We heard only the breeze and the waves hitting the shore.

And Tally whimpering.

We went back inside. I leaned against the door. How to word my unease?

Haylee did it for me. "Something's off about that girl," she said.

23

"Cassie was certainly cagey," I agreed.

Haylee made a show of turning the dead-bolt and locking my front door. "She seemed to stretch the truth a lot this evening, ending with saying she brought her car, but when she left, she walked toward the beach."

"Maybe she left her car in the beach parking lot?" I suggested.

"Okay, I'll give her the benefit of the doubt on that one. But she also said she'd seen us on the beach this evening. Wouldn't you think she might have followed us on foot instead of hopping into her car and driving here?"

I had an excuse for lying about a car. "Maybe she did come on foot. Maybe, when I offered to walk her back, she made up an excuse so we wouldn't go out of our way. More likely, she didn't want to admit that she'd been in that cottage."

"We should have followed her down the hill." Haylee unlocked the door. "It's not too late to learn something."

We scrambled out. I took time to lock the door behind us, and then we raced as quietly as we could down Lake Street.

Two cars were in the beach parking lot. No one appeared to be in either one.

We jogged all the way to the water's edge and peered west.

A solitary figure tramped through the hard, damp sand.

"Is that Cassie?" Haylee breathed.

"I think so." Although I didn't quite trust Cassie, I couldn't help feeling sorry for her. Her posture projected a bravado that reminded me of my first morning of kindergarten. I'd reluctantly let go of my grandmother's hand and had held my head up in a show of courage that I didn't feel. Although I'd wanted desperately to run back to safety, I'd kept going, into the scary unknown. Now I wanted to protect Cassie from whatever was frightening her.

She turned away from the water, toward one of the cottages, perhaps, or onto one of the walkways that would take her to Beach Row and eventually to the Lazy Daze Campground.

"Are you certain she was the person you

saw in a cottage?" Haylee asked me.

"Not positive. I only caught a glimpse."

We turned around and started up Lake Street toward In Stitches. "What got me most about Cassie," I said, "wasn't the lie about having brought her car and maybe lying about being in that cottage, but the way she seemed to be angry at Neil for dying. Dying? He was murdered. Shouldn't she have been angry at his murderer, not at him?"

"And she took it so personally. Neil was dead, so she was out of a job."

"Self-centered," I said. "On the other hand, did you notice the way Neil looked at her in the bakery tent at the picnic? Like he really liked her?"

"It didn't seem appropriate for an employer-employee relationship," Haylee agreed. "Do you suppose she had to fight him off, and she fought a little too hard, and he, as she put it, died on her?"

"She's kind of small to drag someone into my yard."

"Neil was slight, too," Haylee reminded me.

"But I suspect he was very muscular and therefore heavier than he looked."

"Cassie is muscular, too," she said. "Did you notice her forearms?"

"I didn't think about it, but you're right. She must work out."

All of the stores except the restaurants we passed on our way up the hill were closed for the evening. As usual after hours, though, a few men were sitting around inside The Ironmonger. We waved, and they waved back.

I pointed out, "Another thing that was odd about Cassie was that she happily took credit for organizing most of the picnic, but never mentioned Yolanda by name. She said she *might* have given a brochure to Mona. But I think she wrote down Yolanda's phone number and gave that to Mona."

"And then there were the kittens." Haylee's voice took on somber tones. "Cassie said she'd never seen them before, but they acted like she was their favorite person."

"Those two!" Just thinking about them made me smile. "They climb everyone they see. I think they were glad for a warm lap to curl up in. It's the way they greet people, even strangers." However, if Cassie had a connection with the kittens who were dumped in or near my yard about the same time that Neil's wrapped corpse was dragged there, Cassie could be very dangerous.

Haylee and I both laughed when we saw

my shop's front door. I'd left lights on inside. Both dogs pressed their noses against the glass. The two kittens stood up on their hind legs and batted at the pane as if they expected to burst through it and hoist themselves up to our shoulders to purr against our necks. I opened the door and we each scooped up a kitten and patted a dog.

Haylee handed me Mustache. "What can we do with the information we have about Cassie?"

"Do we have any?" I asked. "Other than that her answers to our questions weren't very straightforward and her stories don't hang together with what Mona said? The only concrete information we have is Yolanda's phone number. What can we do with that, call and ask her if she stole asparagus and failed to wash it before adding it to salads and selling it to people? Bow-Tie, please don't bite my ear." I tucked the mischievous kitten into the crook of one elbow. "I suppose we could give Yolanda's phone number to the police, but they probably already have it."

Haylee bit her lip. "And we'll end up being accused of meddling and investigating things that don't concern us."

I snapped my fingers, causing Bow-Tie to

attack them. "How about doing a reverse lookup? That number looks like a landline from Elderberry Bay. We can get the address."

I handed Bow-Tie to Haylee and logged on to my computer.

Yolanda's address was on Beach Row.

"Ice cream for lunch tomorrow!" I crowed.

Haylee gave me both kittens and then raised her arms in a victory sign. "Maybe all we really had to do was walk along Beach Row this evening instead of along the beach. Maybe that white van has been parked in front of Yolanda's place all along."

As Haylee left, she again reminded me to lock my doors. "Call me or my mothers if you need anything," she added. "Have a good night."

Having a good night was not easy in the company of two kittens who were convinced that darkness was when everyone was supposed to practice stalking and pouncing. Fortunately, I was the proud owner of a cat-herding dog. Sally-Forth was determined to lie beside my bed, and did her best to train those kittens that sensible creatures should sleep at night.

We all woke up early and more or less ready

to open the shop and greet our customers.

Ashley and I showed our students hardanger embroidery, which was named after an area in Norway, and had nothing to do with difficulty or anger. This neat, disciplined style of embroidery was like a cross between drawn work, in which threads are pulled out of the fabric, and cutwork, where shapes are cut out of the fabric.

First, we started embroidery software programs, and then each student created a pattern of small squares and crosses on the screen.

After the women created the designs, complete with stops for removing the hoop from the embroidery machine, Ashley and I helped them hoop sticky stabilizer with the backing paper up. We showed them how to score an X across the hoop through the paper without puncturing the stabilizer itself, which could cause it to tear. Carefully, our students peeled the backing away, leaving the sticky side of the stabilizer uppermost in their hoops.

I gave everyone a square of monk's cloth. The next step was the most crucial of all, and caused a lot of distressed muttering. They had to keep both the warp and the woof absolutely straight as they smoothed the fabric onto the sticky stabilizer. Ashley and I checked every student's work before they attached their hoops to embroidery machines and started stitching. The machines obediently sewed straight stitches around neat little squares.

The women in our workshop removed the hoops from their machine and we examined the stitching under a strong light. These women were experienced, and because the fabric had started out straight, their little squares were exactly on the straight and crosswise grains.

With sharp, teeny-bladed scissors, they cut out the insides of the little squares, leaving the stitching.

They reattached their hoops and started the embroidery machines again. The machines stitched around the open squares with narrow satin stitching and added the crosses that made up the rest of the hardanger designs.

While the others stitched, I considered ice cream flavors. Mentally tasting them was almost as good as the real thing. Almost.

The women unhooped the fabric and painstakingly tore off the excess stabilizer. Everyone was happy with the work they'd done.

At noon, I took my dogs and lunch to the bandstand.

Haylee was already there. "I can't go for ice cream after we eat," she said. "I have to *present* myself at Opal's. Will you come along? Please?"

"Of course I'll come with you to Opal's," I answered. "What's up?"

"Those *people* are coming to see her." She chomped at her sandwich.

24

I asked Haylee, "Who's coming to see Opal? Max and Zara Brubaugh?"

She nodded.

"I see you're keeping an open mind about them," I teased.

"And about missing out on ice cream." She took another vicious bite of her sandwich. "*Again.* Thanks to them."

"We'll definitely need our ice cream fix tonight."

She brightened. We polished off our lunches and hurried up Lake Street. Haylee went straight to Tell a Yarn while I ducked into In Stitches and put the dogs into the apartment with the kittens. I told Ashley where I'd be, then rushed out the front door. And practically into Detective Gartener.

He was in jeans, blazer, and a white oxford cloth shirt, a very nice look on him. Except for his impenetrable policeman expressions,

no one might ever guess he was a detective.
He put his hands out as if to catch me.
"Whoa! Have a second?"

I glanced away from his dark eyes to the
street. No BMW yet. "Sure."

"Any idea why Max Brubaugh has been
hanging around Elderberry Bay?" He
couldn't possibly have known I was thinking about Max and his sister.

"He's a reporter."

"Yes, in Pittsburgh. So what is he doing
up here? He was here before Chief Smallwood found Neil's body, and before Snoozy
Gallagher was dug up, too. So what story is
he following?"

"I don't think he's here on business, but
on a personal quest. He suspects that Opal
might be his long-lost aunt."

"What are you rushing off to?"

I knew I didn't have to answer his questions, but I trusted him. "Max and his sister
are coming to Opal's shop. Haylee's a little
ruffled about the whole thing and asked me
to the reunion, if it is one." Glancing up
into those dark, amused eyes, I bit my lip.

He slanted a grin down at me. "Mind if I
come along?"

"No." Did he notice my slight hesitation?

If he did, he didn't show it. "And can you
please call me Toby and not let on I'm a

state trooper?"

"Okay, but I can't vouch for the others."

"Let's go, then, and ask them to keep my dirty little secret." He crossed the street with me.

Opal was sure to think I'd completely lost it, bringing a detective to what could have been, and maybe should have been, a private family gathering.

Detective Gartener — Toby — opened Opal's door and stepped back to let me in first. Speechless for once, Opal, Naomi, and Edna stared at us. Lucy, as always, was far from speechless. I picked her up and held her close. Her insistent meows changed to contented purrs.

Haylee grinned. She was probably certain that Max and Zara were involved in a scam and that our favorite detective was about to arrest them.

Opal recovered first. "Welcome, Willow and Detective Gartener."

"Please," he said in that resonant made-for-radio voice. "Call me Toby. And when the others show up, don't tell them that I'm with the state police."

Eyes gleaming, Haylee nodded, but the other three tilted their heads and raised their eyebrows.

I attempted to explain. "He was just asking me about —" Outside, a silver BMW pulled up to the curb. "Them. Why they're here."

Opal followed my glance. Max unfolded himself from the driver's seat and stared into the store. The tentative way he licked his lips made him appear both hungry and a little anxious.

Opal clapped a hand over her mouth.

Edna squeaked, "It *is* Max. I'd know him anywhere."

"From watching the news, no doubt," Haylee murmured out the side of her mouth. Probably only Toby and I heard her, but Toby was obviously memorizing everything he could about that BMW.

Zara got out and stared at the store with a saucy expression. Her brother might have been nervous, but she certainly wasn't.

Haylee crowded me. I was not only going to stand by her, I might need to hold her up.

Max opened the shop door. Her face nearly expressionless, walking tall in a way that showed off her long neck, Zara preceded him into Tell a Yarn. Max let the door close behind him and stood still, gazing from face to face. The confidence I'd seen in him the day before had been replaced by caution doing battle with boyish expectation.

Finally, he tossed Haylee a sheepish grin, and walked right up to Opal. "It really *is* you," he said.

Haylee crossed her arms across her chest. Toby and I were probably the only ones besides the purring cat to hear her grunt of disapproval.

Max's attention did not stray from Opal's face. "When I was little, I called you Auntie Elbow. Do you remember me at all? My mother is your sister Pearl." He added names, dates, and an address. "I made you read *Winnie-the-Pooh* to me, the story about the heffalump, over and over again. You gave me a toy cat that you said looked like a Lucy, so that's what I called her, but it probably came out more like Wucy."

Opal seemed to have problems finding her voice. She glanced at the cat in my arms, cleared her throat, held her palm flat, and bent forward until her hand was close to her knee. "You were about this tall."

He said, quite simply, but quite believably, "I missed you."

Opal managed a quiet, "I always hoped I might see you again. How's your mother?"

"She's fine. She'll be thrilled that we finally found you."

"But —" Opal's face crumpled and her eyes glistened. Naomi and Edna moved closer to her.

Max seemed to notice them. "Naomi and Edna. Didn't you used to babysit me, too?"

"You remember us!" Naomi was obviously flattered.

"Of course. I made you read about the heffalump, too." He nodded toward the corner where Haylee, Toby, and I stood like three monkeys refusing to hear, see, or speak evil, or anything else. "Hi, Willow. Hi —"

That seemed to break the trance Opal had been under. "I should introduce you to your cousin, my daughter Haylee."

Max came toward Haylee, hand out-stretched. "Sorry I mistook you for your mother. But you two do look alike."

Zara put down a skein of Opal's silk yarn and pushed Max aside. "Haylee's too young to be our aunt. Don't pay him any attention, Haylee. He never could play well with others."

"That's not true," Naomi said in shocked tones.

Haylee shook Max's hand. "It was kind of funny," she admitted.

Max glanced curiously at Toby Gartener but didn't offer his hand, and no one introduced them.

Edna blew her nose. Forthright as ever, she began interrogating Haylee's cousins. "Opal wasn't surprised when your grandparents disowned her. But she expected your mother to stay in touch. Why didn't she?"

Max took a step back. "Disowned? Nana and Dada dis*owned* Opal? They told Mom and Dad that Opal ran away and was living on the streets of Detroit."

"I've never been there," Opal said. "I never had to live on the streets, though I figured that's what they thought I deserved. How did they explain that my best friends, Naomi and Edna, left home the same time I did?"

Max studied his perfectly manicured fingernails. "Mom got the idea that all three of you had been trapped in a cult or using drugs."

Naomi burst out, "But Opal wrote to your mom! Pearl never answered. It hurt Opal dreadfully. Not that being kicked out by her own parents wasn't bad enough." The usually sweet Naomi managed to look very condemning.

"Mom must have never gotten Opal's letters." Max clamped his mouth closed. A muscle twitched in his jaw.

"Letter," Opal said. "One letter. I was told to leave you all alone, so when Pearl didn't answer, I put the old life behind me. By the time I gave up on hearing from Pearl, you were the only one from back home that I still cared about, Max."

Beside me, I felt Toby's tense concentration. What did he think of all this? Was he wishing he could take out his notebook and write in it?

Max touched Zara's wrist. "Mom had a difficult pregnancy with Zara, and had to spend most of it in bed. Nana came over every day to look after me and everything. She easily could have intercepted your letter."

"Nana was mean." Zara's voice was as sharp as chipped glass. "Dada, too. Nothing I could do was ever good enough. Why did they disown you, Auntie Elbow?" She darted a look at Haylee. "No, let me guess. You weren't married and you were preggers." She looked up at her brother. "That explains it. Explains a lot." She gazed into Opal's eyes. "I must have been under two years old when they started warning me against boys."

"They warned me, too," Opal said. "I didn't listen. And I'm glad. I have Haylee."

"We all have Haylee," Edna corrected her. "And we're all glad."

Zara smirked. "I didn't listen, either, but I don't have any children. Yet."

"What about you, Max?" Naomi asked politely. "Any children?"

"No. I may have heeded Nana and Dada's warnings too much. I'm still single."

Finally, Opal asked softly, "How are your Nana and Dada?"

Max frowned. "Dada died a few years ago. Nana's in a home. Alzheimer's."

"She doesn't know who we are," Zara said.

Naomi pressed her hands to her cheeks. "That's terrible."

My lunch hour was over. Haylee's was, too, and judging by her stony expression as she stared at her newfound cousins, she didn't want to stretch it or spend any longer with them. I handed Lucy to Max. "Here's the Lucy I told you about."

His long-fingered hands were gentle as he caressed the cat, and I thought I detected a glint of unshed tears in his eyes.

I excused myself. Toby and Haylee said their good-byes, also. Haylee's was curt, thrown toward her mothers as Opal's shop door closed behind us. I was certain that her mothers could tell as well as I could that Haylee wasn't about to accept these new cousins easily. I could have crossed the street and gone to my own shop, but Haylee seemed about to burst, so I stayed with her.

Toby did, too. He must have noticed Haylee's unusually stormy face. In front of The Stash, he asked, "Are you all right, Haylee?"

She shrugged. "I'm fine."

I suspected that Toby didn't believe her, either, but he didn't say anything. Having learned about the way he used silence to motivate others to talk, I stayed quiet, too.

As Toby probably hoped she would, Haylee gave us a more complete answer. "I don't feel anything about losing grandparents I never knew. I never heard anything good about them."

"No wonder," I muttered.

"And these cousins," Toby prodded. "Do you believe they're really Opal's sister's children?"

Haylee's eyes could be merry, but at the moment, they were bleak. "I don't know. Their story holds together with the little I've heard. I think Opal's going to have to meet their mother. She should know for sure if this Pearl person is her sister." She crossed her arms. "But I can tell you one thing. If they hurt my mom, I won't answer to the consequences." She glared at him with resolve — a definite improvement over the desolation I'd noticed earlier. "And that's a threat I don't mind making in the presence of a state trooper."

I would have kicked her or found another way to hush her, but Toby would have noticed.

He held up a hand. "Please, Haylee, if you think anything needs to be done, tell me first, okay? I promise to do whatever I can legally do to keep Opal or anyone else from being hurt. Do you really think that pair is out to harm your mother?"

She rubbed the top of one sandal against the back of her other leg. "I don't know what to think." She gave Toby a crooked grin. "But I'll talk to you or Chief Smallwood before I act, don't worry."

"Good," he said.

"And *then* I'll do what I was going to do in the first place." But her smile had gone impish, and I was happy to see her more like herself.

"No you won't," Toby told her. "Speaking of Chief Smallwood — can she and I come talk to you two this evening?"

"We have firefighting practice from seven to nine," I said.

"How about nine thirty, if it's not too late? We have some questions for you. They won't take long."

Haylee glanced at me. I was sure she was thinking the same thing I was — another delay before we'd get our next taste of that fantastic ice cream. "Sure."

Toby turned to me. "You'll come, too?"

"Okay."

The universe was conspiring against us and our desire for ice cream. But if I couldn't decide which flavor to order, maybe it didn't matter.

25

A few months before, I might have bitten my nails at the idea of Detective Gartener and Chief Smallwood wanting to talk to Haylee and me. Now, I felt gratified. Maybe they hoped our knowledge of the community could help them solve crimes.

Then, as I guided my afternoon students through their attempts at hardanger embroidery, I began to wonder if I should be worried, and by the time everyone left the shop, I was certain I was going to be grilled by the two police officers.

Meanwhile, I had to take the dogs out. We ran to the beach and were almost back at our front porch when I heard Mona yoo-hooing behind us. "Willow!"

I stopped. Huffing and puffing, she caught up. She shook her head so briskly I could tell she was excited. "You hang around with the dreamiest men!"

I did? I hadn't seen Clay since Sunday

morning — more than two whole days. "First that yummy detective, and then . . . Tell me my eyes weren't deceiving me. Did I see Max Brubaugh go into Opal's shop after you went in with that hunky detective? Max *Brubaugh*?"

"Yes, that was Max Brubaugh."

She clapped a hand over her chest as if about to have a heart attack. "If men like that are spending time in yarn shops, I need to learn how to knit! What's *Max Brubaugh* doing in tiny Elderberry Bay? Surely he can't be interested in a small village, even when there's a death involved. It must be the treasure, right? Snoozy Gallagher's treasure? If you found that, it would be a national story. I didn't realize you were that clever, but now I understand why you turned it in to the police. Max is going to make you a *star*!"

"Not likely. I think he's merely on vacation." If Opal wanted the world to know she was Max Brubaugh's aunt, Opal could tell the world.

Mona's eyes widened and she shook her head even harder. "He must be staying at the Elderberry Bay Lodge! I looked him up and he's not married, so I don't know who that woman with him was. If she hasn't gotten her claws into him yet . . ." She shook her head. "Excuse me. I have to go talk to Ralph. Maybe he'll know what's going on."

If Max and Zara were in the market for costumes, Ralph could know something about them, but Halloween was more than four months away.

Mona dashed toward Disguise Guys and I went inside for a quick supper. On the off chance that Haylee and I might have time for ice cream after Vicki and Gartener talked to us, I skipped dessert.

Firefighting practice had become much more fun than when Haylee and I first joined the force. Clay was still a volunteer firefighter, and we had a new fire chief and deputy. Ralph and Duncan had joined, too, and were sometimes full of surprises, like the time Ralph had come dressed as a fire-fighting clown and everyone had laughed so hard that Duncan forgot to be shy.

Haylee liked to drive her red pickup truck to firefighting, and Sally and Tally, who were always welcome at our practice sessions, happily hopped up into the cab. I had eight doggie feet, two doggie rumps, and a pair of fuzzy tails in my lap all the way to the ballpark near the state forest on the east side of Elderberry Bay.

Clay was already there, joking with Ralph and Duncan and an older gray-haired man in jeans and black sneakers. Clay introduced him as Fred Zongassi. I would have recognized Fred if he'd been playing a clarinet and wearing a band uniform with one white satin pant leg caught in his high-tops. At the moment, the legs of his jeans hid the tops of his sneakers.

Clay told us that Fred used to be a volunteer firefighter years ago here in Elderberry Bay, had been an active volunteer firefighter ever since, and was transferring to our force.

I tried not to stare at the man that Chief Vicki Smallwood seemed to think may have murdered both Snoozy Gallagher and Neil Ondover.

Fred had a slow, easy smile, like he knew I was considering him as a possible murder suspect and found it funny. His amused confidence should have made me wary. Instead, I decided, based on nothing more than a hunch, that he couldn't be a murderer, and even though I warned myself not to trust him, I liked him. How could I not admire someone who knew how to drive the heavy equipment I'd been eyeing? Sally and Tally certainly had no qualms about him. They nuzzled his hands as if he were an old friend.

During practice, we all, including Sally and Tally on their leashes, ran around the bases of the ballpark. I'd become so used to the exercise that I was able to chat with Ralph, who pumped his arms, panted, and turned red. Duncan loped around easily, but detached from the rest of us, as usual. He seemed to be watching his father as if concerned that Ralph could be overdoing it. Clay and Fred kept up a pace that none of the rest of us, except for a couple of teens, could match.

After the exercise, we sat on the bleachers. Yes, Fred's sneakers were the high-tops he'd worn at the picnic, which proved nothing.

But, I reminded myself, I had seen the prints of sneakers about the same size as Fred's in the sand near Neil's body.

We discussed recent fires and how we could have fought them better, and then everyone else was going out for ice cream.

Haylee and I declined. We didn't tell them we had an appointment with Gartener and Smallwood. We both said we had sewing we needed to do, which was always true, but Clay gave us a skeptical look and again said he'd pick us up on Friday at six thirty.

After we got back into Haylee's truck, she sighed. "I guess we can't very well go out for ice cream later tonight for fear the firefighters will still be there and think we were trying to avoid them."

"They may already think that."

She gulped down a laugh. "Or that we're afraid that Fred Zongassi is a killer."

"He has quite a sense of humor."

"You and Clay aren't trying to throw him and me together, are you?"

"Of course not. Even if he weren't too old for you, we wouldn't want you going out with a murder suspect."

Haylee shuddered. "I wonder if he's the guy who asked Naomi out, the one she said would never compare to the man she once planned to marry."

"And no wonder," I said, "if he killed Snoozy Gallagher all those years ago." I bounced on my seat as well as I could when two dogs were sitting on my lap. "*Z*s!"

"What?"

"Snoozy Gallagher's belt buckle had *Z*s on it, and everyone said they stood for Snoozy. But couldn't they have stood for Zongassi? Maybe Fred killed Snoozy over a stolen belt buckle."

"Maybe," she said in a dry voice. "If his last name was ZZZZZZZongassi."

I accused, "You sound like a chain saw."

"And your theories are about as good as theories a chain saw might come up with."

I stared at her. "Huh?" But we were

already in front of In Stitches. The dogs and I hopped out. "See you at The Stash in a few minutes." I closed Haylee's truck door.

The dogs went down to the apartment where the kittens woke up and decided that Sally's tail was their favorite toy. I copied the phone numbers Mona had given us for Yolanda and Cassie and stuffed the originals into my jeans pocket. At half past nine, I went, without pets, to The Stash.

I loved Haylee's fabric store. She was featuring summery fabrics, a light, bright, and cheerful array. Who doesn't like touching cotton? And bamboo fabrics that are softer than cotton and smoother than silk?

However, Haylee ushered me past the bolts of intriguing fabrics to her classroom. She had four long tables arranged in a rectangle with a walkway into the middle, and several sewing machines and sergers on each table. Finished garments hung on the walls like the works of art they were.

Detective Gartener — I didn't think he wanted us to continue calling him Toby — and Vicki Smallwood sat together facing the door. Their notebooks and pens were on the table in front of them, and Gartener held several loose sheets of letter-sized paper printed in black ink. His white shirt was still spotless, and Vicki's uniform was crisp.

Haylee and I sat around the corner from them. Gartener was on my right. I held my knees stiffly together and my feet pulled underneath my chair for fear of accidentally brushing against his jeans.

"I ran the plates on that man's BMW, Haylee," he said. "The car's owner is listed as Max Brubaugh."

"Can you tell me his birth date?" Haylee asked in a small voice.

"Not officially." He consulted the printed pages in front of him. "He must have had some exciting birthday parties, with everyone dressing up and going door-to-door for treats." Watching Haylee's face, he tilted his head.

Who wouldn't have understood that hint?

Haylee thanked him. "I'll ask Opal if it's —" She scrunched up her face and rattled off the date of the Halloween three and a half years before she was born.

"You got it," Gartener confirmed.

"And you already know," Vicki added, "that the man potentially posing as your cousin works for a TV station in Pittsburgh, and his reports are often broadcast up here."

Haylee nodded. "My mother has been paying attention to him for the past six months, ever since she first saw him. I'm sure that the name alone was enough to make her want to believe he was her nephew. She can convince herself of nearly anything. But maybe this guy stole my real cousin's identity."

And his appearance, also? "Why would he come after Opal?" I asked. "She makes a comfortable living like we all do, but it's not like she's wealthy."

Haylee clenched her hands. "I don't know. But if he's up to anything, I'm going to be prepared."

"He has no record," Gartener said. "A couple of speeding tickets."

Haylee stared down at her fists as if wondering how her knuckles had gotten so white. "Thanks for looking into it."

Gartener was quick to tell her, "I didn't do it only for you. I'd been wondering what brought them here."

I volunteered, "Max and Zara are staying at the Elderberry Bay Lodge. Haylee and I are going to the gala there Friday night. Is there anything you particularly wanted to know about them?" I asked him.

"Not really, now that we know why they're here."

"Why they *say* they're here," Haylee muttered.

Vicki offered, "It was a bit of a coincidence that they arrived around the time the area was hit with a spate of food poisonings."

Haylee raised her head. "Food poisoning? Haven't you been saying it was the flu?"

"That was before the tests were completed." The chief tapped her pen on her notebook. "You two guessed right in the first place. The cause of the outbreak turned out to be food poisoning, not the flu. The bacteria came from recently fertilized asparagus that had not been thoroughly washed. The problem is that the farmers around here swear that they did not sell any asparagus after they spread manure on it. A couple of them admitted that they hadn't waited for the manure to compost because they figured it would be thoroughly composted by next spring's harvest."

"Don't they risk burning their plants?" I asked. "With, I don't know. Something too strong?" I made a face. "Besides the smell."

Vicki didn't try very hard to hide a grin. "Apparently not." She had definitely gotten over her tummy troubles.

I reached into the pocket of my jeans and fished out the hand-printed slips of paper. "Mona DeGlazier organized the community picnic. Cassie, Neil's assistant, helped. Mona said that the woman who catered the salads was named Yolanda."

Vicki asked me, "And you're sure that the salad caterer was one of the women who fought during your sidewalk sale, right?"

I nodded. "I'm sure. So she must be this Yolanda. Here are the numbers that Cassie gave Mona for herself and for Yolanda." I passed the numbers to Gartener. "We think Yolanda may have used stolen asparagus in one of her salads. Perhaps she didn't wash it."

Vicki asked, "Why are you jumping to the conclusion that the asparagus was *stolen*?"

I put my hands palms up on the table. "As you said, farmers wouldn't sell asparagus immediately after spreading manure on it. Besides, we saw —" I broke off, trying to figure out how to word it so they wouldn't know we'd been snooping.

But of course Vicki guessed. "I know you two go wandering around at night poking your noses where they don't belong —"

Haylee regained her sense of humor. "Not in crops recently fertilized with manure!"

Vicki rolled her eyes in mock disgust. "Did you two see anything unusual while on one of those dog-walking jaunts you two take?"

I leaned forward. "We did. A man was picking asparagus in the moonlight, in a field where it was obvious — from the smell

— that manure had been spread recently. When we shined a flashlight at him, he hid his face. I drove a little farther, but then turned around and came back in time to see him get into his van and speed away."

Gartener had been writing. "Did you recognize him?"

"No," I answered. "Or his van."

"Description?" Gartener asked.

"The man was tall and broad-shouldered," Haylee said. "About your size, Detective Gartener."

"About the size of Fred Zongassi," I added. "Or Tom Umshaw. But Tom drives a pickup truck, and this was a minivan."

"An old one," Haylee contributed, "with lots of dents. A dark color, like brown or maroon. No logos or company names on it."

Vicki raised one eyebrow. "Where and when did you encounter this?"

I was sure she guessed the answer, but I confirmed it. "On that road where you found us sweeping up broken bottles, a few minutes before you came along. I'd been following the van and had dropped back, hoping its driver wouldn't notice us."

"And you turned off your headlights," Vicki accused.

I went on as if she hadn't spoken. "He

turned toward Elderberry Bay, and then that harvesting contraption blocked our way."

"Was the driver of the harvesting contraption working with the man in the van, would you say?" Gartener asked.

Haylee shook her head. "It didn't look that way."

I added, "Teens were riding on the thing, drinking beer and throwing empties onto the road." Why did the detective and the police chief want to know all this? To arrest someone for not washing asparagus?

Or . . .

I blurted, "Did Neil die of food poisoning?"

Vicki shook her head.

"He was poisoned, all right," Gartener said.

"Tests showed he had the same thing that poisoned me." Vicki looked a bit green again. "Manure — ick! But the food poisoning wasn't what killed him. No, our friend Neil ingested something more deadly."

"What?" Haylee demanded.

Vicki looked at Gartener as if asking his permission to answer.

"Rat poison," Gartener said.

26

I felt sick. "How did Neil manage to ingest rat poison when he probably didn't feel like eating anything?" I asked Vicki, remembering how she'd barely been able to down flat ginger ale.

She thinned her lips.

And then the obvious explanation hit me. "Let me guess," I said. "Neil was sick to his stomach like you were, Vicki, and, unlike me, Neil kept medicine on hand for settling stomachs. And someone added rat poison to the medicine. And he took it."

Vicki and Gartener's neutral expressions were a dead giveaway that I'd come up with a good theory — maybe one that was the same as theirs.

"I'm just guessing," I told them quickly. "I have no way of knowing how the rat poison was . . . er . . . administered."

Vicki seemed to stare right through my eyes and into my brain. Surely she didn't think I'd had anything to do with poisoning Neil.

"Feel free to search my premises for rat poison," Haylee offered.

"Mine, too," I echoed, possibly too late.

Vicki pinned us with a look she might have given rookie cops. "More likely we'd need to sift through everybody's garbage for empty containers."

I grimaced as if I would be the one assigned to delve into bags of smelly trash. "Have you searched the bakery? Maybe the poison was there."

"If it was," Gartener answered, "it's long gone. Except for —" He gave me a curt nod. "Except for upstairs in Neil's apartment, in the dregs of that medicine bottle you suggested."

"Lucky guess," I managed in a weak voice. "Whose fingerprints were on the bottle?"

"Nobody's," Gartener said. "The outside of that bottle was cleaner than if it had come out of a dishwasher. And the bottle was wrapped in tissue in the middle of a wastebasket."

I stared at Gartener in something like shock. Someone had cleaned the outside of the medicine bottle and hidden the bottle in the trash, and I doubted that Neil, who must have been very sick when he took the medicine, would have done all that. The strange disposal of his body pointed to murder, but now I was convinced. Again, I wondered who could have done such a thing to the baker that everyone seemed to like, and again, I felt very sad about Neil's life being cut short.

Gartener had been watching my face as I thought it all through, but he didn't comment. He stood and handed Yolanda and Cassie's phone numbers to Vicki. "Here, you might like to follow up on these. Let me know if you need help from the state police."

She gave him a radiant smile, then turned to us with a much less radiant look. "And you two — no more playing detective."

"Don't worry," I said. "We were only curious about what caused everyone's flu-like symptoms. Now we know. Thanks for telling us."

They gathered their things.

"Wait," I said. "Didn't you say you had questions for us?"

"We got our answers." Vicki could be very stern.

Gartener softened it with a smile. "We were curious about what you might have learned about the Brubaugh pair. And what other gossip . . . um . . . information you might have picked up."

Gartener and Vicki thanked us for our time and left Haylee's shop.

The moment the door closed behind them, I burst out, "What do you suppose they came to find out? How we reacted to Neil's being killed by rat poison?"

"Probably, and when we didn't immediately confess, 'Oh, officers, you found us out!' they realized we weren't the culprits."

I squeezed my face between my hands and moaned, "And then I had to go and guess how someone gave Neil the poison in the medicine! I was sure they were about to arrest me."

"Vicki may never consent to be your houseguest again, especially if she may need medicine." Haylee could always make me laugh. She dropped the sarcastic tone and asked what I was wearing to the gala.

"I don't know." I gazed at the perfectly made outfits hanging around The Stash. "Are you wearing one of these?"

"I'm already tired of seeing them. Probably not."

"Come check out my sample dresses at In Stitches. Maybe we could make a trade for that evening."

At In Stitches, Haylee fingered the hem of a white linen dress I'd made and embroidered with cutwork around the neckline. "You could wear this. Maybe Clay will think wedding bells."

"On our first date? A date that is not really a date?"

"Want me to *not* come?"

"No! Sorry for shouting. You have to come. But think of it as three friends going somewhere together. Not a date for any of us."

She sighed. "Sure, sure."

"Besides, white linen cutwork might only make him think of his grandmother's dresser scarves."

"What do you know about his grandmother's dresser scarves?"

"Nothing. But my grandmother had white cutwork dresser scarves and doilies, inherited from her mother. Every time I look at that outfit, I think of those."

"Well, at least you'd be what they call a snappy dresser."

I groaned.

She pointed across the shop to another dress I'd made in fuchsia dupioni silk embellished with simple touches of silver machine embroidery. "You'd be stunning in that. I can't wear that color. It shows up the red in my cheeks. And I refuse to wear black in the middle of the summer. I have some periwinkle silk that would make up beautifully. I'll go start it now."

It was Tuesday evening, nearly eleven. Wednesday night would be partly taken up by that very necessary trip for ice cream. Haylee would have to finish the dress Thursday night.

If anyone could do it, she could.

And sure enough, on Wednesday afternoon, some of my students who had attended morning classes at The Stash reported that Haylee had shown them a beautiful periwinkle silk dress she'd already begun piecing together.

And by the time I leashed the dogs for our after-dinner stroll, Haylee confirmed that the dress she was making would easily be ready by Friday night, and of course she could take a break for ice cream.

Instead of following the water's edge, we strolled along Beach Row, the lane leading past the cottages that had backyards on the beach. Naturally, we hoped to see the white van that Yolanda had driven away the night of the community picnic.

We didn't.

But I did find the little gray cottage between a pale yellow one and a two-story robin's-egg blue one. While many other cottages were obviously occupied, with bikes and toy trucks in sandy front yards, towels and swimwear hanging over clotheslines, and barbecues standing open on front porches, the gray cottage where I'd caught a glimpse of someone resembling Cassie had an air of being abandoned, and there was no vehicle of any sort in the driveway. However, Sally and Tally had to sniff the edge of its front yard, exactly as they had all the others.

Vicki was right that walking my dogs gave Haylee and me excellent opportunities to snoop while we waited for the dogs to figure out which animals had passed that way. I tried to look like a casual observer as I stared at the windows of the gray cottage. No faces.

Haylee said out of the corner of her mouth, "Look at the address."

Surprise, surprise, a house number on the front door matched the address we'd found for the phone number that Cassie had given Mona for Yolanda, the mysterious salad lady who may have given food poisoning to Vicki, Edna, Neil, and a whole bunch of other people.

I mumbled, "You know, firefighters in Elderberry Bay are supposed to help people check the batteries and best-before dates on their smoke and carbon monoxide detectors whenever they ask. Do you think the owners of this cottage could be encouraged to ask?"

"I'm sure they could."

Sally lifted her head and tested the air. She whimpered. Haylee braced herself to keep the determined dog from going up the small gray cottage's front walk. "Sally pulled toward the back of this cottage Monday night, too, when we were on the beach." Her arms jerked as Sally-Forth tugged at her leash. "Did Tally want to investigate it?"

"No, but he was anxious to catch up with you and Sally."

Looking mulish, Sally stiffened her legs and wouldn't move her feet.

I jogged ahead with Tally. It was enough. Sally gave in. She and Haylee quickly caught up with us.

By the time we got to the ice cream stand, I had not made up my mind what to order. How could I, when I didn't know what flavors they might offer, and everything I'd ever tried at that stand had been delicious?

However, when I saw the evening's latest new flavor — roasted garlic and caramelized onion — I decided to go for an old favorite, dark chocolate with bits of candied ginger sprinkled through it.

Having learned not to try to walk with

leashed dogs while we ate our gourmet ice cream, we sat at one of the bistro tables on the patio outside the ice cream stand. The dogs were very good about lying down and not begging.

The ice cream was even yummier than I remembered. We finished and continued west to the entrance of the Lazy Daze Campground. Leaving Haylee holding both leashes, I started into the office.

"No dogs," the woman behind the counter barked.

Either two women in Elderberry Bay had long blond scraggly hair and ropy muscles like that, or this was the woman who had fought with Yolanda at the sidewalk sale.

27

I showed the woman my empty hands. "I left the dogs outside."

"We're full up," the helpful woman announced, pointedly returning her gaze to her TV.

"I'm looking for a friend," I said. "Cassie. How do I get to her campsite?"

The woman stared at the TV. "If she's your friend, she'll tell you where to find her."

"She said she was staying at Lazy Daze. She gave me her cell phone number, but she said she often keeps it turned off, and when it wasn't on, I could ask for her here."

The woman hunched one tanned, bony shoulder, effectively creating an invisible wall between us. "That's your problem."

I tried, "Do you know where I can find Yolanda?"

Impatiently, she drummed long nails on her counter. "I don't know of any Yolanda registered here, and if I did, I wouldn't tell you or anyone else. Our guests have the right to privacy." Intent on a yogurt commercial, she ordered, "Get those mutts away from my door. They'll scare people away. And don't slam that screen on your way out. It will come off its hinges."

Having been thoroughly put in my place, I slunk out of the office and carefully shut the screen behind me.

The score was Campground Woman — 1, Willow — 0.

An RV had just pulled into a parking space outside the office, and a cheerful middle-aged woman with wavy red hair jumped out of the driver's seat and headed toward the office. With an apologetic smile, she raised a hand to stop me and murmured, "Is she okay?"

Dumbfounded, I asked, "Who?"

Haylee inched closer with the dogs. I could tell she was listening.

The woman's shorts and matching blouse were creased as if she'd driven all day with the RV's air conditioner off. She stared toward the screen door I'd just closed. "Her. Bitsy. I heard her ex-boyfriend was recently murdered. When I was here last summer, she told me she regretted breaking up with him and wanted to get back together with him, even though I got the impression it had been a few years since they broke up."

"I don't know." All sorts of possibilities and conjectures suggested themselves.

"I'd better go pay for my campsite." She dashed up the stairs to the office and carefully let herself in through the screen door.

I collected Tally-Ho's leash from Haylee. "I couldn't pry one bit of information out of the woman in the office," I muttered.

Haylee grinned. "But I overheard her name from the lady in the RV. It's Bitsy."

"Yep!" With Tally's help, I led the way back toward Beach Row. "I'm sure Bitsy is the woman who had the spat with Yolanda at your sale table last Friday evening."

"Vicki and Gartener might be interested in that information."

"That *gossip*," I teased. "Bitsy informed me that even if a person named Yolanda was registered here, she wouldn't tell me. We'll *have* to sic Vicki and Gartener on her." The idea, I had to admit, pleased me.

"And also tell them what the woman from the RV said. Neil and Bitsy were once a couple! And Bitsy wanted to get back with him."

"I can see why he didn't go for that," I said. "He was much nicer than Bitsy."

"I wonder if he dumped her, and she

waited until she thought people might have forgotten about her relationship with him before she did him in."

"With," I guessed, "help from Yolanda."

Agreeing that our theories had merit but that our favorite police chief and detective would pooh-pooh them since we had no tangible evidence, we sauntered toward home along the beach. When we reached the part of the beach near the small gray cottage's backyard, Sally-Forth stopped to sniff. Wagging her tail, she looked at Haylee and me with an expression that seemed to ask why we were so stubborn about not letting her barge into someone's cottage. "Maybe," I said to Sally, "if we ever see a vehicle in the driveway, we'll ring the bell. Meanwhile, don't you want to return home to the kittens?"

Heaving a heartfelt sigh, she plodded along the beach with the rest of us.

I wanted to know more about the cottage where I'd seen Cassie, the one that really seemed to interest Sally, but the June evenings were long and the sun hadn't set. I grinned at Haylee. "Now that Vicki knows we drive around most evenings after dark, shouldn't we take time off from driving, and *walk* to do our snooping later tonight?"

She nodded solemnly. "Yes. The beach

251

after dark should be glorious. The moon won't quite be full, but it should give us lots of light, even if we decide to bypass Bitsy's office and venture into the campground with its shade trees."

"And in the meantime," I added, "you have that periwinkle silk to work on."

"It's nearly done."

We returned to our shops to sew and embroider until after dark. Just before eleven, I changed into black slacks, pulled on a long-sleeved black T-shirt, and hid my hair under a black sun hat. I left my face and hands pale.

But what could I do about the dogs? Normally, we took them on our snoopy drives or walks, but their patches of white fur would shine in the moonlight. Someone in the cottages would be sure to notice us.

However, Sally-Forth had seemed determined to investigate that gray cottage, so as a compromise, I put a leash on her. Tally obviously wanted to come along, but I told him to stay. With a sad and confused expression on his cute brown and black brindle face, he did.

Naturally, Haylee was also dressed in black. At the beach, far from streetlights, we considered using the flashlights we'd brought, but the moon peeked between clouds, rimming their edges in silver. We meandered through soft sand to the water's edge where waves had darkened and hardened the sand underfoot. Wind gusted from the north across the lake, pushing clouds past the moon and frothing waves into whitecaps. Laughing, we jumped away from spreading, hissing water.

As I'd hoped, lights were on in many cottages, and if people had drapes or blinds, they hadn't pulled them. At the cottage colony, almost everyone knew what everyone else was doing, anyway.

The gray cottage was completely dark, and as far as I could tell, no drapes were pulled. Sally sniffed and turned toward the cottage.

I let her pull me closer.

We were still officially on the beach when Haylee grabbed me and whispered, "Were those things on those chairs earlier?" The wind and waves were so noisy I could barely hear her.

She pointed at a small wooden deck outside a sliding glass door.

A striped beach towel hung from the back of one lawn chair. A shirt was draped over another.

Sally cooperated and pulled me almost to the deck.

Haylee came, too. Near the deck, she

flicked her flashlight on for the briefest of seconds.

I recognized the shirt.

It was pink plaid and short-sleeved, either the one we'd seen Cassie wear or one exactly like it.

28

Haylee and I stopped at the edge of the low wooden deck, but Sally-Forth never had concerns about people's notions of etiquette or privacy. She leaped onto the deck and sniffed the pink plaid shirt as if she also recognized it, then strained toward one side of the deck, where bulging plastic bags leaned against overflowing recycling bins. The tops of the bags were gathered into twist-tied ruffles that bobbed and rustled in the wind.

Elderberry Bay's garbage was usually picked up on Wednesday mornings. Either someone had forgotten to put their garbage out, or they had accumulated this much during the day. Sally jumped off the deck, pulled me to one of the bags, and nearly buried her nose in the plastic. Before I could stop her, she raised a front paw and tore the bag from top to bottom.

Bits of paper fluttered out into a gust that

swirled them upwards. Most of the scraps somersaulted between the gray cottage and the robin's-egg blue one. Haylee took off after them.

Sally, however, had no interest in the storm of paper scraps. She sniffed at the growing pile of sand at our feet.

I didn't need the olfactory sensors of a dog's nose to realize that the sand falling from inside the bag stunk. A rolled aluminum edge of a turkey roasting pan clued me in to what I was smelling and why.

I wasn't the only one who used disposable aluminum baking pans as kitty litter trays, but while I had filled my turkey pan with nicely deodorized kitty litter, the person who'd filled this pan had simply walked out her back door and scooped up beach sand.

My cute little Sally-Forth smelled cats, and probably thought she had to mother every one of them. Another scrap of paper floated out of the bag. I lunged, but Sally refused to budge, except to paw more sand out of the bag, and I missed. The scrap flew off toward where Haylee had disappeared.

Because of the wind and waves, I couldn't hear anyone inside the cottage, but what if someone inside heard us? Explaining that I was only walking my dog wouldn't pass muster, since we were so close to the cottage's rear wall that we were practically inside.

Sally nosed something out of the bag and dropped it beside me. Moonlight reflecting off clouds showed me a catnip mouse. Sally stuck her snout into the bag again, and this time, I was nearly as curious as she was and didn't stop her.

She hauled out a tiny pet bed upholstered in sheepskin-like fleece. She snuffled it, whimpered, and wagged her tail. Now she wanted to adopt a pet bed? She was going overboard with her motherly instincts.

Remembering Gartener's comment about searching people's trash for empty rat poison containers, I pulled Sally away from the gashed bag.

Haylee zipped out from between the cottages and pointed back toward Beach Row. Grasping bits of paper like a pale bouquet in one fist, she pretended to turn a steering wheel. I got the message. Someone was driving on Beach Row near the gray cottage.

Haylee bent as if to deposit the scraps she'd collected in the gaping garbage bag. I shook my head violently. With my free hand, I grabbed the bouquet of torn-up paper from her.

Headlights raked the side of the robin's-egg blue cottage. Was someone turning a car around in one of the driveways? Maybe they were parking at the gray cottage.

Hoping that Sally wouldn't yip in excitement about our sudden flurry of activity, I plodded as quickly as I could through deep sand, away from the cottage and toward the water. Still leashed, Sally had to come along.

Haylee zoomed ahead and led us west, away from Threadville, past the backs of cottages. When we were close to the walkway that led to Beach Row and the ice cream stand, we stopped.

"That car," Haylee panted, "could have been Max's."

No one was visible on the moonlit beach, but anyone could be tiptoeing close to the cottages or running along Beach Row, spying between cottages and keeping up with us. I imagined a faceless murderer speeding ahead to ambush us.

Waves crashed. Wind rattled shutters and roared in our ears. We wouldn't have heard a front-end loader or a truck, let alone the engine of a new and probably well-tuned BMW. I saw no reflections from headlights, which wasn't reassuring, since I'd driven without them on a recent moonlit night.

Breathless from adrenaline and running, I handed Haylee Sally-Forth's leash. Thanks to Sally, I had already used both of the stoop-and-scoop plastic bags I'd brought along, and had tossed them in one of the beach's trash barrels before we came to the gray cottage, so I didn't have a convenient way of carrying the bits of paper that Haylee had collected. I untucked my T-shirt in the front to make a sort of kangaroo pouch, thrust the scraps into the pouch, tucked the shirt in with the loose section hanging down over my waist, and hoped that no one besides Haylee would see me. Or would come close enough to smell me, either. The paper had apparently absorbed some of the odors from inside that garbage bag.

"Phew," Haylee said. "Those things stink."

I heaved a sigh. "Tell me about it."

Sally wagged her tail.

"Why did you come this way?" I asked Haylee. "Now we have to pass that cottage to get back."

"I didn't want to lead anyone to our apartments."

I had to admit that her idea had merit.

"Besides," she continued, "if we go up to Beach Row and walk west, we'll come to the road to the wharf, the marina, and the driveway to the Elderberry Bay Lodge. That road will take us to Shore Road. We can walk back to Threadville along Shore Road."

She glanced at my hands clasped over my pregnant-looking T-shirt. "No one could guess you're hiding something."

I groaned. "Let's go. Act nonchalant."

Hanging on to Sally's leash, she strolled toward Beach Row. "And you're just casually clutching your stomach. Maybe you'll pass for a victim of food poisoning."

"I'm beginning to feel like one." And not only from the lingering fumes of used kitty litter. Letting Sally tear into someone's garbage was bad enough. Absconding with some of the garbage was worse. I told myself I'd throw it away after I examined whatever might be written on it, and then I'd take a nice long bath.

Before we reached Beach Row, we stopped and listened. There was no sign of a car or a murderer sneaking along after us, so we turned and sauntered along Beach Row as if we were doing nothing more interesting than walking a dog.

The ice cream stand had closed for the evening. We passed more cottages. The Lazy Daze Campground office was dark, and a gate barred the driveway.

"Latecomers don't get in?" Haylee whispered.

"There's a number pad." I could barely make it out in the moonlight. "We could duck under the gate to search for Cassie."

Haylee laughed. "And if we found her?"

"We'd know she wasn't lying about where she was staying. But we don't know what kind of car she drives, so unless she's outside with a light shining on her face, I'm not sure how we could figure out which campsite is hers." I lowered my voice. "More likely she did lie about where she's staying, she's in that cottage where we saw her shirt, and she's scared stiff because someone was just prowling around it."

Although walking west on Beach Row to get ourselves east and home seemed counterintuitive, we kept going. Neither of us wanted to meet up with the person who'd been driving the car that could have been Max's.

In the harbor, the wharf was protected from the wilder waves out beyond the jetties. The moon peeked between scudding clouds, illuminating fishing boats and the backs of boathouses. The boathouse behind Tom's fish market had two garage-type doors, pulled down to just above the water. Sally found the odors around the wharf interesting, but they were a bit too fishy for me. Poor Tally was missing all the fun.

Beyond the wharf, sailboats, yachts, dinghies, and motorboats of every size clung to the marina docks. Breezes jangled metal fittings against masts. Inside one sailboat, a couple at a candlelit table shared a bottle of red wine and a card game. Music, laughter, and chattering voices came from the deck of a massive yacht moored farther out. We continued west until we saw the Elderberry Bay Lodge. Beyond the wide, pillared porch stretching the entire length of the building, lights made the lodge appear cozy and welcoming. We'd be back Friday night, dressed to party. With Clay.

By then, I hoped to have lost this strange paunch and washed off the kitty litter odors.

We turned onto the road leading uphill. Max's BMW wasn't among the few vehicles in the lodge's parking lot. Where was it, near the gray cottage? I was glad that Haylee had led me this way, and not into the arms of the person who had been driving along Beach Row.

Shore Road ran high above Beach Row, and more or less parallel to it. Finally, we were walking toward Threadville — and home. Trees on the slope below us sheltered us from the wind and diminished its sound. Breaking waves were farther away. Hearing each other became easier.

"Why did you want all that garbage?" Haylee asked. "To find out what Cassie has been doing around Yolanda's cottage when she was supposedly staying at the campground?"

"Partly. Also, I suspect that the kittens who were dumped in my yard the night Neil was dragged there may have come from Yolanda's cottage. Sally was very interested in kitty litter that spilled from the bag. She also dragged a catnip mouse and a kitten-sized pet bed out of the bag."

"People throw those things out. Especially kitty litter. They may have nothing to do with Mustache and Bow-Tie."

"The pet bed and catnip mouse looked new. Vicki is understandably curious about where those kittens came from." I patted my stomach. "Maybe I'll find the name and address of whoever left them behind. I won't have to tell Vicki I helped myself to garbage unless something important is written on the paper." But did people tear up *unimportant* garbage?

At the foot of the hill below us, the roofs of tents and trailers peeked between trees in the Lazy Daze Campground.

On the shoulder ahead of us, the tops of signs suddenly glittered. I whipped around.

On Shore Road behind us, headlights crested a hill.

Maybe the driver who had been near

Yolanda's cottage was searching for us. His lights hadn't touched us. Yet.

We sprinted to a drainage ditch leading toward the campground. Sneakers dislodging rounded stones, we clattered down its sloping side. Sally seemed quite pleased to join us in a new and different adventure.

Breathing heavily, we crouched, our fingers on the ground. The paper in my impromptu kangaroo pouch shifted, but my shirt stayed in place, and none of the scraps fell out. Sally flopped down between us and panted, her tongue hanging out and her eyes bright in the moonlight.

Haylee muttered, "If anyone saw us run, we could be in worse trouble than if we'd just kept walking."

We waited, watched, and listened. No lights approached. What had happened to that vehicle? Sally's panting made it hard to hear anything else, but I thought maybe tires crunched on gravel as if a vehicle had stopped beside the road not far from us. And had turned its headlights off.

I didn't know who might be chasing us or if he knew that I'd helped myself to some of the garbage outside Yolanda's cottage.

An enormous concrete pipe ran underneath the road, from the far side to the drainage ditch we were in. What if I crept into the culvert and left the bits of paper under a stone, then came back later with a bag to collect it all?

What if someone reported to Vicki that two tall women, dressed in black and walking a distinctive black and white dog, had rifled through someone's garbage?

Someone's? Cassie's, probably. I was positive I'd seen Cassie in that cottage on Monday evening, and a shirt like hers had been hanging on the back of a lawn chair a little while ago. Yet Cassie had told Mona — and Haylee and me — that she was staying in the campground.

At that cottage, had Sally smelled the kittens she had adopted, or other cats?

Cassie didn't seem like a murderer, and she didn't seem like someone who would dump kittens.

While all this was spooling through my brain, I tensely and silently waited with Haylee for the sound of a car door, maybe for footsteps on the shoulder of the road.

I mentally prepared to crawl into that culvert.

I'd been staring at it blindly, but my eyes adjusted to the darkness under the road.

Something was in the culvert, something lumpy and bulky.

29

I gasped.

"What?" Haylee whispered. She still had Sally on a leash. If my dog had noticed the thing in the culvert, she wasn't particularly interested. She stared up toward the road. The vehicle still hadn't passed.

I pried my flashlight out of my pocket and shined it into the culvert.

I told myself that the black plastic garbage bag was only litter tossed from a car, but there was something disturbingly organic about the lumps in the bag. And if it had been only tossed, it probably wouldn't have ended up neatly underneath the middle of the road.

Still squatting among rounded stones, Haylee and I stared at the thing. Haylee's breathing sounded as uneven as mine. Sally just went on panting in her slaphappy, grinning way.

What was that other sound? A furtive

footstep on the gravel shoulder above us?

I flicked off my light and steadied myself with one hand flat on the ground. My position cramped my lungs. Holding my breath became painful.

Vicki Smallwood's voice rang out. "This is the police. Come out with your hands up."

"Vicki!" I shouted, finally letting my breath out in one whoosh. "Don't shoot. It's just me."

"And me," Haylee added.

"Who's 'me'?" Vicki demanded, her voice still sharp.

I called back, "Willow and Haylee. And Sally-Forth."

"Is anyone else down there with you three?"

I glanced at the bag. "Not that we know of." No one who was alive, anyway.

We clambered up the stony slope.

Vicki took one look at us and shook her head in apparent disbelief. "What on earth were you two doing, running off the road and hiding from an approaching police car?" She shined a flashlight on our clothing. "In black again, too. Snooping? After we told you not to?"

I defended our actions. "We didn't *know* it was you. We didn't hear a siren or see

267

flashing lights." Vicki could undoubtedly hear the tremors in my voice. Trying to calm myself, I added, "And you never know who might be coming along this dark, deserted highway."

"There's been a murder," Haylee contributed, as if that explained our actions. And as if our intrepid police chief didn't already know about Neil's death.

"If it's that dangerous, why were you out here in the first place?" Vicki asked.

This time, I answered. "Walking the dog. We went to the beach and were taking a different route home."

Vicki peered down at Sally-Forth. "Only *one* dog?"

I couldn't blame her for being suspicious. I had never walked only one of the dogs before. Siblings, they were devoted to each other. Tally-Ho was probably going into deep mourning alone in our apartment. Well, almost alone. Would the kitties' presence comfort him? I waved my hand in dismissal. "It's a long story, and not important compared to . . . something in the culvert. I think you should see it."

"What is it?" she asked me.

"I'm not sure."

As far as I could tell, she didn't even try to hide her impatience. "Show me." In her police-issue boots, she negotiated the gully's clacking, rounded stones as if they were pavement. "Is Tally-Ho okay?"

I kept my answer short. "He's fine."

We didn't go into the culvert. She swept her powerful flashlight over the garbage bag. "Good thing Detective Gartener is on his way." Lit from below, her grin looked more devilish than she probably realized. "There might be maggots."

I shuddered. "Oh, please."

Vicki sniffed in the direction of the garbage bag. "I don't smell anything terrible coming from it. Do you?"

We had to admit that we didn't. I added, "And Sally isn't acting like anything in that bag is interesting to a dog. But I was freaked out because —" Oops, I didn't want to tell her I'd been scared that someone was chasing us after perhaps seeing us root through garbage. Let Vicki think that finding Neil's body in my yard was still freaking me out. Actually, it was.

Vicki turned her head toward me and sniffed again. "Maybe I do smell something. It's like used kitty litter, but it seems to be coming from you, Willow."

Not good. "Could be."

She crouched at the edge of the culvert.

"Let's have a look. Hold my flashlight for me?"

Haylee hung on to Sally's leash and stayed back while I aimed Vicki's flashlight at the garbage bag. "It can't have been there long," I pointed out. "It's not dusty."

Vicki put on gloves, duckwalked into the culvert, untied the bag's red drawstring, and opened the top.

Something white puffed out. A sweater?

In the confines of the culvert, Vicki hefted the bag. "I think we've found the yarn-bomber's cape. Except that the part I can see of it is all white, it's knit like the *thing* that managed to get itself onto my car inside my garage. And the bag is about the right weight for a garment that size made of bulky yarn." Leaving the bag behind, she scooted out of the culvert and aimed her flashlight at Haylee. "Know anything about who hid this here?"

Haylee blinked and shaded her eyes. "No, but I'm guessing that she didn't want her husband finding her disguise — or is it her next yarnbombing project? — in an upstairs closet. Which lets Willow and my mothers and me off the hook. We each live alone."

Vicki shined her light down on the ground. "Except when my car was yarnbombed, Willow had a temporary roommate — me.

270

Maybe Willow was going to take this back home after I left, and hadn't gotten around to it? Maybe you two were here to pick it up tonight?"

Naturally, I defended myself. "I'd have brought a car. Besides, Haylee and I were talking to Detective Gartener when your car was yarnbombed."

Vicki snapped her fingers. "That's right."

I was sure she'd remembered all along. Police college had probably taught her how to keep people on edge. I added, "Besides, Trooper Jeffers said that the person in the cape ran like a man."

Above us, a car door slammed. "Vicki?"

Detective Gartener's deep melodious voice. Great. Now we'd really be on edge.

"We're down in the gutter, Toby!" Vicki was, perhaps, a little too cheerful.

"Are you okay?" He slipped and slid down to join us.

"Sure, we're fine," she answered. "Haylee and Willow were searching for maggots, but all they found was the yarnbomber's cape."

"They *did*?" The admiration in that resonant voice was patently fake. "Let's see."

She showed it to him. "What do we do," she asked, "leave it here for the yarnbomber to retrieve later?"

"Sure! And deputize Willow and Haylee

to hide in the culvert twenty-four-seven watching for him. It might keep them out of mischief."

Uh-oh. Did he know what else we'd been up to that evening?

He radioed for troopers to come check out the bag in the culvert, then turned to me. The flashlights gave him a devilish grin, also. "Where's your other dog, Willow?"

I might have known he'd come up with the question Vicki had asked.

"She said it's a long story," Vicki told him. "We have time, Willow, while we wait for the troopers to show up. I don't think anything is about to jump out of that bag at us."

I'd left Tally behind because I was afraid we'd be more than twice as noticeable with two dogs, but I'd had another reason for taking only Sally, and I gave it, rather tentatively. "On our walks to and from the ice cream stand, Sally had seemed very interested in one of the cottages. I thought maybe the kittens had come from it, and I didn't bring Tally along because he might distract her." I made up the last part, but in retrospect, it was a pretty good excuse for leaving Tally at home.

"Let me guess." Vicki pinched her nose. "Sally found some kitty litter."

I said in a small voice, "Yes."

Gartener folded his arms across his chest. "What else did your dog find?"

Confession might not be good for the soul, exactly, but it was a relief. "She ripped open a garbage bag that was outside that cottage. Kitty litter spilled out, and she hauled a catnip mouse toy and a small pet bed out of the bag, too."

"Before you could stop her." Vicki hadn't lost her sarcastic touch.

This time, I had my excuse ready. "You asked me to let you know if I found out where the kittens came from."

"I also asked you — told you — to let us do the investigating," she scolded me.

But Gartener still seemed interested in our exploits. "Where did your dog find all these things?"

Haylee quickly rattled off the address.

I held my breath. Would they know that the street number wasn't on the back of that cottage, and that we'd paid particular attention to the front? Would we have to confess that we'd done a reverse lookup on Yolanda's number?

Gartener stared at Vicki. "Isn't that —" He paused.

"Yes. Same address." Her answer was clipped.

"Same address as what?" I asked, hoping I wouldn't have to divulge what I already knew.

Both officers stared at me. "Might as well tell her," Gartener said, finally. "It's not exactly a secret."

Vicki heaved a sigh. "That's the address for the phone number you gave us for Yolanda, the woman who made the salads at the picnic."

"You've talked to her?" Haylee put a friendly, interested smile in her voice.

Vicki shook her head. "She doesn't answer that number, or the door."

I leaped into the fray with an obvious statement. "You need a search warrant for that cottage."

30

"What would we base a search warrant on?" Gartener challenged me.

It was probably the scraps of paper in my shirt that gave me the sudden desire to fidget. "To find out if the kittens came from that cottage, in case someone dumped them along with Neil's body? They showed up about the same time."

Vicki turned to Gartener. "Assuming that Yolanda Smith concocted her world-famous bacteria and bocconcini salad there, can't we ask to search for rat poison?"

Thinning his lips, Gartener nodded.

I should have been proud of myself — and of Sally-Forth — for discovering that those kittens might have once been in Yolanda's cottage. Instead, I felt like the scraps of paper in my shirt were probably glowing or something, and I might as well make a complete confession before Vicki and Gartener noticed them. I offered in a small voice, "Bits of paper blew out of the bag."

Haylee jumped in. "But I collected them."

I patted my stomach. "And I have them here."

"You ate them?" Vicki asked in exaggerated shock. Then at the expression that must have been on my face, she relented. "Just kidding. You tried to hide them in your shirt, right?"

I mumbled, "I guess I didn't succeed."

"Considering the odd bulges, not to mention the odor, no, you didn't. Why did you stuff them into your *shirt*?" she asked.

"I didn't have a bag, and they wouldn't have fit in my jeans pocket. I would have thrown them in the trash, but I thought they could be important, and could maybe give us proof of who dumped those kittens."

"You realize," Vicki scolded, "that anything that you removed from a site can't be used as evidence, even about dumping animals, no matter how 'important' it seems?"

I nodded miserably, waiting for her to add that I could be arrested for interfering in an investigation.

"I'd like to see what's on those papers." Gartener's deep, warm voice could actually be comforting. "But the wind's too strong and Haylee might have to retrieve them again. I'll get them from you in the shelter of my car." While he was hauling me off to jail, most likely. I decided that studying my feet, which seemed to need to wiggle around, was probably the most worthwhile thing I could do right then.

"Did you remove anything else from those premises, Willow?" Vicki asked.

I dragged my gaze back to her face. "No, but we saw a shirt hanging from a deck chair. It looked like the pink plaid shirt we saw on Cassie, the woman who was Neil's assistant at the bakery."

Both police officers became very still, and so did my feet, finally.

"And it hadn't been there after supper," Haylee chimed in, "when we went out for ice cream."

I added, "On another of our outings for ice cream, I thought I saw Cassie in that cottage."

"When?" Detective Gartener's voice was as rich as ever, but his question sounded urgent.

I turned toward Haylee. "The night that Max and Zara caught up with us on the beach and we didn't actually get any ice cream."

"Monday night." Her dry tone showed her scorn for her cousins.

"Did you also see Cassie at that cottage

that night, Haylee?" Gartener asked.

"No," Haylee answered. "I was in a hurry to get away from Max and Zara."

"Why?" Vicki sounded on the verge of laughter.

"Max called me his *aunt.*"

Vicki covered her mouth.

"Max hadn't seen his aunt Opal since he was three and Opal was sixteen," I explained. "And Haylee does look older than sixteen."

"And Max Brubaugh looks like a fake," Haylee retorted. "Maybe he's the real Max Brubaugh, my cousin, but he doesn't act like Opal or me." She swept her palm across an invisible surface. "We're not that smooooooth."

I defended him. "He had to learn that for his job."

"Exactly." Haylee turned to Gartener and Vicki. "You two must be good at telling when someone is lying. Have you interviewed Max and Zara yet?"

"No reason to," Gartener said. "And I got a good look at both of them in Opal's store."

Haylee folded her arms. "But . . . they arrived in the vicinity right before Neil was murdered!"

"Lots of people were in the vicinity," Vicki pointed out, "including all of us standing out here in a gully."

Helpful.

"We may get to the Brubaughs yet," Gartener said. "Meanwhile, Haylee and Willow, you two come with me and let's have a look at the scraps of paper you found."

Vicki muttered, "I'll stay here in the ditch with the garbage bag until your team arrives to pick it up."

"I'd wait with you," Gartener said, a smile in his voice, "but I need to see what Willow found, and then I need to arrange for that search warrant."

Vicki looked straight at me. Her eyes flashed in the moonlight. "At least the garbage bag in the culvert doesn't *stink.*"

"Willow doesn't, either," Gartener retorted. "At least not much." How magnanimous.

He scrambled up the slippery slope, with Sally close behind him and Haylee and me nearly keeping up.

At the top, he stopped and looked down the hill at the lights in the campground. "That's Lazy Daze, right?" he asked us.

We said it was.

"So it would be simple for someone to haul a garbage bag up here in the dead of night and hide it in the culvert?"

Again, I agreed. "The yarnbomber took

off in a boat, though. If she —"

He interrupted, "Or he."

I went on, "If she *or he* took the boat to the marina, what did he or she do with the cape in the meantime?"

"Good point," he said. "But it was dark when it all happened. He probably took that cape off, stowed it in the bag in the boat, and then tied up the boat and brought the bag here. Trooper Jeffers and I looked for him that night, but we didn't find him or the boat or the cape. Or anyone walking along the road carrying a full trash bag." He opened his passenger door, cleared notes and an empty paper coffee cup off the seat, and then stood back. "Here, Willow, you can put the scraps on the seat out of the wind."

I leaned forward, untucked my shirt, and shook it over the car seat. One scrap blew out of the car, but Haylee, with help from my enthusiastic Sally, grabbed it.

Gartener put on plastic gloves. "It's like a jigsaw puzzle." The paper had been hand-shredded into a slew of little pieces. He turned them right side up and shoved shapes together to fit, sort of. "There are two pages," he said after a while. "And they were torn together, so we have two nearly identical jigsaw puzzles. Probably only the words on them will differ." He lined up part of the top of a page, one with hand-printed capital letters across it. I made out: *ILL AND TEST L ONDOV.*

Gartener translated under his breath. "Last will and testament of Neil Ondover."

Oh, no. Now I was really in trouble for removing evidence. "And someone tore it up and threw it out?" I asked. It was getting worse and worse. Wasn't there some way I could teleport myself somewhere far away? The moon, perhaps?

"Looks like it." He gathered the pieces and dropped them into an envelope. "You said you found these scraps in a bag near Yolanda Smith's cottage? Can you give me an exact description of the location?" He took out his pen and notebook.

"On the beach side of the cottage, right behind it, under a window, to the right of the deck if your back is to the lake."

Haylee added, "Some of the pieces of paper blew between that cottage and the next one. I was only trying to pick up litter, not collect evidence, so I may have missed a few bits."

Gartener frowned at us. "I hope we find them. I also hope that most of the rest of the will is still in the bag and can be entered as evidence."

Maybe I should aim myself toward Venus, not the moon. Venus was farther away. I asked, "Who was the beneficiary of the other will you found?"

But he was watching a vehicle speed toward us. A state police van pulled up behind his cruiser, and two troopers hopped out. "It's going to be a long night," Detective Gartener muttered. "I'll have to go all the way to Erie, get that search warrant, and meet these guys back at that cottage. You two can go. But please, stay away from that cottage and from any investigating. Can we reach you at your home numbers tonight if we need you?"

We said he could and he wrote our numbers in his notebook. He gave Sally-Forth a pat, suggested to her that she could join a K-9 unit, pointed his colleagues to the gully where Vicki waited with a non-smelly garbage bag, and tore off toward Erie.

I took Sally's leash. After Haylee, Sally, and I put a lot of distance between us and the officers, I murmured to Haylee, "He didn't want us to know who Neil's beneficiary was, did he?"

"He sure didn't," Haylee answered. "Whoever it was, I wouldn't want to be in that person's shoes."

"Or in the shoes of the person who ripped

up the will," I said. I wasn't overjoyed about being in the shoes of the person who had removed the will from the scene, either. I made a silent vow that I would never, ever, be curious about anything again. If I came up with a question, I would leave it to others to answer. I was through with sleuthing. Finished and done. Period.

"The mysterious Yolanda Smith threw out the will?" Haylee suggested. "Or Cassie, who has apparently been hanging around that cottage?"

"Cassie and Yolanda obviously know each other, or Cassie wouldn't have given Yolanda's number to Mona. And Yolanda fought with Bitsy from the Lazy Daze Campground office, who wouldn't tell us anything about Cassie. But if Cassie's staying in the cottage, not the campground . . ."

"She's moved in with Yolanda?"

"Whom we haven't seen since Saturday night," I said. "Oops. We didn't tell Vicki and Detective Gartener that we tracked down the woman who fought with Yolanda at the sidewalk sale, and that she supposedly used to date Neil and tried to get back with him."

Haylee slanted an amused look at me. "Which is just as well, considering that our evidence is all hearsay, and we'd only get another scolding."

I laughed. "You're right. But those three women must be involved in something. Saying it was a conspiracy could be stretching it, but I'd sure like to know what their secrets are."

"Thanks to us, the investigators already have all three women in their radar," Haylee said.

Right. And I wasn't doing anything resembling investigating, ever again.

The closer we got to home, the faster Sally walked until we, with our longer legs, were nearly running, while the dog seemed to be only hurrying.

Haylee said good-bye at The Stash. It was after two.

I unlocked the door to In Stitches and unleashed Sally-Forth. Downstairs, Tally-Ho barked. Sally rushed to the door leading to the apartment, and dashed downstairs as soon as I opened it. I followed at a less breakneck speed. Tally and Sally had an emotional — and very noisy — reunion, but where were the kittens?

I found them, their eyes approximately the size of saucers, peeking out from under the cabinet above the fridge. I hauled the kitties down and hugged them, but they didn't purr. When Tally looked their way, they puffed up.

"Tally," I said sternly, "did you chase Mustache and Bow-Tie?"

Tally wagged his tail and ducked his head, and he didn't look any less dejected when Sally bounded to me and stood on her hind legs to sniff her charges.

I set the kittens on the floor. They arched their backs, hissed, and hopped sideways toward Tally.

The cute little guys didn't frighten me at all, but Tally slunk away and curled up on his bed. I looked at him more closely. He had a tiny scratch on his nose.

I told the fierce kitties, "I think you've taught him what you wanted him to learn."

Sally sat down and stared at the kittens in obvious bewilderment. They were still twice their normal size.

I patted Tally. "Sorry we didn't take you along." The kittens probably were, too.

He wagged his tail and snuffled at the hem of my T-shirt. Great. Whatever he might think of kittens, he seemed to relish the smell of used kitty litter.

I dumped my clothes in the laundry, took a shower, and went to bed. It was already Thursday morning, so Friday night, and my almost-date with Clay, was officially one day away.

31

All the next morning, I kept thinking of Friday night's outing with Clay and Haylee. I could hardly wait to see what happened when Clay introduced Haylee and Ben. Mona had said that Ben was widowed. Haylee had assumed that would put him into the same age group as Fred Zongassi, or maybe Snoozy Gallagher, but knowing Clay, I suspected that Ben would be closer to our age. I liked Clay more than I wanted to admit. If I agreed with him about Ben, I'd probably like him even more.

On the other hand, if Ben turned out to be horrid, I might be able to stop thinking and wondering about Clay.

Our students wanted to try hardanger embroidery on a finer weave than monk's cloth, so Ashley and I helped them hoop an evenly woven mid-weight linen and try it on that. At lunchtime, I left In Stitches in Ashley's capable hands and went off with the dogs to meet Haylee in the park.

Naturally, we had to plan our evening outing with the dogs. Haylee had nearly finished her dress and said she would definitely have time to go out for ice cream again. Although we were both curious what, if anything, we would find out by walking past Yolanda's cottage, we agreed that we wouldn't venture close enough to upset any investigators who might still be searching it.

Ashley's and my afternoon workshop was a bit more challenging than the morning class. One of our students failed to make the linen in her embroidery hoop absolutely straight on the grain. She threw the crooked result down and muttered, "I see why they call it hard*anger.*"

Ashley apologized for not making sure the grain was straight, and then helped the woman hoop another piece of linen. That one came out fine.

After supper, the sun was still high overhead, and the dogs were quite happy to go for yet another walk on the beach. Because of the day's warmth, the waves washing up on our feet had lost some of their chill, and we neither gasped nor shrieked.

The towel and pink plaid shirt were gone from the deck chairs behind Yolanda's cottage, and the trash had been taken away.

Sally seemed to expect me to ignore the yellow tape and let her explore the cottage's backyard and deck, and probably the inside of the cottage, too.

Imagining running into Gartener and telling him, "The doggie made us do it," I kept moving, and Sally, who didn't have much choice since she was on a leash, came along, wagging her tail.

The coffee ice cream was delicious, and Haylee liked her butterscotch swirl.

We sauntered back along Beach Row. Catching a glimpse of Bitsy glaring at us through the campground office window, we sped our pace. Except for the crime scene tape, the front of Yolanda's cottage looked the same as it had the night before, unoccupied and lonely. Not that I was sleuthing. I'd given that up.

Sensibly, Haylee focused on the gala. "Clay said he'd pick us up tomorrow night," she said. "His truck doesn't have an extended cab, so how will we fit?"

"I could drive. Or we could walk."

"Carrying our heels?"

"I thought I'd wear sandals."

"Great idea. And the three of us can have a romantic stroll back home along the beach. Are you sure you want me to go?"

"Positive. Maybe Clay has a plan for getting us there and back."

She laughed. "Knowing him, he does."

"Renting a limo?"

"I wouldn't put it past him."

Actually, he did have a plan, introducing Haylee to the lodge owner, Ben Rondelson. Maybe Ben figured in part of Clay's travel arrangements, too?

But the next evening, devastatingly handsome in a navy linen suit, white shirt, and red tie, Clay arrived alone at In Stitches. I stepped onto the porch.

"Mmm," Clay said. "I told you that you'd outshine jewelry."

I laughed. "I'm not wearing any besides earrings, so it's pretty easy to do."

He ushered me toward a silver SUV. "You look lovely."

I thanked him, and he helped me into the passenger seat.

Fred Zongassi was at the wheel. "Evening, Willow," he said, "I'm your chauffeur tonight." He wore a suit and polished leather shoes. No high-tops.

"I'll be back in a minute with Haylee," Clay said. He closed the door gently.

A determined look on her face and a gorgeous periwinkle silk dress hugging her curves, Haylee marched toward us. Did she fear that Clay had shut me into a vehicle with a murderer?

Smiling, Clay helped her into the seat behind Fred, and then went around the car and sat behind me. "Fred offered to take us tonight. He said my truck wasn't suitable."

Fred said, "It's not." He drove to the lodge, pulled into the circular drive underneath the porte cochere, dropped us off at the front door, and drove away. Haylee looked puzzled, probably wondering if I'd lied when I'd told her that Clay and I weren't trying to set her up with Fred.

Clay offered Haylee and me each an arm. "I'll be the envy of every man at the gala tonight." He led us around the side of the lodge to the long, wide porch that faced the beach.

Haylee darted a questioning glance at me.

I put on an innocent face. I could hardly wait to meet Ben. Would he and Haylee find each other interesting?

"Willow! Haylee! Claaaaaay."

Only Mona could draw a man's name out into that many husky syllables.

We turned around. Clinging to the arms of Ralph and Duncan, Mona wobbled on stiletto heels toward us. Her white sequined mini-dress showed off a substantial amount of tanned skin. She shook her head. "Hay-

lee and Willow, you seem short of a man."
She dimpled. "But I'm not sharing either of
mine tonight!"

Ralph winked at her, but poor Duncan
pulled at the knot of his navy blue tie. It
took me a second to notice that the tie was
made from lightweight brocade, with tiny,
detailed giraffes woven into the silk. Duncan must have inherited some of his father's
love of whimsy.

"I suppose we could all sit at the same
table," Mona conceded. "Unless —"

Duncan pulled the door open onto a vast,
windowed sunroom that overlooked the
porch and the beach.

A buffet table stretched along the lake side
of the room. A dark-stained oak dance floor
took up one end, and white-draped dining
tables filled the rest. The architecture was
Victorian, and although there was no red
velvet or brocade — other than Duncan's
tie — in sight, the bouquets and gleaming
silver candlesticks and cutlery on the tables
all had a decidedly Victorian flair. The entire
effect was of sparkling glamour. Whatever
Ben Rondelson might need, it was not the
decorating advice that Mona had hoped to
give him.

Mona undulated into the hall first, and
then stopped and squealed. "There's Max

Brubaugh! Excuse us, Willow and Haylee. *I* have to go meet him." She teetered to a table where Max, in a retro white dinner jacket, sat by himself. Ralph rushed after her, but before he could catch up, she pulled out a chair next to Max and plunked herself into it.

Haylee turned to me and Clay. "Let's sit on the other side of the room."

Duncan blushed.

"Not from you, Duncan," Haylee clarified. "From Max Brubaugh. I've already met him."

Duncan continued to stare at her. "Will you —" His Adam's apple bobbed. "Save a dance for me later, Haylee?"

"Glad to."

Duncan glanced past her at me. "And will you, too, Willow?"

Dancing? I shot Duncan a smile. "Sure!"

Mona stood and waved. "Duncan, over here!" She patted a chair beside her. Shaking her head, she beamed at Max. She probably thought he had risen to greet her, but he was staring at us.

He couldn't politely walk away from Mona, who held her right hand toward him, obviously introducing herself, and coincidently blocking him from coming our way.

Haylee stalked to the opposite corner of

the room. Although a crowd had already gathered in the banquet hall, Haylee found a table set for four with a card — *Reserved for Fraser party* — beside the silver candelabra in the middle of the table. Smiling, Clay pulled out chairs for Haylee and me. Duncan continued toward Mona and his father, but turned and waved at us.

We waved back.

Edna came in from the porch with Gord. Edna's dress must have started out black, but she'd covered it with crystals of nearly every size, shape, and color, and she'd fastened tiny, functioning lights all over the dress. Silver glitter glimmered in her hair. Gord wore a black suit I'd seen on him on another formal occasion, a suit that wouldn't have looked out of place onstage at the opera. Someone, Edna, most likely, had added rhinestones and lights to his boutonniere. Later, if the lights were turned down, those two would be easy to find.

Beaming in more ways than one, Edna waggled her fingers at us, then led Gord through milling people to a table for two near the dance floor.

And that's when The Beauty entered from the lobby.

32

Trust Zara to dress like a Greek goddess and pause on the threshold until all eyes were on her and her curling blond tresses and her flowing white gown. Slowly, she walked to Max and touched the sleeve of his dinner jacket.

For once, Mona didn't shake her head. She simply gaped.

Beside me, Haylee murmured, "Mmmmmmm." She probably didn't know she'd hummed. Startled, I turned toward her. She wasn't looking at her cousins.

She gazed in apparent awe at the man standing in the doorway that Zara had just vacated.

No wonder Haylee had made that admiring sound. Compared to this man, her cousin Max became a mere mortal. The new guy was at least six-five, with muscles to match and a face made more handsome by smile wrinkles. He wore an impeccably tailored black tux. He glanced around the room.

Zara waved girlish fingers at him. Mona gave him a broad smile.

Greeting people on the way, the man walked to our table. "Clay," he said, "good to see you." If anything, his voice was more resonant than Detective Gartener's.

Clay turned to us. "Haylee and Willow, I'd like you to meet Ben Rondelson. Ben, Haylee and Willow are some of my friends who own Threadville shops."

Smiling, Ben shook our hands, first Haylee's and then mine. His strong hand encompassed mine.

His dark good looks contrasted perfectly with Haylee's slender figure and beautiful face. Best of all, the man had kind eyes, brown like Clay's. I tried to wipe the smug smirk from my face.

Yes!

Clay was right. If Ben's personality matched the warmth in his face, Ben might be perfect for Haylee. It was all I could do not to improvise a little tap dance right then and there.

Across the room, Zara stared hungrily toward Ben. He would, of course, also set off Zara's beauty, but in my opinion, Haylee outshined her cousin. Still, apprehension teased at me. Zara must have already spent several days in Ben's vicinity. Had Clay waited too long to introduce him to Haylee?

Poor Mona looked absolutely torn. She'd engineered a place at a table with three eligible men. She probably didn't know yet that Zara was Max's sister, but now that Zara had joined Mona's table, Ralph and Duncan seemed to have forgotten Mona.

And Clay and Ben were all the way across the room from her.

Ben murmured to the three of us, "I'll have to go say a few words before I can join you." He touched the back of the one empty chair at our table. It was, of course, between Haylee and me.

I could tell that Clay was struggling not to show how satisfied he was with his match-making.

I hoped that Haylee wouldn't notice that Edna's smile was nearly as bright as her gown as she stared at the four of us and whispered to Gord. Haylee would think we'd *all* been part of a plot to throw her and Ben together. Clay and I had been the only members of the conspiracy. Me, conspiring with Clay . . . I kind of liked the sound of that.

Mona must have decided that Ben was a

better prize than the three men at her table. She started toward us, but Ben headed for the podium on the stage beside the dance floor. Mona sat down again.

Ben turned on the mike and welcomed all of us to the opening of the Elderberry Bay Lodge. We were to help ourselves to dinner and drinks, and a dance band would arrive later.

Crowds converged on the buffet table.

Taking my cue from Clay and hoping that our table's foursome would end up at the buffet together, I stayed at our table. Haylee remained seated, too, but instead of admiring Ben, she was staring at Max and Zara. She probably didn't realize she was gathering her white linen napkin into tight pleats.

She saw me watching her and leaned forward. "I wish I knew why they were really here."

Was it that hard to believe that Opal's sister and Max loved Opal and wanted to find her? Maybe I was being too optimistic, too ready to believe the best of others. Being around Clay tended to have that effect on me.

Ben started toward us, but Mona waylaid him. Tugging at her tight, stretchy dress, which was riding up her thighs, Mona talked to him until he made a gesture toward the buffet table. Max and Zara had joined the end of the lineup. Mona wobbled on her precarious heels to them and said something to Max. He bent toward her with a totally believable air of attentiveness.

Ralph and Duncan joined them and turned to talk to Edna and Gord behind them. I suspected that the Disguise Guys would soon add lighting displays to costumes they crafted. Sharing skills in Threadville was always fun. I imagined embroidery designs that incorporated lights. Sounds, too . . .

Ben must have noticed us hanging back. He returned to our table. "I can't eat until I'm sure everything is going well in the kitchen and with my staff." His eyes were on Haylee more than on Clay and me. *Score.* "You three go ahead, and I'll be with you when I can."

We didn't need more urging to help ourselves to the yummy feast at the buffet. When we returned to our table, Ben was there, opening a bottle of champagne. He poured some into each of our glasses, and, speaking only to the other three of us at his table, toasted Clay for the restoration work he'd done to the lodge. "Without you, I never would have been able to carry out the plans that —" Suddenly, his face went sad.

"You had the vision," Clay said quietly.

We all took a sip. It was excellent champagne. Ben set his glass down and hurried off to the kitchen.

Watching him go, Clay frowned.

"What's wrong?" I asked him.

He took a deep breath and leaned toward Haylee and me. "This lodge was a dream that Ben and his wife shared. She died of breast cancer about two years ago, and he's completed everything in her memory. I hope he has the heart to stick with it."

Haylee gazed toward the kitchen door. "This place is beautiful, but it must remind him every day of his loss. For the lodge's sake, I hope he stays, but for his sake . . ." She didn't need to finish the sentence.

"I hope he stays because I like him," Clay said. "Selfish, I know."

I lifted my glass. "And he brings us good champagne." But the only lightness in the evening seemed to be in the bubbles rising through the liquid in our glasses.

The food was delicious, and when Ben returned with a plate for himself, his moment of grief seemed to be over.

Haylee complimented him on the evening and the entire lodge. "You seem to have everything running well. Did you own other inns before this one?"

"This is my first, both to renovate and to manage. I was a mechanical engineer for the aerospace industry. It was pretty intense, and then my wife . . ." He swallowed. "My wife became ill, and we decided to live the way we wanted to. We believed she'd have longer."

Haylee and I expressed our sympathy, but I wasn't certain that he registered our comments.

We'd barely finished our dinners and a few too many desserts when Mona dragged an empty chair from a nearby table and placed it between Haylee and Ben. "We didn't get to finish our discussion," she told Ben. "I was about to tell you how I can help decorate your lodge."

Ben looked as flabbergasted as I felt, and Haylee and Clay seemed to be stunned speechless, also.

Mona didn't appear to notice. "I've already talked to Max Brubaugh, you know, the reporter from Pittsburgh?"

Ben nodded.

Mona took that as encouragement. "I told him he should do a show on how the right finishing touches can bring your little hotel here from ho-hum to wow." She smiled and shook her head the way she did when she wanted someone to agree with her, though it often had unplanned results. "I even gave him the title for the show. 'From Ho-Hum to Wow!' " She shook her head again as if marveling at her brilliance. "Isn't that cute?"

Poor Ben continued to be at a loss for words.

I told Mona, "I don't think I've ever seen Max Brubaugh report on 'cute.' "

"I have," she insisted. "He often reports on the repurposing and refurbishing of architectural gems. There was this mansion in Pittsburgh . . ." She stared off into the distance. "So I've also told him how we turned the quiet little village of Elderberry Bay into Threadville — a thriving metropolis that crafty women flock to from all over to learn how to decorate their homes! He's going to come to Country Chic this week to learn all about how we created Threadville."

Haylee made a noise like a very fake cough. Haylee and her mothers had established Threadville before I moved here, and Mona had opened her shop *after* I'd opened mine. Clay's brows lowered, but Haylee must have nudged him under the table. He jumped. I winked at him, and he winked back.

Ben turned to me. "Were you also one of the first to open a Threadville shop, Willow?"

I suspected he knew the answer, but I explained, anyway. "No, Haylee was the first with The Stash, and then her mothers, then me."

"But *they* don't do home dec," Mona explained. "I'm the go-to girl for interior decorating."

Musicians carrying instrument cases wandered in from the lobby. Ben excused himself and strode off toward them.

Mona stared at his back. "I'll have to speak with him when he's not so busy. Sorry, but I'll have to leave you three to your own vices." She simpered to show she'd made a joke. "I need to make more plans with Max for our joint TV shows."

Haylee, Clay, and I carefully did not look at each other until she was out of earshot, and when we did, Haylee had a coughing fit while Clay and I simply smiled at each other.

Haylee subsided and wiped her eyes. "You know," she said, "I think I might start watching Max Brubaugh's reports, after all."

For once, she didn't frown when speaking about Max. Maybe Mona had done some good.

Haylee focused on the stage behind the dance floor. "Our chauffeur is in the dance band."

I sat up straight for a better look and recognized most of the band members. Some of them had moved Blueberry Cottage up the hill in my backyard, and I'd probably seen all of them at one time or another in the Fraser Construction Marching Band. Now they wore dark suits, white shirts, gold ties, and shined shoes.

"How come you're not playing tonight?" Haylee asked Clay. "Trumpets can be in dance bands."

"I intend to *dance*. Besides, Ben wanted me here tonight as his guest, not as a member of the band."

"If we're going to dance," Haylee said, "we'd better check our hair."

Taking the hint, I followed her to the ladies' room. Like the dining room, the ladies' room didn't need Mona's decorating touches. It was beautifully finished, with linen towels and designer soaps and lotions.

Haylee checked under the stall doors. No feet. We were alone. "You two planned this, didn't you?"

I tilted my head, pretending I didn't understand.

Haylee tapped a foot. "The Fraser party that just happens to include Ben Rondelson. Someone's playing matchmaker."

I grinned. "Clay. I merely went along with

it. But having met Ben, I've decided Clay has excellent taste. What do you think?"

She ran a comb through her hair. "I think he does, too." She sighed. "I also think that Ben is light-years away from looking at another woman."

"That's no reason to avoid him," I pointed out. "You're like your mothers. You can't *help* being friendly. Or sisterly."

"Great." She made a face at herself in the mirror.

"And look at it this way," I continued. "If Clay arranges events where you and Ben can be together, Clay and I will have to spend more time with each other."

"You conniving —" But she was laughing.

"Hasn't that been your goal all along?"

"Yes. You two are so slow!"

"Maybe Ben will join the fire department," I said with exaggerated enthusiasm.

"Be still my heart."

"And we could go out together after practices."

"All sweaty and messy."

Well, there was that. But Clay seemed to like me no matter what I got into, and if I assessed Ben correctly after such a short acquaintance, he could be as tolerant as Clay . . .

The door to the ladies' room banged

open, and Mona tottered in and removed her high heels. "Ah, that feels better. Listen, you two, what I said tonight about Max Brubaugh was in confidence. I don't want you two horning in on my plans with him."

"No problem," Haylee answered quickly. "I don't even like him."

Mona stared goggle-eyed at her and shook her head. "What's not to like? And that woman is not his girlfriend — she's his sister! So he's available." She licked her lips. "Yummy yum yum. Dibs!" She stuck a forefinger up in the air. "And don't look at me like I'm robbing the cradle — he doesn't need to know how old I am, and I'm sure he's older than Duncan, and Duncan likes me. So does his father." She attempted a girlish giggle. "But Ralph and me — now in that case, Ralph would be robbing the cradle."

Well, sort of.

"Age doesn't matter. I'll take 'em all. And just between us, Ralph has a certain something that his son lacks." She wagged her finger at us. "But what I meant was those TV show ideas are mine and I don't want you stealing them."

"Don't worry," I said. "But remember, Max Brubaugh has already been in some of our shops" — Opal's and mine, anyway —

"so he may have his own ideas about Threadville stories."

"He'd better not." She cocked her head. "The music's starting. I need to get out there."

If she could hardly walk, how was she going to dance?

She had a solution. Shoes in hand, she wandered out barefoot.

Haylee heaved a dramatic sigh after the door closed and we were alone in the ladies' room again. "There go *all* my chances with Ben."

"Nah," I said. "She's after Max first. Then Ben. We should go out there before she claims him, too, though."

Haylee laughed. "She's really chalking them up tonight — Ralph, Duncan, Max, and Ben, so far."

"And she's already told me if I wasn't interested in Clay, she'd take him."

"Clay really likes *you.*"

We gave each other a high five and left the ladies' room.

Turning the corner toward the banquet hall, I heard a waltz. I hurried, but stopped in the doorway when I saw the dancers. My excitement withered.

Ben and Zara were dancing together. The

stately pair were head and shoulders above everyone else on the dance floor.

33

Clay's and my plans to throw Ben and Haylee together might be too late.

Ben danced gracefully for such a big man. Zara snaked her right hand up to his neck. Squaring his jaw, he again took her hand in his and clasped her in the classical waltz position.

Beside me, Haylee muttered, "His grief for his wife might be easier to compete with than *that.*"

"Don't give up," I murmured. "He looks embarrassed."

"Right. Without even getting to know him, I've gone from friendly to sisterly to . . . well, um . . . and the entire relationship is all in my mind."

"It's a start."

She laughed. "I guess so."

Edna floated by in Gord's arms. He was humming. The crystals and flashing lights on Edna's dress couldn't compete with the glow in her eyes as she smiled up at him.

Barefoot, fluttering her eyelashes at Ralph, Mona danced past us.

Duncan appeared at Haylee's elbow and swung her into the waltz, and a trained broadcaster's voice said in my ear, "May I have this dance?"

Max.

I would have preferred dancing with Clay, but Clay was striding toward the band and probably didn't know that Haylee and I had returned from the ladies' room.

Max was a good dancer, light on his feet, and he didn't hold me too tightly. I relaxed and concentrated on following him. And tried not to concentrate on wondering how well Clay danced. Except for Max, Ben, and Gord, most of the male dancers appeared uncomfortable with waltzing.

"How long have you known Haylee?" Max asked me.

"Over ten years. We worked together in New York City."

"Where you were both financial advisers."

"Yes."

"And you two did some investigating and blew the whistle on your boss?" He sounded amused.

"Yes."

"That cousin of mine is really something."

"Yes." Maybe I should think of another word.

"How long have you known my aunt Opal?" he asked.

"About two years." There, I'd increased my vocabulary.

"You have no idea how thrilled I am to find her, and to discover that my family was wrong about her living on the streets. Their story didn't match my memories of her, but I was only three, so I figured I may have not known some bad things. Turned out, my memories were right, and my family's stories were . . ." His sigh seemed genuine. "Fabrications."

"Opal's a wonderful person."

"I hoped she'd be here tonight."

Maybe he could have invited her, I thought uncharitably.

"I asked her to come," he said as if I'd spoken aloud, "but she said she had something else tonight."

"Storytelling evening. Lots of us are missing it, but she can't. She hosts it."

"Naomi's not here, either? I haven't seen her."

"No."

"But Edna is. Has she been dating that man for long?"

"Several months."

His questions made me uneasy, like he was an imposter and would use the information I gave him to "prove" to Opal that he was the adult version of the three-year-old Max Brubaugh she remembered.

I was saved by the end of the tune. And by Clay, heading purposefully toward me.

Max — or whoever he really was — might as well have dissolved. All I noticed was Clay, and the smile in his eyes as he took my hand in his. The music started slowly, but sped up, and soon I was laughing and twirling under Clay's arm, spinning away from him and being reeled in close.

Gord had grabbed Zara. She towered over him, but the man had all the moves, and she kept up.

Ben bowed down to talk to Edna. She waved her hand in front of her face as if fanning herself and pointed him to Haylee. A little heavy-handed of her, but it worked, and the next thing I knew, three couples were flying around the hall, all of us smiling, while most of the rest of the crowd backed off and watched.

Mona hauled Max out onto the dance floor, and they did a reasonable job of keeping up with the music.

By the time the dance ended, I was giddy. Gord claimed me for a tango, which we hammed up with great glee but sober faces. Clay and Haylee danced together, Ralph took Edna out onto the floor, and Zara dragged Duncan, who blushed furiously, into the melee. Ben danced with an older woman I didn't know, and Max danced with Mona again.

I yearned to dance with Clay again, but like Ben and Gord, he seemed to be trying to dance with every woman in the banquet hall. After dancing with Zara, Duncan took turns between me, Haylee, and Mona, while his father danced with the three of us and with many of the other women as well.

I wanted Ben to dance with Haylee again, but he kept choosing other partners.

During a break, Clay asked me, "Will you save the last dance for me?"

I nodded gladly. The band struck up "Bridge over Troubled Water" and I grabbed his hand. "Will you dance this one with me? It's your song."

He gave me a questioning look. "Sure."

As he took me in his arms, I said, "Don't I remember you once suggesting I should use a bridge to cross a river?"

He laughed and pulled me closer. I wanted to tell him that he was like my bridge, too, always concerned about me, but I couldn't bring myself to do it. I melted into him, his arms tightened around me, and we danced in silence until almost the end of the song, when I asked him, "How are we going to get Ben and Haylee together? I like him a lot, and she does, too."

He bent to murmur in my ear, "He was going to ask her for the last dance."

"I hope he did," I whispered, shivering at the memory of his lips against my ear, "and that she hasn't already agreed to dance it with someone else."

"If she did, you and I will have to find another way to throw them together."

I smiled up at him. "Okay."

The last chords sounded. Clay pulled me into a bear hug and rested his face in my hair for a second, and I could have sworn he brushed a kiss against the top of my head. The evening was going very well.

Ralph and I did a fast dance together, and after several more fast dances with men I didn't know, Ben claimed me for a slow dance.

Good. I could talk to him. I congratulated him on how well the gala was going.

He took a deep breath. "I was afraid it wouldn't. Neil Ondover was going to supply the bread and baked desserts, and you know what happened to him. All of us are new here, and to top it off, one of my kitchen staff disappeared."

I backed away to look up into his eyes. "Disappeared?"

"Didn't show up for work and hasn't answered her phone."

"Did you contact the police?"

"I didn't think she was missing like that. She was renting a cottage on the beach, so I wasn't surprised that she gave up a summer job. Probably got one somewhere else."

"A college kid?" I suggested.

"No. A middle-aged woman."

"Was her name by any chance Yolanda Smith?" I probed.

"Do you know her?"

"No, but I know of her. Which day did she fail to show up?"

"Sunday morning."

I nearly tripped. "But that was —"

"The morning Neil Ondover's body was found. I know."

The morning that Neil's body was found *in my yard.* And, perhaps more to the point, it was also the morning that somebody dumped two kittens in or near my yard, two kittens that I suspected had been staying in Yolanda's cottage.

34

As Ben expertly led me through the dance steps, I looked around the banquet hall. Where were Chief Smallwood and Detective Gartener when I really needed them? I said, "The police would probably be interested in hearing that Yolanda disappeared the day Neil's body was found."

Ben looked contrite. "I've been planning this evening and getting the lodge and dining room up and running. And I needed to find new staff, plus extras for tonight. I will tell the police, I promise."

"Chief Smallwood doesn't actually bite."

He missed a step. "She looks like she might."

I had to laugh. "She's tough. She has to be. But she's fair. Did you get someone to take Yolanda's place?"

"Yes, and she's a better worker than Yolanda, but —"

"But?"

"She was Neil's assistant at La Bakery. But don't worry. I don't think Cassie's a murderer." His grin held a spark of mischief. "Unlike Chief Smallwood, Cassie doesn't even *look* like she could bite! And I don't plan to suffer the same fate her last — I mean previous — boss did."

"You'll be careful?" I asked.

He had a deep, lazy laugh. "I'm not worried. It's no wonder Clay likes you so much."

I was appreciating Ben more and more. If only he would dance with Haylee . . .

To my gratification, he claimed her for the next slow dance. While I shuffled around the floor with Duncan, I glanced at Haylee and Ben every chance I got, but Duncan seemed to be keeping them in his sights, too, which meant he kept turning my back toward them.

Haylee and Ben both looked very serious, and Duncan was practically morose. He didn't say a thing except for a terse thank-you as we parted.

I was glad that my next dance was with Duncan's father. Ralph kept up a cheerful patter about costumes. We conspired to tackle Edna for information about adding batteries and electric circuits to fabrics, clothing, and costumes.

Outside, twilight turned to darkness. Inside, reflections of candle flames sparkled from the wall of glass doors leading to the porch. The last dance was called, and I was in Clay's arms, next to Ben and Haylee. For a while, the four of us danced side by side, chatting, then Clay moved us into the crowd and held me close, gripping my right hand against his chest. I didn't want the dance to end.

"Thank you for a wonderful evening, Willow," he murmured.

I smiled my thanks up into his eyes, but the serious question in them made me turn my face away. Yes, I would welcome a kiss from him.

But not then and there. Later, after he took me home and we were alone.

He seemed to understand, and spread his fingers out on my back.

Every good thing had to come to an end. The music stopped. Clay let go of me, but we still faced each other. He gently placed his hands on my shoulders and stroked his thumbs across the hollow of my throat. "None of those necklaces we found could make you look more beautiful than you already do," he said.

"I'll bet those women whose necklaces were stolen didn't have nearly as nice an evening as I've had."

He moved his hands down to my shoulders. "Rumor has it that their party was completely ruined. But they probably got over it after the insurance settlement. Their husbands were jewelers, after all."

"I wonder if any of them will buy their jewelry back from the insurance company."

He squeezed my shoulders. "You're a romantic, aren't you?"

"What's wrong with that?"

He lifted my chin with a forefinger. "Absolutely nothing."

I backed away and gestured at the banquet hall, bright with twinkling candles. "It's this beautiful room, and the lake and stars outside."

And Haylee and Ben across the room, seriously discussing something. A date, I hoped.

I'd forgotten Fred until he walked up to us. He was carrying his clarinet case. "You kids need a ride?"

Clay looked down at me. "What do you think? Feel like a ride or like strolling back along the beach?"

"The beach, definitely," I said. In only one evening, I had become a hopeless romantic.

Now, if only Ben would decide to see Haylee home . . .

I returned to our table for the evening bag I'd embroidered and decorated with crystals I'd bought from Edna. Clay came with me, and Haylee met us there. Without, I was sorry to see, Ben.

Clay asked Haylee if she'd like to walk home along the beach. "Or I can grab Fred — he'll drive us back to Threadville."

"The beach would be great," she said.

I glanced toward Ben, who was tidying the buffet table.

Haylee tossed her hair back. "He has to stay here. Not that I asked him, or anything. I know this evening means a lot to him. It's been perfect, and he'll want to end it on that note."

Carrying her shoes, Mona was hanging around Ben. Max had disappeared, but Zara looked ready to accost Ben, too. Ralph waited patiently for Mona, but when Duncan saw us heading for the doors leading to the wide front porch, he followed. Ben watched, but made no move to join us. I waved and he nodded. His eyes had gone serious again. I hoped he wasn't choosing that moment to mourn his wife.

Clay opened the French doors. We walked down to the beach. By the time my toes were in the water lapping on the sand, Ralph and Mona had joined Clay, Duncan,

Haylee, and me.

I turned around. A man stood outside the kitchen end of the lodge. I couldn't be certain, but I thought it was Detective Gartener. No one else had quite that military, watchful bearing.

At the other end of the lodge, moonlight showed a dark-uniformed figure beside a tree trunk. I caught a glimpse of blond hair beneath a police hat. Vicki Smallwood? She seemed to be keeping that tree between her and the lodge, and she also seemed to be watching us. I gave a tentative wave, but she turned away and peeked around the trunk toward the lodge.

What were Detective Gartener and our police chief doing?

"Let's run!" Haylee called, splashing through the shallows. Duncan jogged beside her, and Clay and I caught up, leaving Mona to stroll at a more sedate pace with Ralph.

Haylee and I put our sandals on again to walk along the marina's boardwalk and through the wharf's asphalt parking lot, but beyond the wharf, we came to the larger, cottage-lined beach and removed our shoes.

The moon was bright enough for us to search for flat stones to skip, though we didn't find many. I stopped near the cottage

Yolanda had rented and pretended to look for stones. I managed a reasonable visual survey of the cottage. Still no sign that anyone was staying there. Yellow tape fluttered in the breeze.

We left the beach at Lake Street. Haylee and I put on our sandals and walked up the hill with Clay and Duncan. Mona and Ralph had lagged so far behind we could no longer see them. As we passed Naomi's shop, Batty about Quilts, Duncan looked across the street toward Country Chic and said, "Mona invited us in for coffee. Want to come?"

All three of us declined. If Mona had wanted us at her party, she'd have asked us herself.

Besides, it was late, around two, and I was hoping for a few minutes, at least, alone with Clay after we saw Haylee safely to her door.

Duncan said good night and loped off toward Country Chic.

I glanced across the street toward In Stitches. Something moved on my front porch.

Had I imagined it? I squinted into shadows beyond the door.

Setting a rocking chair thumping, someone vaulted over the far side of the low wall surrounding the porch.

35

The person who had fled my porch crashed down through bushes beside the foundation. Branches snapped.

Hoping the intruder would jump up and run away, preferably far from me, I stood stock-still with my hand over my mouth.

Clay, however, sprinted across the street toward the side of my porch where the person would have landed.

Haylee pulled me out of my shocked stupor. "Come on."

Tiptoeing across my yard, I heard leaves rustle and a distinctly female squeal. "Leave me alone!"

"Who are you," Clay growled, "and what are you doing here?"

"I could ask you the same thing." Cassie's voice, tart with fear. She cowered among hostas with leaves the size of unfurled umbrellas.

Clay stood over her, not touching her, but

looking tall and formidable in his navy blue suit.

Cassie struggled through the giant leaves toward me. "Willow, can I talk to you?" She was breathing quickly. She brushed her hands down her denim cutoffs, and then childishly swiped the back of a fist across her eyes. Light from the streetlamps and the moon showed tears welling up in her eyes. "Please? You can come, too, Haylee." She must have retrieved the pink plaid shirt from the cottage deck before Gartener got there with his search team. It looked like it had been washed by hand and dried in a heap.

Clay didn't budge.

"Where?" Haylee asked.

"Can we go into your shop, Willow?" She glanced from me to Haylee. "I need to talk to you two. Alone."

As if she hadn't added that last word, Clay asked her, "Why were you hiding on Willow's porch?"

Cassie took a deep, shaky breath. "I wasn't hiding from *Willow.*"

I put my hand on Clay's sleeve. The muscles of his forearm were hard with tension. "You don't have to worry about Clay." I sounded surprisingly calm and reassuring. "He's a friend, and I'd like him to come

324

inside with us." I knew there was no way he'd leave us alone with her.

She gulped. A car whooshed up Lake Street. Except for her noticeable trembling, Cassie didn't move until it passed. "Can we go inside, now? Quickly?"

That car had frightened her. She was hiding from someone, either on foot as we had been, or in a car. I noticed that she stayed between us — all of us were taller than she was — as we rushed up the stairs and onto my porch. I unlocked the shop door. Clay opened it for us.

Instead of staying in their nice, comfy beds, Sally and Tally must have climbed the stairs. They whimpered on the other side of the apartment door. The kittens were probably with them.

"It's okay, guys," I called toward them.

"Don't turn on any lights," Cassie squeaked.

Haylee asked, "Why not?"

Cassie wailed, "I don't want anyone seeing me!"

I'd had enough of these cloak-and-dagger heroics. "I need to turn on some lights, or you three will trip over things." I touched Cassie's elbow. "I'll guide you to a seat at a sewing machine where you won't be visible from outside."

"Really, all I want to do is borrow a phone," she objected. "I . . . forgot mine."

Leaving Haylee and Clay by the front door, I started Cassie toward the rows of sewing and embroidery machines in my shop. "And you don't want to go back for it?"

She shuddered. "No."

"Weren't you working at the lodge tonight?" How could the cleanup be done already?

"Yes, but the . . . someone was looking for . . ." She corrected herself. "*Stalking* me. I crawled out a window."

I suspected she'd been about to say the police had been looking for her, but thought better of it and changed her words. This was quickly going from bad to worse. "Who was stalking you?" I asked.

"Someone who wanted to hurt me."

Which didn't necessarily eliminate the police. "Sit down here and I'll turn on just enough light for Clay and Haylee to see where they're going."

"A phone?" she whispered.

"Just a second." I ran to the switches beside the front door and turned on lights near the back of the shop.

Clay and Haylee marched to an arm's length — their arms, not Cassie's shorter

326

ones — of Cassie and lounged against sewing tables. Haylee managed to look dangerous despite, or maybe because of, the smashing periwinkle silk dress. Clay folded his arms and stared down at the disconsolate young woman in front of him.

This was not the romantic ending I had visualized for the evening. I grabbed the cordless landline phone off its cradle and handed it to Cassie.

"Thank you," she murmured. "Is it okay if I make a long-distance call?"

"*How* long-distance?" Haylee asked.

"Cleveland. I'll pay you back, Willow." A smudge of dirt on one cheek added to her girlish appearance.

"Don't worry about it. My phone plan covers it."

I noticed that she didn't need to look up the number. Her fingers shook as she pressed buttons.

I went around to the next aisle to put bolts of fabric between us and give her some semblance of privacy, although I could still see and hear her. Haylee came with me, but Clay paced only a few sewing machines away from Cassie and appeared to be studying one of the hardanger examples displayed in an embroidery machine's hoop.

Cassie partially covered her mouth with a

hand. "Hi," she said quietly. "It's me." Her voice was soft, but her tone wasn't. "You have to come to Elderberry Bay." She listened for a second. I couldn't make out the other person's words, but the voice sounded deeper than most women's voices and higher than most men's voices. If I'd had to bet on it, I'd have said Cassie was conversing with a woman. Cassie whined, "No, really. You have to come back. Just take my word for it. None of this would have happened if you hadn't —"

The woman said something.

Cassie shut her eyes and muttered between her teeth, "I would have been fine. He wouldn't have hurt me. Didn't hurt me." She glanced up toward me, hovering beyond the rack of linen. Tears ran down her cheeks. "He didn't do *anything*. If you hadn't meddled —"

Listening to the other person, she took deep sobbing breaths. "Fine," she blurted. "When they allow me my one phone call, it won't be to you. You don't care. I don't suppose you even know of a good lawyer." Bitterness mixed with hurt in her voice, yet she didn't seem surprised at the other person's reaction. I suspected it wasn't the first time that person had dashed Cassie's hopes.

Cassie paled as she listened to a rapid-fire rant. Finally, she cried out, "I didn't do anything! But you did. And you're going to let me go to jail for what *you* —"

The woman on the other end must have interrupted her again. Cassie ducked her head and sagged down in her seat. Barely controlling sobs, she grated out, "And I wouldn't visit you in jail, either."

Carefully, she disconnected the call. Head still down and shoulders shaking, she held out the phone. "Here, Willow. Thanks," she managed.

I took the phone from her limp little hand. "What's wrong, Cassie?" From what I'd understood, not much was right.

Haylee found a box of tissues and handed it to her. Clay stood nearby, silent, not threatening, and ready, as always, to help. That last dance seemed like eons ago.

Even the dogs had become quiet.

Cassie wiped her eyes, blew her nose, and raised her chin. She stared somewhere between us. "Well, that was useless. I should have known. Sorry for wasting your time, Willow. I'll pay you back as soon as I find my purse." Her mouth twisted.

I didn't want to pry, but Haylee had no qualms. "What was that about, Cassie? What was all that talk about jail?"

36

Cassie must have wanted to hide the trembling of her hands. She clamped them between her knees. "I'm scared the police want to arrest me. I tore something up and threw it away, but the police must have gotten hold of it and put it together. It . . . it showed a reason why I might have been tempted to kill my . . . my boss. Neil. But I didn't, and I wouldn't have."

Tore it up and threw it away — the last will and testament of Neil Ondover? And I'd found the pieces in a garbage bag outside the cottage where I'd seen Cassie, and, later, the pink plaid shirt she was again wearing? As I understood it, Neil had known Cassie only about two weeks. During that time, had he written a will in her favor?

But if that were true, why would she tear it up and throw it away? Maybe he had changed his mind and written a new will that cut her out, and that's the one she had destroyed.

Clay urged, "Talk to the police." His empathy made me want to hug him. Actually, there were lots of reasons I wanted to hug him. Instead, I focused on Cassie.

She sniffled. "They'll arrest me and put me in jail for a crime I didn't do."

"What makes you think that?" I asked. Vicki could be difficult, but she wasn't irrational.

A tear wandered through the smudge on Cassie's cheek. She looked younger than ever. And nearly desperate. "They were hanging around the lodge this evening, watching for me to come out. I . . . I ran away. I thought I'd be safe with you, Willow."

The accusation was flattering, in a way, unless she actually believed I would harbor a criminal.

Clay flicked me a glance that warmed me. "People do feel safe with Willow. And they are. But are you sure they were watching for you and not for someone else?"

Cassie rubbed her fist in her eye. "Yes. One of the other kitchen staff went outside for a smoke and some cop asked if I was inside. My friend — or I thought he was a friend — said I was, then he came inside and warned me, so I crawled out the bathroom window. I couldn't go back where I was staying." She wiped her eyes. "I ran here."

Haylee grabbed for a sewing machine as if to support herself. "Maybe they just wanted to talk to you, ask a few questions."

Cassie bit her lip. "Maybe. But it scared me."

The phone was still warm from her touch. I offered it to her again. "Call them and ask if they want to talk to you. If they say no, you can stop worrying. If they say yes, tell them where you are."

She held me with that clear gaze. "Should I?"

"Yes," Haylee answered.

"I'm not a lawyer or anything," Clay said, "but I agree."

"We'll stay with you until they leave," I promised, tilting my head in question toward Haylee and Clay.

They nodded.

Cassie twisted her hands in her lap. "I guess I could."

I offered, "I'll dial Chief Smallwood for you." Vicki didn't answer, so I left a message. "Cassie is at In Stitches with Haylee, Clay, and me, and she's heard that you want to talk to her. Can you give me a call?"

When I was done, I patted Cassie's shoulder. "Sorry I didn't get a yes or no after all."

"Maybe I should just go," Cassie suggested, "or you three might wait all night for nothing."

I shook my head. "Chief Smallwood will phone back. Who did you call earlier? Was it Yolanda?"

Cassie shot me a suspicious glance, which wasn't surprising. Maybe she'd seen me prowling around Yolanda's cottage. "How do you know Yolanda? She didn't stick around Elderberry Bay very long."

"I was curious about who provided the asparagus that made so many people sick, and I figured out which cottage she'd been renting. Didn't I see you inside it one night?"

She started to shake her head.

I pressed, "Monday night, right before you came here to wait for me on my porch? You said you'd seen me on the beach."

"Yes, that was me in my . . . that was me you saw in Yolanda's cottage. She gave me the key so I could use it until the rent ran out. But she had already left Elderberry Bay."

"How do you know?" Haylee asked.

"I had a fight with her about it. I said she

333

should stay and confess about the asparagus. She said it smelled, but I don't think she bothered to wash it very well before she served it raw to people. She bought it from some guy named Brad. She said he was a farmer, but she was lying. I can always tell, with her." A casual acquaintance would not have sounded as bitter.

Remembering the man that Haylee and I had seen gathering armloads of asparagus in a field that reeked of manure, I suggested, "Maybe she guessed that Brad had stolen it, and she didn't want to admit that she may have bought and sold stolen produce." And she'd handled that asparagus, too, ick.

"Yeah, maybe," Cassie agreed with a sad little shrug, "but that doesn't make it much better, does it? I found Brad's address written on the telephone pad in her cottage. He may be a farmer, but his address is in the village."

I didn't know anyone named Brad, but I hardly knew villagers who weren't Threadville customers or fellow firefighters. "Is Yolanda —" I wasn't sure how to word it so that she wouldn't feel worse. "A relative?"

"Yeah."

"Your mother?" Haylee asked.

"How did you find that out?" Cassie wasn't very good at hiding things. At least not her relationship with Yolanda. But maybe she was hiding other important things. Like that she had murdered Neil. Or that she suspected who had. From the half of the conversation I'd eavesdropped on, and from the pain in Cassie's eyes, I guessed that the girl was afraid that her mother had murdered her boss.

"I guessed," Haylee answered. "She's older than you, and you sounded like you were talking to someone you knew well. Some mothers and daughters develop that, well, a certain *tone* with each other."

"Hateful, you mean," Cassie spat out. "We don't get along."

That was obvious, if each of them was going to blame the other for Neil's death.

"My mother didn't kill Neil, if that's what you're thinking." Again, I felt pity for Cassie and the bitter edge in her voice whenever she mentioned her mother. "She left early Sunday morning. I said she should stay and confess about the asparagus, but she just laughed and said no one would find her in Cleveland. Our last name is Turcotte, but she told everyone here she was Yolanda Smith. She made it up. Anyway, she said I was finally going to get my own way and stay here with my . . . new job."

Neil beaming proudly at Cassie, and possibly writing a will that mentioned her . . . Cassie resembled Neil more than she resembled Yolanda. As Neil had been, Cassie was slight and wiry, with gray eyes, freckles, and curly brown hair. I asked softly, "Did you almost say your father? Was Neil your father?"

She covered her face and struggled to control her sobs. "Yes, he was," she finally managed between her fingers. "And I only just got to know him. My mother's second husband adopted me, but I don't remember him, either. I was raised to believe that my real father, Neil Ondover, was a terrible person. My mother took me with her and left him when I was a baby, and she took me and left my adoptive father, too, and as far as I know, he died a long time ago. She threw a hissy fit when I told her that I'd found out where my real father lived and that I was going to go work in his bakery. She said I would become just like him. But you knew him. He was nice. He cared about people. *She* doesn't." She hiccupped. "If either one of them was abusive in that relationship, it had to be her, not him. It's all so unfair. He died before he even got to *know* me. He probably didn't even like me."

"He did," I said. "I could tell by his face when you were talking to us at the bakery tent on Saturday night."

"Yeah, well, I guess he did, but two weeks is not long enough to get to know your father."

"It's more than some people have," Haylee muttered.

Cassie gave her a sharp look.

"But I have three mothers, all of whom spoil me," Haylee admitted.

And they all got along with Haylee better than Cassie's mother got along with her. "My kittens," I asked, using the word "my" to show I wasn't giving them up to anyone who dumped them or who knew that someone else had gotten rid of them and had not done anything about it. "Were they Yolanda's?"

"I don't know what she was thinking, buying kittens. She can't keep them in her apartment in Cleveland. So I guess she just dropped them off in the street the night she drove away. She probably knew that one of you Threadville ladies would take them in."

I doubted that Yolanda had cared about the kittens. Maybe they'd only been possessions she could get rid of the moment they got in her way.

I *really* didn't like Yolanda.

I also suspected that she'd done a few

337

other things before she drove away that night.

She could have poisoned Neil, wrapped him in quilt batting, pinned the batting shut with knitting needles, driven his body up the riverside trail, trampled the snow fencing, dragged the batting-wrapped body into my yard, dumped it in the hole, and shoveled dirt over it.

Yolanda would have needed to leave car doors open while she hauled Neil's body out and attempted to bury it. Maybe the inquisitive kittens had jumped out of her car that night and she didn't know, didn't care, or didn't dare take time to round them up.

Poor Cassie. Yolanda was a very unpleasant person, to say the least. I hoped that the woman would never return to Elderberry Bay except under heavy police escort.

As if my thinking about police had conjured some up, Detective Gartener and Chief Smallwood walked quietly onto my porch.

37

I beckoned to Vicki and Gartener and mouthed, "Come in." They did. My sea glass chimes jangled. Vicki switched on the rest of my shop lights, causing me to blink in the sudden brightness.

Cassie seemed to shrink within herself. She didn't get along with her mother, but would she protect her from the police? Would she tell them everything she'd told us?

"Cassie Turcotte!" Vicki's authoritative police chief voice rang out, as startling as my door chimes at three in the morning.

Cassie struggled to her feet. "Yes." Below the short sleeves of that wrinkled shirt, goose bumps popped out on her forearms.

Gartener asked in gentle and very resonant tones, "Did you want to talk to us?"

She shrugged. Although her arms were muscular, her shoulders were so thin that they resembled blades, and something like a knife twisted in my stomach. I wanted to protect this woman who was really little more than a child, who hadn't lived a very happy life, and who had, perhaps, only been trying to make herself and her father happier.

"I heard you were looking for me," Cassie mumbled toward her feet.

"We were." Vicki seemed to relish playing bad cop.

Gartener could do it, too, especially if Vicki wasn't around. Mostly, though, he seemed to stay silent and observe, especially when he wanted to make someone uncomfortable enough to confess — to just about anything. This time, he said in a friendly way, "We have some questions for you."

I was going to be very interested in those questions, and in Cassie's answers.

"Okay." Cassie was trembling again, and so was her voice.

"We'd like you to come with us," Vicki added.

Cassie folded her arms as if the action could control her shuddering. "Do I have to?"

"No," Vicki snapped, "but if you refuse, we'll arrest you, and then instead of going to my office here in Elderberry Bay, you'll have a nice long ride to state police headquarters in Erie with Detective Gartener."

Cassie glanced at me. "Can Willow come?"

The poor thing, I thought, *barely more than a kid.* I stepped forward.

Gartener held up his hand. "Just you, Cassie. Do you have ID you can show us?"

She shoved her hands into the front pockets of her cutoffs. "Not with me."

She looked so miserable that I answered for her. "She left her phone at the lodge where she was working in the kitchen. Your wallet, too, Cassie?"

"Yes," the girl whispered.

Vicki rolled her eyes as if telling me to butt out.

"They're fine," Gartener said. "Ben locked them in the safe in the lodge."

I had a nervous desire to giggle. The safe in the lodge? Where all that jewelry had definitely *not* been safe thirty years ago?

Smallwood and Gartener guided Cassie toward my front door. Between the two officers, Cassie looked diminished and forlorn.

"Vicki . . . Chief Smallwood?" I called.

She barely turned her head. "What?"

All I could think of saying was, "Kittens." I meant, "Try to be like Sally and look after young and helpless creatures." But I couldn't tell Vicki what to do, and she probably wouldn't appreciate it if I did.

"I'll talk to you tomorrow, Willow," Vicki said. "After we clear this up and get some sleep." Maybe she thought I was offering the kittens to her.

"Cassie can tell you who provided that asparagus —"

Cassie wrenched herself around to face me. "Don't tell *anyone* what I said." Her twisted face and tone were strangely fierce.

None of us could promise, and Vicki and Gartener ushered Cassie out the door and across the porch. Was Cassie sacrificing herself to save her mother, or trying to make *certain* that the police would interrogate us, and then Cassie wouldn't have to accuse her mother directly?

"I should go, too," Clay said. "I'm supposed to be at a construction site in four hours."

"Cancel it," Haylee and I both said at the same time. Unfortunately, my romantic mood seemed to have evaporated.

Clay looked as tired and dispirited as I felt. "I wish I could. Walk you home, Haylee?"

"No, thanks. It's only across the street, and Neil's murderer is either in Cleveland or —" She pointed outside. "In police custody."

That was possibly true, unless the culprit

was Neil's former girlfriend, Bitsy, hiding out at Lazy Daze Campground and plotting how to continue getting away with murder. "I'll watch until Haylee locks herself in," I said. "Do you need a ride home, Clay? It's kind of late to call Fred."

"No need — he met me at the beach parking lot this evening. My truck was still there when we walked past a while ago." He rested one hand on my shoulder and the other on Haylee's. He gave my shoulder a squeeze. "Thank you both for coming to the gala with me. Talk to you later." He waved and went out the door behind the others. The chimes jingled and subsided into silence.

I heaved a tremulous sigh.

"I'm sorry," Haylee said. "The evening was a total bust."

"No it wasn't. I had a *great* time. Until —" I nodded toward Vicki's cruiser easing away from the curb. All I could see of Cassie was the profile of her lowered head.

"What?" Haylee asked me. "Are you feeling sorry for Cassie? What if she murdered her own father?"

"What if she didn't? What if she spends the rest of her life in jail, serving a sentence that someone else — maybe her mother — should serve? What if her mother goes on a murderous rampage and kills other innocent people?"

"How many ex-husbands do you think Yolanda hates?"

"I'd like to know what — or who — killed Cassie's adoptive father, what's-his-name Turcotte."

Haylee tapped the toe of her sandal on my polished black walnut floor. "I told you there was something off about Cassie, last time we saw her."

"Unless she was lying, she was too young to have murdered Turcotte. But now we know what she was hiding that night, don't we?" I asked.

"What?"

"That Neil was her father and Yolanda was her mother."

Haylee scoffed, "She didn't have to hide any of that."

That was true. "She's young."

Haylee yawned. "Vicki and Gartener will have to figure it out. But I agree with you about Yolanda. If nothing else, she deserves to be arrested for poisoning half the community and for generally being a horrible person."

"And I'll bet she murdered Neil. Even if she didn't dump those kittens, even if they escaped and she didn't notice at the time,

Yolanda didn't do anything to find them. She just drove away, and abandoned her daughter, who's only about twenty-two, to cope with everything, including the murder of the father she'd met only recently. Yolanda is not only horrible, she's evil, and if Vicki and Gartener don't come to that conclusion, I'll . . . I'll —"

My diatribe seemed to have amused Haylee. "You'll what?"

"Well, for starters, I intend to report everything Cassie told us tonight."

"What a night." Haylee patted her hand over another yawn.

"Why did you say it was a total bust?"

"I didn't expect to meet the man of my dreams and have him come running after me with glass slippers or anything, but then to meet a guy like Ben and discover he's way beyond my reach . . ." She wrapped her arms around herself. "It's disappointing."

"He's not beyond your reach. He likes you. He danced with you."

"The first time, he told me about the lodge being his late wife's dream, and then about everything he'd been doing to follow her plans. I can't compete with his memories of her. He obviously loved her very much."

"He's a good man."

"I know, and his devotion makes him even more appealing. But there's other competition, too. Zara —"

"He asked *you* for the last dance."

"And then there's Mona." With great exaggeration, she moaned the first syllable of Mona's name.

I laughed, both at her pronunciation and the memory of Mona's persistence in chasing Ben around the banquet hall to talk him into her schemes. "The poor guy — he tried to give her some attention, but I could tell he wasn't impressed about her calling his lodge 'ho-hum' and he also wasn't about to hire her to redecorate a lodge he's already finished decorating."

"But he hasn't finished decorating it." Haylee's eyes glinted with excitement. "The last dance with him wasn't romantic, if you discount what a good dancer he is, and being in his arms — mmmmm — but at least he didn't go on and on about how he missed his wife. We talked about decorating the lodge, instead. He wants you and me to help him with some of the recreation rooms he's outfitting."

"Us? Why?"

"He found an entire stash of old photos, and he would like you and me to visit the lodge, go through the pictures, and choose the most interesting ones for him to enlarge, frame, and hang."

I clapped my hands. "Aha! He wants to see you again!"

"I'm not sure."

I insisted, "He does!"

"And you," she pointed out.

"Yeah, well, maybe he figured that was a good way to get you to do it. Besides, he's probably heard of my excellent taste when it comes to interior decorating."

She glanced up at my soaring white cathedral ceilings. "Your shop *is* beautiful."

I let out a gurgle of laughter. "Yes, because *you* designed it and Clay carried out your plans!"

"But I wanted you to fall for it, and I knew your taste."

"And Ben probably figures you'll know his, too. When does he want us to come?"

"ASAP. Before Mona discovers he actually does have some empty walls in the lodge. He suggested tomorrow night." She glanced at the clock. "That would be tonight. I guess we should try to get some sleep, if we can unwind."

"That means he doesn't have a Saturday night date with Zara!"

She dampened my enthusiasm. "He didn't

say *he* was going to look through the old photos with us."

"But we'll definitely see him."

Smiling, she turned around and walked toward the door. "Yes. He's adorable."

I agreed, said good-bye, and watched until she safely crossed Lake Street and let herself into The Stash.

Finally, I went down to my apartment. The animals frisked about, welcoming me home. I took them outside, into the part of my yard we were allowed to use. I knew from past experience that the investigators might not release the crime scene for weeks.

I crawled into bed. I didn't know about the dogs and kittens, but I was exhausted and fell asleep almost immediately.

38

To my surprise, I managed to wake up in time to rush through the morning chores and open the shop.

What had happened to Cassie during what was left of the night after Vicki and Gartener took her away? Had they questioned her, sent her back to Lazy Daze, and then sent someone to arrest her mother? Would anything ever go well for that girl? Perhaps what bothered me most was having no way of reaching her except through the police. I didn't want Cassie to think that no one would ever give her the benefit of the doubt.

Luckily, Ashley's wide-eyed fervor kept our students occupied. I hoped that while worrying about the twenty-two-year-old Cassie, I wasn't leaning too heavily on Ashley, who was only sixteen. She seemed to thrive at the job, though. She'd gained confidence.

Halfway through the morning, Clay called.

"I just wanted to hear your voice," he said.

What was I supposed to say? I probably managed something like a grunt. Very romantic.

"And to thank you again for last night," he added.

"Thank you, too. It was wonderful." I told him about Haylee's and my plans with Ben for that evening.

"Our matchmaking worked?"

"I'm not sure yet. Ben may need more time to grieve and heal before he can be interested in another woman."

"At least the three of us can be around when and if he needs to talk."

"Starting tonight, with Haylee and me."

"I wish I could join you, but I'm working late on a house we're building down toward Erie. After we finish that, I'll have more time to create occasions for Ben and Haylee to get to know each other."

"Haylee and I walk the dogs on the beach most evenings, to the ice cream stand and back."

"I'm missing out on a lot."

He didn't know the half of it. Stinking of kitty litter, crawling in culverts . . .

He added, "You won't be surprised if I show up at the ice cream stand, say, around eight some evening with Ben in tow? We locals need to show him around."

I laughed. "It's a deal."

"Meanwhile, I'll swing by the lodge on my way home tonight. If your car's still there, I'll come inside to talk to you and Haylee. And Ben."

We said our good-byes and I put the phone back in its charging station. The evening was looking better and better. I'd planned to walk to the lodge, but if Clay was going to check for my car in the lodge parking lot, I'd have to drive, and drag the night out as long as I could until Clay arrived. I'd never want to leave, in case Clay would appear two minutes later. With any luck, Ben had plenty of photos for us to sort through.

Vicki showed up just before my lunch hour. She was carrying a plastic supermarket bag, not the sort of thing I was used to seeing cops carry. I took her down to the apartment. She whipped a jar of homemade raspberry jam out of the bag. "I have raspberry canes all over the back of my place," she said.

I thanked her and offered peanut butter and jam sandwiches for lunch.

"I thought you'd never ask," she teased. Together, we made our sandwiches.

With Sally-Forth's help, I left the kittens

inside and ushered Vicki out to the patio. "The kittens are yours if you want them," I told her.

Again, she said she couldn't deprive Sally of them.

I plunked my plate onto my picnic table. "Well, they're not going back to Yolanda. Or to Cassie, who could have confessed much earlier that she knew who owned them and had abandoned them."

Vicki set her plate and glass of milk down gently, but pinched her lips together in a severe frown. "Cassie may not be in a position to have pets for a very, very long time."

I could look almost as stern. "That girl didn't kill her father."

"How do you know?" Vicki challenged.

"I think her mother did it. Yolanda is mean and evil, didn't like Neil, doesn't treat Cassie well, and she left two innocent kittens outside to fend for themselves."

"But what actual evidence do you have against Yolanda?"

I blew strands of hair away from my forehead. "According to Cassie, Yolanda bought the asparagus from someone named Brad, and then failed to wash it properly. So she ended up poisoning you and Edna and a bunch of other people with some horrible bacteria. She could have gone one step further and given her ex some rat poison in his medicine. Cassie said her mother left Neil when Cassie was a baby. Yolanda remarried, someone named Turcotte, and then left him, too. Cassie thinks Turcotte died long ago. Maybe you should look into his death, if all of Yolanda's ex-husbands have been dropping off before their time."

Vicki put her sandwich on her plate, took out her notebook, and scribbled in it. "Will do. Anything else?"

"Yolanda taught Cassie that Neil was a bad man, and well, you knew Neil. He was sweet, and Cassie noticed that, too. She said that if anyone was abusive in the relationship, it would have been Yolanda, not Neil."

"So most of your opinion of Yolanda comes from the food poisoning and from what *Cassie* said?"

I defended myself. "Don't forget the sidewalk sale. Yolanda fought with that blond woman. I found out who she is, by the way. She works at Lazy Daze."

Vicki licked raspberry jam off her finger. "I figured it out, too. She's Bitsy Ingalls, the campground's owner."

"I hear she broke up with Neil, at least a year ago, and wanted him back."

Vicki gave me one of her stern looks. "Investigating again?"

"Someone told me." I didn't want to mention that I'd been in the campground at the time. Vicki would want to know why.

"So it's A-B-C?" she demanded.

"What does that mean? I didn't get much sleep last night, so I'm a bit slow today," I reminded her.

She frowned. "Neither did I, though I was standing around outside the dance instead of having fun inside like the rest of you. A-B-C. Anybody But Cassie." She gave me a weak grin. "Just kidding."

I returned an even weaker grin and a dismal argument. "Cassie seems more like a victim than a villain to me."

"Look, Willow, I understand why you identify and empathize with someone who's hardly more than a girl. You want to rescue her. I do, too, but I can't let emotion overcome reason."

And I could? "It's just that she seems so defeated. By a horrid mother, by her circumstances, by life. And she tried so hard to rise above it. She located her father. She went to work with him in his bakery. She said it was a dream job. She liked him. She wanted to get to know him better. She wouldn't have killed him."

"Maybe she's been defeated by her own choices."

354

But I wouldn't give in. "After Yolanda and Bitsy fought, Bitsy may have tried to start a fight at my table. And while all this was going on, someone shoplifted those purple knitting needles from Opal and stole the quilt batting out of Naomi's back room. Yolanda and Bitsy were going around that night causing distractions. On purpose, I suspect."

Vicki raised her eyebrows. "And you already told me that you didn't think the shoplifter and quilt-batting-lifter could have been Yolanda or Bitsy."

I saw where this was going. "I guessed they had an accomplice," I admitted reluctantly.

Vicki put her sandwich down again and flipped pages of her notebook. "And who did you tell me you figured might have been that accomplice?"

"A small woman wearing a pink plaid shirt, a woman with brown curly hair."

"Like Cassie."

"Exactly like Cassie," I agreed, though it hurt to do it.

"And you know those scraps of paper you found?"

I nodded.

"They pieced together with scraps that were still in the torn garbage bag. Neil had handwritten a new will only two days before his death. In it, he left everything he had to Cassie. The bakery business and building and all his other assets."

"Yeah, but . . ."

"Not to his ex-wife, Yolanda, or to his ex-girlfriend, Bitsy, but to his daughter, Cassie, who has educational debts, had been unemployed until she found that short-lived job with her father, and has been living in a tent and a car."

39

"So if I hadn't found those scraps and given them to Detective Gartener, you might never have searched through that garbage bag, and Cassie might still be free." Still, evidence was evidence, and I would never have withheld it. But one torn-up will couldn't serve as proof, could it? Surely, the police would need more than that to charge Cassie with murder.

Vicki gave her head a small, decisive shake. "Even if we hadn't found the pieces of that will, we would have known Cassie was Neil's heir. The will you found was a copy. We'd already taken the original from his apartment."

No wonder Gartener had been able to make out the title from the bits we'd pieced together — he'd already seen it, whole.

"An exact copy?"

"Both were handwritten, but the wording was the same."

I continued my defense of Cassie. "If Cassie needed money, why did she destroy Neil's will? Wouldn't she have gone running to his lawyer with her copy the minute he died?"

"Not if she realized we could use her inheritance to tie her to a murder."

The logic didn't quite make sense. "Then she wouldn't have killed him!"

"Lots of people act before they think."

I wasn't about to argue that with her — she would probably cite some of my behavior as proof. I asked, "Did Neil leave a lot behind?"

"He'd been saving nearly everything he had. Maybe it wouldn't be a lot to some people, but to most of us, it would be, and to Cassie, it could have seemed like a fortune that would lift her out of her debts and poverty."

"Who was his previous will made out to? Yolanda? Bitsy? Maybe Neil felt threatened by whichever one of them he left his fortune to —"

"Willow —"

I barreled on. "Maybe he feared that Yolanda or Bitsy was going to kill him for his money —"

"Willow —"

I didn't pause for breath. "Maybe he made

this new will in Cassie's favor —"

"Willow —"

"And Yolanda or Bitsy didn't know about it, and killed Neil, still hoping to inherit!"

"Willow —"

"And then Yolanda or Bitsy *found* the will where he gave everything to Cassie."

"Willow —"

"Last night, Cassie said she tore it up and threw it out, but maybe Yolanda or Bitsy really did that, and Cassie's taking the blame."

"Willow —"

"Maybe she was trying to protect her mother. Yolanda was renting that —"

"Willow —"

I was out of breath.

But Vicki wasn't. She explained calmly, "We searched for an earlier will and didn't find one. In addition, Neil used a lawyer for routine things involving his business. Shortly after Cassie came to town, Neil told his lawyer that he had never written a will, and thought he should. He said he'd look on the Internet for how to write one. We're sure the will we found was Neil's very first."

I gave Vicki my version of a baleful eye, whatever that was. "Trust you to deflate my theories."

She only laughed.

But I wasn't done questioning her. "Who witnessed the will made out to Cassie?"

"Do you have to know everything?" she countered. "If I don't tell you, will you race off and do your own investigations?"

"You never know," I warned in an ominous voice.

"Okay, it's not exactly confidential. Bitsy Ingalls and Yolanda Turcotte witnessed that will."

"Turcotte? I thought she was calling herself Smith while she was here."

"Not for this."

"Did Yolanda and Bitsy sign both copies of the will?"

"Yes."

"So they knew there were two copies." I chewed on my apple. Finally I conceded, "Cassie may not have known about the other copy."

"You've got it, Willow."

"It still doesn't make sense. Why kill him for the inheritance and then destroy what she thought was the only copy of the will?"

Vicki tilted her head. "Because after the courts were done with it, Cassie could have inherited anyway?"

"Not as much. The courts and the government would probably take a chunk."

Vicki shrugged. "But she may have

thought that if she destroyed the will, no one would realize she had a motive for killing Neil. And what was left from the lawyers and government might still be a fortune, to her. But we'd have caught up with her, eventually."

"You've charged Cassie with Neil's murder." I didn't bother to make it a question.

She held up a hand. "Not yet. We require better evidence against her before we can charge her."

"Good. Just get the murderer, okay?"

"We will. Especially if you and your friends keep out of it."

I carefully did not look at her. In the past, if I hadn't interfered in investigations, a couple of people could have gone to jail for murders they didn't commit, and the real culprits could have gone free. Vicki knew that, but if she preferred to pretend the police would have arrested the right people without my interference, I would let her.

We finished our apples, and Vicki said she had to head out toward Erie to talk to Clay.

"And Haylee?"

"I just came from there. You and she told me basically the same things."

"We were all really tired last night when Cassie came here, so we may be unclear."

"And you'd been drinking."

"Not much." Only champagne. The gala seemed like a distant memory, but a warming one.

We went up the hill and I let Vicki out my side gate.

Although I was worried about Cassie, and still believed she couldn't have killed the father she'd been happy to locate, I couldn't stop thinking about the evening ahead. I wasn't certain, since I didn't know Ben well, but he seemed like a great guy for Haylee. Someday, maybe, he would emerge from the depths of his grief, look around, and recognize that Haylee was a gem.

And maybe, if we took long enough looking at Ben's photos, Clay would show up. I could hardly wait.

Fortunately, working with our students on yet more complex hardanger embroidery projects made the afternoon fly by. After Ashley and I closed the store, I took the animals out. The kittens had already become proficient at using my garden as a litter box and then trotting inside with their self-appointed surrogate mother.

After a short, much-needed catnap and some supper, I phoned Haylee and explained that I needed to drive to the lodge so that Clay could check the parking lot on his way home from Erie. "He'll come in if he sees my car there."

Haylee understood immediately. "Then we'll need to take our time over those pictures."

And maybe Ben would spend the entire evening with Haylee . . .

I ran to the beach and back with the dogs before I met Haylee at my car.

I drove the longer way, taking Beach Row. Yellow tape still surrounded the cottage Yolanda had rented, but no police vehicles were nearby. We went on, past the wharf and the marina and up the hill. I parked in the lodge's lot.

"Hey, look!" Haylee yelped in glee. "Max's BMW is nowhere to be seen! Maybe Mona scared Max away."

Cheerfully, we hurried down the hill, underneath the porte cochere, and into the lobby.

Zara had not left.

Wearing a halter top and a tiny pair of shorts that showed off her long, tanned legs, she was talking to Ben, who was behind the black marble reception counter. He was handsome as ever in a white dress shirt but no jacket or tie. He gave us a smile that nearly blinded me.

Zara turned around and scowled for a second before she rearranged her face into an expression that was, I figured, supposed to be welcoming. "Hi, Cuz," she trilled. "And Willow." She leaned back with her elbows on the counter. Like she owned the place.

Like she owned Ben, too.

Ben called someone on the house phone, and a teenage boy in a suit ran into the lobby. Ben showed the boy a list of people he still expected that night, patted him on the shoulder, and told him he'd be fine on his own, especially with Zara there to help him.

Zara frowned.

Ben came out from behind the counter and shook Haylee's and my hands. "Glad you two could make it. I've got everything I want you to see in my office."

The dismissal might not have worked for Mona, but Zara got the hint.

Well, sort of. She bounded toward the stairs. "I'll be in my room, Ben, if you need me." So much for helping the kid with reception. Not that she should be expected to, but she'd obviously been content to hang around the desk as long as Ben was there.

Ben led us to a spacious office done in dark oak and touches of red that were a nod to Victorian styling. An ornate mahogany desk was positioned so that natural light from glass-paned French doors would come in over Ben's shoulders. If he wanted to be cozy on winter nights, he could pull red velvet drapes over the doors and build a fire in the fireplace, which was centered in a wall of oak bookcases and cabinets. Two red-upholstered wing chairs faced a sturdy fumed oak table on the wall opposite the windows. Ordinarily, they probably flanked the side table, which was alone and isolated in front of the fireplace.

Only two chairs at the long work table? Uh-oh. Maybe it was a sign that Ben wasn't going to stick around for the evening. Or that I should find a reason to leave — I should suddenly remember that I had pets, for instance?

Besides the rearranged chairs, the only things out of place in that tidy office were cardboard cartons with flaps turned back showing piles of black and white photographs.

I loved old pictures. All thoughts of departing fled my mind.

Before I could dig into the boxes of photos, though, I gave the oriental rug an appraising look. I wanted to kneel and stroke my fingers between the rich blue, dark red, black, and ivory fibers. From their sheen, I guessed they were silk.

Ben must have noticed my covetous glances. "This office is mostly the way Snoozy Gallagher left it. The rug and furniture needed cleaning, and I've sent the books and paintings to restorers." He pointed at the bookshelf between the fireplace and the windows. "Want to see the safe that was robbed?"

40

Haylee nodded as if the beautifully restored room had stolen her powers of speech. I was breathless with admiration, both for the room and for Clay and Ben and their success in bringing it to this stunning glory.

Ben gave Haylee a wide smile, then locked the office door.

My face must have shown my surprise.

He explained, "I don't want to reveal the lodge's secrets to everyone in the world."

Zara, for instance? Didn't he trust her? Interesting . . .

He crossed to the bookcase next to the window, pressed something beside a book, and swung the bookcase open on its hinges.

The safe was at eye level and surprisingly small. A painting could have hidden it, but trick bookcases were definitely more fun. Had the room been originally like this, or had Snoozy Gallagher added the safe and bookcases in anticipation of a future heist? I imagined Snoozy in this office, decorated much as it was now. He'd have been planning his little escapade, smiling to himself, and dozing off.

The safe's door wasn't locked. Ben opened it. "Empty, I'm afraid. For some reason, no one seems to want to entrust me with their jewelry." I detected a twinkle in his eyes.

Haylee smiled back at him. "That safe doesn't exactly have a great reputation."

I asked, "Weren't Cassie's belongings supposed to be in there?"

"Chief Smallwood picked them up," Ben told us.

Peering into the safe's shiny black interior, I hid a shiver. "I was one of the first to see the jewels after they were removed from this very spot and buried for thirty years." My voice came out barely above a whisper.

"Clay told me about it," Ben said. "That must have been something." He placed his palm flat on the bare floor of the safe. "Can you imagine all those leather and velvet pouches in here?"

"And the ladies in their designer gowns parading down your staircase," Haylee contributed.

"And the looks on their faces when they came to the office for their jewelry and found the safe door open and empty like this, and Snoozy nowhere in sight," Ben added. "I hope you two aren't afraid of ghosts."

Haylee backed away from him. "Why? Have you sensed anything?"

He closed the safe. "No, but if they'd be anywhere in this lodge, they'd be in this room, don't you think?"

"Was Snoozy killed in here?" I asked.

"The police say he wasn't." He glanced out his French windows at shadowed woods looming beyond lawns and flower gardens uphill from the lodge. "They're sure he was killed out in the woods, close to where he was buried."

"Does it bother you, owning property where someone was murdered?" Haylee asked.

"That was a long time ago. I knew this place came with a wealth of history when I bought it. Willow, though —" He gave me a sympathetic look. "You've had a much tougher time of it, from what I've heard."

I helped him swing the bookcase over the safe. "I try not to let the actions of evil people spoil a place I love."

He studied my face. "Would all the things that have happened in your yard make you consider moving?"

"Only if I felt threatened."

369

"And do you?" he persisted.

Did I? Sometimes. I took a deep breath. "Not really, not when Haylee and her mothers live right across the street."

He latched the bookcase. "That was one of the reasons we — my wife and I — chose this lodge. We'd heard about how, pardon the pun, close-knit Threadville was. Deirdre particularly wanted to live near such wonderful women."

Haylee looked about to cry. "Did we ever meet her? Was she ever in our shops? I hope we were nice to her."

"She was never here, but we read articles about Threadville and about the lodge, and we knew we had to see it all. Just reading about you — she was sure she'd like all of the Threadville store owners — and planning to live here gave her a lot of pleasure. But she . . . didn't make it." He spoke those last three words barely above a murmur, then turned abruptly, grabbed one of the cartons, picked it up as if it weighed nothing, set it on the oak table, and lifted out a handful of sepia-toned photos. "I thought we could start with this box. These photos look oldest."

Haylee glanced at him from under her lashes. "Love to." She pulled three pairs of simple white cotton gloves from the bright, striped canvas bag she'd made. "We can wear these to handle the photos."

Ben stared at the gloves. "They look like they wandered in here from some of the old photos."

Haylee laughed. "Archivists wear them. I brought you an extra large pair."

"Okay." Leaving the gloves behind, he went around to the other side of his desk, grabbed his antique leather desk chair by its wide back, and rolled it to the work table between the two wing chairs. "You two can have those chairs. This desk chair looks better than it feels."

We sat down and put on the gloves. Haylee was the first to pick up a photo and study it. "Look at this gown," she squealed.

Even in the old photo, the richness of the black satin, embroidered all over with faceted jet beads that Edna would have craved, gleamed. The woman in the picture sat staring sternly at the camera while her husband stood behind her with one hand on her shoulder. "Late 1890s?" I guessed, looking at the clothing and the consciously immobile expressions of the couple.

"I think so," Haylee agreed. She turned toward Ben. "You're probably interested in hanging other pictures, too, besides the ones showing off fashions. But you must have an entire costume history beginning in the 1890s!"

He rumbled a deep laugh. "And ending in the 1980s. Some of us notice faces more than outfits, so I also like these pictures. It's too bad they used painted backdrops. I'd really like to find old photos of the lodge and of people participating in activities besides sitting still for the photographer."

We sorted the photos into three piles, one for photos that were boring or blurred, one for photos we thought might suffice, and one for those that seemed perfect. Ben told us he didn't intend to hang the originals. He planned to have the photos professionally cleaned, and then have many enlargements framed, more than he could hang at once, so he could change the displays frequently. He said he would store the originals in acid-free archive boxes.

We carefully went through loose photos, then eased old, leather-bound albums open and inserted bookmarks near the pictures we liked best. Many of those had captions, handwritten in white ink. Ben became excited about having the captions photographed, too, and framed with the photos.

Outside, twilight settled to dusk. Ben turned up the lights. We progressed from sit-still-for-a-whole-minute portraits to beach scenes from the early twentieth century. Women wore bathing dresses and men did not yet go topless. In wooly, vested bathing suits, they clowned around wooden rowboats that must have weighed a ton.

Realizing that we were selecting way too many photos as perfect, we tried to force ourselves to be more critical. It was difficult, though, especially when we got to the 1920s and the flappers.

Ben pointed to a photo of cars parked under the lodge's porte cochere. "Flivvers," he said. "What a wealth of antique cars."

Dusk darkened to night beyond the French doors. We worked in warm camaraderie, nearly always agreeing about which photos would fascinate the lodge's guests.

Ben took off his gloves. I was afraid he was going to send us away before Clay showed up, but he only said, "Time for a refreshment break." He glanced at the office door. "I already locked that, didn't I?"

41

Ben strode to the side of the fireplace that didn't house the safe, fiddled with that bookcase, and swung it away from the wall.

By now, I shouldn't have been surprised, but I was.

Laughing at our expressions, he said in a scary voice, "Come with me." He opened an almost full-sized door and turned on a light.

Curious, we crowded in after him. A dim passageway stretched in front of us.

"Clay discovered this." Although he whispered, his voice was eerily loud, magnified by the passage's bare wood floors and unpainted plaster walls. "We figure it was built during Prohibition. Liquor smuggled across the lake from Canada could have been stored here."

"In this passage?" Haylee breathed.

Ben tossed us a mischievous grin. "Someday, when we're sure it's safe to enter, I'll show you the hidden wine cellar. It's in a basement underneath the wine cellar that everyone else knows about." He walked on and opened a pair of double doors. "This is a normal closet, if closets in secret passageways can be considered normal, but the door leading to the stairway to the secret wine cellar is hidden inside it." He pointed to the wall opposite the closet. "The banquet hall where we ate and danced last night is that way. And the kitchen is straight ahead."

Aha. The promised refreshments.

Ben turned a corner, opened another door, and we emerged into a pantry. After he locked a narrow cabinet back into position, I would never have guessed that it hid a secret passage.

He pointed to a door showing the night through its rippled antique glass window. "I can go outside here and take a path through shrubbery that I'm deliberately keeping overgrown. In seconds, I can whip through the French doors in my office and be sitting at my desk. Like Snoozy, I can come and go and be in different places than my employees and guests expect me to be." He opened his eyes wide in pretend amazement. "It gives me all sorts of opportunities for sneaking around."

Haylee gave him a huge smile. They were definitely kindred spirits.

I wondered if the secret passage and the overgrown shrubbery had provided Snoozy's murderer with similar — and deadly — opportunities for sneaking around.

Ben opened a normal, steel-clad door with a round porthole window near the top. As he had probably expected, no one was in the bright, state-of-the-art hotel kitchen. He went to a huge refrigerator and grasped the door's handle.

"What does that lead to?" Haylee teased. "A hidden swimming pool?"

Ben laughed. "No, a bowling alley."

Somewhat disappointingly, the opened door revealed only the interior of a refrigerator. Ben brought out a tray of strawberries dipped in chocolate, first white chocolate, then dark, slanted to form a V neckline to make the strawberries appear to be wearing tiny tuxedos, complete with dark chocolate buttons and bow ties on the white chocolate shirts. He set the tray down. "Sorry to feed you leftovers from last night, but help yourselves. And what can I get you to drink? How about pineapple punch from last night? It's nonalcoholic, but we can spike it."

I waved my hands in front of my face. "I'm driving."

Haylee found three glasses and set them on the counter. "And I'm sorting through photos."

Ben poured us each a glass of punch, and encouraged us to eat as many strawberries as we wanted. In addition to being cute, the tuxedoed strawberries were yummy. We gorged ourselves and had second glasses of punch. After we tidied everything away, Haylee said we needed to wash our hands before we put on our cotton gloves to handle the photos.

Ben led us into the banquet hall. From there, we knew the way to the ladies' room.

Haylee and I smiled at each other's mirrored reflections. Haylee lifted up one hand and pinched the back of it with the other. "I'm not dreaming."

"A gorgeous man, a secret passageway, and strawberries wearing tuxedos," I said in mock wonder. "What more could you ask?"

"That's easy," she answered. "But first he has to *notice* me."

"I think he has."

"And notice me *more* than he notices Zara."

"I think you're fine on that score, too. He locked her out of his office."

She pointed one finger in the air. "He locked *everyone* out of his office."

"And us in."

She gave a pretend little shudder. "It's very gothic, isn't it?"

"It's whimsical and fun." And Clay had been the one to find the passageway. Two lord-of-the-manor types. "If only they had smoldering eyes," I wailed.

She tapped my arm. "Ha! Have you seen the way Clay looks at you?"

"Not recently."

"Last night."

"That wasn't recent," I moaned.

Laughing, she pushed the ladies' room door open.

Ben was waiting for us beside his open office door. This time, he didn't lock us in.

We donned the gloves, pulled up the chairs, and delved into the next box in the series. Admiring slinky, bias-cut satin gowns, we worked our way through the thirties and forties. By the fifties, dresses and gowns hardly showed up in the pictures except at banquets and dances. At a beatnik party, the women wore black tights and bulky, tunic-length sweaters while the men wore high-waisted black jeans with tucked-in T-shirts, their short sleeves rolled up to show off their biceps, and, in a couple of instances, their cigarette packs.

I found photos from annual jewelers' conferences. I sat up straighter in the comfy overstuffed chair. "Some of these gems may be the very ones that were stolen, and that Clay and I found."

Haylee leaned close to Ben so she could see. "Recognize any of them?"

"No," I answered, "but the jewelers could have reset the same stones year after year, or simply borrowed different jewelry from their stores when the time came for the ladies' maids to pack for the conference." I pitched my voice low in imitation of a suave male voice. "What gems would you like to wear this year, my dear?"

Haylee fluttered her white-gloved hands near her heart and mimicked in a high voice, "Oh, *dah*ling, you *know* that diamonds go with simply everything!"

Ben's deep, appreciative laughter made our goofing around worthwhile, and we might have continued if someone hadn't tapped at the door.

Clay? My heart danced a little jig.

42

But it wasn't Clay at Ben's office door.

Without waiting for an answer, Zara threw the door open and sashayed in. She wore black leggings covered by a voluminous sweater that had been hand knit, complete with a kangaroo pocket, from chunky black yarn. Not her usual svelte look, though she did have her hair pinned back in a sleek hairstyle that went with her black ballerina flats, each embellished with a black satin bow. Maybe she'd gotten cold in the shorts and halter top she'd been wearing earlier, or maybe she'd been looking through the beatnik party photos. "Ben, did Max say when he was coming back?" she asked.

Ben stood. "Late tonight or early in the morning." His voice was warm and friendly, but he didn't move toward her. "He had to go to Pittsburgh on business, but didn't want to take more than a day from his vacation."

A vacation that seemed to be lasting forever, especially to Haylee, suddenly thin-lipped and silent on the other side of Ben's vacated chair. And how interesting that Max had told Ben his plans, but not his sister. His supposed sister. Or maybe he had told her, and she'd devised an excuse to come into Ben's office and find out what we were doing.

Zara pouted. "But I need Max's car." She rubbed a forefinger along the carved edge of Ben's desk. "May I borrow the lodge's truck? You can drive me if you're afraid of my driving."

Ben pulled off his white gloves. "I don't think anyone else needs it tonight." He walked across the office to the other side of his vast desk from her. "Here, catch." He slid a ring of keys across the shiny mahogany to her.

She grabbed it. "Another thing — I'd like my trunk brought downstairs so when Max does arrive, I can put it right into his car. Can you help me carry it?"

"Give me a couple of seconds. I'll be right up. Which room is yours?"

She pursed her lips in a coy smile, but looked at Haylee instead of Ben when she answered. "Edelweiss. As if you didn't know. Coming?"

His face darkened in a flush that could be embarrassment, but looked more like controlled anger, as if he didn't appreciate the innuendo. "In a minute. I have a couple of things to finish here, first."

Zara peered toward the table where Haylee and I were not paying much attention to the photos in our gloved hands. "What are you folks doing, anyway?" She wrinkled her nose. "Why were you talking about diamonds?"

How long had she been listening at the door, and did she think Haylee had been talking to Ben in that exaggeratedly flirtatious voice? And calling him "*dah*ling"?

Luckily, Zara didn't notice me trying to control a snicker. She gazed at Ben. "Why were you wearing those weird gloves, Ben?"

"Just going through some old stuff." The way he tried to make it sound unbearably dull almost brought on another involuntary snicker.

Haylee sneezed. I knew her well enough to know it was a fake sneeze, but it sounded real.

Ben returned to the table, grabbed his discarded white cotton gloves, and frowned at some rather obvious dark smudges. "It's dirty work," he said.

Zara brushed a white fleck off her sweater.

"Okay. Meet you upstairs, Ben." Singing, she flitted away. I had to say one thing for her — she had a really good voice.

Ben stood perfectly still, watching her go. When her song reached the foot of the stairs, he muttered, "You would never believe the amount of luggage that woman brought with her. Would either of you take a steamer trunk on a two-week vacation?"

"I didn't know they still made them," I said.

He waved the gloves past his face. "Maybe it's a foot locker. It wasn't very heavy when I carried it upstairs for her. But she could almost hide a body inside it."

I defended the need for luggage. "We've been known to take sewing machines on sewing, quilting, or embroidering retreats. And bunches of fabric. It can add up really fast."

Ben leaned back against his desk. "Good point. I'm forgetting. Zara also brought an easel, canvases, and paints. She's been wandering around, painting pictures."

I asked, "Is she good?"

He nodded slowly. "I think she is. And Max says she's had several exhibitions."

Upstairs, something crashed.

Ben winced. "She could also be good at gouging woodwork with that trunk's sharp metal corners. I'd better go. I'll be back as soon as I can." Leaving the door standing open, he dashed out of his office. I heard his feet pound up the stairs, then his voice. "Here, Zara, let me take that."

"See? What did I tell you?" I whispered to Haylee.

"Are there no limits to that woman's talents? Alluring men, singing . . . and painting, too?"

"No, didn't you notice? He doesn't like her."

She tried to prick holes in my theory. "Or he's putting on a show of not being interested, for our benefit."

"No! He got the message when you faked that sneeze! He started talking about *dirt*." I clasped my white-gloved hands over my heart in phony awe. "You two belong together."

"Would you stop?" But she was laughing. She grabbed another photo. "Look at these mod mini-dresses from the sixties. Aren't they amazing?"

They were. "What's even more astonishing," I commented, "is the outfit Zara was wearing. That bulky sweater didn't exactly flatter her, and she's dressed all in black, like we often do when we're —"

"— not wanting to be seen at night," Haylee finished for me.

For once, she and I were out after dark in light colors. She'd put on khaki shorts and a neatly tailored pale blue linen blouse. When I'd closed In Stitches for the evening, I'd left my aqua tank top on, but had switched my skirt to cutoffs. We both had on sandals, not the running shoes we sometimes wore if we thought we might have to . . . well, maybe not run, exactly, but hurry.

Listening for Ben to return and hoping that he wouldn't abandon us for Zara, I continued sorting through photos. Color photos from the seventies showed a preponderance of brown, avocado, orange, and gold clothing, color combinations that had probably looked crisper in real life than in these slightly pinkish, faded photos.

Outside, a vehicle honked a couple of little toots.

Seconds later, Ben returned to the office and pulled on his dust-specked white gloves. "Didn't she say she only wanted help bringing that trunk downstairs?" he asked us. "So she could put it into Max's car later?"

We agreed.

"She had me carry it outside, then she stayed with it while I got the pickup for her, then she had me help her lift it into the truck bed. And she drove away. But I could have sworn that foot locker was empty just now. It barely weighed a thing."

I looked at Haylee. Gazing back at me, she plucked at an invisible bulky sweater.

"The yarn in Zara's sweater looked familiar," I said slowly, gauging Haylee's reaction. "But I'm sure it's not like anything Opal carries in Tell a Yarn."

"It looked like craft yarn to me," Haylee agreed.

I jumped out of my chair, knelt on Ben's silk oriental rug, and picked up the white fleck that Zara had brushed off her sweater. "And so's this." I rolled the short piece of yarn between my gloved fingers. "Super bulky."

It was time to take off the gloves. I threw my dusty white cotton pair onto the table, grabbed my bag, excused myself, and headed outside.

No one was anywhere near the porte cochere. I took out my phone and dialed Chief Smallwood's number.

She answered right away. "Hi, Willow, what's up?"

"I know who your yarnbomber is," I said.

43

Naturally, Vicki fired back, "Stay out of police business, Willow."

I bristled. "I am. That's why I'm telling *you*. Zara Brubaugh just borrowed the Elderberry Bay Lodge pickup truck and loaded a lightweight foot locker onto it and drove away. If anything gets yarnbombed tonight —"

"Know which way she headed?"

"No, sorry."

"I'll have a look around. I know the truck — dark green with a logo of a stylized sprig of elderberries in a circle. Thanks, Willow."

Convinced that she'd never catch up with Zara, or that I was wrong about Zara being the yarnbomber and Vicki would scold me the next time I saw her, I trudged inside.

I cheered up as I approached the office. Haylee and Ben stood close together with their backs to the door. They were so interested in what Haylee was holding that at first they didn't hear me coming.

When they did, Haylee whirled around. Excitement turned her eyes a more brilliant blue than ever.

Ben faced me, too. His smile was wide and proud. "Look at what Haylee found in the last batch of photos." He held up a snapshot. "The date scribbled in the margin at the bottom is only about a week before Snoozy Gallagher disappeared. We definitely have to display this one."

We. Wondering if he could be thinking, perhaps unconsciously, of running the lodge with Haylee's help, I leaned forward to study the photo.

I'd hoped for a glimpse of the gowned but not bejeweled women at that final banquet at the jewelers' convention, but this was a simple snapshot taken on the grassy slope between the lodge's porch and the beach. A short, bald man was with four teenagers. The two boys and one of the girls faced him. Standing to one side, the other girl smirked toward the camera.

And then I saw the belt buckle the man wore. Silver, with three *Z*s embossed on it.

"That can't be Snoozy Gallagher," I exclaimed.

"That's what I'd have thought, too," Ben said. "Supposedly, he never let anyone take his picture. But he was looking at the boys, so he probably didn't notice that someone was sneaking up on him."

I shuddered. Had his death the next week occurred because he didn't notice someone creeping up on him one last time?

Snoozy appeared to be in his mid-sixties. Because his head was turned, I could see only part of one of his eyes. It was heavily lidded and drooped down at the outer corner in a way that made him look, from the side, both wily and half asleep. His wide belt cinched his paunch with limited success. He had tucked his orange checked shirt into his brown slacks, but it bloused out in irregular pleats, making his upper body resemble a pudgy pumpkin.

The boys wore tight jeans and baggy T-shirts advertising rock bands. Their mouths were open wide, as if they were shouting at Snoozy, and their hands hacked at the air. The boy next to Snoozy was the tallest in the picture. His brown hair was wiry and he'd grown a wispy attempt at a beard. The other boy was smaller, with enviably curly hair. The girl next to him wore turquoise capris and a gray off-the-shoulder sweatshirt. She glared at Snoozy, and her mouth was open, also.

It looked like those three teens were yelling at Snoozy, who found them slightly amusing, while the other girl flirted with the photographer.

Careful not to touch the rare snapshot of Snoozy Gallagher, I pointed to the girl who seemed to be yelling. Except for the long frizzy hair and bangs, prominent cheekbones, and apparent anger, she could have passed for a younger version of Cassie.

"Could that be Cassie's mom, Yolanda? It looks like her."

Haylee answered, "Could be. When we last saw Yolanda, her hair was an odd shade of purplish red, like she was trying to replicate the auburn of her youth, and this girl's hair was reddish brown." She adjusted the photo in Ben's hand so that the light fell on it differently. "And this guy next to Yolanda — I think it's Neil."

I bent for a closer look. "I think you're right. He looks like Neil, only younger, and he also resembles Cassie, with the freckles and light brown curls."

After we all agreed about Neil, it didn't take us long to recognize the taller boy. His height, wiry hair, and pale eyes gave him away. He was a younger version of Tom Umshaw, the fisherman.

The flirty girl wore a pink and gray striped cropped top with big shoulders and a short, ruffled pink skirt that showed off long, colt-ish legs. Her hair was brown, long, and tied in a ponytail over her left ear. "That's Bitsy," I said, "before she was blond."

After this picture had been taken, Tom and Neil had stayed friends through the years. Neil and Yolanda had eventually married and had a daughter, but the marriage hadn't lasted. At some point after Yolanda left Neil and took baby Cassie with her, Neil and Bitsy had become a couple, but, according to the lady in the RV at the campground, they'd broken up.

Ben summarized what I was thinking, "Tom, Neil, and Yolanda were all yelling at Snoozy Gallagher shortly before he died, and Bitsy witnessed the argument. Chief Smallwood might like to know about the disagreement, if there was one, and also that Tom, Bitsy, and Yolanda might be able to tell her who else was around the lodge the week that Snoozy died."

"Supposedly, Fred Zongassi was," I said. "Mona said that he had a fight with Snoozy and took off around the time Snoozy disappeared."

Haylee turned the photo over. On the back, someone had printed, *Found in waste-basket in Zongassi's room in staff cottage. If anything happens, look for Z. No one else ever got past my guard.* Three *Z*s were scrawled beneath the note.

I asked, "Did Snoozy mean if anything happened to *him,* like if he was injured or killed, or did he mean if anything happened to the jewelry stored in his safe? Maybe Snoozy planted this picture among Fred's things in the hope that the heist he was planning would be blamed on Fred, except I guess that no one read the back of the photo until now, or everyone would have suspected Fred of the robbery at least as much as they suspected Snoozy."

I still couldn't picture Fred as a murderer, but I didn't know what he'd been like in his late twenties and early thirties. However, if Snoozy's and Neil's murders were connected, Fred was a much more likely villain than Cassie, who hadn't been born yet when Snoozy died. Tom, Neil, Yolanda, and Bitsy had been in their teens, old enough to kill.

Ben took off his gloves and went to the phone on his desk. "Do either of you know Chief Smallwood's number?"

I had it programmed into my cell, but maybe Vicki would be more receptive to a call from Ben's landline. I read her number aloud. While Ben dialed and stood listening to a recorded message, Haylee said to me, "We know that Snoozy was killed shortly before Fred left town, and that Neil was killed shortly after Fred came back."

I murmured, "But they took Cassie away for questioning, not Fred."

Ben covered the mouthpiece with his hand. "As far as we know. I haven't seen Fred since last night, but I didn't expect to."

"Chief Smallwood doesn't want me investigating people based on hunches —" I started.

Haylee let out a burble of laugher. "She doesn't want you investigating people, period."

I lowered my eyebrows in a fake glower. She was as willing to snoop around as I was. Had been. I suddenly remembered that I was leaving snooping to the experts. But all I said was, "Neither Cassie nor Fred seem like murderers. But Yolanda and Bitsy do."

Ben raised an eyebrow. Still covering the mouthpiece, he asked, "What about Tom? He was around at the time of both murders, also."

Haylee and I shook our heads, and I told them about Tom and Neil joking together during the sidewalk sale, a pair of buddies, totally comfortable teasing and being teased by each other.

"I've seen them together, too," Haylee

said. "They were friends. Bitsy and Yolanda fought with each other at the sidewalk sale, and Yolanda had no qualms about feeding questionable food to people. *Poisoning* people."

"Including Tom," I said. "He told Haylee and me he'd been sick, too. And he looked it." I counted on the fingers of one of my gloves. "Bitsy seems mean and irrational, but Yolanda fled Elderberry Bay about the time Neil was murdered. Worse, she was willing to see her daughter go to jail for Neil's murder." And Cassie was going along with her mother's lies, to save a mother who maybe didn't deserve saving. "And Yolanda may have dumped helpless kittens in my yard about the time Neil's body appeared."

Ben left a message asking Chief Smallwood to call or come see him next time she was free.

Originally, I had hoped that sorting through the photos would take a long time and that Clay would join us, but it was almost midnight, and we'd all been up late the previous night. Clay might reasonably assume that Haylee and I had left hours ago, and he might drive past on Shore Road without checking the lodge's parking lot.

Besides, now I wanted to get into the car and drive around. If Haylee and I found

Vicki, we could tell her to go see Ben. He could show her the photograph of Bitsy witnessing what appeared to be Neil, Tom, and Yolanda yelling at Snoozy Gallagher. And supposedly, the picture had been taken by Fred Zongassi who, if he *was* the photographer, had been able to sneak up on Snoozy at least once. And he had also brawled with Snoozy, and then had left town around the time Snoozy had disappeared.

If we didn't locate Vicki, she would eventually listen to Ben's voice message.

Naturally, if Haylee and I went searching for Vicki and *happened* upon another yarn-bombing, no one could possibly accuse us of snooping.

Ben must have been tired, also. After we scraped the last snapshot out of the box, he told us to leave all the photos in their piles, and he'd finish another time. He glanced at the antique wooden clock on the mantel. "Zara hasn't brought my keys back yet. She said she wasn't going far."

I could see Haylee struggling not to say something catty about her supposed cousin, and I wanted to tell Ben he was too trusting. Instead, I asked if she'd ever borrowed anything before, and if she'd been late bringing it back.

"She's gone out in lodge boats from time to time, but was never gone long enough to worry anyone. She's not exactly late this time, either. I'm not worried, only curious."

"Boats?" The yarnbomber had escaped in a small motorboat. "Like rowboats?" I asked.

"And motorized rowboats. Probably canoes, kayaks, and paddleboats, too."

"Could your truck have run out of gas while she was driving?" I asked.

He had a wonderfully boyish grin. "Not this soon. The tank was half full."

I asked if he wanted to join Haylee and me in my car to search for her. "Maybe she had a flat."

He hesitated as if going with us appealed to him. "No, thanks. I have a car here, too, but I'm not leaving the lodge with only that one new hire out there at reception to look after everything. And Chief Smallwood may still show up. If she does, I'll let her see the picture and what's written on the front and the back. Thanks for all your time and work. After I go through everything again, want to help me decide which of these so-called 'perfect' photos are best, how they should be framed, and where to hang them?"

"Sure," I answered for both of us. "Anytime." Maybe Clay would be able to join us for the entire evening next time.

Come to think of it, when I could use my entire backyard again, I could have them all over for a barbecue, and Clay and I could ask Haylee and Ben for suggestions about finishing Blueberry Cottage. And Ben would walk Haylee home . . .

Haylee and I said our good-byes and hurried toward the parking lot.

"Did you call Vicki when you went outside earlier?" Haylee asked. "Is she looking for Ben's truck, Zara, and a new yarnbombing installation?"

I knew she had figured it out. I raised my hand and we did a self-congratulatory high five.

We didn't have to discuss what to do next. Of course Haylee would want to hop into my car and search for Ben's truck, Zara, and a yarnbomb. And if we found Vicki, we'd send her to Ben.

I drove to the top of the hill, where the road from the lodge, marina, and wharf met Shore Road.

We had no problem deciding which way to turn. A glow hovered above a dip in the road between us and Threadville. Parts of the glow blinked brighter and dimmer, red, white, red, white . . .

I turned toward it. The road sloped downhill toward a gully and a culvert that we knew all too well.

Vicki Smallwood's cruiser was parked, lights flashing, behind the Elderberry Bay Lodge pickup truck. The truck's tailgate was down. The foot locker, its lid propped open, was on the tailgate.

Vicki had turned on the cruiser's interior dome light. Zara sat in the front passenger seat, talking quickly, it appeared, and gesturing with her hands while Vicki took notes. Zara had pulled a black stocking cap over her pinned-up hair.

"My so-called cousin looks like a burglar," Haylee said, obviously pretending that she never dressed in a similar way. "She must have been trying to pick up the cape, and it was, surprise, surprise, gone. Ha!"

We high-fived again.

I turned my car around, went back to the cruiser, and stopped in the road beside it. I pushed the button that opened Haylee's window. I planned to tell Vicki to go see Ben.

Vicki kept writing, and Zara kept talking. About the tenth time Zara glanced past Vicki to us, Vicki turned and scowled at us. She didn't open her window. She waved her hand in a cop-like gesture that could mean only one thing.

Get out of here.

44

Our police chief refused to talk to us. Fine. I took my foot off the brake, pressed on the gas, and eased away from her cruiser.

"What shall we do now?" Haylee asked.

I accelerated, leaving our police chief and Zara Brubaugh behind. Because I'd turned the car around before attempting to talk to Vicki, we were heading back toward the lodge, and not toward home. However, we could return to the village and avoid passing our cranky police chief again if we drove past the lodge, the marina, the wharf, Lazy Daze Campground, and all the cottages along Beach Row. Naturally, I didn't want to drive *past* the lodge. What if Clay showed up?

I parked in the Elderberry Bay Lodge parking lot again.

"Still hoping that Clay will find us?" Haylee teased.

"Just being cautious." Vicki would have

noticed which direction we went. Maybe she would follow, which would lead her straight to Ben and the interesting photo.

Haylee nodded at the lodge. "I suppose tattling to Ben that my delightful cousin was pulled over in his pickup truck might be seen as unkind, huh."

"Unkind to your delightful cousin, maybe," I retorted, "but not to Ben. He might be staying awake worrying."

We tiptoed to the porte cochere. No lights were on behind the French doors leading to Ben's office, and even without going into the lobby, we could see that Ben wasn't there. The lights had been dimmed, and no one was near the registration desk. A bell to ring for service had been placed on it.

We turned around and headed toward my car. "Too bad Ben didn't accept my offer of a ride," I muttered. "He'd have seen Zara after she'd been pulled over or whatever."

"I wonder what story she'll tell him when she does bring the truck back."

"*And* wants him to carry that empty foot locker upstairs again," I added.

Haylee giggled. "She must have gone to that culvert looking for the bag she left there, and thanks to your quick call, Vicki got there in time."

I opened the driver's door. "I wish I'd seen

Zara's face when Vicki showed up."

"I can just hear our police chief, 'Did you lose something?' " Haylee imitated Vicki's inflection perfectly.

I wanted to hoot with laughter, but didn't, for fear of waking people in the nearby lodge.

Haylee slid into the passenger seat. "Do you see Max's car anywhere?"

"No. Clay's, either. But I'm not going back home past our ornery police chief!"

Haylee laughed. "She really got to you, didn't she?"

"Waving us on as if we weren't important!" I exaggerated my complaining tone.

At the foot of the hill, I steered into the potholed parking lot that served the marina and wharf. Breezes blowing off the lake through the car's open windows smelled watery but fresh.

Near the row of boathouses, something beeped.

"What's wrong with your car?" Haylee asked.

Uh-oh. "I don't know." I stopped and listened. Another beep. "I don't think it's coming from my car." I turned off the engine. After about a minute, we heard the beep again, distorted by wind.

"Smoke detector," we said in unison. It

was either in a yacht or a boathouse.

"As firefighters, we should investigate," Haylee pointed out.

"And help change the batteries if they need it." The warning didn't sound urgent, but we needed to figure out where it was coming from and notify the owners that one of their smoke or carbon monoxide detectors possibly needed new batteries. The yachts and boathouses were very close together. A fire in one of them could be disastrous. And carbon monoxide killed with no warning.

Haylee grabbed my flashlight from the glove compartment. We got out and listened.

The beeps drew us east. We stopped in front of Tom's fish shack.

The moon was three quarters, but since it had just risen, the earth's atmosphere magnified it. Light from the lot's only fixture slanted down onto a notice tacked to Tom's front door: *We will be closed on Monday to celebrate the life of our good friend, Neil Ondover. RIP, Neil, old buddy.*

I breathed out a mournful sigh. Neil's death was all so sad and so needless.

Another notice said that the door stuck and to push hard.

I rammed it with my shoulder the way Tom had shown us.

The door was locked.

We peeked in through cobwebby front windows. "I think there's a light on inside," Haylee said.

Both of us knew that meant nothing. We had night-lights in our shops, also.

From this close, the beep was more like an angry chirp. If the batteries died and a fire started before new batteries were put in, I would have a hard time forgiving myself for not investigating. I suggested, "Let's check around the back of Tom's shack, where he parks his boats, and see if we can pinpoint where the smoke detector with the low batteries is." Even if Vicki showed up, she couldn't scold us for snooping. We were only doing our job as firefighters. And she could patrol the area frequently during the rest of the night until we managed to call Tom.

"Okay." Haylee handed me my flashlight. "And then let's go home. This place gives me the creeps. Doesn't the water lapping at the posts beneath the pier sound like something licking its lips before it pounces?"

I smothered a laugh. "Not to me." Haylee wasn't usually a wimp. Maybe she just wanted to go back up the hill and take a few more longing looks at Ben's lodge.

I nearly chickened out, though, when I

shined my light on the catwalk leading to the back of Tom's shack. The line of wooden planks was barely wide enough for my feet, and the water below was a deep, ominous, oily black.

And did Haylee have to mention that lip-licking sound again?

I reminded myself that I'd heard of record-setting catfish and sturgeon in Lake Erie, but the lake couldn't possibly harbor women-eating monsters.

Gamely, Haylee followed me down the catwalk. Narrow boards sagged and creaked as we shuffled along them.

Tom's commercial fishing boat was moored to the wharf running along the shore ahead of us.

The closer of the two garage doors at the back of Tom's fishing shack was rolled all the way up. A motor launch swayed gently in the far bay of the boathouse, but nothing was in the nearer section.

"Does Tom usually keep another boat in here?" Haylee asked. "Does he fish at night?"

"Maybe he uses a smaller boat to commute to and from his home. Or he rents out space."

The catwalk running along the inside wall of the boathouse was almost as narrow as the one outside.

The smoke detector chirped again. This time it sounded louder.

From where we stood, trembling in the suddenly chilly evening, it was easy to tell that the smoke detector with the dying batteries was inside Tom's fish shack, and not in the one beside it or on his fishing tug.

Just one look, and then we'd go, I promised myself. I shined my flashlight around the interior of the boathouse.

The door leading inside to the sales area was ajar.

45

Something groaned. Haylee grabbed my arm.

I extinguished the light, but then we couldn't see our way out of Tom's boathouse. I heard the groan again and turned on the light. Had the door leading into the sales area of his fish shack moved?

I dug in my bag for my cell phone.

Our police chief's answering system went straight to messages, but I didn't feel like going through the entire rigamarole about investigating smoke detectors with low batteries after midnight on a Sunday morning — she would undoubtedly say we were snooping — and I didn't leave a message. "I'm going to peek inside," I said. "It's probably only the door creaking in the wind, but what if Tom's in there, and all he can do is groan? What if he fell off a ladder while trying to change the smoke detector's batteries, and now he's too injured to move or yell for help?" In that case, I'd call emergency. Bothering Vicki would be pointless. I thrust the cell phone back into my embroidered bag.

"Okay," my intrepid friend said. "I'll come with you."

The smoke detector let out another loud beep.

We tiptoed around coiled ropes, floats, nets, and cans of motor oil. I pushed the door open.

Inside the boathouse, a restaurant-style sink and stainless steel counter dominated the first room on our right. That would be where Tom cleaned the fish.

Another beep sounded, so we kept going, into the familiar shop, with its refrigerated display unit, counter, scales, and cash register. Between the wind, the smoke detector, and the eerie echoes in the fish shack, we couldn't be sure where the groans originated.

I whispered, "Tom?"

No answer

I opened the door beside me and found a small, shelf-lined storeroom. Something heaped on the floor made both of us jump and catch our breath, but when I shined my flashlight at the thing, we clutched each other in relief. It was only a fishnet made of thick green plastic rope.

The smoke detector made another insistent beep. It was on the ceiling above the display case, too high to reach without a ladder, and there was no ladder in sight.

Who had moaned? I went back into the storage room and shined my flashlight around the walls. No one was near the net on the floor, and the shelves along the walls were too narrow to hold anyone, groaning or not.

Behind me, Haylee gasped.

"What?" I didn't see anyone.

"Shine your light up to the right again."

I did.

"See that small box?" she whispered. "That's the box of water-soluble thread that went missing from the sidewalk sale."

"How did it get here?" I asked.

"I don't know, but . . ." She plucked the box from the shelf. A small paper packet like a seed envelope must have been underneath the box. The envelope drifted down and landed on the fishnet. "Shine your light on this box."

I did.

"It sure looks like what I lost." She turned the box over. Spools of thread fell out and bounced into some of the holes in the fishnet.

"Oops." Haylee added a few stronger words. "I should have checked if the box was closed before I tried to read the words on the bottom." She stared down at the net. "I'm sure I had more spools than the few that fell out."

"So maybe it's not your box of thread," I said sensibly. "But we should pick them up, anyway." I leaned forward, grabbed a spool, and handed it to her. She put it into the box. I couldn't reach the next spool without stepping onto the mounded net.

My foot slipped between the ropes of the net. I fell, and both my hands slid into holes in the net, too. This was getting ridiculous.

"Here, grab my hand," Haylee said.

Flashlight and all, I forced my right hand out, and reached back toward her. She took the light and pulled at me, which helped extricate my left hand, but as I twisted toward her, pain shot through my right ankle, and to take pressure off it, I let my free foot land on the net. It slipped into the mess of connected ropes, too. Worse, my left foot was now pointing north while my right foot was pointing east. "Stop pulling," I panted. "I hurt my ankle and we need to untangle this net so I can get my feet out."

She set the flashlight on one of the lowest shelves. Together, we tried to move the rope netting so we could squeeze one of my ankles out, but the ropes were thick and stiff and wouldn't budge. I couldn't wriggle out of my sandals, either. Both of my feet were stuck, and I couldn't straighten one without causing a lot of pain in the other.

Haylee shined the light at the storage room shelves. "Tom must have a knife."

Naturally, I had to be stubborn. "I'd like to get out of this mess without damaging Tom's net." The smoke detector beeped again.

Haylee grabbed my flashlight, jumped up, ran into the fish-cleaning room, and returned carrying a knife with a long, serrated blade. She handed me the flashlight, got down on her knees, and edged the knife between my right ankle and the rope. Holding the knife away from my ankle, she began sawing.

After what seemed like an hour but, considering the number of times the smoke detector beeped — exactly once — had to be less than a minute, she rocked back on her heels and rubbed her wrist against her forehead. "Either this knife is duller than it looks or that fishnet is made of very tough ropes. And I'm afraid I'll hurt you."

Not worse than I've already hurt myself. I didn't say it. Haylee would only worry and

I needed her to think clearly, since, thanks to the pain in my ankle, my reasoning seemed fuzzy. "Let me try," I said.

She left the knife where it was, between my bare ankle and the rope. "I'll call for help. Vicki Smallwood?"

Despite my pain, I laughed. "That would be a last resort. She didn't look very pleased with us."

"Well, she should have been. We found the yarnbomber. I know — I'll call Ben! He can be here in a few minutes. I'll tell him to bring sharp tools. Or a chainsaw," she teased.

"Ouch. Maybe I can free myself in the meantime."

"Do you know the lodge's number?" she asked.

"No, but information . . ."

She stood and looked down at me doubtfully. "I don't want to leave you here alone, but how about if I run up toward the lodge while I try to phone Ben? That way, if I don't get his number before I arrive at the lodge, I can grab him and his chainsaw and we can zip back down here."

My bag was on a shelf high above my head. I nodded toward it. "Get my keys and take my car."

Her laugh held no humor. "Running while

talking on the phone will be faster than teaching myself to drive a stick shift. Your car might end up on the deck of a sailboat."

Not a good plan. "I'll be fine waiting for you and Ben. Or watch for me to come jogging up behind you." Hobbling would be more like it.

She sprinted to Tom's front door, unlocked it, pulled hard until it opened, and called back to me, "I'll leave this door unlocked so Ben and I can rush back in. Maybe I'll be lucky and find Clay. He'll have tools."

Yes, he would. He always did. Would he be pleased because I'd found an innovative way of throwing Haylee and Ben together? Or would he think I'd gone a little far?

Clenching my teeth, I plunked the flashlight on the net and hacked at the rope.

The smoke detector chirped, and chirped again. I was getting nowhere.

I should have known. Haylee was strong. If this fishnet was going to surrender to a serrated knife, it would have already done it.

In weird, shifting shadows, I glimpsed fishing line wrapped around the intersection where two of the ropes in the net joined. Fishing line would be strong, but at least it was thinner than those ropes.

413

I set my flashlight on its end to shine upward and give me a steadier source of light.

It tipped over and rolled just out of my reach.

I quickly changed my mind about being left alone.

Was Haylee still nearby? In the gloom, I called her. No answer, only that peculiar moan. It seemed to happen each time a breeze touched the door leading to the boathouse. We'd come inside for no good reason, and I'd been suitably punished.

Okay, now that I'd admitted that I'd been wrong, smoke detector or no smoke detector, to barge into Tom's boathouse, shouldn't the knife slice through the fishing line uniting a couple of those ropes?

I strained toward the flashlight, and managed to graze it with my fingertips. I tried harder, and nudged it. Its plastic outer shell grumbling against the plank floor, it rolled completely out of reach. I would have to continue working by what little light it shed.

Meanwhile, that smoke detector was becoming really annoying.

My hand brushed against the paper that had drifted down off the shelf when Haylee grabbed the box of thread. I picked up the small envelope.

The world went suddenly still.

I didn't hear the beeping smoke detector, the moaning door, or the jingling marina. I didn't hear the licking, lapping water out in the boathouse. All I heard was a deep, red roaring inside my head.

Even in the dim light, I recognized the skull and crossbones on the paper envelope. I didn't need to read the biggest word, but I could, and I did.

Poison.

A straight red line slashed across the silhouette of a rat.

I dropped the envelope and sawed furiously at the fishing line joining two of the net's ropes.

I reasoned that of course Tom would have rat poison in a shack where he cleaned and sold fish. Rats could swim. They could probably climb up the posts supporting the pier. They could have been the critters that gnawed the holes I'd seen in the shack's wooden siding when Haylee and I bought fish here last Sunday evening. Rats could pose a real problem for Tom.

He wouldn't have poisoned his longtime friend. Tom himself had been sick when Neil died.

Mouth suddenly dry, I whispered again, "Haylee?"

Of course she wasn't there. She'd be back any minute, with Ben. How much time had passed? By now, she should be almost at the lodge. Or she had called directory assistance and was talking to Ben. They'd both be here soon. The moaning noise became more frequent, coupled with a creak as the back door swung on its hinges. The breezes had accelerated. Gusts seemed to rock the shack.

The smoke detector griped.

I chopped at the thinner cords lashed around the ropes. I couldn't tell in the lack of light, but those cords also seemed impervious to Tom's knife.

Panting through my open mouth, I concentrated.

And then I heard a noise that made me clamp my mouth shut, hold my breath, and tighten my hand on the knife's wooden handle.

An outboard motor chugged softly, coming closer. Wavelets brushed an aluminum hull.

No. A boat couldn't be coming here, not to this boathouse. Tom couldn't be returning in his boat. He'd left, for the night, probably.

I told myself I was imagining things. I was imagining the smell of exhaust. I was imagining the engine shutting off. I was imagining water rippling against an aluminum hull . . .

I told myself that no one could possibly have driven a boat into that empty bay in the back of the boathouse.

A woman whined, "I'm cold."

The woman's voice sounded familiar. She wasn't Haylee.

But whoever she was, her voice was coming from that previously empty bay in the back of the boathouse.

46

"I'll get you a sweater," a man said. Tom.

"I'm freeeeeezing. What's that beeping?" I placed the woman's sharp voice. Bitsy from the campground was with Tom. Great. The woman had never seemed particularly helpful.

"Smoke detector. Gotta change the batteries. Wind's coming up fast. Let's go inside out of the wind and warm you up."

My heart beat with sickening thuds. The storage room door had been shut when Haylee and I arrived. Now it gaped open, and I was inside, unable to get up to shut the door, and spotlit in the glare of a flashlight I couldn't reach.

Maybe Tom and Bitsy wouldn't come into the front of the shack. Maybe Tom would find the sweater and they'd go back out to the boat and putter away.

Maybe . . .

There was the sound of feet scraping

against wood. A scuffle?

Bitsy yelped, "Don't push me!"

"Shh! Stay behind me. There's a light on." His whisper was hoarse. "Someone might be in there."

Maybe he would call the police without investigating. Either way, I was about to be very embarrassed. I opened my fingers and let the knife drop into the net behind me. I grabbed the rat poison packet and stuffed it into the pocket of my cutoffs. I didn't want him thinking I'd brought poison to his shack. Or that I'd guessed he could have poisoned Neil. *No,* I told myself, *he wouldn't have hurt his buddy.*

I heard Tom tiptoe closer. There was no point in pretending I wasn't here. He might attack the supposed intruder first and ask questions later.

Beep.

"Tom?" I called out, but my voice quavered as if I were stuck in a nightmare. "Is that you? Can you help me?"

He ran to the storeroom and knelt in front of me. "Willow! What happened?"

Bitsy yelled, "What is it?" Her voice was more piercing and grating than ever.

Tom called over his shoulder. "It's okay, Bitsy. Stay where you are." Quietly, he asked me, "What are you doing here?" In the dim light, his usually pale eyes seemed dark.

I stuck to the truth, but my words sounded unbelievable even to me. "I heard the smoke detector, and then I heard someone moan. I was afraid you'd fallen off a ladder while changing batteries and were too hurt to move or yell, so I came in to investigate." My shudder was real. "I thought this net might be you." That was a stretch. "So I came closer, but I stumbled and one foot got caught. When I tried to lift that foot, I hurt my ankle, and my other foot got caught."

He picked up my flashlight and shined it on my legs and feet. "Whoa, you really are snarled up."

"Who is it?" Bitsy hollered. "Want me to call the police?"

"No," Tom shouted. He grinned at me. "You don't want the police, do you?"

He was nice. He couldn't have hurt Neil. I grinned back. "No, thanks. I'm glad you understand that I barged in uninvited because I was trying to help. I'm also glad," I added belatedly, "that you didn't fall off a ladder and that you aren't injured."

Moan.

"Tom!" Bitsy yelled. "What was that?"

"Yes, what is it?" I asked Tom. "That's what I heard and thought could be you, too

420

hurt to talk. *Is* somebody else in here?" I had no trouble sounding frightened.

Tom patted my hand and called over his shoulder to Bitsy, "It's only the door blowin' in the wind. Don't panic."

But she'd obviously had enough of being relegated to the creepy, watery part of the boathouse. She ran inside and stopped beside the storeroom door. "Who's your girlfriend, Tom?"

"I'm not —" I began.

Tom stood and put his arm around Bitsy. "She's not my anything, Bitsy. You're my girl. You know that."

Bitsy had been Neil's girlfriend, and now she was Tom's . . . Could a love triangle have been responsible for Neil's murder? Could Tom have killed Neil due to jealousy, or had Bitsy killed Neil because she couldn't have him? Or maybe it was money. Had either or both of them expected to inherit from Neil?

Beep.

Bitsy was not about to be put off. "Then what's she doing here?"

"She was explaining that. She heard that door, too, from outside and came in to see if I was okay."

I added in the most sensible-sounding voice I could muster, "I'm a volunteer fire-fighter. He needs to change those batteries." While he was doing that, Ben and Haylee would show up. They'd free me, and we'd have a good laugh. And then we'd all go home.

And the police could continue their investigation into Neil's death. Snoozy's, too.

Bitsy peered more closely at me. "Oh. She's the one who came pestering me at work one night. Seems to me she likes asking too many questions and going too many places where she doesn't belong."

Maybe the gloom in Tom's shop would prevent them from noticing my struggle to look innocent.

"Bitsy, darlin'," Tom scolded, "she thought I was hurt and was only trying to help."

Bitsy folded her arms. "Sure, sure. Where's that sweater?"

"Hangin' by the front door. Go get it and put it on, would you? There's a sweetie." He bent toward me. "Here, Willow, I'm going to try to pick you up. When I do, see if you can kick the net off your feet."

Considering that Tom was hardly taller than I was, I didn't have much hope that his plan would work. Besides, my ankle hurt.

"Could we cut the net off my foot?" I asked. It wasn't a very nice request. I'd invaded his fishing shack, and now I wanted him to damage his equipment for me.

"I hope we won't have to resort to that."

He was being remarkably good-natured about it all.

I raised my arms and let him grasp me in a bear hug. He stood, taking some of the pressure off my ankle, which was a relief.

"Kick your feet," he grunted.

The fishnet probably weighed just short of two tons. I could barely move my feet, let alone kick them.

Wearing a gigantic beige sweater with dark brown moose heads knit on the front, Bitsy stood glowering behind him. I attempted to shake my feet out of the heavy net, but all I shook out of it was something that rolled across the uneven floor.

Bitsy picked it up. "She brought a spool of thread? She sells the stuff, you know."

"Hang on to it for her, will you?" Tom growled.

I didn't want to admit that the spool wasn't mine, or that Haylee had been here, or that we'd been snooping among the things on his shelves. And I certainly was not about to tell Tom and Bitsy that Haylee was coming back. What if they set a trap for her?

I told myself to calm down. I reasoned that if Tom had knowingly poisoned Neil, he'd have rid his shack of all traces of rat poison, not merely stuck the packet underneath a box of thread. It was only a coincidence that the packet was there. Tom couldn't have murdered his friend. Wouldn't have. Tom had told Haylee and me that he'd been sick, too. Maybe someone had tried to dose him with rat poison, but he hadn't taken his medicine. Maybe the poisoner was right here with us . . .

"Put her down," Bitsy said. "That's not doing any good."

I was afraid she was right, but I was sure that wasn't her real reason for wanting him to stop hugging me.

"Tom's a nice person," I managed, "but don't worry, I have a boyfriend." *I wished.*

Bitsy just sniffed.

"None of the Threadville women would be interested in old Tom," he told Bitsy. Did I detect an offended note in his voice? Was Tom the man whose advances Naomi had rebuffed? I could easily see how Naomi might be Tom's — or any man's — first choice. But no one, not even easygoing Tom, would live up to Naomi's memories of her long-gone fiancé. "I'm all yours, Bitsy babe." In a pleasanter voice, he said to me, "Let's see if we can drag this thing off you, Willow. It's so heavy that maybe it will stay behind while we move." He went around behind me, grabbed me by the armpits, and pulled me toward the back of his shop.

Something else clattered to the floor. Bitsy swooped down on it. "She had a knife!" she shrieked in a shrill voice.

"Relax, babe, will you? That's my knife."

"What was she doing with it?"

"I lost it. No telling what all's fallen into that net since I dumped it on the floor."

No telling, indeed. Did he know that he'd actually left that knife where he cleaned his fish? Maybe he was trying to protect me from Bitsy. He was certainly trying to dampen her jealousy. He was a nice enough man, but he wasn't Clay. Besides, the smell of fish around Tom — and his fishnet — was not entirely pleasant.

Bitsy bent and grabbed the fishnet with both hands. "Put her down and maybe we can just pull the thing off her feet."

"It's too heavy," he panted.

"Yeah, she might be lighter than it is." She braced her feet and tugged, anyway.

I attempted to help by bending my knees and trying to pull my feet out of the net. I heard a wad of paper land on the floor. The crumpled rat poison envelope had fallen out of the front pocket of my cutoffs. I gasped.

"What?" Tom asked. From the sound of it, he toed the balled-up envelope aside.

With any luck, he didn't recognize it and hadn't noticed it tumbling out of my pocket.

In the silence between the smoke detector's complaints, I attempted to explain my involuntary gasp. "I wrenched my ankle when I fell." It throbbed, and I was certain it had swollen, which would make it even more impossible for me to shake the net off.

"Stop yanking at her, will you, Bitsy?" Tom could have spoken in nicer tones to his girlfriend. "Come around here and give me a hand." With Bitsy's help, he dragged me and the fishnet past the moaning door, out of the shop, and into the boathouse. I was becoming seriously frightened. We were much too close to those narrow catwalks.

"Can't we just cut the net?" I asked loudly, hoping someone might hear me and come to my aid. Where were Haylee and Ben? They should be on their way, unless Ben had already fallen asleep and was hard to awaken. Would the teen looking after the lodge's reception desk be any help cutting a fishnet off my feet?

"That's what I'm plannin'." Was it my imagination or had Tom's tone with me changed, also? He now sounded peeved with both Bitsy and me. "I've got the right tools, but not here. Let's see if we can get you into my boat."

"Boat?" Bitsy parroted. "Wouldn't your truck be simpler?"

"How would I lift that fishnet into a truck?" He was more than peeved. He was angry. He and Bitsy dragged me onto the catwalk. It bent underneath the weight of the fishnet and three humans.

"Don't take me anywhere." I tried to hide my rising panic. "Call the fire department. They'll bring the jaws of life." I was becoming as shrill as Bitsy.

"Nah," Tom scoffed. "That'd take too long. We can get you fixed up sooner than that."

"No!" I yelled. Maybe someone in one of the yachts would hear me and come out to investigate. Despite Vicki's complaints, snoopy civilians could come in handy.

The smoke detector beeped.

Grunting, Tom pulled me up the catwalk. Bitsy pushed at the fishnet, which might have been more effective if I'd straightened my knees, but I wasn't about to cooperate. I made myself go limp. Still, they managed to haul me all the way to a boat.

It had to be the one Tom had piloted into his boathouse only minutes before. It was large, made of aluminum, with an outboard motor in back, a steering wheel and windshield in front, storage containers that served as seats lining the gunwales, and the floor between the seats puddled and smelling of slime.

"Bitsy," Tom ordered. "Help me get this thing into the boat."

He and Bitsy hopped onto the nearest seat. The boat tilted, putting its gunwale at the same height as the catwalk. They reached over the side and rolled me and the heavy fishnet onto the seat. Pain seared my right ankle.

I twisted my body enough to lever myself up to a lounging position with my elbows as props. My legs were stretched out on the seat, and my feet were still tied together as if I'd created a clumsy mermaid outfit for myself. "This is not a good idea," I protested.

Tom had stepped out of the boat again and was kneeling on the catwalk, breathing heavily. His face was only slightly above mine. "You think I can't handle a boat?"

"Of course you can, it's just —"

By the feeble reflections from the glow of my flashlight inside his shack, his teeth looked wolfish. "I have a radio on board. I can radio for help. I can also whisk this boat up the river. I can land it behind your house so quietly no one will notice."

And he could do all that, and probably had done all that with this boat, and after he'd landed, he'd dragged a body wrapped in quilt batting up the riverbank, had dumped it in my yard, and had shoveled dirt over it until the sound of my sliding glass door or of Sally-Forth's collar had scared him. Then he'd jumped into his boat and drifted off down the river, steering between silent eddies without bothering to restart his outboard motor until he reached the lake . . .

It was probably as much of a confession as I would ever receive from him.

Obviously, he didn't expect me to ever repeat it.

"Haylee!" I yelled.

As if I hadn't made even a peep, Tom directed Bitsy to undo the last line and jump into the boat. Calmly, he hopped in and started the outboard motor.

Bitsy clambered out, unwound the line from a cleat on the catwalk, leaped in, tumbled onto the fishnet, and landed on the floor. Shrieking, "It's wet," she crawled up onto the seat opposite mine and sat hunched over, her arms wrapped around Tom's huge sweater, holding it closed.

We roared out of the boathouse and into the harbor.

I yelled for Haylee. I yelled for Ben.

I screamed Clay's name.

The wind blew off the land. It pushed my voice out over the lake.

47

Tom had hinted he might head toward the mouth of the Elderberry River and pull his boat up behind my shop and apartment. Maybe he'd drag me up the riverbank and leave me on the trail beside my yard. Eventually, if I couldn't rouse my neighbors with my shouts, early-morning birders would find me and get help.

But Tom steered his boat straight out into the lake. Maybe he needed to avoid the shallows close to the beaches? The good news was that I could no longer hear that annoying smoke detector.

Tom cut the motor. The boat bobbed up and down. From the tops of waves, I could see the shore on both sides of downtown Threadville. The state forest and the river's mouth — close to home but unbearably far away — were dark. A row of streetlights marked Lake Street. Lights shone from a few beach cottages and the lodge's veranda.

A pair of headlights wended down the hill from the lodge toward the wharf. Ben, in the car he said he kept at the lodge, bringing Haylee and a long, sharp pair of shears? Clay, searching for me?

Maybe Haylee and Ben would see Tom's boat out here and race to my rescue in one of Ben's boats. The moon was fairly bright, and Tom should have running lights on.

I couldn't see any. What were the chances of anyone on land spying a small boat riding up and down on waves?

Tom crept between boxes of fishing gear toward me.

He reached for me.

I shoved him away.

He merely laughed. "Bitsy, get over here and give me a hand."

Scowling, she boosted herself off her seat and joined him. "What do you want me to do?"

I noticed insignificant details, like she still hadn't buttoned the sweater.

Focus, Willow, focus.

On what?

Saving myself.

Right. How? It's a little late . . .

Tom growled. "Let's get this net into the water where it belongs."

Bitsy slapped at him, but it seemed more

432

playful than violent. "We can't. It's still attached to her. She'll be pulled under. She'll drown."

"She knows too much."

"What does she know? Nothing. All she did was dig up those jewels you promised me." She huddled into the sweater. "Easy come, easy go. I didn't believe in those jewels, anyway."

He straightened and glared at her. "Didn't believe in them? Didn't you believe in the money I gave you, either? Didn't I buy you a whole entire campground?"

"The campground is real. And it's a lot of work, besides. Jewelry, though? What woman believes a man who offers her diamonds and rubies?"

He clenched his hands into fists. His muscles bulged with the apparent difficulty of keeping his arms at his sides. "The campground's too much work for you, is it? Cleaning bathrooms is beneath you? How would you like to gut fish all day every day, instead? You help me push this fishnet into the lake, or there won't *be* any campground. You'll be cleaning bathrooms in prison."

"I never did anything. I never hurt those guys. I was in high school when Snoozy disappeared. We were just kids — you and me and Neil and Yolanda. We didn't have anything to do with how he disappeared. And Neil wasn't bad. He was your friend. Why did you have to . . . ?"

"For you, babe. And for him. Neil was deathly sick from that flu. He *begged* me for medicine. I had some medicine for upset stomachs in the shack, so I took him there in my boat, joked he couldn't blame seasickness for the way he felt, you know, just trying to jolly him into feeling better. And I had just the right thing to fix him up. Lucky thing he got that flu, because until then, I wasn't sure how to give him the other medicine he was going to have to take. But I was smart. I mixed the two medicines together, then took the empty bottle to his apartment and put it in the trash there." He studied her face. "You told me you didn't like him anymore."

"I didn't." She didn't meet Tom's eyes. "Not as a boyfriend."

"You're lying," he accused. "You still liked him."

Shaking her head, she backed away from Tom. "No. I always liked you best."

Tom snorted. "You should have. Neil wasn't the smartest cookie in the box, but sooner or later, he was going to figure out why Snoozy never made it to Mexico with his loot, and who really went to Cleveland

and bought a ticket to Mexico in his name, which, by the way, I cashed in later." He tapped the side of his head. "I was always the smart one, but Neil was getting suspicious. If he'd clued in, I'd have been in hot water, and *you'd* have lost that campground that I thought you liked. Or was it all about being Mrs. Snooty-Tooty landowner? You thought you weren't going to have to work."

She whined, "You said I wouldn't have to work after you cashed in those jewels. And we were going to build a mansion where the campground is. Lakefront, almost."

"Yeah, well that's not an option, thanks to this Willow broad prowling around where she shouldn't have been. Bitsy, last chance — are you going to help me or not?"

She folded her arms. "Not. Don't do it, Tom. Don't. It's . . . it's wrong."

"Right, I'm going to just sit here and let her put me in prison?"

I tried to give him a way out. "Did Snoozy *force* you to help him steal that jewelry and cash?"

"Him? No, that gig was all his. I knew he was up to something, though, and watched him. Dumb guy went out in plain daylight, carrying his chest of treasure out to the hole he'd dug in the woods. So I followed. Taking the box from him wasn't easy, though.

He fought. He shoulda known better. Luckily, he'd dug a nice, big hole. He tried to bury me in it. I had no choice."

"And then you had to cover his body," I prompted, "and go off to Blueberry Cottage and dig underneath there, too."

"Nah, didn't have to dig. Part of that cottage was sitting on stone piers, with a big, bare hole underneath. I just took out the cash, then slipped the box between the piers where no one would see it while I waited for everyone to stop looking for those jewels. I didn't go near there for a whole year, and when I did, I couldn't find the box."

Clay must have guessed right. Floods and ice may have moved that box.

Maybe I could make Tom believe he could get away without hurting anyone else. I suggested, "Take us back to shore. Let us off the boat. Or just me, if Bitsy wants to go with you." Just how anyone was going to *let* me off the boat, I didn't know. "Then take your boat and leave."

"You think I'm stupid, don't you. Stupid old fisherman Tom, not good enough for the shopkeepers of Threadville."

"What do you mean, not good enough?" Bitsy's voice was as bitter and squeezed as a dried-up lemon. "That's the second time you've hinted something about that. Did you go and ask one of them out?" She glanced down at me. "Her?"

"Of course not, babe. You're my girl. But talk about snooty-tooty, Willow — you and those snooty-tooty friends of yours would send someone after me. Stupid old fisherman Tom was pretty smart after all, getting stuff from those women's shops before I needed it. As soon as the police figure out whose stuff that was, Willow and her snooty-tooty friends will be blamed for burying poor old Neil."

I didn't tell him that the police already knew whose stuff it was, and I didn't inform Bitsy that I suspected Tom had asked Naomi out — what would be the point? "I won't say anything for a week," I promised rashly and not exactly honestly. "Go get the rest of the cash you took from Snoozy and do what he planned to do — go to Mexico. Go anywhere. Just take me back to shore, first."

"That cash is gone. Spent. I bought my first fishing boat with some of it, and bought Bitsy her campground with the last of it." In the light of the three-quarter moon, his eyes seemed wide with a combination of simmering rage and canny determination.

I told myself he wouldn't push me into the cold, dark water. No one would be that evil. He was bluffing, trying for more concessions from me.

Bitsy must have thought so, too. "We'll never tell anyone what we know about you," she pledged. "If you just disappear, we'll never say a thing."

"And you wouldn't come with me, Bitsy babe? You'd just let me go? You wouldn't miss your old Tom, who gave you your very own campground? And Willow is buddy-buddy with the police. I'm surprised she's not dialing 911 in her pocket."

I would have been if my cell phone had been in my pocket and not in my bag in his shack, and if I weren't still propping myself up on my elbows with my hands behind my back.

Suddenly, he came at me and shoved. Knocked off balance, I lashed out with my fingernails, but didn't do more than scratch his arm, maybe.

And then I was tipping sideways, scrabbling with my fingers for the gunwale, the oarlock, anything. And that heavy fishnet was being pushed, with my feet trapped inside it, over the side. And Bitsy was screaming.

As Lake Erie, colder than I'd guessed it would be, closed over my head, my most encouraging thought was that Haylee knew where I'd been, and Tom wouldn't get away with murder, at least not with *my* murder.

48

I never really believed that the entire life of a drowning person could pass before her eyes as she sank into the water. How would there be enough time?

But I also wouldn't have believed what I saw. Not my past, but a future, a future that might never exist. Me cuddling babies that belonged to Haylee and Ben . . . Clay at my shoulder . . .

I had instinctively filled my lungs before I hit the water, but I wasn't going to be able to hold my breath much longer. My lungs burned.

Clay, I thought, *Clay.*

Which way was up? I held as still as possible in hopes that my air-filled lungs would raise my head close to the surface and then I could flutter my hands and lift my face out of the water for another breath.

A lessening of the inky darkness penetrated my eyelids. A breeze whispered across the top of my head. I opened my eyes. My nose cleared the water. My mouth did, too. Bitsy was still screaming. I let out my breath and gulped in another. Something splashed nearby. Another wave washed over my head.

This time, I was able to see the bright moon and keep track of which way was up. I surfaced long enough for another gasp of breath.

A motorboat roared. Away from me. Tom and Bitsy must have been leaving.

Another wave knocked me under, but I let my natural buoyancy carry me up again. Why wasn't the fishnet dragging me under? The floats attached to it were designed to keep the edges up, but the rest of the net would sink, allowing fish into the net. The whole net was bunched up, though, so the floats were keeping the net from plummeting. It and my trapped feet stayed just underneath the water.

Near me, a reedy voice gasped. "Help!"

Bitsy?

Instinctively, I kicked my feet. The water was so cold that my ankle had stopped hurting.

Hypothermia would be next.

I could breathe between waves, but if I became too cold for my organs to function,

I would never know Haylee and Ben's babies.

I heard wild splashing and another small, hopeless call for help. It had to be Bitsy.

I treaded water with only my arms and hands again, and the movement seemed to warm me up a little, but the sluglike fishnet kept me from turning quickly toward Bitsy. In a trough between waves, I called to her, "Tread water!"

"I don't know how!" Another splash and a burble. "I can't swim!"

At least I had a good excuse for not having worn a life jacket. Bitsy and Tom hadn't bothered with them.

Where were Haylee and Ben? Where was Clay?

And . . . what had happened to the fishnet?

It was no longer stuck on my feet. My normal swimming reflexes had caused me to kick, and what had been impossible on land had happened easily in the water.

I had kicked myself free.

I could tread water. If I watched for incoming waves, I could keep my head above water. I could float. I could swim back to the wharf. I shook water from my face. It wasn't far, wasn't far, wasn't far. I'd live to see Clay again.

"Help!"

I could save myself, but if I didn't at least try to rescue Bitsy, who had told Tom not to throw me into the water, I would never be able to live with my conscience, would never be able to look Haylee and Ben's mythical babies in the eye . . .

"Relax!" I shouted to Bitsy. "Lie on your back with your arms straight out like a cross."

"I can't!" The woman would drown in panic before she drowned in water.

Finally, I saw her, only one wave away from me. She was still wearing Tom's sweater, which was soaking up water like a sponge. "Kick off your shoes," I yelled, "and take off that sweater and let it go."

I'd heard that people who were drowning would fight with potential rescuers until they both drowned. Sure enough, as soon as I swam close, Bitsy grabbed for me. I ducked out of her reach, treading water backward toward shore. She lunged toward me again. She'd obeyed me and removed the sweater.

I shouted at her, "You're swimming! Do that again, and keep your head above water."

I backed away from her.

"I can't!" With her awkward attempts to reach me, she kept moving forward.

"You can!" She was on her stomach.

"Straighten your knees, point your toes, and kick your feet. Do the doggie paddle with your hands and keep your chin up."

I demonstrated, always leading her toward the calmer water of the harbor.

Bitsy might have been cantankerous, but her desire for self-preservation was strong. That night, in the cold, wavy waters of Lake Erie, I gave Bitsy Ingalls her first swimming lesson.

It was the first swimming lesson I'd ever taught, also. Almost drowning was causing clichés to pass before my eyes. Now it was the one about necessity being the mother of invention.

And inventing a mother. As Bitsy and I neared the wharf, I admitted to myself that Haylee's future children existed only in my imagination. I would have to try not to plague my best friend with the insistence that she had to have children because I'd *seen* them during my near-death experience.

I didn't have to warn Bitsy to be quiet. Both of us needed all of our strength just to stay afloat in that cold water. And she probably knew as well as I did that if Tom discovered that we'd survived, he'd do everything he could to finish the job he'd started out there in the wave-torn lake.

We were almost back at the wharf when I had second thoughts about returning to it. For one thing, unless I'd gotten turned around out there, Tom had sped his boat toward the wharf. For another, the wall between the wharf and the water was made of steel. The wind was still coming from the land, so waves weren't exactly slamming into the wall, but they could scrape a person against it. Crawling out onto a beach would have to be easier than scaling rusty, algae-coated steel.

However, I wasn't sure I had the energy to turn around, tackle the deeper water again, and swim to a beach. Bitsy was probably more exhausted than I was.

I'd hoped I was wrong about where Tom had piloted his boat after he pushed me out of it, but I wasn't. His boat was again in his boathouse.

Bitsy must have seen it, too. She flinched. I led her, still practicing her doggie paddle, underneath the pier jutting out from the wharf until we were close to Tom's market. Both of us grabbed for posts. They were slimy. I let the next wave carry me upward where I could grab a less slippery section of the post.

Bright light filtered down between planks. I'd seen headlights when we were out in the lake. Had that vehicle stayed, or was Tom in his truck, about to go home and pretend he knew nothing about Bitsy's and my disappearance?

There was no way I was showing myself until I was certain I was safe from him.

That smoke detector was still bleating. I almost considered swimming back into deep water.

Something sharp banged into my elbow. A scrap of plywood swayed back and forth under the pier. I shoved it toward Bitsy, and both of us rested our forearms on it. But my teeth were chattering loudly enough to alert Tom, if he were still nearby, to our hiding place. And hypothermia had to be threatening Bitsy, also. With her hair pasted to her head, her mascara streaked, and her eyes wide with fear and anger, she resembled a sea monster. I probably did, too.

"Where's Willow?" Haylee shouted.

"How would I know?" Tom answered.

"She was in your shack with her feet tangled in a fishnet, and now she's not there." Haylee was *very* angry.

"I was out fishing. I just got back. I haven't been inside. Maybe she's still there. And I have to ask you what you think you were doing inside my fish market after I closed it."

He sounded very threatening. Was she confronting him by herself?

Leaving Bitsy and the plywood behind, I glided toward where I might get a better look at the situation, but for my own safety, I stayed hidden underneath the pier.

The night was bright with lights — including reassuringly red and white strobing ones — and noisy with voices, everyone yelling at once.

Despite Haylee and the cruiser's presence, though, I felt vulnerable. If Tom saw or heard me, he could throw a stone that would accomplish what his fishnet had failed to do.

I swam back to Bitsy. She clung to the piece of wood, but her eyes seemed to roll back in her head. I touched her shoulder and murmured, "Is there a ladder so we can get out of the water?"

She nodded and pointed at a narrow channel underneath the catwalk leading to the back entrance of Tom's boathouse.

Great, the last place I wanted to go. Together, we kicked our improvised raft to a ladder dangling off the catwalk I'd navigated with Haylee approximately a lifetime ago. At least I wouldn't have to go into that dreadful boathouse again. We'd be able to skirt around it.

First, though, we had to climb the ladder. Bitsy trembled so violently that I didn't think she could pull herself out of the water, but she managed, with me right behind her.

My legs felt too heavy to move, but my ankle supported me, barely. Sure I was about to slip back down into that black, licking, lapping water, I heaved myself up onto the narrow catwalk and sidled along it. Splinters tore at the soles of my feet. My sandals were somewhere in Lake Erie, maybe in a jumble of fishnet.

Bitsy seemed to have lost her fear. Although her feet were bare also, she dashed down the lined-up planks. She caterwauled like a fishwife, "Tom Umshaw, you promised me money and you promised me jewels, and all you did was throw me into the lake so I'd drown."

"Bitsy!" I heard him run toward her. "She fell out of the boat. I was coming to get help when you all started yapping about Willow, and I didn't get to tell you I needed someone to go out on the water and help me find Bitsy."

"Don't you touch me!" she screamed. "He pushed me out of the boat. He knew I couldn't swim."

Beep.

Hanging on to the handrail, keeping my

weight mostly off an ankle that began throbbing again in warmish air, I crept closer.

"Then how'd you get here?" Tom had to be sarcastic.

"That's a very serious allegation, Bitsy." I'd never been happier to hear Vicki Smallwood at her sternest.

"She's wrong," Tom said. "She was falling overboard. I went to grab her, but couldn't save her. I musta touched her, so she says I pushed her. Don't charge her for false accusations, Chief. She's not herself."

"After all I did for you," Bitsy screamed. "You told me to get someone to help me pick fights at that sidewalk sale so everyone would be distracted while you set something up, but you didn't tell me what it was until just now, out there, when you told us it was so you could steal things that would make it look like those store owners killed and buried Neil. Get your hands off me! You promised me jewels, but you didn't bother digging them up until someone else got there first."

"Where's *Willow*?" Haylee managed to outshout Bitsy. "Did he push her overboard, too? When her feet were stuck in a fishnet?"

"Yep." Bitsy was at her shrillest. "And he wanted me to help him. But I refused. That's why he pushed me."

"And Willow is out in the water?" Clay's voice this time, full of pain, and very little hope. "Fred and Ben, let's get three of Ben's boats and go out and search for her."

Men ran.

Bitsy faltered, "No, no, she's not out there."

The men continued running, farther and farther away.

It was time — past time — for me to make my entrance.

49

The problem was that planning to make an entrance and actually doing it were two different things. Bitsy had been able to screech. My voice didn't work at all.

Not only that, I could almost stagger, and I resembled a drowned rat, besides.

I wasn't going to let that bother me. Clay was nearby, and about to rush off and board a boat on a futile mission, and I wanted to be in his arms.

"I'm here," I croaked.

I might as well not have said anything. No one responded, and I could no longer hear the men running away.

I limped out from behind the corner of the building and stopped at the sight in front of me. The parking lot's one streetlight cast a dim yellow funnel over Vicki's cruiser and an unmarked state police car. Both flashed their rooftop lights. Because my eyelashes were wet, everything shimmered with haloes.

Ben, Clay, and Fred were racing away from the wharf and toward the dock where Ben moored his boats.

Vicki held Tom in the glare of her flashlight, and in the glare of her eyes, in front of his fish market. Vicki's right hand hovered over a holster hanging from her belt.

Detective Gartener's back was to me, but he was facing Tom, and obviously ready to leap if Tom so much as twitched.

After Haylee had left me in the fish shack, she'd not only rounded up Ben, Clay, Fred, and the police, but she'd apparently also called her mothers and Gord as well.

Haylee, Opal, and Edna stood in a semicircle around Bitsy, who was lying, shuddering and sobbing, on the broken asphalt of the parking area. Gord knelt beside Bitsy with his hand around her wrist. Someone had covered her with a large sweatshirt. Crouching, Naomi patted Bitsy's shoulder.

Edna looked down at the top of Gord's head, but Haylee and Opal scowled, watching Tom, and obviously ready to support Vicki and Detective Gartener if they needed it.

I pointed at Bitsy. "She tried to save me," I rasped.

With a strangled cry of relief, Haylee

leaped over Bitsy, bounded to me, and hugged me. "Clay!" she shouted, nearly rupturing my eardrum. "Willow's here!"

Vicki took out a whistle and nearly ruptured my other eardrum.

Tom simply stared at me with his mouth hanging open.

My voice came back. I pointed a shaking finger at him. "You must have mended your nets with the thread you shoplifted from Haylee at the sidewalk sale. You didn't read the fine print. It was water soluble."

He folded his arms over his chest, but he still looked like he'd seen a ghost. Two ghosts — mine and Bitsy's. He answered me, though. "I used thread that I bought from you. Monofilament, you said. Invisible."

I shook my head and pointed at my feet. "After the net was in the water for a while, the thread you used dissolved, or I'd still be out there."

Clay, Fred, and Ben must not have heard Vicki's whistle. They were beyond the marina, and still running. Vicki sprinted to her cruiser and started its siren.

That brought the men to a halt that was almost comical. Vicki blew her whistle again, three sharp blasts, and they all pelted back toward us.

With Haylee supporting me, I staggered toward Clay. He put on a burst of speed, and after what felt like a couple of agonizingly long minutes, he caught me to him and held me close. He didn't say a thing, and neither did I, not even when he took off his jacket and draped it around my shoulders. He pulled me close again.

The smoke detector inside Tom's fish shack was becoming frantic.

Leaving Vicki to cover Tom, Detective Gartener strode to me and asked quietly in his deep warm voice, "What happened tonight, Willow?"

"My feet were stuck in a fishnet." Gartener raised his eyebrows, but I didn't take time to explain how I'd gotten into that predicament. "Tom said he'd help me remove it. He put me into his boat, drove the boat out into the lake, and dumped me overboard. Bitsy tried to stop him, and she ended up in the water, too. And you heard him — he knew she wasn't a swimmer. And he as much as told us that he killed both Snoozy and Neil."

Gartener watched me steadily. I took a deep breath and filled the silence he created. "I'd found an empty packet of rat poison under a box of Haylee's water-soluble thread in his shack and had already

454

guessed he could have used the poison on Neil, but I didn't want to believe it." I patted the front pocket of my sopping cutoffs, and babbled on as if I had to spew everything out before something worse happened. "The packet fell out of my pocket, and he must have seen it and figured out I could have suspected he'd poisoned Neil with it, and he decided he had to do away with me. And I think Bitsy also figured out that Tom murdered Neil and Snoozy. She's been enjoying the cash from Snoozy's haul and planned to enjoy the jewels, too, only Tom hid them underneath Blueberry Cottage, and ice or floods must have moved them." I was out of breath.

Gartener touched my shoulder. "Thanks, Willow. I'll get your full statement in a while. Would you like to sit in one of the cruisers in the meantime?"

I shook my head. If my car keys hadn't been in my bag inside Tom's shack, I could have sat in my own car. Either way, I didn't want to move. Leaning against Clay took the pressure off my ankle.

Gartener spoke directly to Clay. "Warm her with your body until we get more help for her, okay?"

Clay crowded closer. "No problem."

Detective Gartener marched to Tom and

told him he'd have to take him in for questioning. Tom protested, but allowed Detective Gartener to lead him to the back door of Vicki's cruiser. Gartener opened the door, and jumped back as if startled.

Still all in black, Zara erupted from the backseat and yelled, "Ben!"

He strode toward her.

Detective Gartener helped Tom into the cruiser and shut the door.

Zara ran to Ben. They met underneath the light fixture.

Zara walked two long fingers up Ben's bare forearm. "Do you have any idea how cramped it is in the backseat of one of those things?"

Ben edged away until her hand dropped from his arm. "What were you doing in there? And where's my truck?"

Haylee must not have tattled on her cousin.

Zara unpinned her stark hairdo, shook her head, and ran her fingers through her hair as it cascaded around her shoulders. "A misunderstanding about one of my art installations."

Vicki stopped in the process of opening her trunk. "She vandalized my cruiser."

Zara shrugged. "It was only a yarnbomb. No big deal. It was art. And besides, that was days ago."

Vicki snorted. "*Art*. If your *art* had delayed me in a life-or-death situation, you'd have gotten worse than a fine and a reprimand."

Zara shot back, "*And* an hour of being cramped in the back of a police cruiser for no good reason."

Vicki opened her trunk and gave a nice imitation of Zara's usually careless shrug. "Yeah, well, a civilian's in our cruiser and we get called to an emergency, the civilian has to go sit in the back until the situation is resolved. It's for your own safety."

"You could have let me out. I'd have driven Ben's truck back." She turned to Ben. "Sorry. Your truck is up on Shore Road, but it's close to the lodge. I'll walk there with you and you can drive us both back."

Despite trembling like I was about to freeze, I had to admire her persistence.

"You still have the keys, don't you?" he asked.

She patted the kangaroo pocket of the black sweater she'd knit from the same kind of bulky yarn she'd used in her art installation. "Yep."

He held out his hand. "I'll take them."

She hesitated, pouted, then fished the keys

from her pocket and dropped them into his hand.

Leaving Zara standing under that one light, Ben walked away from her and returned to the group surrounding Bitsy, Clay, and me. He stopped right next to Haylee.

Zara wandered off and sat on one of the boulders edging the parking lot. With her knees together, her shins angled out, her elbows on her knees, and her chin in her hands, she made the complete picture of an abandoned waif.

Fred also joined the group supporting Bitsy. Gartener looked him up and down. "Fred Zongassi, do you understand how close *you* came to being the one sitting in the back of a police cruiser? Why did you wait an entire hour before reporting those bones you found? Don't you know how that made you look?"

Fred bowed his head. "I recognized that belt buckle and guessed whose bones they might be, and I had a lot of thinking to do. I knew someone was sure to remember that I'd fought with Snoozy before I left town, and if those bones were his, I could land in a whole heap of trouble. Finally, I decided to own up to uncovering those bones in the hopes that no one would remember the fight, but someone did."

Vicki pawed around among things in her trunk. "Everyone in the village over the age of forty remembered that!"

Gartener asked Fred, "What did you fight about?"

"Not really a fight — despite the way the rumor grew, I didn't touch him. More like an argument. I'd found him digging a hole out in the woods, damaging a lot of tree roots in the process, and asked him why, since I was the gardener. He fired me on the spot, and I was fed up with him anyway — he was nasty and didn't know the first thing about landscaping or gardening, and he always ordered me to do idiotic things like dig out shrubs that only needed pruning. It nearly killed me to destroy those plants. So I yelled at him and told him exactly what I thought of him, and he yelled back, and finally, I just left him there in the woods. I was so mad I didn't care who all had heard the things I said to him." He shrugged in the dim light. "You know, I wanted nothing to do with Elderberry Bay after that, so I never even heard that he and the contents of that safe went missing. I guess he was digging a hole to put the treasure in, but he ended up in the hole himself."

"I guess so," Detective Gartener agreed. "What made you come back to Elderberry Bay?"

"A place like this just stays on inside you, and I couldn't help it. I had to return to this shore I loved. And then I dug up that skeleton and Snoozy's belt buckle. It was a shock, I can tell you, especially when I realized the bones were in or near the hole I'd argued with Snoozy about." He rubbed his hand over his chin, which had developed a two A.M. shadow. "Sometimes, it takes a while to figure out what the right thing to do is."

Vicki snorted and pulled two foil packages out of her trunk. Striding toward the rest of us, she opened one package with her teeth and tossed the other one to Clay. "Survival blankets." She nodded at me. "Put it around her and keep hugging her."

Gord and Edna wrapped Bitsy in one of the blankets while Clay and Haylee wrapped me in the other. It was supposed to trap my body heat, but I wasn't certain that I owned any. My shivering was so violent that my teeth didn't chatter. They clashed.

But I could still hear that smoke detector. If someone didn't fix the thing soon, I would. I didn't need Vicki or Detective Gartener to tell me that Tom's fish shack was now a crime scene, and none of us were going to be allowed inside to fiddle with a smoke detector. Or retrieve my bag, wallet, phone, keys . . .

Burrowing into Clay's warmth, I asked Fred, "Did you ever sneak up on Snoozy Gallagher and take his picture?"

Fred squinted as if confused. "Not sure. Maybe. If I did, it was a long time ago."

"Neil was in it," I suggested, "with Tom, Yolanda, and Bitsy. They were teenagers. Neil, Tom, and Yolanda looked like they were shouting at Snoozy."

"That does sound familiar." Fred nodded slowly. "All four of those kids worked for Snoozy, and they wanted more pay. From Snoozy Gallagher, of all people. What I earned barely covered the rent for my room in the staff cottage. But I threw out nearly everything to do with that job when I was packing to go. Who needed to be reminded of a nasty boss? I tossed out that photo, too, so how would you know about it?"

I managed through my shivers, "Your nasty boss retrieved it from your wastebasket and kept it. Ben has the photo now."

Fred nodded toward Ben. "You're welcome to it. I still don't want it."

Light jounced down the hill toward us, and Max's BMW drove slowly into the parking lot. He parked beyond the cruisers and climbed out. A tall, lean, middle-aged blonde unfolded herself from his passenger seat and stood stock-still, looking at the rest of us.

I gaped at her, then quickly checked the faces around me. Opal was not beside Max's car.

Opal was next to Naomi.

Opal's mouth was open, and she was staring toward the woman I'd mistaken for Opal.

50

Time seemed to stop, and then start again in a rush as the Opal lookalike broke loose from Max and started running toward us.

Zara let out a startled yelp. "Mom! What are you doing here?"

But if Zara's mom heard her, she didn't let on. She rushed to Opal, threw her arms around her, and cried out in a mixture of pain and joy, "Opal! I was afraid I'd never see you again!"

"Pearl," Opal said, and then the two women were hugging each other and laughing and crying.

Detective Gartener sauntered to Haylee. "So I guess they really are your cousins?" he asked her quietly.

"I guess."

"Opal looks happy," he pointed out. "Except that she's crying."

Vicki was still beside us. She elbowed Gartener. "That's what women do when we're happy."

"Remind me never to make some woman happy, then," he retorted.

Vicki and I exchanged glances and laughed. She eyed Clay with his arms around me and my silvery blanket. "Are you warming up, Willow?" she asked.

I nodded.

"Next thing we know, you'll be crying," she joked.

"No way," I said. "Tears are wet and I'm already soaked."

"Doc Wrinklesides — Gord — called an ambulance for Bitsy. Do you need to go to Emergency, too?"

"I'll be fine when I'm warm." My voice wavered.

She scrutinized my face, then teased, "For a second, there, I thought you were crying."

Clay chuckled and hugged me tighter.

I told Vicki, "Those two kittens are yours if you want them." Actually, I hoped she'd say she didn't.

"I think I should leave them with Sally-Forth, don't you?"

I nodded.

She added, "But if you ever need a pet sitter, just ask. I'll do it if I can."

I asked her, "And Cassie's in the clear?"

"Yep. She'll be okay."

I shuddered. "With a mother like that?"

Vicki frowned. "One good thing about this, if anything can be good, is that Neil's mother, Cassie's grandmother, hasn't seen Cassie since she was about two, and wants to meet her."

"Did you ever find out about Cassie's adoptive father?"

Vicki gave a decisive nod. "Turcotte died of lung cancer when Cassie was four, two years after Yolanda left him. There was absolutely no suspicion of foul play."

"So you'll charge Yolanda only with selling stolen goods and dumping kittens? And you'll charge that Brad guy with stealing asparagus?" I demanded.

"We'll charge them with whatever we can make stick. That guy, Brad, actually has no sense of smell. Can you believe it?"

I laughed. "Easily."

Opal and Pearl stood arm in arm, beaming at each other. Up close, I could see that Pearl was older, with careworn creases in her face that Opal did not have. But while Pearl must have worried about what had happened to her little sister, Opal had probably never had to worry whether Pearl was healthy, fed, and housed. And Naomi and Edna had supported Opal emotionally all

465

these years.

I turned to see how Opal's best friends were taking the reunion. Her eyes glittering, Naomi beamed at the two sisters. Edna stood behind Gord, who was still kneeling beside Bitsy. Edna smiled down proudly at Gord's shoulder. Her left hand rested lightly on it.

And then I saw what she was smiling at. Her hand. Her ring finger.

It sported a ring with a colossal diamond. Bling for our bling-loving Edna.

I shrieked, "Edna!"

She jumped and placed her left hand over her heart. "What? What's wrong, Willow?"

But I was smiling so hard that my lips hurt. That diamond twinkled, and Haylee noticed.

She shrieked Edna's name, also, then grabbed Edna's hand and held it where Naomi and Opal could see it. "You didn't tell us!"

Edna tilted her head in her birdlike way. "I was waiting for someone to notice."

Gord rose to his feet and accepted our congratulations. Everyone, even Zara, who had abandoned her waiflike posture but not her pout, crowded around to admire Edna's ring.

Leave it to Gord to begin humming. Mendelssohn's "Wedding March," of course.

He smiled down at his fiancée. But she and the two women who called themselves The Three Weird Sisters were gazing fondly at Haylee, standing very close to Ben, whose gaze also appeared to be turned in her direction.

Vicki sidled to me and whispered, "Don't you look so smug, Willow Vanderling. It's late now, but I'll talk to you tomorrow about how you just *happened* to entangle your feet in one of Tom's fishnets."

That smoke detector was becoming almost unbearable.

"Okay." I fingered the thin, silvery blanket. "Do I get to keep the blanket?"

Vicki shrugged. "Sure."

I called to Edna and Gord, "I know what I'm wearing to your wedding!"

Edna cocked her head. "But how can you embroider it?"

I answered seriously, "Very carefully."

Clay tightened his arms around me and the blanket.

Pearl's eyes were wide and her hand covered her mouth. Suddenly, she dropped her hand and started laughing. "Oh! The survival blanket! I thought she meant the *man.*" And then she and Opal were clutching each other and laughing so hard they could barely keep their balance.

Smiling down at me, Clay murmured, "May I have this dance?"

WILLOW'S EMBROIDERED
JEWELRY POUCH

You don't need an embroidery machine to make one of these cute embroidered pouches, but life is more fun with an embroidery machine. Or two.

You Will Need:

1. Fabric:
Two squares of fabric about 12 inches across.
Two squares of fabric about 9 inches across.
Note: the fabric can be all the same, or you can choose coordinating fabrics.

2. Embroidery thread:
As many colors as your design requires, plus an additional color, if desired, for stitching around the edge.

3. Stabilizer — the correct weight for the

fabric you're embroidering.

4. Circle of plastic (you can cut one from a flat-sided juice container) about 2 inches in diameter.

5. Pretty cord in a color coordinating with fabric(s).

6. Spring-loaded cord lock like those found on outerwear (usually sold with buttons).

Construction:
1. Use a dinner plate to draw circles on the wrong sides of the two larger pieces of fabric. Don't cut them out.

2. On the right side of the fabric, mark the center of the circles.

3. Place stabilizer underneath one piece of fabric and place the fabric and stabilizer in your embroidery hoop with the right side of the fabric on top.

4. Embroider a design, about an inch and a half in diameter, in the center of the circle.

5. Embroider buttonholes that are just long

enough to accommodate a safety pin (for inserting cord, see step 16 below) side by side about an inch and a half from the edge of the circle. If you can't make the buttonholes with your embroidery machine, use your buttonhole attachment.

6. If you didn't have to unhoop your fabric for step 5, unhoop it now.

7. Pin the two larger pieces of fabric, right sides together.

8. Stitch around the circle you drew, leaving a gap for turning. Trim close to the seam, snip raw edges without snipping the seam, turn right side out, press, and edge stitch around the outer edge, being sure to close the previously unsewn gap neatly.

9. Stitch two more circles concentric with the edge of the project, one on each side of your pair of eyelets or buttonholes. This will form a channel for your drawstring.

10. Use a dessert plate to draw circles on the wrong sides of the two smaller pieces of fabric. Don't cut them out.

11. Pin the two smaller pieces of fabric,

right sides together.

12. Stitch around the circle you drew, leaving a gap for turning. Trim close to the seam, snip raw edges without snipping the seam, turn right side out, press, and edge stitch around the outer edge, being sure to close the previously unsewn gap neatly.

13. With the help of spray adhesive or double-sided sticky tape specially designed for use with fabrics, center the plastic disk on the unembroidered side of the larger circle.

14. With the help of spray adhesive or double-sided sticky tape specially designed for use with fabrics, center the smaller circle over the plastic disk.

15. Being careful not to stitch over the embroidery on the lowest level of the project, stitch around the edge of the plastic disk, through all four layers of fabric. You have now encased the plastic disk between the two double-sided fabric circles.

16. Using a ruler, mark four evenly spaced straight lines from the outer edges of the smaller fabric circle to the circle of stitches

around the plastic disk. Stitch along lines, stopping at the center circle of stitches.

17. Attach a safety pin to one end of the cord and insert the pin in one of the eyelets or buttonholes. Pull the pin around the circle and out through the other eyelet or buttonhole. Keeping the project flat, pull the cord about three inches beyond each outlet. Remove the safety pin. Pressing down on the button of the spring-loaded cord lock, push the ends of the cord through the hole in the spring-loaded cord lock. Knot the ends of the cord to keep it from unraveling, and adjust cord lock.

There. You have a pouch with a center section and four inner pockets, very handy for the next time you attend a jewelers' convention . . .

WILLOW'S TIPS

1. Keep water-soluble thread in a dry place, preferably in a well-marked box. You wouldn't want to accidentally use it when stitching up swimwear.

2. Experiment with different types of threads, but for metallic threads, which are extra fragile, be sure to use needles rated for them. Slip a fine mesh "stocking" over spools of stiffer threads to keep them from unwinding too quickly and snarling.

3. If you're wiring your sewing project for lights and/or sounds, avoid metallic threads in your designs.

4. Protect all thread from light, dust, and damp.

And don't forget to visit my website at www .threadvillemysteries.com.

WILLOW

The employees of Thorndike Press hope you have enjoyed this Large Print book. All our Thorndike, Wheeler, and Kennebec Large Print titles are designed for easy reading, and all our books are made to last. Other Thorndike Press Large Print books are available at your library, through selected bookstores, or directly from us.

For information about titles, please call:
(800) 223-1244

or visit our Web site at:
http://gale.cengage.com/thorndike

To share your comments, please write:
Publisher
Thorndike Press
10 Water St., Suite 310
Waterville, ME 04901

CPSIA information can be obtained
at www.ICGtesting.com
Printed in the USA
FFOW05n1519030214

9 781410 462558